Witch Born

BOOK II OF THE WITCH SONG SERIES

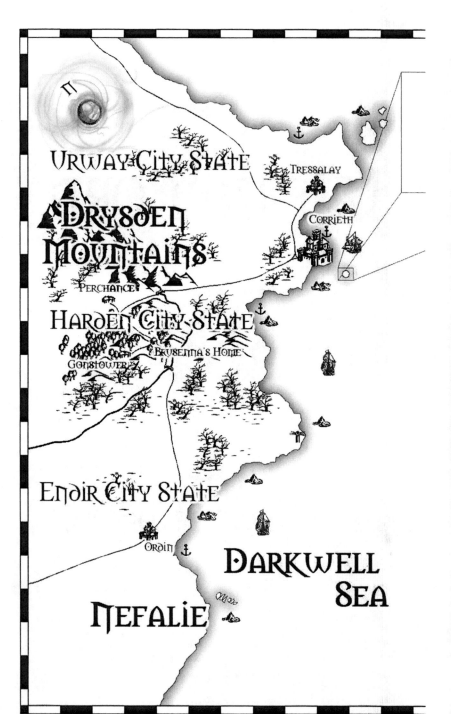

HAVEN

TARTEN

ENDALL SEA

SENNA'S LANDING

KAEN'S FARM

SHIOK

ICAR MOUNTAINS

CARPEL

ESPEN'S REALM

EPAL

ZAEN

SHIPS' GRAVEYARD

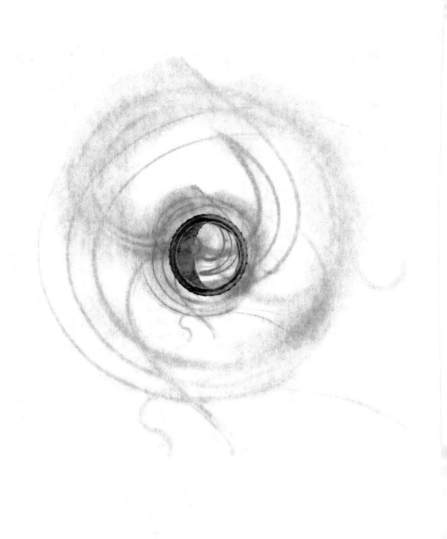

Author's Note

While the world in Witch Song and Witch Born is strictly a fantasy setting, the author wished to use America's resonance with the Salem Witch Trials. Therefore, the technology and setting for Nefalie are loosely based off of seventeenth century New England. Conversely, Tarten is loosely based off an amalgamation of South American landscapes, mostly Columbia.

WITCH BORN

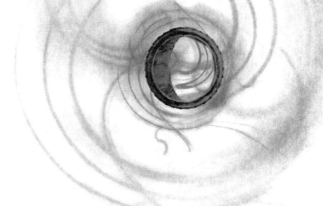

BOOK II OF THE WITCH SONG SERIES

BY AMBER ARGYLE

Starling Publishing

Editing by Linda Prince
Text design by Kathy Beutler
Author photo by Emily Weston
Map by Robert Defendi

Cover art by Eve Ventrue. Contact Eve by visiting her Web site at http://eve-ventrue.weebly.com/

ISBN-13: 978-0-9857394-0-9
ISBN-10: 0985739401

Also available as eBook.

Library of Congress Control Number: 2012945651

Printed in the United States of America
10 9 8 7 6 5 4 3 2 1

Visit Amber Argyle at her author Web site:
http://www.amberargyle.com

DEDICATION

To Derek Smith
For giving the greatest gifts.

1. SHADOWS

The night was so deep the shadows seemed to bleed darkness. Senna glanced toward the hidden sky, searching for the moon that would not come. Not tonight. Even the strongest starlight was strangled by the dense canopy of trees. The temporary blindness was frightening, but it ensured no one would notice her slipping away.

With each step she took, the roar of the waterfall grew louder. Finally, she reached the staircase carved into the side of the cliff. Mindful of the slippery steps, she climbed upward until her muscles burned and sweat broke across her skin despite the chill.

When she'd crested the top and crossed the bleak expanse, she glanced at the frothing sea far below. Sea spray misted her skin. She faced westward, towards the distant land of Tarten. Closing her eyes, she cast her senses across the vast ocean, searching and feeling the faraway echoes of the Four Sisters—Earth, Water, Plants, and Sunlight. She concentrated until she could hear their pain, an aching melody.

Senna's tears started again, wetting the salty tracks already on her cheeks. At night, her dreams haunted her. Dreams of a withered land and a dying people. With all the strength she had, she sang.

> Let not the curse of Witches
> Destroy a land of natural riches.
> Plants, preserve life in thy roots,
> Seeds sleep in earth, send forth no shoots
> Until the Witches shall disperse
> This terrible and unjust curse.

She came to the cliffs every night she could manage to slip away. Hoping to right the wrong she'd done, she sang for Tarten—the lands she'd helped destroy months ago.

When her throat was scratchy and she could no longer hit the high notes, she stared at the land she knew was struggling to hold onto any life at all. Because of the Witches' curse, no rain had fallen in Tarten for over two months—death to any jungle, but this one held on deep in the ground, waiting for the promise of her song to be fulfilled.

She withdrew her senses back to her home, Haven. Above the crash of waves, Senna thought she heard the scuff of a boot against stone. She whipped around and peered in the direction she'd come, her heart pounding in her throat. If the Discipline Heads discovered she was subverting their curse, the punishment would be severe.

"Who's there?" Her whisper sounded like a shout in the darkness.

No answer. She wished Joshen were here. The Discipline Heads had done their best to keep her apart from her Guardian. She hadn't seen him in two months. Not since he and Leader Reden had gone on a recruitment assignment.

Hugging herself, Senna trotted back to the staircase and began the long descent into the uninhabited quarter of Haven. At the base, she plunged between trees that towered above her, the tallest over eight stories high, the smallest just over two. Some were so wide it would take twenty witches stretched arm to arm to encircle one. Each tree was hollow and had once been inhabited by a Witch. Now they were empty, proof of the Witches' lingering decline into ruin.

Here, everything still bore faded signs of the Witches' final battle with Espen. A door in a tree creaked on its rusted hinges, a hole yawning where the latch should have been. Broken windows gaped like mouths with hungry, serrated teeth. The destruction was at odds with the life bursting all around.

Still, Senna couldn't shake the feeling she wasn't alone. There was no indication anyone had marked her sneaking away, no indication she'd been followed. But some instinct inside her seemed to chant a warning—through the gloom, someone was watching.

The feeling grew, and with a start, Senna heard music again. But this wasn't the distant music from Tarten. This was closer. *Here.*

She halted and tipped her head toward a sound so soft and natural she realized she must have been hearing it for a while and mistaken it for the sounds of nature.

But there was no mistaking it now. The melody carried a warning.

The wind picked up, snaking along the path and tugging at her cloak. Senna held her hood close. The thick vegetation before her shifted against the breeze. Someone was coming. Trying to calm her ragged breathing, she reminded herself she was safe on Haven. The Witches' headquarters were an impenetrable fortress—surrounded on all sides by cliffs that were in turn surrounded by the frigid ocean. The only way in or out of the island was for a Witch to sing you through an underwater cave.

So this was simply another Witch out for a stroll in the middle of the night in the abandoned part of Haven. The witch would see Senna and wonder why she was out for a stroll in the middle of the night in the abandoned part of Haven.

The tempo increased, matching the pounding of Senna's heart. She backed off the path and hid behind a plant with leaves the size of her chest. Her hand strayed to her seed belt, her practiced fingers automatically finding the pouch of Thine seeds. She waited, as motionless as a mouse at the mere whisper of a wing.

A figure emerged onto the path, features hidden by the dark. Coming level with Senna, a muscular hand brushed some of the overgrown vegetation out of the way.

The hand was distinctly male, but there were no men on the island. They weren't allowed, not without the Discipline Head's permission. If this man shifted a mere fraction, he would touch her cheek. She gasped softly.

He paused and cocked his head as if listening. Holding her breath, she closed her eyes so they wouldn't catch a stray bit of light and reveal her. The man hesitated before moving forward, his pace faster this time.

Senna let out her breath in a rush. She bit her lip as the man disappeared back into the shadows that had birthed him. Steeling herself, she stepped onto the path.

A man where no man should be? Perhaps she was mistaken. After all, it was so dark. But there was a way to find out. Obscured by time and neglect, the gravel path held a perfect imprint of a boot. She eased her foot inside. It was easily half a dozen sizes bigger.

She hadn't been mistaken. But why was a man here? The music changed, luring her forward. Her fingers buried in Thine seeds, Senna slipped after him. She kept him just in sight—the solid darkness of his form, the scrape of his boots. He rounded a bend. She crept forward, but when she glanced down the path, he was gone.

She paused, listening. The hollow tap of a boot on wood. There. He was slipping up the steps to a tree house. Dropping into the shadows of the plants, Senna parted a leafy branch and peered upward.

The man glanced around before tugging the door closed behind him. It shut soundlessly, as if someone had oiled the hinges recently. Senna heard voices that were too muted for her to make out the words. The tempo of the music picked up, pounding out a savage beat.

Something was wrong, and she had to know what. Her breath catching in her throat, she eased silently up the steps. At the top, she couldn't help but notice the creepers had been carefully pulled away from the doorframe. Whoever this was, they'd met here before.

Senna peeked past the vines that partially covered one of the broken windows. Through the gloom, she could only make out two distinct silhouettes. That meant there wasn't just one man on the island. There were two.

"Why?" asked a bass voice.

A tenor answered, "Because I had to know for certain."

"And *now* you're certain?"

"Yes. She'd put the rest of us to shame. Even Krissin." He paused. "Have you spoken with our contact?"

The bass grunted. "She'll make sure we're clear to depart with our captive tomorrow. And she guarantees our forces will breach the island."

Senna gripped the sill until her fingers ached. Why would anyone attack Haven? And who would help them?

"Good. I'll be glad to go home and stop pretending."

The other man chuckled. "Easy for you to say."

A sigh left the tenor's lips. Senna saw movement and thought he must have stood. "We'll meet again tomorrow after sunset."

A vague shape started toward the door.

The music grew louder, pounding a warning.

Senna gathered herself and rushed down the stairs. She heard the door behind her swing open, followed by a startled cry. "We have to stop her!"

Hauling her skirt above her knees, Senna ran. Her cowl slipped off her head. She glanced back. Her hair swept over her face and partially blocked her view, but she could see two hooded figures chasing her.

The smaller of the two stopped and swung something around above his head. A rhythmic, whooshing sounded around her. Before she could understand what was happening, something solid smacked into the back of her head.

Lights exploded behind her eyes. She pitched forward and hit the gravel hard. And then he was on top of her. Senna didn't have time to think. Acting on reflex, her mouth opened and a song poured forth.

Plants, stop the man who'd halt my flight.
Bind him, though he flails and fights.

A rustling slither filled the air as the plants responded. The man yanked her into his chest, into his arms. His breath washed over her face—he smelled of something dark and sweet, like licorice. Repeating the same verse, she tried to kick free, but his grip was too tight.

A vine shot past her and snatched his arm away. More plants responded, twisting around him and pinning his other arm. Still singing, Senna kicked her way out from under him. One more song, and he'd be wrapped up completely.

Something snapped behind him. She had forgotten about the tenor! She clambered to her feet, a song on her lips. Before the first syllable fell, he barreled into her. She slammed back into the dirt.

Plants, stop—

He shoved a gag into her mouth. Knowing how vulnerable she was without her song, Senna drove her elbow back, catching his wiry frame in the gut. The attacker grunted in pain. His grip loosened enough for her to spit the gag out. But she didn't have enough breath to sing. She twisted until she was chest to chest with him. All she saw was a face wrapped in shadows, dark eyes glinting. She punched as Joshen had shown her, putting all her strength into it.

An explosion of pain spider-webbed through her hand. Her attacker tottered. She shoved him. The man tried to hold on, but his movements were slow and clumsy. Senna kicked her way free and started running. She panted out a song.

Plants of the forest, hide my trail,
For an enemy, I must quell.

She was too winded for the song to be very effective, but it was the best she could manage. At the sound of a sawing knife, she knew the smaller attacker was freeing the larger. They'd be after her soon.

Even with her song weaving the plants behind her, Senna didn't think she could outrun two men. She needed some kind of weapon. Her head whipped from side to side as she searched for something.

All she saw were enormous plants, broken doors, and *windows!* She darted into the dense foliage. Plants whipped her face, stinging her eyes. She erupted onto another of the hundreds of Witch-sung paths that wound between Haven's trees. She followed it for half a dozen steps before darting back the way she'd come.

Beneath a tree's broken window she flattened herself against the ground, her face pressed into the damp soil. Her movements slow and even, her fingers searched for a piece of glass to use as a weapon. All she could find were worthless bits.

She froze as footsteps pounded past her. The men paused uncertainly, but they were good at this game, better than her. Without a word, they split up. Senna could hear them hunting for her.

She tried to slow her breathing. Sweat soaked through the back of her dark green dress. She started searching again. Something sliced her finger—a shard of glass about the size of a knife blade. Keeping her movements smooth, Senna wrapped the edge of her cloak around her hand and picked it up. She chanced lifting her head. Sweat rolling down her temples, she listened for any sign of the men before she scooted backward. When she bumped into the tree house, she eased to her feet and edged to the other side.

Now she was near where they'd first attacked her, hopefully the last place they would think to look for her. Her heart pounding in her throat, she waited. Nothing. She moved away from the tree, toward home, her senses straining for any sign she'd been spotted.

Some instinct made her turn around. By then it was too late. The gag bit into her mouth and the knot pulled tight. But the attacker had underestimated the rest of Senna. She whirled and struck with the glass shard.

A gasp slipped from his lips. Under his hood, the bass's eyes went wide with shock. A gush of warm blood soaked Senna's hand, and she stumbled back in horror.

The attacker fell to his knees, his large hand on his stomach. Senna retreated, fear clawing her insides.

He watched her, the skin around his eyes creased with pain. "You're not safe, Brusenna. Soon, all the Witches will be dead."

2. Nips

The attacker's threat made Senna's heart thump painfully in her chest. Who was this man? How had he known her name? She stepped closer and squinted at his face, trying to make out something besides his dark outline.

Somewhere out of sight, the plants rustled as if someone was running through them. The tenor!

Senna turned and fled, not daring to look back. Three times she fell, once so hard she feared she'd broken her wrist. She yanked on the gag, her lips cracking, before finally managing to pull it off.

Ahead, the warm lights of Haven came into view. She caught glimpses of lanterns gleaming inside the trees like distant stars. Had she really gone so far?

When she finally reached her tree house on the outskirts of the inhabited quarter, her breathing came in ragged gasps. She ran inside the tree, up the spiraling central staircase, and wrenched open her mother's bedroom door.

Her mother sat up. "Brusenna?" Her voice was heavy with sleep.

"We're not safe!" Senna snatched her mother's hand and dragged her outside and deeper into Haven.

"What happened? Why are you covered in blood? What happened to your face?"

Senna ignored her. She had to warn the others. Were there more attackers? Was anyone safe? She didn't stop until she reached the

Ring of Power—a circular clearing ringed by tall, ancient trees. She darted to the center. Tipping back her head, she sang.

Wind, carry my song through all of Haven.
An enemy with purpose craven
Has breached our everlasting border,
Wreaking havoc and disorder.

The wind whipped around her song, carrying its message all over the island. It reverberated off the impassable cliffs. Within moments, Witches were pouring into the Ring of Power, most wearing little more than their shifts.

Prenny, her short gray hair sticking up like the scruff of an aggravated dog, marched straight up to Senna. "What's the meaning of this, Sprout?"

Senna held up her hand to shield her eyes from the lantern Prenny held. The older woman seized her by the wrist.

Her mother gasped and turned Senna's palm toward the lantern light spilling through the clearing.

Exhaustion crashed down on Senna as the two studied her hand. "It's not my blood."

"Some of it is," her mother said.

Her mouth forming a small "O" of surprise, Senna stared at the cuts in her palm, her blood mixing with that of her attacker to run in garish streaks down her sleeves. The glass must have sliced her when she'd stabbed the deep-voiced man. She hadn't even felt it, but now she did. It stung, more by the moment.

Her mother lifted her skirt. "I'll get my kit."

Prenny clicked her tongue as she examined the wounds. "It'll keep for now, Sacra." The older woman smelled of herbs and dirt, but it was not unpleasant.

When her mother didn't pause, Senna reached for her with her good hand. "No! They're still out there!"

"Who's out there?" Coyel, Head of Sunlight, asked as she arrived with Drenelle half a step behind.

Senna winced. "Two men attacked me."

"What?" her mother cried.

More Witches gathered around Senna. All of them gaped at her, fear in their eyes. Senna felt their stares like a mantle of lead and wanted to disappear.

Coyel clapped her hands. "To the middle of the Ring, all of you."

Drenelle grabbed Senna's arm and dragged her away from listening ears. "By the Creators, why would two men attack a sixteen-year-old girl?"

"That's impossible," Prenny growled. "There are no men on the island. And no one can get inside without our permission."

Senna's mother met the old woman's gaze. "Like they didn't get on the island before?"

Prenny stepped back as if she'd been slapped. "The traitor is dead. All the other Witches are accounted for."

Senna shook her head. "I heard them. They're part of a plan to attack Haven. And they're working with a Witch here."

Prenny opened her mouth, but no words came out.

Coyel held herself very still. "You're sure?"

Senna met the woman's blue eyes. "They were guaranteed egress from the island for themselves and a captive."

The three Heads exchanged glances. Senna could see they didn't want to believe her. But the blood on her hands and the bruise swelling on the back of her skull were proof.

Chavis marched toward them. The Witch was Head of Water and therefore their leader in battle. She was dressed in men's clothes. Strapped across her chest was a crisscross harness for her pistols, with a water-emblem coin where the leather straps met. Her long gray hair hung in a braid down the center of her back. "How many? Where?"

Senna pointed a shaking finger back the way she'd come. "Two of them. On the west side of the island."

Chavis whirled around. "Witchlings and Apprentices in the circle. Arianis is in charge."

"But if there's a traitor in our midst—" Drenelle started.

Chavis turned toward her. "Have you a better idea?"

Drenelle slowly shook her head.

Chavis went on, her tone commanding, "Keepers assume battle formation—one Witch from each of the Four Disciplines, with a Water in charge. Search the island. Senna with me."

"I'm coming with my daughter," her mother declared.

Chavis tightened her lips but nodded. "Fine."

Drenelle blanched. "Shouldn't we wait till morning?"

Chavis didn't bother responding.

Arianis glanced at the Witchlings and Apprentices before jogging forward. "Head Coyel, I can help search the island."

Coyel answered without looking at her. "You're still an Apprentice."

Arianis glowered at Senna. "So is *she*."

Senna had to stop herself from rolling her eyes. This really wasn't the time for Arianis' petty jealousies.

Chavis shouldered past Arianis. "Yes, but she knows where she was attacked and you do not. Now move!"

Arianis clenched her jaw and started shouting for the Apprentices and Witchlings to form up. The Apprentices locked forearms and started singing.

The area around them surged with a blast of wind. Shimmering like an aurora, a cylindrical barrier rose into the night sky. Nothing and no one could cross until the Witches released each other.

As long as the circle held, the young Witches would be safe. Unless the traitor…Senna pushed the worry away.

Chavis handed a musket to Prenny and one of the pistols to Coyel. The three women loaded the gunpowder, wad, and ball before tapping the powder into the frizzen.

Senna had just stabbed a man. Watching them load the guns made her stomach hurt. "We have our songs," she said.

"Sometimes a musket works better than Witch song," Chavis said.

Drenelle grabbed her lantern off the ground. "This is a bad idea. We should stay where it's safe."

"Douse the lantern. It will only make us targets and blind us to the night." Chavis started forward without another word.

Drenelle pursed her lips before blowing out the light, but she didn't put the lantern down.

Senna stared at the pistol in Coyel's hands, her whole body loath to go back into the darkness. She listened for the music again, somehow doubting she'd ever heard it in the first place. Hollow silence echoed back to her.

When Senna made no move to follow them, Chavis turned. "Senna, you may need to show us where to go."

The memory of being shot burned through her, and her long-since-healed arm ached anew. She could taste the gunpowder on her tongue from the night her dog, Bruke, had died saving her. She couldn't seem to move.

Gently, her mother took her arm. "Chavis won't shoot anyone unless she has to."

Going back into danger went against Senna's every instinct. Fear seemed to lift her stomach into her throat. Steeling herself, she left the lantern-lit clearing behind.

Her mother pressed herself against Senna's side, and Senna had to admit she was grateful for her presence.

Passing other groups of searching Witches, the five Keepers hustled as fast as they dared, their hands outstretched to feel their way forward, towards the only way in or out of Haven—the underwater cave. If Senna's attackers wanted to flee, it was the only place to go.

Etched in the side of one of the cliffs was a stone archway. Briars and thistle guarded the entrance and grew thick over the cave's name: Velveten.

"No one's been here," Coyel said, her voice heavy with relief.

"Unless a Witch sang them inside." Chavis checked the powder in her pan and half cocked her gun. "Drenelle, light your lamp."

Senna heard the scrape of a rare match. A flame burst to life, burning afterimages into her vision—the sight of Drenelle in a chemise that practically vomited lace. The air was filled with the smell of burning sulfur. Drenelle lit the wick and twisted up the lever on her small, ridiculously ornate lamp.

As light flooded the area, Senna sighed in relief. For the first time since leaving the clearing, she could make out the other Witches' faces instead of amorphous shapes.

Coyel sang away the briars and thistle that hid the elaborate entrance. It was a place that could only be created by Witch song. The intricately engraved arch was just the beginning. Carved into the rock wall all along the island were perfect trees, mountains, curls of wind, the sun, moon, and stars, even the faces of the

Creators. Every image important to the Witches was present. But the once beautiful carvings were worn by time and weather until they were mere shadows of their former majesty.

Much like the Witches themselves.

Chavis took the lantern and eased down the steps. The light threw harsh, crawling shadows on the walls and gave the carvings the appearance of movement, as if they were writhing away from the light. At the bottom, Senna stood on the mosaic stone floor, staring at the black surface of the pool.

Coyel breathed in sharply. "One of the boats is missing."

"They're gone then." Chavis cursed. "How badly was he injured?"

Senna started to clench her fists. Pain shot from her palm up her arm. She made a sound that was somewhere between a grunt and a whimper. "About a hand's span of glass in his stomach."

Chavis chewed her lip. "The other one either carried him out or abandoned him. Come on, back to the place they were last seen." She grabbed the lantern out of Drenelle's hands and shoved it at Sacra. "You stay here just in case. Make sure no one gets past you."

Sacra shot a concerned glance at Senna before hurrying after Chavis. "I'm not leaving my daughter."

Chavis handed her one of the pistols. "We need Brusenna to show us where she was attacked. We need four of us to control the Four Sisters. You are extraneous, therefore you stay."

Sacra stumbled to a halt, her mouth open as if to argue. She swallowed. "You brought me here for this—to guard the door."

"Obviously." Chavis started moving out. "Keep your back against the wall so they can't sneak up on you. If you see one of them, shoot. Aim for the stomach—that way they'll live long enough to be interrogated."

Senna paused beside her mother. She couldn't bring herself to leave her alone. "We shouldn't—"

Coyel gripped her arm and propelled her forward. "Your mother is a very capable Witch. She'll be fine."

Senna turned to watch her mother in the small orb of lantern light. Sacra cocked back the hammer of the pistol and glared into the darkness. Hoping Coyel was right, Senna hurried to catch up with Chavis.

When they moved into the uninhabited quarter of Haven, Drenelle glanced at Senna askance. "What were you doing *here?*"

Senna's mouth went dry, and she had to swallow several times before the words would come. "I couldn't sleep."

After a few minutes of blundering around, she stepped on something hard and oddly shaped. Her veins aching with dread, she stopped to pick it up. She turned it over in her good hand a few times before she realized what it was. A slingshot. Her head seemed to throb in response. "Here."

Chavis pulled out her pistol. "Prenny and Coyel."

Prenny handed her musket to Drenelle, who held it away from her body like it might sully her white chemise. Then the older Witch pulled out four glass vials. "Ready?"

Coyel crooned to the wind.

> Wind, spread these Nips and blow them straight
> To any who may lie in wait.

Wind gushed down on the tops of their heads, swelling away from them when it hit the ground. As Coyel continued the song, Prenny circled them and tossed the contents of each vial into the air. The wind caught the powder, billowing it outward.

Even with the currents blowing it away from their packed group, the Nips made the back of Senna's throat itch and her eyes smart. She held her cloak over her face and squinted through watering eyes.

Coyel stopped singing and rested a hand on Senna's shoulder. "Anyone the powder touched would erupt into a helpless fit of coughing."

The Witches strained, listening. But there was no sound.

Chavis stared into the shadows. "We're not going to find anything on a night like this. Best lock ourselves in and wait till morning. We can do a thorough search then."

"Whoever it was, they're either gone or dead," Prenny said in obvious relief.

Coyel stared into the dark depths of the forest. "Don't be too relieved, Head. Someone brought them inside, which means we still have a traitor on the island."

3. Pendant

After setting her healing kit on the table, Sacra poured a measure of medicine into a cup. "Drink this. It will help with the pain."

Senna's hand shook so badly she could barely keep from slopping the medicine over the brim. She threw back the bitter stuff, gagging at its strength.

Every time she closed her eyes, she heard the bass's gasp as she'd slipped the knife into his guts. She could still taste the metallic fear on her tongue. Her body seemed to store the impression of his arms wrapped around her, the licorice smell of his mouth. A tremor coursed through her body, and the mug slipped from her fingers, clattering to the floor.

Her mother glanced up. "You're starting into an apoplectic fit." She grabbed another potion from the shelf. She held it to Senna's mouth and helped her drink it before wrapping her up in a blanket. But the shudders just kept getting worse.

"Senna, listen to me. You have to calm down."

Senna half shook her head. Without the frenetic rush of fear to hold her emotions at bay, they came crashing down on her. "I just—I wish Joshen were here." She needed him to hold her and reassure her that all would be well.

A hurt look crossed her mother's face. "Slow your breathing. Come, breathe with me." She inhaled slowly and held in the air.

Senna mirrored her until the dizziness passed.

Soon, Senna noticed the edges of her vision softening. Her eyes went unfocused and she tingled everywhere.

"Good. The potion's beginning to work. Just concentrate on breathing." Her mother relaxed a bit. "You're going to be all right."

Senna hissed through her teeth as her mother gently poured salt water onto her wounded hand. Blood welled into the lines of her palm. They formed dark, curling patterns that swirled in the water like incense smoke shifting with the breeze. It was almost pretty.

"What happened out there tonight, Brusenna?"

She only wanted to forget, but her mother needed to know. Senna had repeated her account so many times her head spun with it. Each time, it seemed more dreamlike, less real. With a sigh, she recounted it again.

Her mother held her curved needle over a candle flame. She waited for it to cool before threading it with thin strips of sheep intestines. "The cuts aren't wide, but they are deep. It should only take five or so."

Senna glared at the needle.

"Hold out your hand."

Shutting her eyes, Senna turned away. The needle dug in. She gasped, but it would be worse without her mother's herbs. She squirmed and fought the urge to clench her hand and pull away.

"Hold still. It'll hurt less."

Senna tried to think of something to distract her, but her thoughts danced out of her head before she could catch them.

She was silent until her mother tied the last stitch. "Finished."

Senna studied the ugly cuts in her hand, black string sticking out of her flesh. She wondered what a palm reader would make of the new lines crisscrossing her palm. "Do you think he's dead—the man I stabbed?"

"With a gut wound, probably."

How much must he have hated her to use his dying breath to threaten her, threaten all the Witches? "Then where is his body?"

"Probably hidden somewhere we'll never find it. Or maybe they really did escape."

Senna shivered inside. "Am I a murderer?"

"There's a difference between defending yourself and killing someone who's helpless against you." Her mother smeared some salve onto a bandage and wrapped Senna's hand. "Keep it still for about a week or you'll reopen them."

Staring at the shockingly white bandages, Senna nodded.

As her mother began carefully packing her kit away, she put to words the question that must be on every Witch's tongue. "How did men get onto the island?"

Senna cradled her hand to her chest. "Someone sang them in." She'd thought the Witches were past such dangers when she'd imprisoned the Dark Witch in a tree.

The sounds of her mother repacking her kit stilled. "You know what we must do."

Senna shook her head in an effort to clear the drugs dulling her wits along with the pain. "What do you mean?"

Her mother rested her hand on Senna's arm. "We must leave."

Suddenly more awake, Senna sat up. "I've finally begun to learn. We can't leave now!"

Her mother leaned forward. "I can teach you as well as anyone here. And you said it yourself. The man claimed all the Witches would soon be dead. I can't risk it. I can't risk you."

Senna didn't exactly have friends here, but Joshen was tied to Haven. The Discipline Heads had made it clear time and again that he was their Guardian, not Senna's. And she would not leave him. "So we run again? Is that your answer for everything?"

Her mother's expression tightened. "Senna, sharks and falcons and wolves chase. Deer and mice and sheep run. That's the way of our world."

Senna shook her head. "It wasn't always this way. We haven't always chosen to act like prey."

"Those days are far gone."

"And you'd have us going back to Gonstower, would you? See how long it takes for them to hang one of us?"

Her mother withdrew her hand. "It wouldn't have to be Gonstower. Just...away."

Senna remembered the taunts she'd grown up with. The hatred. "No. I won't live like that. Never again."

Her mother sagged in her chair. "Dying is easy, Senna. Living is hard."

Senna started out of the room, her good hand out to steady her from the vertigo caused by the herbs. "No. Choosing to do the right thing, no matter the consequences, is hard." She swayed into one of the walls, her eyes closed against the spinning.

Her mother carefully draped Senna's arm across her shoulders. "You're not going to make it by yourself."

Senna screwed up her face. "No. I've always had to have help from someone."

"I imagine most of us are like that." They started up the curling stairs. It was a tight fit, especially because Senna kept stumbling and swaying.

"Well, at least I know what kind of drunk you are—philosophical. Could be worse I suppose." Her mother grunted with effort.

Senna stiffened. "I'm not drunk!"

Her mother chuckled. "The herbs I gave you were stronger than your grandfather's whiskey. And they used to mix that with lacquer."

Senna bumped into the railing. "Grandfather? You never talk about him."

Her mother braced her feet to steady her daughter. "He made very strong whiskey."

They'd finally crested the stairs. Senna felt like they should celebrate somehow. "What about Father? Was he your Guardian?"

Sacra shook her head. "He gave it up when we had your sister. Someone had to raise her, and I was too busy."

It was more than Senna had heard about her father in years. "That makes sense."

Her mother helped her into the bed. "Good night."

Senna hitched herself up on her elbow. "But why didn't he—"

Her mother closed the door to her words.

Senna flopped back onto her bed and quickly forgot her frustration. The patterns the tree's leaves made against the backdrop of the stars fascinated her—black on black with a scattering of pinpoint light. She was grateful that for once, sleep came on hard and dreamless.

***

Two days later, Senna sat inside a tree house shaped like a bulging onion. Her stitches itched like mad. To distract herself, she stared westward out a window with peaked tops and bottoms and a swelling center, like a bubble trying to escape from a seed pod.

She was haunted by her attack of a few nights ago, by the land and people dying in Tarten, and by the sweet licorice smell of a dying man.

Her whole body ached with the need to do something—find her attacker, release the curse on Tarten. *Something.* But after only a day, the Heads had insisted all the Apprentices and Witchlings go back to their regular classes, while they continued the search alone.

So Senna studied the trees of Haven. They never ceased to amaze her, especially their variety. For instance, some doors opened right onto the white gravel path. Others sat above curving steps made of woven roots or expanses of living wood. All the windows and doors were peaked and bubbled outward, though they varied in size.

Arianis took down a map from the wall and placed it on an easel. "We begin studying a new nation today. Can anyone tell me what country this is?"

Silence echoed through the room.

"Senna, care to enlighten us?"

She suppressed a groan. The Heads had insisted she take some Witchling classes to fill in her somewhat-spotty education. Unfortunately, some of those classes were taught by Apprentices. This one was taught by Arianis, who had been trained from infancy to defeat the Dark Witch, and whose exceptionally powerful song had ensured a clear path to the highest level of Haven's hierarchy.

And then Senna had come along. She'd defeated the Dark Witch. And there were whispers among the Keepers of her strength—whispers that Senna's song was even stronger than the Dark Witch's.

No one spoke of the astonishing strength of Arianis' song anymore.

Senna tore her gaze from the window and glanced at the map before turning back to her vigil. "It's Harshen."

Arianis crossed her arms. "And what can you tell us of Harshen?"

Senna sighed. Sometimes Arianis gave up at this point. Apparently, today wasn't one of those days. "It's far to the south—a land of deserts and scrubby mountains. The people live in large pavilions and have dark skin. Rivers run high and furious once a year, before dwindling to barren puddles by midsummer. Harshen is isolated by deserts in the interior and horrible storms along the coast."

Arianis grunted. "Almost word for word from *Desert Countries*, by Jennalee Odd. Do you have any original ideas in your head?" Senna didn't respond. It was clear Arianis hadn't really expected her to. "And what do the Harshens think of Witches?"

"They blame us for their country's lack of water," said Nilly, an Apprentice with enormous ears and pretty brown eyes.

"They hate us. The whole world hates us. By destroying Tarten, the Heads only make that perception worse." The words darted from Senna's mouth like a flock of startled birds.

Arianis gaped at Senna. "This is a geography class, not a political debate."

Senna didn't regret what she'd said. After all, it was true. "You asked what the Harshens think of us. I told you."

Arianis answered, her voice dripping with scorn, but Senna had stopped listening. Outside, someone was calling her name.

"Senna! Senna!"

She knew that voice. She shot from her chair.

Arianis startled. "Sit down. Class isn't dismissed yet."

"Senna!" the shout came again.

Senna lifted her skirt and ran from the tree house. In the sharp sunlight of midday, she caught her first sight of Joshen in two months. His brown hair hung over his forehead in waves. His gray eyes—the color of snow in the shade—stood out on his tanned face. The skin around his eyes was creased, as if he never stopped smiling long enough for the lines to smooth out. With an involuntary shriek, she launched herself into his arms.

He caught her and swung her around. She molded her body to his. This was where she fit. It was where she would always fit.

Joshen released her and ran his fingers lightly over the bump on the back of her head, his body tense. "Are you all right?"

She winced. "I'll be fine. When did you arrive?" He'd been in their home country, Nefalie, on a recruiting assignment to find more Guardians.

He inspected her bandaged hand with a frown. "A few hours ago. We had to meet with the Heads first."

"Do you know why someone would attack you?" Senna started at Reden's Tarten accent. She hadn't even noticed him coming up the path behind Joshen.

The Leader of the Guardians wasn't a tall man, but he was well built. His eyes and hair were nearly black, his skin a creamy brown. His face had a certain ageless quality. He could be anywhere from twenty to forty, but Senna had learned over the last few months he was only twenty-four. He'd become Leader of all Tarten's armies at sixteen. His brilliance as a soldier and a tactician had assured his rise to the Leader of the Guardians mere days after he'd rebelled from Tarten, leading the Witches safely away from the armies he'd once commanded.

His keen eyes seemed to bore into Senna. And he wasn't the only one staring. Senna became aware of dozens of eyes watching them. Clearly reluctant to obey Arianis' attempts to shoo them back to their seats, Witchlings peeked out the window and door of the tree. Senna felt the weight of their stares like stones in her pockets.

"I need to borrow your student, Apprentice." Reden gripped Senna's arm and steered her away.

Arianis' eyes narrowed to slits, and Senna could see her trying to come up with some reason to deny his request. But Reden only answered to Chavis and the other Heads. Not to upstart Apprentices.

"Fine, but I want an oral report on Harshen mountains and trade routes, due tomorrow," Arianis said.

She no doubt knew how much Senna loathed public speaking. But it was a small price, one she'd gladly pay for the chance to be with Joshen again.

Before either Guardian pelted her with a barrage of questions, she told them of feeling like someone was watching her the night of her attack. The secrets whispered in an abandoned tree house. Being attacked by the two men. Her narrow escape. The terrifying trip back into the darkness with the Heads. "I took them back the next morning. All we found was broken vegetation and some bloody soil to go with the slingshot."

Reden pursed his lips. "You realize they were after you? You're the captive."

Senna's head spun. "No—that's not possible."

Joshen raked his hands through his hair. "How do we know they didn't simply attack her because she overheard them?"

Reden scanned the trees around them. "If that were the case, she'd be dead. Instead, they tried to subdue her. That means they wanted to take her alive. The question is why."

"Maybe they just didn't want to kill anyone," she murmured.

Reden's expression hardened. "You don't come on a mission like this unprepared to kill someone."

Joshen nodded westward. "The Tartens? But why would they want Senna?"

Reden shook his head. "We don't know it was the Tartens. As for why someone wants her, we don't know that, either."

She stared in the distance without seeing anything. "Their accents didn't sound Tarten."

"What did they sound like?" Reden asked.

Shuddering, she tried to match the accents to anything else she'd heard. She was usually good with all kinds of inflection, but she was pretty sure she hadn't heard this one before. "I don't know."

Reden ground his teeth. "Is your Witch song as strong as they say it is?"

Senna lowered her gaze. Her song had always been exceedingly strong, but since the Creators had gifted her with the Dark Witch's song, the power of her voice had shot up like a summer weed. "Yes."

Reden hesitated. "The Heads have searched the island. They believe whoever attacked you is gone. I'm not so sure."

Joshen grunted in agreement. "This place has more burrows than a field full of gophers."

Senna pressed her hands into her stomach, just over the crescent-moon tattoo that circled her navel and marked her as a Witch.

Reden eyed the foliage between the trees. Senna tried to see it as he would—cover for anyone sneaking around the island instead of a beautiful byproduct of hundreds of daily songs.

"I tried to convince them to move the island," he said. "They refused, claiming the Witches' numbers are too low to attempt it. Nor do they believe they are in any real danger."

Senna halted. "But the man said—"

Reden held out a forestalling hand. "I know. But the Heads trust in their walls and their songs to protect them."

Senna's wounded hand pounded in rhythm with her racing heart. "So they won't do anything?"

Reden gestured to Joshen. "I convinced them to bring Guardians onto the island to watch the entrance and send out patrols. That way there will be no more men sneaking inside."

Senna's mouth fell open. Men had never been allowed on the island for longer than a few days. That the Heads had agreed to let the Guardians stay spoke volumes of their fear.

Reden started off again, and Senna fell into step beside Joshen. She didn't know where the two were going, and she didn't care, as long as she was with Joshen.

"Will they let you Guard me now?" she asked him.

His jaw was tight. "No. They say safeguarding the entrance should be enough to keep you safe, and my presence would only distract you from your studies. Besides, it's against the rules."

She managed a tight smile. It wasn't enough, but that Joshen was here at all was a miracle. "They're probably right—you would distract me."

They arrived at the tree house Reden had used during his last stay on the island. He unlocked the door and pushed on it, but it stuck fast. He dropped his shoulder and rammed the door. It flew open and banged into the opposite wall, making Senna jump.

Reden's desk was just to the left of the entrance. He brushed the dust from his chair before collapsing onto it. "You need to tell me the truth about what you were really doing in the uninhabited part of the island in the middle of the night. None of this, 'I couldn't sleep' business you gave the Heads."

How had he known? She closed her eyes.

"Senna?" Joshen prodded.

Despite how many times she had told her story, she'd always left this part out. "I've begged the Heads to release the curse on Tarten. They've refused me time and again. I would lift it myself, but it takes an entire choir...so I do what I can."

Joshen brushed her hair over her shoulder. "Oh, Senna."

She met his gaze. "They saved our lives, Joshen, at risk to their own. How can we just forget that?"

"I haven't forgotten," Reden said, his voice thick.

Her face burning with shame, Senna stared at the perfectly smooth floor. Of course Reden hadn't forgotten. He *was* Tarten. And he'd sacrificed his country for the world. Senna wondered if she had that kind of strength. She measured herself and came up dreadfully short. "I'm sorry."

Somehow, this was her fault. After all, she had agreed to curse Tarten. Had asked Reden to betray his people. Had helped sing that curse into being.

"I'm where I should be." Reden's voice had softened.

Senna nodded.

The Leader started searching his desk. "How did you know to hide from your attacker in the first place?"

Her breath caught in her throat. Haltingly, she told him she'd heard music nearly every night—the song of the Four Sisters. And that the night she was attacked she'd heard music all around her, warning her.

"Has it happened since?" Reden asked.

"Not like that."

He opened his mouth to say something but hesitated, as if measuring his words carefully. "Senna, sometimes a lie is better than the truth—if that truth does more harm than good. I think it best that your singing for Tarten stay among us. Do you understand?"

Senna stared at him in disbelief. She thought she knew Reden, just like she knew Joshen. Reden was a career soldier, a man of honor, a man who saw the world in terms of defensibility and tactics. She'd never expected him to encourage her to lie. Especially not to the Heads. But then, he'd betrayed his country and his men to save the world. Some might not call him honorable at all.

As if uncomfortable under her scrutiny, Reden waved them toward the door. "Joshen, see that she gets to her next class."

His hand on the small of her back, Joshen held open the door. They stepped out of the tree and moved down the steps made of the tree's roots. Senna eyed the horizon expectantly. She sensed a storm would be rolling over the cliffs soon—after all, she had helped sing it into being this morning.

As she listened, it seemed the wind's fingers strummed branches like strings; the sound resonated in hollows and crevices. She could almost taste the mineral rain, see the color melt away into shades of gray, and feel the cool damp.

"Senna?"

She realized Joshen had been speaking to her for a while and she hadn't heard any of it.

She forced a bright smile. "How are you?"

He shrugged. "I missed you. And I'm starving! Are you sure you can't sing a steer to swim to the island? I could use a steak."

She laughed for real this time. "You know Witch song doesn't work on animals. If it did, I'd have sung you here weeks ago."

Grinning, he glanced up and down the trail as if making sure no one was watching before pulling her off the path. They ended up hidden by the plants, cradled in the buttressed roots of an enormous tree.

Turning suddenly serious, Joshen studied her, his gaze seeming to unearth everything she wanted so desperately to keep hidden. "Now, tell me why you're so sad."

She let out a bitter laugh. How could he so easily see the darkness she was desperately trying to hide? "I thought being with all the other Witches would mean I'd finally find a place I belonged, but I'm more alone here than anywhere I've ever been." It was true. Even when her mother had left her, she'd had her dog Bruke, and later Joshen. Now Bruke was dead, and they'd taken Joshen away.

But he was back now. It would get better.

"What about your mother?"

Senna fought to keep her emotions from overwhelming her. "The only words that ever pass between us are angry. So we keep silent." She didn't say her mother wanted them to leave Haven forever. Nothing good could come of his knowing that. She gripped his shirt and buried her face in his chest. "And there's the nightmares. Nearly every night."

His arms tightened around her. She wet her lips. Dare she tell him the next part? "Something's happening to me, Joshen. It's not just that my song's getting stronger. My senses are, too. I truly hear the pain of the Four Sisters in Tarten. It haunts me."

With the tip of his thumb, he traced the tattoo on her stomach— his touch unerringly accurate. "What can I do to make it better?"

By the Creators, she'd missed the smell of him—horses and the sea. "Make me forget, for just a little while."

He tipped her chin up and kissed her. He was always soft and gentle, but today she felt an undeniable hunger somewhere deep inside him. He was trying to suppress it. But she didn't want that. She wanted him to banish the lingering foulness of the curse and the fear that had never released her from its sweaty grasp, replacing all of that with the sweet taste of his mouth.

Gripping fistfuls of his dark hair, she pulled him down and deepened the kiss. His lips crushed against hers, Joshen responded, kissing her like he'd never kissed her before. The stubble along his jaw was rough against her chin. She felt herself melting, going soft inside.

Breathless, she pulled away before things grew more heated. "Mother will call out the Heads if I'm not home for supper." She wanted to invite him, but she feared his presence would upset the fragile silence in her home. "And after, I have another class."

With a groan that sounded like half frustration and half pain, Joshen rested his forehead against hers. "This late?"

"Three of the Four Sisters are more awake at night. On the next dark phase of the moon, the chesli harvest will begin. That lasts until dawn every night until the moon starts to outshine the flowers." Senna let herself linger next to him. "Drenelle says communing with the earth works best at night during a rainstorm."

"Mmm hmm." She could tell he wasn't really listening. He ran his fingers along the edges of her face. "How much longer until I can marry you?"

Senna licked her swollen lips, savoring the taste of him. "Apprentices aren't allowed to marry. You know that. "

He cradled her face in his hands. "Well then, how much longer until they graduate you to a Keeper?"

She tried to imagine their future, but she couldn't picture spending the rest of their lives on this tiny little island, hidden away from the rest of the world. Joshen would never have his horses. She would never have the freedom she longed for.

Putting a little distance between them, she pulled her necklace out from under her dress. From it hung her pendant—a circular amber piece that had been cut into a waxing crescent and a waning gibbous.

She tried to unclasp it, but her injured hand wouldn't cooperate. Joshen brushed her hair to the front of her shoulder and fumbled with the catch until he had it free.

With a click, she detached the waning gibbous and slipped it from the cord before settling the crescent back in the hollow of her throat. The gibbous felt warm and familiar in her palm. "I meant to give this to you earlier."

Taking Joshen's hand, she placed it inside. "The moon is the sign of the Witches. Each phase represents our power as individuals. The full moon is the combined power of all of us. This pendant was cut to represent that. You and I, we're stronger together than apart. And if you ever need to find me, just tap the pendant against a piece of metal. It will vibrate and lift, pointing in my direction. I'll be able to do the same for you."

Joshen stared at the pendant. "I don't know what to say."

She smiled. "Say you'll always be there. No matter what."

"Always."

She fingered her necklace. Next to the pendant was the ring Joshen had given her over two months ago. It was a simple thing, made of willow branches that Coyel had sung to wrap around a pearl.

Senna's mother and the other Heads had had a fit over it. Apprentices weren't allowed to have contact with men, let alone be betrothed to one. So Senna had quietly moved it from her hand to her neck. For her, the meaning was still the same, regardless of its location.

Joshen rubbed the pearl with the edge of his thumb. "If it were just you and me on a horse ranch somewhere, we could marry whenever we pleased."

Senna leaned toward him, inhaling the air he breathed. "Someday."

He kissed her again, but there was a taste of goodbye in it. She wouldn't risk being late for class—not when she still had so much to prove.

4. EARTH SONG

A cold trickle of rain dripped through Senna's soaked hood and slid down her back. Wishing she'd left her long hair down, she shivered under her heavy cloak. Thunder grumbled in the sky. Lightning stabbed the sea beyond Haven's high cliffs. Senna used the brief illumination to glance back at the long line of sopping-wet Witchlings trailing behind her.

"Come along. The storm will only remain this strong for an hour at best. We mustn't dally."

Senna had to resist the urge to strangle Drenelle. She'd left Joshen for this. All because the Head insisted they commune during a storm. Something about the earth opening up to receive the rain, and therefore opening up to them as well. She also claimed the earth came awake at night.

So here they were, traipsing through Haven in the middle of the night. In the pouring rain. Drenelle and the other Heads believed the attackers were gone. Senna suspected at least one was still out there. The whole outing was utter madness.

It wasn't like Senna needed to slip into a trance to feel the Four Sisters—Earth, Water, Plants, and Sunlight—all around her.

As the class finally reached the Ring of Power, the clouds parted briefly, revealing the crescent moon.

Four was a sacred number for the Witches. There were four phases of the moon in direct opposition to each other—half moon, crescent moon, gibbous moon, and full or new moon. Four seasons. Four Sisters or elements. Four Creators who'd formed the world by combining their mastery of their respective elements. Four Discipline Heads who were patterned after the Creators to administrate over their respective elements.

Drenelle peeked out from under her umbrella. "Perfect. This is all going perfectly. All of you spread out. Make yourselves comfortable."

Comfortable? Sopping wet in a lightning storm. Under a tree. Comfortable? More like suicidal. But Senna kept her thoughts to herself. In Drenelle's earth lessons, they mostly identified rocks, meditated to map out valuable deposits, identified soil composition, and studied earth-tremor detection and reduction.

Tugging her hood further down, Senna did her best to arrange her cloak so it protected her from the damp grass, then leaned back against the smooth trunk of one of Haven's trees, which managed to keep a little of the rain off her.

"All right, everyone," Drenelle said in her most soothing voice, which reminded Senna of a cawing crow. "Dig your feet into the earth. Spread yourself into it like a seedling, sending forth roots—searching, feeling, being. Send away your conscious thoughts. Feeling the earth does not happen in your consciousness, but deeper, in your unconscious mind. Let yourself flow with the natural rhythms, like sand slipping between your fingers."

There was no way Senna could keep her bandage dry, which meant after Drenelle's class, she'd have to suffer through another of her mother's scoldings. Grumbling, Senna untied the laces of her boots and slipped them off. Despite her sour mood, she couldn't help but be drawn into the earth. Much as she hated to admit it, Drenelle was right. The Fourth Sister was more open during the storm, like the earth expanded upward, stretching to receive the rain, even as Senna extended down.

While Drenelle was still droning on, Senna was already deep within her unconscious mind, flowing with the natural rhythms of the earth. Her connection with the Four Sisters allowed her Witch senses to travel further and deeper than she'd ever gone before.

She heard something…something far away. She shifted toward it, but no matter how fast she moved, the sound grew no closer. She paused, frustrated. And then she remembered what Drenelle had said.

Like sand slipping between your fingers. Senna stopped chasing the sound and imagined her soul as a grain of sand, sifting wherever the wind or the rain or the earth willed. Imagination became reality. Her soul pulled out of her body.

It should have been frightening—terrifying, even. But it wasn't. It was liberating.

Smelling the wind all around her, she twirled on the currents like a handful of dandelion fluff. The wind set her down gently. She opened her eyes to find herself caught on a mountaintop. She stood immovable as the peak. Her soul was buffeted by wind and rain, yet she was not afraid. All was as it should be. As it would be for eons to come.

But her soul was not as patient as a mountain. She allowed herself to sink into rich, dark earth with the rain. Deeper, where precious stones lay like lumps of sugar. She reveled in the darkness, in the pressure and stillness.

All her life, she'd searched for this kind of communion—this sense of belonging, of oneness. She'd never felt more complete. More at peace.

From far away, she heard the sound again. It was music. Deep-throated drums and echoing horns in a song that was seductive with a texture so cavernous she'd never reach the end of it. Senna swayed to the rhythm, her throat aching to sing.

So she did. She wasn't conscious of the words she sang, but the music paused as if listening. After half a heartbeat, it started up again, its rhythm melded with hers. Delighted, she sped up the tempo and lifted her pitch. The music matched her.

She cast her senses wider, her heart full of wonder and her voice eager to find something else. She explored, dancing with the Four Sisters as the music swirled around her, teasing her with its beauty.

And then she slammed to a stop against some kind of block or barrier. She held out her hand. Colors rippled outward where she touched the barrier. The music hummed beneath her fingertips. This was Witch made. And if a Witch made it, another Witch could unmake it.

She tipped her head, listening to the faint tinkling song until she had it memorized. She sang again and the song changed to match hers. The barrier faded a little, like darkness before the dawn.

Best not to completely destroy it. After all, she only wanted to see what was beyond it. Smiling, she passed through the weakened barrier. She cast about, looking for landmarks as Drenelle had taught her. An island surrounded by briny water. A shore in the distance with mountains. Change the mountains out for hills and it was eerily similar to Haven bordering Nefalie. But Senna's body was so far away, an ocean away from where she sat in the pouring rain and—

She froze as the sound of the music changed. Earth song squeezed and pressed against her. She gasped and listened hard. And then she understood. Witch song was all around her like pelting hail. And not just one Witch. Hundreds of them. They were singing against her.

But that was impossible. There couldn't be hundreds of Witches outside of Haven.

Was it because she'd damaged their barrier? Confused and frightened, Senna fled back the way she'd come. She opened her eyes to find herself standing in the center of the Ring of Power with no memory of having moved there. Her hood was thrown back, rain streaming down her face. Whatever she'd experienced had stirred up a savage fear, awakening instincts that overrode rational thought. She tipped her face into the rain and sang.

> *Haven lift up thy stakes,*
> *Winds a path to make—*

A stinging pain spread across her face. Her hand to her cheek, Senna stumbled back in shock. The earth trembled all around her.

Hand raised for another slap, Drenelle stood before her, chest heaving. "Who taught you that song?"

Senna suddenly grew conscious of the mud squelching between her bare toes. Bewildered, she searched for some kind of explanation. The Witchlings were on their feet, their expressions stunned. Feeling the perfect imprint of the woman's hand, Senna dropped her head. "I— What song, Head?"

Drenelle scrutinized Senna like a dead spider in her tea cup. "Don't lie to me!"

Senna opened her mouth, but the right answer refused to fill it. "Head?"

Drenelle seemed to remember where they were. She pointed to three Witchlings. "Go find the other Heads. Tell them to meet me at the Council Tree." They pivoted and started away. "Run!" Drenelle shouted. The girls sprinted through the storm.

Drenelle gripped Senna's arm and hauled her through the Ring and towards the largest tree on the island. Its buttressed roots were so wide and tall it would take a rope to climb them. The Council Tree.

Senna's heart seized in her chest. "What have I done wrong, Head?"

Drenelle squeezed her arm so tight Senna winced. "Inside."

The Discipline Head swung open the ponderous door between the two widest roots. Before them was a wooden desk set just in front of a set of spiraling stairs so smooth they appeared to be made of liquid frozen in place.

Mistin started out of her chair. Her eyes widened, and she shot Senna a concerned glance. The small Apprentice was the closest thing to a friend Senna had on the island.

Drenelle hauled her up the stairs, her footsteps heavy. At the top was a circular hallway with five doors. Drenelle marched for the largest door, directly opposite them. Inside was a crescent-shaped room with warped windows fitted between rifts in the tree. Bookshelves lined the walls.

Coyel sat beside the well-bricked-in parlor stove, a book in her lap. She looked younger with her blonde hair hanging loose down her back. "Brusenna? Drenelle, what's this about?"

Drenelle started pacing from one side of the room to the other. "I don't want to explain it three different times. We'll wait for the others."

Chavis came in moments later. She swung off her cloak and set it on a hook beside the fire. Today, her graying hair hung in twin braids. Senna nervously eyed the pistols Chavis never took off.

Drenelle shucked off her dripping cloak and threw it on a hook by the fire. Her wine-colored skirts were damp around the edges. "Where's—"

Another voice overrode hers. "This better not be more idiocy about mining deposits in the middle of the Darkwell Sea."

"There's enough precious stones there to buy a whole fleet of ships!" Drenelle tried to growl, but it sounded more like a spitting cat.

Prenny went on as if Drenelle hadn't spoken, "I was in the middle of creating my Ioa potion after Brusenna stole my last batch. It takes months to prepare. And I had to leave it in the care of a trembling Witchling. If that girl ruins it—" Prenny's tirade stumbled to a halt when she finally noticed Senna. "What's the Sprout doing here?"

Senna folded her arms across her chest. "I had to have that potion to save all of you from Espen."

Coyel rolled her eyes heavenward. "Drenelle, is this about the earth tremor we felt earlier?"

Drenelle turned her scorching gaze from Prenny to Coyel. "Brusenna started to sing the Relocation Song. We're lucky I stopped her before she moved us."

Chavis sat up straighter. "She what?"

Senna knew she'd sung something forbidden, but she still didn't know what. "The words were just there!"

Ignoring her, Chavis dropped into a chair. "And the island began to respond?"

"That's impossible," Prenny said as she held her hands over the stove. "Even a Seventh Level couldn't make the earth shift. Not alone. A song that powerful takes *hundreds* of Witches."

For the first time, Senna noticed that Drenelle looked rather pale—almost frightened. "I heard it."

Every Head was silent. Senna moistened her lips. "I—I don't know what's happening."

Coyel's over-bright eyes fixed on her. "You began the song that moves the island."

Senna took a step back. "I— What? No. I was only meditating on earth, like Drenelle said. And I heard music. It was so beautiful I sang along. And then I became frightened and the words came to me."

"You heard music?" Chavis repeated with an undercurrent to her voice Senna didn't understand. Anger or fear, or both.

Coyel laced her fingers over her stomach. "Did anyone teach you the Relocation Song?"

Senna shook her head. "I was just frightened, and words were there."

"Frightened of what?" Prenny asked softy. She'd opened the grate and was staring into the fire. It was almost as if she were speaking to the flames.

Senna studied the oldest Head's profile. For a woman in her sixties, Prenny had amazingly few wrinkles—probably because she knew of potions to diminish them. "You wouldn't believe me," Senna finally replied.

Her face flushed from the fire, Prenny studied Senna with a hard expression. "I might."

Senna took a deep breath and told them everything that had happened in the Ring of Power. They listened without interrupting. Drenelle slumped in a chair, Chavis wore a grim expression, and Prenny stood stiff and unmoving beside the fire.

When Senna finished, Coyel's expression revealed nothing. "Is it possible for that many Witches to gather without our knowledge?"

Chavis blew out a breath. "Surely we would have felt such a thing through the Four Sisters—every time they sang together, the elements would have shifted."

Drenelle sniffed. "Are you certain you didn't just fall asleep?"

Senna didn't bother answering.

Coyel rubbed her neck. "Foreign Witches would explain how two men entered the island uninvited and would relieve of us of finding a traitor."

Senna bit her lip. "Can't you strip the Dawn Song away from the other Witches?"

Chavis snorted. "We need a name or the actual person to banish him or her."

Coyel sighed. "All right, Senna, we'll take care of this. You go on home."

Senna paused. "I'd like to help."

Coyel smiled tightly. "Remember your place, *Apprentice* Brusenna. From now on, please remember that a Witch's song is also a weapon. Best not to do something if you don't understand the consequences."

Her head hanging, Senna nodded.

Coyel motioned toward the door. "Please don't repeat the song. We don't want the words to become common knowledge. And don't tell anyone about what happened tonight."

Senna nodded again and had to stop herself from running out the door. As she started to pull it shut behind her, she heard Drenelle's high voice. "You're just going to let her go?"

"It's begun." Senna just caught sight of Prenny turning away from the fire. "I tried to warn you."

At the old woman's words, Senna froze and left the door open a sliver.

Coyel groaned. "I had hoped Senna would be spared."

"You should tell her," Chavis said softly.

What *are* they talking about? Senna wondered.

Coyel straightened to her full height. "Absolutely not. No matter what transpires, none of us can tell Senna. We all agreed to this."

Chavis rubbed her forehead. "It's not fair. She's just a child."

Prenny rested her hand on the Head of Water's shoulder. "We're not going to let her die."

Die? Senna held her hand to her mouth to keep from gasping and alerting the Heads to her presence.

Prenny seemed to shake herself. She reached for her cloak. "I have a potion to tend to."

The four women rose to their feet.

Senna backed away from the door, her mind numb with shock. Knowing they would come out at any moment, she pivoted and ran down the smooth steps two at a time.

"Brusenna?" Mistin called as she shot past the secretary's desk. "What's wrong?"

Senna didn't pause. Didn't even turn around. She just threw open the door and sprinted across the now-deserted Ring of Power.

5. TRAVELING

Lightning flashed, dressing the island in white. Stinging rain pounded against Senna's face. She crossed the Ring of Power and shot inside the trees again.

Spared? Dying? By the Creators, what had the Heads meant? What was happening to her?

Senna wanted to run straight out of Haven and hide. She darted off the path, into the dense foliage. Gasping, she collapsed against a tree. With her forehead pressed up against its moist bark, she tried to slow her galloping heart. Her injured hand pounded in rhythm to the blood pumping through her.

Suddenly she stiffened and the hairs on the back of her neck rose. Someone was watching her. She stole a look around, but saw nothing besides shadows skulking from the light.

Was it one of the attackers from the other night? She shouldn't have wandered off alone again. All the trees around the Ring of Power were inhabited. But in her desperation to get away, she'd left the inhabited quarter. She was alone now, in the dark forest.

She saw no movement, no hint of anything. She cursed herself for leaving her seed belt in her tree house, but she hadn't wanted to risk getting the seeds wet. Unable to bear it anymore, Senna backed deeper into the foliage. The plants in front of her suddenly shivered. She opened her mouth, a scream on her lips.

"Senna?"

She let out all her breath in a rush. "Joshen?"

He was breathing hard, as if he'd run to catch up to her. "What happened? Why did Drenelle haul you into the Council Tree?"

"How did you know about that?"

He shifted his feet uncomfortably. "Reden and I both disagree with the Heads. Merely guarding the entrance to the island isn't enough. You'll be watched by one of us at all times."

She gaped at him, partially horrified by the lack of privacy, partly relieved she wasn't alone.

Before she decided which emotion was stronger, Joshen wet his lips and stepped closer. "Was that earth tremor—was that really you?"

Hugging herself, Senna nodded. "I heard music."

He pulled her deeper into the buttressed roots of the tree and put his hands on both sides of her to shield her from the rain. "You think this has to do with Espen giving you her song?"

The cold had settled so deep in Senna's bones she wasn't sure she'd ever be warm again. She tugged up Josh's shirt and pressed her cold hands against the hard muscles of his stomach. She heard his sharp intake of breath, but he didn't push away. She snuggled her cold nose against the crook of his neck.

When she didn't answer, he tipped her face up. "Senna?"

She met his gaze as the rain splashed off his hood onto her face. "I don't know. Maybe." She told him everything—well, almost. She glossed over the part where she'd overheard the Heads saying she would die. Joshen was unbearable when he was worried. "All my life I've been surrounded by secrets, forced to hide while the world falls apart around me."

When he didn't respond, she pulled back. Lightning lit up the sky, illuminating his face. His brow was drawn. "What secrets?"

She wiped away a rivulet of rainwater dripping from her nose. "All I know is the Heads are hiding something from me. I plan to unearth those secrets, and then I'm going to save Tarten."

Joshen closed his eyes as if he were in pain. "How?"

The enormity of the task nearly crushed her. "I don't know yet."

He was silent for a time. "It's late. I need to get you home. Come on, I'll see you there safely."

He walked with her toward the inhabited quarter.

From off to the side, Senna saw a flash of movement between the trees. "Joshen, did you see that?"

He glanced up sharply and stepped in front of her. "What?"

She studied the shadows. Joshen couldn't have been the one watching her earlier, because he'd been chasing after her. "Just before you came, I thought someone was watching me."

He cursed softly. "Powder's damp. Worthless."

He pushed her in front of him and pulled his knife free. They crossed the barren Ring of Power. She only stopped long enough to grab her abandoned boots. She hesitated when she saw the lantern light in her parlor. A lecture was surely waiting for her inside.

Joshen squeezed her hand. "You want me to go in with you?"

Senna shook her head. "It's probably better if you don't."

His broad shoulders drooped a little. He had to know Senna's mother didn't like him.

"Don't worry. She doesn't like anyone. Me included."

"I or one of the other Guardians will be here in the morning. Bolt the door and stay inside until then." He kissed her piously and stepped back, then waited while she mounted the steps. She knew he wouldn't leave until she'd locked the door.

Through the window, she watched him go, but her gaze was drawn back to the darkness. She *felt* someone out there. She stepped back and pulled the drapes closed.

Behind her, Senna's mother used a dried leaf to mark her place in her book. "Why are you barefoot?" She found a towel and tossed it to her daughter.

Senna dropped her boots by the door and started cleaning her feet.

"The rest of Drenelle's class came home long ago."

The words that hung unsaid made the air hard to breathe. Senna considered telling her mother everything, but she didn't want to relive that conversation again. Besides the Heads had asked her not to tell anyone; she'd already broken that promise by telling her Guardian, but that was Joshen. "I spoke to Joshen for a moment afterward."

"Guardians aren't to have contact with Apprentices."

Senna said the one thing she knew her mother wouldn't argue with. "Reden and Joshen feel I'm still in danger. They plan on watching over me."

Obviously flustered, Sacra took one look at Senna's wet bandages and hauled out her healing kit. "That doesn't explain why you're late."

Senna sat at the table, her cheeks burning as her mother cut away the soiled, damp wrapping. She knew what her mother thought—that she'd sneaked away to meet Joshen—but she couldn't tell her the truth.

Sacra inspected her daughter's wound. "There's a very good reason Guardians were not allowed on the island before now. Your studies come first."

"They do." Senna's palm was wrinkled and waxy. The stitches stuck out, black against her pale skin. The puckered wounds almost looked like the pursed lips of an old man.

Sacra applied a strong-smelling salve and started rewrapping the hand. "See that it stays that way. Because if that changes, so will your privileges."

"I'm sixteen, Mother. Old enough to be married."

Her mother tied off the bandage. "Senna, I don't think you're ready for this. The only man you've ever known is Joshen. And you're so very young. How can you know what you want when you're still discovering who you are?"

Senna cradled her hand against her chest. "He's a good man, Mother. Why won't you give him a chance?"

Sacra repacked her kit, each item in its place. "This isn't about Joshen. This is about you. If you're not strong enough without him, you'll never be strong enough with him." Leaning forward, she rested her hand on Senna's arm. "You owe it to him, to yourself, to become the woman you're meant to be."

"Just because you failed doesn't mean I will," Senna said coldly.

Sacra's gaze went distant, it was like she wasn't here at all. "Failed? Yes, I failed. Your father. Your sister. You." Her pain was almost visible, as if grief had been etched on her skin. "So you should learn from my mistakes instead of repeating them."

As though some unseen weight bore down on her, Sacra took a labored breath. "It's healing nicely. Try to keep it dry this time." She trudged up the stairs.

Senna watched her go, regret building in her chest. Long ago, someone had told her she should pray that she would never experience the hurts her mother had, that she shouldn't judge her mother without knowing those hurts. "Mother, I'm sorry. I just... have you ever heard the music that wasn't really there? Have you ever danced with that music and found yourself somewhere else entirely?"

Sacra half turned, tears shining bright in her eyes. "Traveling? No. Such a thing is of legend."

Traveling... Senna straightened. "What legend?" Legends were sometimes based on fact, after all.

Sacra shook her head. "The legends of women long dead." She started back up the stairs with a set in her shoulders that indicated she would speak of it no more.

The open, loving relationship Senna had once had with her mother seemed far away and long ago. All Senna felt now was the hollow ache where once light and warmth had been.

After hanging up her sodden cloak by the stove, Senna went to her own room. *Traveling.* If her mother knew the name for what Senna had done, then so did the Heads. Why hadn't they told her? Why were they keeping things from her?

Perhaps because by Traveling, she could unearth the truth they were hiding. Which meant she had to try it again. She had to go back to that hidden land.

She changed out of her damp clothes one-handed, put on a fresh shift, and crawled under her blankets for warmth. She imagined herself as a grain of sand at the mercy of the Four Sisters. It came easier this time. No sooner had she let her mind relax than her soul left her body again.

The wind caressed her skin and wrapped around her with the sound of high strings and the tinkling of hundreds of raindrops. Her senses wanted to dance with the music, to sing and be sung to. Though she'd only experienced this once before, her soul seemed to crave it.

She danced across the waters, her feet kicking up drops that sparkled with captured moonlight. She flew with birds, the wind tickling hair and feathers, like she was simply one of them in a different form.

But her joy ground to a halt when the barrier shimmered to life before her. She didn't want to cross it. Not just because it couldn't exist, but because she somehow knew they would be waiting for her. But she had committed herself to finding answers, and this was the only way she knew how.

Going through the barrier felt a little like crossing a curtain of honey, but it didn't seem as thick this time. It was as if it was somehow diminished.

The wind set her down in water up to her ankles. The rocky shore bruised her feet and the chill water splashed the hem of her shift. Trying to discover where she was, she cast her senses of the Earth Sister outward.

An island. Westward, beyond the ocean, was more land—a desert, mountains. Just as she drew upon the Plant Sister, the ground vibrated beneath her feet, and she heard Witch song again. The rocks and dirt stirred beneath her. No, not stirring—shifting. Shifting away from her, as if she'd grown so heavy the ground couldn't bear her up.

All at once she realized her danger. She bolted out of the water, but with every step she took, the ground only sucked her in faster. Faster and faster she sank until she was buried up to her waist. She called for the wind to carry her away. It surged around her, whipping her hair around her like something alive.

But the wind wasn't strong enough to lift her out of the mud. All at once, rain pelted her, making the ground softer beneath her feet. Plants and vines reached out to snag her arms, immobilizing her as the dirt swallowed her up to her breasts, then up to her neck.

She was going to die.

She screamed, her mouth filling with dirt. She couldn't breathe, couldn't move. Using the last air in her lungs, Senna sang.

Stop.

The trembling ceased, and the plants loosened their grip. Senna clawed her way out of the rough hole and staggered to her feet.

Her injured hand ached fiercely, and she was covered in welts and scratches. Breathless, she sang for the wind to take her home. She was lifted from the mud and hurtled across the skies into her own bed, into her own body.

Gasping, Senna tried to sit up, but blankets tangled her limbs. She fell to the floor with a thud and kicked her way free. Her shift was spotless. Lifting her shaking hands, she stared at her clean skin, her pristine bandages.

But her fingernails were torn and bleeding, and she was covered in scratches and welts. Her hand throbbed.

She hadn't actually been there. It was just her soul. What had her mother called it—Traveling?

But if her soul had died, what would have happened to her body? Suddenly dizzy, she rested her head against her drawn-up knees. A sharp ache stabbed her chest. She felt so out of control. So helpless. It was as if the Four Sisters—the source of her power—had turned against her. Was it some kind of punishment from the Creators, for failing to convince the Discipline Heads to save Tarten?

One thing Senna knew—she needed answers. That required help, and the only person she trusted was Joshen.

What if her attacker was still watching? But there had been only two of them, and one was either dead or badly injured. One person couldn't watch her all the time, could he?

She fumbled to dress, found her damp cloak, and wrapped it around her shoulders. Then she slipped from her tree house. She ghosted down the path at a jog, breaking all the brand-new rules the Discipline Heads had put in place—rules about Apprentices and Guardians, rules about going out alone after dark.

Twice she had to dart off the trail and wait for other Witches to pass. When she reached Joshen's tree in the Guardian quarter, she tapped on the window. Nothing. She tapped louder. After her fifth try, he stumbled to the window and stood looking down at her, his chest bare. At the sight, a warm tingle spread from the top of Senna's head to the tips of her toes.

Moments later, he opened the door. After she'd slipped inside, he locked it behind her. "Senna?" he said, alarm in his voice. "I told you not to go out by yourself. What if your attackers had been waiting? You're not even supposed to be here." He pulled the drapes shut but then peeked out the window. "I don't think anyone saw."

"I heard the other Witches again." Senna wrapped her arms around herself. "Maybe I shouldn't have risked it, but I'm tired of feeling helpless. I need to figure out what's happening to me."

Joshen took her hand and led her into his bedroom. His tree was short and rather fat, so everything was on the same level. "What did you see this time?"

Feeling awkward, she sat on his rumpled bed and told him of her second experience Traveling.

Joshen took a deep breath. "Senna, I want to help you, but I don't know how. I'm not a Witch."

"Were you watching me the whole time I was in the Ring of Power earlier?" she asked carefully.

He nodded.

"And I was there the entire time? I never…disappeared?"

He blinked a few times. "No. You just looked like you were asleep. After a while, you stood up, all graceful, like a dance. I didn't realize at first you were even singing, it was so soft. When you were loud enough to understand, Drenelle started to panic. She shouted for you to stop, but it was like you couldn't hear her. I almost left cover to see what was wrong, but Drenelle is one of the Heads, and they made it very clear we're to stay away from the Apprentices. Besides, you didn't look like you were in danger."

He said the last bit apologetically. She bumped his shoulder with hers. "I only asked because I wanted to know how much of me really Travels."

"Isn't there someone you could ask?"

Senna studied her hands fiercely. "I tried with my mother—she won't tell me. The Heads are already keeping the truth from me. It's almost like they're afraid of something—afraid of *me.*" She knew that was ridiculous. "If they were going to tell me anything, they'd have done it by now."

Joshen rested his palm against her back. "Is there no one else?"

She grunted. "There's always Espen..." She'd meant it as a joke, but as soon as she'd said the words, she straightened.

He shook his head. "Oh, no, Senna. We can't trust her!"

She took his hands in hers. "But if I really can Travel...what harm comes in trying?"

He shot to his feet. "What harm? The woman would've had me kill you!"

"Joshen, I'm in danger now. Can't you see that? The other Witches sang for the earth to swallow me whole."

He trembled with rage. "What if these other Witches find you again?"

"I refuse to live in ignorance and helplessness."

He started pacing back and forth across the room. Senna waited for his anger to fade. Eventually, he thumped down beside her. After a while, he rubbed the stubble on his face thoughtfully, and she knew she'd won.

"You're not really with her, are you?" he asked. "I mean, she can't hurt you, right?"

She tried to quell her fear. "Joshen, I turned her into a tree."

"I thought it was over," he muttered.

Senna was grateful he didn't seem to notice she hadn't really answered his question. She rested her head on his shoulder. "So did I." She was beginning to understand that her power came with a price—a burden every Witch born bore, especially one as strong as her.

He kissed her hair. "When do you want to try?"

"Now."

Joshen winced. "She'll ask for some sort of payment—just don't give her anything that would put yourself or anyone else at risk." His hold on Senna tightened. "It's going to be all right."

By the Creators, she'd missed him. "How do you know?"

"Because I'll make sure of it."

She smiled and tipped her face back for a kiss. He brushed his lips across hers. His lips were so soft. He leaned his forehead against hers. "You can do this."

Senna scooted back until she sat in the center of the bed. "You won't leave me?"

Joshen took her hand. "No."

She took a deep breath, closed her eyes, and listened for the music she knew was there, just under the surface. Leaving her body came even faster and clearer this time, almost as if the Four Sisters had been waiting for her. Waiting to take her back.

But she shifted her destination away from the mysterious island, speeding across the ocean in a blur. Within the space of a few dozen heartbeats, she was in Tarten again, in a clearing now bereft of trees. Save one, a kind of weeping willow whose leaves formed a faultless circle. Without ever having to touch it, Senna knew the bark was as soft as flesh.

The branches shifted aimlessly in the breeze. The once-glossy leaves were now covered in a crusty blight. Half of them seemed to litter the base of the tree. Wetting her lips, Senna stepped forward, leaves crunching underfoot. "Espen?"

The tree heaved a little as if stirring in its sleep before going still again.

"Espen," Senna tried again.

This time the tree seemed to rouse itself. Senna almost felt it looking at her. The leaves quivered as if in recognition. The branches snapped toward her.

Senna had prepared for this reaction. After all, she was the one who'd forced Espen into this form and stolen her song.

Stop.

The branches struggled as if against an invisible current, but Espen was in essence a plant, and plants obeyed Witch song. Though the Dark Witch trembled with anger, she couldn't move.

Espen retreated into herself. A clump of bark dropped from her trunk. With a start, Senna realized the Dark Witch was dying. The drought wasn't just killing the Tartens.

Suddenly, Senna didn't feel frightened anymore. She could still feel Joshen's hand in her own. And for once, she was in control of the situation. "I have questions the Discipline Heads refuse to answer. As payment, I can ease your suffering. Water. A song to take away the blight."

Her eyes never straying from the tree, Senna crouched down and brushed the ground free of leaves, revealing dark, dry earth.

Espen slowly stretched a branch forward and wrote in the dirt. "Free me."

Anger flashed through Senna. "I can't free you. And even if I could, I wouldn't. The Creators took your song, remember? You have no fruit and therefore no seed."

The leaves rustled as she wrote, "Not save from life."

Senna opened her mouth, closed it again.

"Free me!" Espen wrote in deep gouges.

Senna stared at what remained of the Dark Witch until the tree stained her after vision. "It's no more than you deserve."

Espen didn't respond.

Senna took a deep breath. "Fine. I will come to Tarten and free you."

Espen seemed to sag in relief.

"What is Traveling?"

A branch came forward and scratched against the earth. "Obvious."

Senna grimaced. "That's what I'm doing—Traveling? How do I control it, stop from being attacked?"

The branch stabbed at the same word, "Obvious."

"No. It isn't. I could have died tonight!" Crouching, Senna brushed the word away and jabbed at the blank earth. "Tell me how to stop it, how to protect myself."

With exaggerated slowness, Espen wrote, "Witch song."

Senna stared at the words as the simplicity of it crashed down on her. Espen was right. It was obvious. You fought Witch song with Witch song. It wasn't a perfect solution. Her song was strong, but not as strong as the whole of those other Witches.

"How is this possible that I can Travel?" Senna whispered.

Espen bent forward and wrote again. "Creator touched."

Senna's breathing came faster. She'd been right. More than just her song was changing. This was bigger than just taking Espen's song. "What happens to someone who is Creator-touched?"

The branch scratched a single word into the ground. "Death."

Senna's breath caught in her throat. Was this what she'd overheard the Heads speaking of? Weighty as the rectangle of earth above a grave, the word lumbered from her mouth. "Death?"

The wind trailed Espen's branches.

Senna's gaze narrowed. "You're just trying to frighten me." Still Espen didn't answer. "Why would I believe anything you have to say? You'd gladly see all the Witches dead."

The tree rustled and the branch scratched in the soil. "Not dead. Rulers!"

Senna flinched. How often had she thought the Witches were meant to be more than a cluster of frightened women hiding on an island? Their songs transformed the world, and mankind hated them for it. "And the hundreds of other Witches outside of Haven?"

Espen went very still, so still the breeze didn't seem to touch her.

Senna rose from her crouch. "I've felt them. On an island much like Haven."

The tree strained forward. Espen swiped the earth blank and wrote, "Don't know."

Senna glared at the trembling tree. "You know something." If Senna didn't know better, she'd think Espen was afraid.

"Impossible," the Dark Witch wrote.

"What's impossible?"

Espen didn't answer for a long time. Finally, she wrote, "Calden. Lilette."

Senna stared at the unfamiliar words. "What do they mean?"

Espen lifted a shaking branch. "Fulfill bargain first."

So Espen wouldn't tell Senna anymore until she came before her. "Please," Senna couldn't help but ask.

Espen made no answer.

Take me home.

In the space of a handful of heartbeats, the wind carried her across the ocean, back to the room where Joshen sat waiting for her. Senna took a gasping breath.

Joshen started. "Did it work? What does Espen want as payment?"

Senna stared at him, her eyes moist. "She wants me to kill her."

6. WASTREL

"Brusenna," Prenny snapped. "Are you trying to fail?" Startled out of her daze, Senna sat upright. Her potion, which had been a cloudy topaz color, was now a muddy brown. Using a rag to protect her hands, she pulled the beaker off the flame and dumped its contents into another to cool off. Then she drizzled a few needle-like princher leaves into the liquid and swirled it gently. It immediately went from a muddy brown to coffee black.

She held the beaker to her nose and sniffed. Burned herbs.

Senna felt like throwing something. She settled for setting the beaker down so hard the potion sloshed angrily. At this stage, it was supposed to be the color of apple cider and smell like resin. She was to put in the princher leaves just before the first bubbles formed. She'd let it get too hot. Now she'd have to start over. Three days worth of work, ruined.

And that much longer before she could be done with her Apprenticeship and finally be seen as a full Keeper. She pried her hair away from her sticky forehead, wishing a breeze would work its way through the outdoor pavilion.

Prenny sniffed the contents. "You've killed it."

Senna buried her head in her hands. Prenny always insisted potions were full of life. It was the life they held that made them work. They had to be treated gently. Never boiled or frozen. Only fresh ingredients. "Yes. I killed it. I managed to save the world, but I can't manage a midlevel potion."

Prenny snorted. "Oh, don't be so dramatic."

"Dramatic? People are dying!" As soon as Senna said it, she wanted to capture the words and shove them back in her mouth. Prenny's voice went from stern to unsure. "Brusenna? Is this about Tarten? I know you and I don't agree with the other Heads, but they really do have the Witches' best interest at heart."

"It's in the Witches' best interest to look after the world, not just themselves." When Prenny didn't respond, Senna dug the pads of her fingers into her tired eyes. The resin made them sting.

Even with Joshen snoring softly on the floor beside her, chaotic thoughts had kept sleep at bay. He'd kissed her goodbye when they'd parted. She still felt the impression of his lips on hers.

Prenny went from soft with concern to rigid so fast it was as if someone had slid a rod up her backbone. "This is an *Apprentice* class. You may have the strongest song on this island, but potions are more than raw talent. It's the three P's." She ticked them off on her fingers. "Patience, practice, and persistence."

Knowing the Head was just warming up for one of her famous lectures, Senna stifled a groan.

Prenny took a breath and settled in. "It's a good thing the harvest is coming up. We're nearly out of chesli pollen, and you squandered at least a pinch on that." She waved at Senna's burnt potion. "Disaster. I told the others it was too soon to promote you to an Apprentice. Now—Mistin!"

Senna nearly startled out of her chair at Prenny's outburst.

The Head marched toward Senna's cowering friend without a backward glance. "You are far too advanced to be adding porfor to a drinking draught! Do you want to wrest the truth from your subject, or keep them hunched over the privy for an entire day?"

Senna could have kissed Mistin for sparing her another of Prenny's tongue lashings, even if the girl hadn't saved her on purpose.

Senna glared at her ruined potion. With a sigh, she abandoned it and marched over to the stack of potion books kept in a waterproof cabinet in the center of the pavilion. She reached for *Intermediate Potions*, but hesitated. Next to it was another book—*Master Potions* by Linsee Chrissin.

After glancing around, Senna pulled it down and flipped through the pages until she reached the potion she had in mind—Ioa. It was extremely complicated—nearly a hundred plants mixed in dozens of different ways on an extremely tight schedule. But she already knew that because she'd tried to make it once already and failed miserably.

Honestly, it was probably still too advanced for her, but if she were going to sneak off the island, the potion would be indispensable. Checking to make sure Prenny was still busy with her scolding, Senna slipped the ponderous book in her satchel and set it down on her table.

Then she wove through the tables of other Apprentices toward the hybrid garden, careful not to crush any vines that had worked their way between the rows, some even growing up the table legs.

The smell of herbs hung so heavy Senna imagined she could reach out and pluck it from the air like a veil. In Haven, there were plants that didn't exist anywhere else in the world. For decades Witch song had crossbred plants, traipsing across boundaries no one else could. Now, instead of a dozen plants of varying strengths to lower a fever, there was one—pesnit. One controlled the potency simply by how many leaves one used.

There were many, many such plants. Simple cures for everything from warts to infections. She struggled to snip a few leaves; she wasn't used to using scissors with her left hand. While she took cuttings, she snuck a few leaves for the Ioa potion into her pocket.

Back at her table, she carefully rolled the leaves for the Ioa potion in parchment and tucked them in her pocket. She'd work on it when there weren't any prying eyes to watch her.

Finished with that, she began the arduous process of creating the olive-green truth serum. As she worked, Mistin pulled up a chair and set up next to her. Senna was on the short side, but Mistin was positively tiny. She had golden skin, almond-shaped eyes, and lustrous black hair that hung nearly to her waist.

"Brusenna, maybe if we work on this together, we can avoid another of Prenny's tirades," Mistin whispered.

Senna eyed her sideways. When she'd first met Mistin, she thought she was twelve. She had later learned the girl was a full year older. Though they weren't exactly close, Mistin was the nearest thing Senna had to a friend on the island.

"I've told you, call me Senna." Retrieving her scraper, she carefully released a scattering of chesli pollen, which would exponentially increase the shelf life of her potion. The little bits swarmed like lightning bugs. With a ring of glass on glass, she stirred clockwise with her stir stick. The potion started to glow softly.

Mistin flipped open her book. "I've been meaning to ask you about that. Don't you like your name?"

Senna shifted uncomfortably. Her classmates rarely spoke to her. At her or around her, but rarely to her. She wasn't used to making small talk. "I like it fine."

"Then why don't you use it?"

Senna slid a dropper back into the bottle then tapped her stir stick against the beaker. Matching her pitch to the clear tone that rang out, she sang.

Truth and honesty extract
Speak in only careful fact.

The potion swirled. She continued the song, her voice sweet and clear, until her sense of the Four Sisters told her it was ready. She added a few drops of alcohol. The potion shifted from clear to amber.

Mistin tipped her head to one side. "Well?"

Senna might not know how to "chat," but she desperately wanted to try. "Brusenna wasn't safe anymore. And I wanted to be someone new. Someone better."

Mistin nodded as if that made perfect sense. "And are you? New and better?"

Senna remembered how terrified she'd been of her village, of the people inside. They wouldn't frighten her now. "Yes, I think I am."

"Then I shall call you Senna." Mistin sang to her potion. The differences between their voices were immediately apparent. Senna's soprano soared and the whole world seemed to still, as if listening. Mistin's alto was like the creaking of old wood. She was one step above a Wastrel, or wasted Witch. A level one. Her potion was many steps ahead of Senna's, but its color and luster were off. Her song just wasn't strong enough for the transformation to take place.

If a Wastrel remained on Haven long, she became little better than a servant.

Mistin's song dropped to silence. As if guessing Senna's thoughts, she said, "Weakness in one area forces growth in another."

Senna found herself aching to say something honest instead of the veiled niceties everyone else seemed to prefer. "Haven only sees one kind of strength."

Mistin's steely gaze met Senna's. "Their mistake."

Why did it have to be that way? Why were some innately more powerful than others, regardless of merit? Sorrow burning in her chest, Senna dropped in a few kenlish seeds. Almost ashamed of the clear ringing of her voice, she sang.

Banish all half truths and lies.
Even silence we decry.

The kenlish seeds slowly disintegrated as they swirled. But Senna's potion wasn't the only one to change. Mistin's potion color went from a dirty yellow to honey. The black flecks floating inside shone like flakes of gold.

Mistin blinked. "How many potions could one strong Witch sing if dozens of Witches were mixing the ingredients for her?"

Senna nodded. "I've wondered the same thing. But it's just not the way they do things here, right or wrong." She studied Mistin more closely. "What's it like where you're from, in Dresdan? What's your family like?"

Mistin hesitated as if considering her words carefully. "The world hates Witches. My mother forbade us from singing. Still, someone always managed to find out what we were, and we'd have to move again. One time, we didn't get away fast enough. Only my brother and I escaped."

How had Senna known Mistin for months and not realized most of her family was dead? "I'm so sorry." Senna had lived with the outside world's hatred of Witches her entire life. "Where's your brother now?"

Mistin gave a small smile. "He followed me to Nefalie. He wants to become a Guardian."

Senna watched a bird fly into the pavilion, circle the heads of the Apprentices a few times, and dart out again. "Why didn't your family live here? It would have been safer."

Mistin's nostrils flared. "My family's songs were very weak. Believe it or not, I'm the strongest of them. There would have been no place for my sisters here. And I would not have left them alone."

Senna couldn't fathom it. Wastrels weren't welcome on Haven. Apparently, they weren't welcome anywhere else either—rejected by Haven for not being enough of a Witch, and rejected by the world for being too much of one. They would belong nowhere. "It shouldn't be like that. There's plenty of room here."

Mistin stirred her potion harder than necessary. "That's why I'm still here, despite the fact that they treat me like a servant and everyone looks down on me. There's nowhere else for me to go. Certainly nowhere safe."

Senna stared at her beaker so Mistin wouldn't see the pity in her eyes.

"Finish up, girls. It's nearly time to shift your studies," Prenny announced.

Senna stopped off her half-finished potion.

"Brusenna— Senna, you're in trouble, aren't you?"

Senna startled. "How could you know that?"

Mistin shrugged. "I told you. Weakness forces a person to develop other strengths. Good singers tell the world what to do. Not-so-good singers are better at listening to what can't be heard."

Things like hearing the music of the Four Sisters? Things like Traveling? Senna rinsed out the dirty beakers and set them in the sun to purify. "What do you mean?"

Mistin straightened her narrow shoulders and assessed Senna from head to foot. "Maybe I can help."

Senna opened her mouth then closed it again. What she needed were answers—answers only the Heads had. "Unless you can tell me where to find hundreds of Witches hidden somewhere outside of Haven, I don't think you can help me much."

Mistin's eyes went impossibly wide. "What?"

Senna sighed inwardly. *And small talk had been going so well.* "Never mind."

Prenny stalked around, pointing to beakers that needed cleaning and books that needed to be reshelved. "The chesli harvest starts at the next crescent moon—that's a little over a week away. Everyone is required to participate. Plan your schedules accordingly. Jassy! If that beaker of acid spills on my book, I'll use your hide as replacement parchment!"

Senna snatched up her last few items before the Head made it to their table. She shoved everything in her satchel as she walked. She was meeting Joshen for lunch, and she didn't want to be late.

"Senna?" She turned back to see Mistin following a few steps behind. The girl bit her lip. "I meant what I said. I can help you."

Senna didn't know how to respond, so she stayed silent.

Mistin glanced around and took a step closer. "I work as a secretary to the Heads to help pay my tuition."

Senna tipped her head sideways. "I know."

Mistin rubbed her palms together nervously. "I make appointments."

The first prickle of unease jabbed Senna's stomach. "What are you trying to tell me, Mistin?"

The girl tucked her hair behind her ears. "You're the closest thing I have to a friend. Everyone else mocks my song. When I said you were in trouble and I could help— Your mother made an appointment to speak with the Heads today."

Senna straightened. Why would her mother be meeting with the Heads? "About what?"

Mistin's dark eyes met Senna's. "You."

7. A Choice

A crawling sense of betrayal skittered up Senna's spine. Mistin glanced around again and took a step closer. "You're mother is trying to force you off the island."

Senna's mind seemed to empty of all thought. "What? Why?"

Mistin shook her head. "I don't know. The meeting has probably already started. Come with me."

Senna followed without question. At the Council Tree, she entered with only a slight hesitation. In the center of the room was a large desk. Behind the desk were a set of spiral stairs.

Mistin shifted from one foot to the other. "She's up there with them now."

Senna shifted in embarrassment. But Mistin had risked her place on Haven to give Senna this chance. She wasn't going to squander that. Nor would she wait for someone to tell her what was going on. She slipped off her boots.

Mistin took a letter from her desk. "I'm to deliver this missive to Leader Reden." She paused just before the door and whispered so quietly Senna barely heard, "Good luck." She gave Senna a meaningful look before pushing the door shut behind her.

Boots in hand, Senna eased silently up the stairs and slipped inside the Council Room. She'd been inside twice before—when she'd plead for the Heads to lift the curse on Tarten and when she'd accidentally sung the Relocation Song. Neither time had been pleasant.

She heard voices coming from the other side of the door. But she couldn't make out their words, only that they were angry. Steeling herself, she pressed her ear against the wood.

"I'm her mother!"

"Sacra, please, you—" Senna recognized Coyel's voice.

"I will not! You've no right to keep her here."

"It's not safe for her to leave," Chavis said.

"And staying here is?" her mother growled. "Someone attacked her!"

"Don't be ridiculous," Prenny's old-sounding voice answered. "We've brought in over twenty Guardians. She's perfectly safe. Besides, she needs to learn."

"I'll teach her," Sacra said.

Prenny snorted. "Like you taught her before."

There was a brief silence. "That was a mistake. I won't repeat it."

In her scratchy voice, Drenelle asked, "What does Senna want? Has anyone bothered to ask her?"

Senna was surprised to hear words of concern from Drenelle.

"What she needs is more important than what she wants," her mother said.

Senna gripped her boots so tight the leather squeaked in protest.

"The answer is still no." Then Coyel's voice softened. "She's nearly a woman, Sacra. You can't force her to leave."

"And if the past repeats itself?" her mother asked so quietly Senna had to strain to hear. When no one answered, her mother's voice gained strength. "All of Haven couldn't stop what happened then. But perhaps, far away from everything, I could—

"Oh, this is absolutely ridiculous," Prenny said. "Sacra, you're two henn extracts short of a trible potion."

"By the Creators, what's that supposed to mean?" Chavis asked.

"It means your argument is like a three-legged horse. A two-legged dog. A one-legged man."

"Stop," Coyel commanded. "I'm sorry, Sacra, but the answer is no. You may not take Senna from Haven."

"Even if she wishes to go?" Her mother's voice sounded broken.

The Heads murmured.

"Even then," Coyel said above them.

Those words sent Senna scurrying down the stairs. In the parlor, she thrust her feet into her boots and shoved the laces inside the tongue. Boots clomping, she bolted through the door just as footsteps started down the stairs.

At the path, she tried to act normally as Coyel's muffled voice leaked through the closed door. "Mistin? Oh, where is that girl! Every time I need a messenger, she just up and—"

The door groaned as it opened. Her mother's voice overrode the Head's. "Brusenna?"

Schooling her expression, Senna turned.

Her mother shut the door firmly behind her. "What are you doing here?"

"I'm on my way to meet Joshen for lunch."

Her mother pursed her lips. "Where were you this morning?"

"I left early for the library." Senna was surprised at how easily the lies rolled past her lips.

Sacra pulled her a little way off the path. "I need to speak with you."

"About?"

"Brusenna, are you…happy here?"

Senna crossed her arms over her chest. "Yes."

Her mother smoothed back Senna's hair. "You don't seem happy?"

A pang stabbed through Senna's heart at her mother's touch. She had the sudden urge to tell her mother that everywhere she went, the other Witches stared at her. Every time she fell short of anyone's expectations, she let down those who believed in her and validated those who didn't. Sometimes she felt like the Heads had set her up to fail. "I'm happier than I've ever been anywhere else." That was more than she could say of their isolated, persecuted existence in Gonstower.

Senna gave a tight smile, pushed past her mother, and started toward the Guardian quarter. After a bit of searching, she found Joshen in the midst of sparring practice. Senna settled down on one of the enormous roots of the tree houses then pulled out her lunch of salt fish, buttered bread, and an apple. She placed the fish between the folded bread and took a bite.

Joshen's chest was broad, his body hard and slick with sweat. He was tan, but whiter skin peaked beneath his trousers. Despite everything, the sight made her feel heady and her mouth go suddenly dry. She struggled to swallow, the remainder of her lunch forgotten.

From the Witches' quarter of the island, a man approached them. Joshen and the other Guardian—a dark-skinned man with beads clinking on the ends of his hair—broke apart. The three spoke and the other two left together. Joshen trotted over to her.

She nodded toward the two men. "Who were they?"

Sitting beside her, Joshen glanced in the direction she'd indicated. "I was sparring with Collum. The one that came up after is Tempnee. He's tailing you today, and he's not too happy about you breaking the Head's rules by coming here."

Senna tucked her hair behind her ears.

Joshen laughed. "Don't worry. Reden has given you access. Just don't tell the Heads."

She pulled her arms in tight. "I thought it was just you and Reden following me."

Joshen reached over and took a bite of her lunch. "Mmm, fish." He gave her a peck on the cheek. "I have to get my training in, and Reden's hands were full. Tempnee spells us."

He stared ravenously at her meal. With a sigh, she broke off half and handed it to him. "Anyone else I should know about?"

Joshen tore into the hunk of fish and spoke through his chewing, "Collum, too." At the look on her face, he swallowed abruptly. "They're good men, Senna. Reden and I can't be there all day every day."

She picked at her crust. "It's just...unsettling."

Joshen licked butter off the corner of his mouth. "If it makes you feel any better, they both worship you. Most men do, especially after they hear you sing."

She picked crumbs off her bandages. "That doesn't make you uncomfortable?"

He grunted ambiguously. "They know their place." He watched her picking at her bandage. "How's your hand?"

"It itches."

"That means it's healing." He finished off the rest of his food. "Hear you had a row with your Mom."

She eyed him. "How do you know that?"

He shrugged. "The island's not that big."

"Timpnee?" Senna guessed. Movement caught her gaze. She looked down to see a spider skittering across her dress and starting up her arm. Shrieking, she jumped to her feet and shook her arm like a madwoman. Her lunch went flying.

Joshen darted to his feet. "What? What?"

"Spider!"

He gaped at her before bursting into laughter.

She lifted a shaking hand to point to where it was quickly escaping. "Kill it! Quick! Before it comes back!"

Still snorting with laughter, he stomped on it. Then he held out a forestalling hand to the other Guardians, who had stopped what they were doing to watch with concerned expressions. "It was just a spider."

She smacked his arm. "Just? It was at least as big as an upice coin."

She eyed the roots she'd been sitting on and decided standing was safer. Joshen picked up their food and brushed it off. He tipped his canteen and washed the dirt off her apple, then handed it back to her. She took the apple, but refused the rest of the bread and fish.

With a shrug, he polished them off. "Come on, I know you're hiding something. Out with it."

She groaned. "Mother tried to persuade the Heads to force me off the island to go into hiding again."

He gaped at her. "And will you?"

"Of course not."

He breathed out. "I agree with Coyel. At least here we don't have to worry about mobs and lynchings."

She nodded. "Joshen, I want to go to Tarten and try to lift the curse."

He turned abruptly away from her, his fists clenched. "Senna, before, we didn't have a choice, but we do now. Besides, there's nothing one Witch can do."

It was obvious he was avoiding the topic. She watched him warily. "You don't know what it's like. I can feel Tarten's pain, and I want to do something about it."

Joshen dropped his head. "I know a little about feeling helpless—watching the person you love go through something when you can't make it better."

She opened her mouth to speak, but emptiness rushed in. She closed it and tried again. "I'm sorry, Joshen. I didn't mean—"

Joshen gave a halfhearted smile and offered her his hand. "I know. Come with me." She followed him away from the sparring field.

"Where are we going?"

"I'm doing my best to help you. You keep running off and taking these unnecessary risks." Joshen's jaw was set. "Senna, you're one Witch. It would take all of them to lift the curse."

Senna was so tired. "But I'm so much stronger now. I think I can lift at least some of it."

"And then Haven would just reinstate it and you would be banished," he said gently.

She dropped her head.

He sighed. "Just let it go for now. All right?"

Not wanting to argue, she nodded.

They stepped into a triangle of sunshine not far from Haven's cliffs, which rose up before them, higher than even Haven's tallest trees and impossibly circular. In a few places, part of the carved face had collapsed, leaving cones of scree butting up against the black rock. Senna saw occasional pieces of carvings—an eye here, part of a sun, even a bit of a foot. In the center of these shattered pieces of Witch history were straw targets.

There were a few muskets resting against a nearby tree's roots. Joshen picked one up and started loading it. "I want you to practice until loading and firing comes as naturally as walking."

Her heart pounding irregularly, Senna's gaze darted between the musket and Joshen. Her hand closed around the puckered scar on her upper arm, a gift from the Witch Hunter, Wardof, and his musket.

Joshen's mouth tightened at her reaction.

Senna took a step back, her heart hammering in her throat. "I–maybe another time. I have another class."

"Not for nearly an hour, you don't. And it's only singing practice, which you often skip."

There were disadvantages to Joshen knowing her schedule so well.

He pulled a pistol from his holster. "Try with this. It'll be better for you anyway. More discreet. Easier to pack."

"Joshen…"

"My job is to keep you safe, but that's your job too. You should know how to protect yourself." He nodded toward her seed belt. "And I want you to carry a knife from now on. I know you have one."

Her mouth set, she took the pistol. It was heavier than she thought it'd be. Gripping it with her injured hand pulled uncomfortably at her stitches. She was glad she hadn't picked up the musket. They were *heavy*.

She'd watched her Guardians load enough guns to have the basics down.

Joshen helped her measure the powder and gave gentle nudges, showing her how to stand. How to aim down the barrel and line up her target between the little notch on the end. How to let her breath out and hold still as stone. How to squeeze the trigger in one gentle pull.

They practiced until her arm was numb, her ears rang, and her hands were sooty with black powder.

Joshen nodded. "That'll do for today." He pushed the loaded pistol into one of the extra loops on her seed belt and handed her a horn of black powder and a pouch of balls. "You'll have to fill the pan before it will fire."

He watched her reaction carefully. "You need to be ready to use it, Senna. You need to make the decision that if someone tries to hurt you or someone else, you'll do whatever you must to stop them. If you're not, you'll hesitate. And hesitation will kill you."

She felt the weight of the gun on her hip and imagined a person between the notch at the end of the barrel, gently squeezing the trigger the way Joshen had shown her. And just like that, someone would be dead or dying.

"Can you do it?" Joshen asked her.

It was an enormous decision to resolve to kill someone—to come to the conclusion your life had more value than theirs. A hard choice, but easy, too. Hard because she valued life. All life. Easy because that included her own. "I can."

8. Earth Tremor

The next morning, Senna received a summons to meet Coyel at her home. The Head answered the door on the first knock. "Let's meet outside, shall we?" Coyel said. "It's such a lovely day."

They circled around the tree and entered a beautiful garden, thick with the smell of herbs and flowers. The Head of Sunlight settled onto her tree's tangled knot of roots and gestured for Senna to sit beside her. A bit of sun leaked through the leaves. Coyel tilted her face toward it, seeming to soak it in like she was a plant herself.

Senna took a deep breath. "What's happening to me? Why am I changing? Why am I in danger?"

Coyel's eyes snapped open. She was silent for a time. "You need to trust me, Senna. Trust me when I tell you there is a time for everything. And this is not yet the time."

Senna ground her teeth. "But—"

"It's better this way. Let it go."

Why didn't they just tell her? Knowing arguing wouldn't do her any good, Senna swallowed her questions and fears. They settled heavily in her belly.

Coyel took a deep breath. "Have you chosen your Discipline?"

Senna slumped against the tree. After she'd defeated Espen, the Discipline Heads had honored her by immediately elevating her to an Apprentice. So she hadn't been forced to choose a discipline as was custom. The problem was, Senna loved them all. "It won't be Plants," she finally said, if for no other reason than to keep her distance from Prenny.

Coyel smiled as if guessing Senna's true motivation, but said diplomatically, "No wish to spend your life in a garden or over a burner?"

Senna didn't really mind either. "I wouldn't want to be a healer." Another of Plant's specialties. All Witches were required to know healing potions and a few simple procedures, such as stitching a wound or setting a break. But blood always turned Senna's innards into a quivering mess and made her wish someone else—anyone else—would take over.

"Nor will it be Earth." She would never willingly sign up for endless days of "communing with the earth" in Drenelle's company.

Coyel sighed. "So that leaves Water and Sunlight." She lifted her palm, holding the sunbeams as if they were tangible. "You know, Sunlight is more than just learning politics or controlling the wind. It's also about power."

Senna frowned. "Power?"

The Head straightened and suddenly all traces of languidness were gone. She pulled a little pouch out of her dress pocket then untied it and reached inside. Her hands came out clutching a white powder. "Chalk."

Coyel pinned her with her imperial stare. "Do you know why I hold more sway among the Discipline Heads?"

Senna slowly shook her head. "Only that in a group of four, someone has to hold the sway vote."

Coyel tossed the powder into the air. Then she sang soft and low. Slowly, the wind stirred. It moved faster and tightened, catching the powder and sweeping it inward until the chalk churned into a shape like a spinning top. Coyel stopped singing. The wind eventually lost interest and moved on. The powder drifted to the ground.

The Head watched it fall. "Sunlight has always been the first among equals because of the nature of our Discipline. We're leaders, diplomats. But it's more than that. It's the natural order of things. The heat from the sun causes the temperature changes that

control the wind and sea, which in turn affect the plants and earth."
Coyel dusted the chalk from her hands. "It's natural for Witches
to gravitate toward Disciplines that enhance their talents."

Shame heated Senna's cheeks. "Which is why I haven't chosen
one of the other two. I haven't the stomach for war or the ability
to lead anyone."

Coyel tipped her head to study Senna. "No one has all the
qualities they need at the start." She shrugged. "Power, remember?
The power to change things. The power to make decisions. The
power to affect how the Witches operate. Sunlight controls the
wind. And what does the wind do? It changes things."

Coyel must know how desperately Senna longed to revolutionize
Haven's structure. And she was obviously using that knowledge
to manipulate Senna.

"I believe you should choose Sunlight as your discipline."

Senna's chest tightened. "But I'm terrified of big groups of
people." Any more than two and her head emptied of thoughts,
her tongue turned to a useless lump of rawhide, and her body
broke out in a cold sweat.

Coyel brushed her hands off in dew-coated grass. "Just
because you are shy doesn't mean you're not a natural-born
leader. Because you are. You have the ability to see what needs
to be done and the initiative to follow it through." The Head took
a deep breath. "Besides, experience is the mediator of many of
our faults. Every few years, I pick one exceptional student to be
my Apprentice. Eventually, one of those girls will replace me as
Discipline Head."

Senna went rigid with shock. "But Arianis is your Apprentice.
You've worked with her for years." Everyone knew Arianis would
someday be the next Head of Sunlight.

Coyel pursed her lips. "I'm meeting with her after we're done
here. Mirrus can finish her training for me." At the expression
on Senna's face, Coyel pursed her lips. "Arianis is a fine Witch.
One of the best. But a Head is always chosen because she's the
strongest in her Discipline. Drenelle has the strongest earth sense.
Prenny is the best at potions. Chavis is an unparalleled tactician.

The Head of Sunlight has always been the best singer. Your song is stronger than Arianis'."

Senna's heart sank. This was about the strength of her song? "But my song is only a part of me, only one kind of strength." Didn't anyone ever look beyond a Witch's song?

"It's the way things are, Senna. The way they have always been," Coyel said gently.

"Well, maybe it's time we started doing the right thing instead of following tradition. A Head should be chosen based on her abilities to lead, not her power."

Coyel raised a single eyebrow. "A good many of the Witches don't look to Arianis. They look to you."

Some of the Witchlings, perhaps a few others. But that didn't mean anything. Not really. They looked to Senna because she'd freed them. They didn't see that she had been defeated by Espen, just as they all had. The only thing that had saved her was the Creator's interference.

"I'm not what they think I am." The words fluttered out of Senna's mouth like wounded butterflies.

Coyel gave a sad smile. "We are never as bad or as good as others believe. We just are."

Senna couldn't understand the sudden swelling of emotion inside her. Maybe she should stay here. In a few years, she'd have enough power to really change things. She could make sure an entire nation was never cursed again.

Coyel opened her mouth and spoke, but Senna couldn't hear her. There was a discordant screech. Senna clapped her hands over her ears, trying to block out the awful sound.

Coyel leaned in, her lips moved, but Senna couldn't make out the words over the shrieking. Judging by the confusion and concern on Coyel's face, Senna was the only one who could hear it.

The sound faded away.

"Senna? Senna, what is it?"

Before Senna could answer, Witch song rang from the clearing.

An earth tremor comes.

"Why didn't Drenelle send a runner?" Coyel shot to her feet and pulled Senna up. "Come! To the Ring of Power!"

They hustled over roots and around the tree. Senna burst out of the foliage and nearly ran into Arianis. The girl was breathing hard and gripping her cloak so hard her knuckles had bleached white. Her face looked open, vulnerable.

She stared at Coyel with such a look of betrayal Senna had to look away. "Drenelle sent me to warn you, about the tremor, but…" She trailed off when she seemed to realize they already knew about the tremor. Turning, she ran in the opposite direction of the clearing.

"Arianis," Senna called.

Coyel's voice went oddly breathless. "I never wanted her to find out like that."

Senna took a step to go after Arianis.

"Leave her," Coyel commanded.

Feeling a little sick, Senna turned to follow the Head.

Before she'd gone a dozen steps, the earth bucked violently beneath her. Senna fell, a scream on her lips, but the sound was lost in the deafening noise as everything shuddered and shook. With a crystalline shattering, all the windows broke. Tree branches and glass rained down on her. She curled into a ball with her arms over her head.

Slowly, the thundering settled to a rumble before stopping altogether. When it was over, Senna found herself on the path, her lip stinging. She tasted blood. Feeling something hard with her probing tongue, she found a splinter and pulled it from her lip. She was lucky it hadn't stabbed her in the eye.

She surveyed the damage. One of the largest trees had split down the middle, leaving the rooms inside exposed—incredibly, the table still held an unspilled jar of milk. Nearly every window in sight was broken. Tree branches and sparkling bits of glass littered the ground. Doors hung ajar. Everywhere, Witches were getting to their feet.

In seconds, Joshen was there, pulling Senna upright. "You all right?"

She nodded dumbly. The world shook again, but not nearly as violently. Gripping his shirt, she watched as the milk sloshed in the jar, spilling over the sides. She vowed to never complain about her Guardian detail again.

The world finally stilled.

"You're bleeding."

She licked blood from her upper lip. "Just a little."

Coyel was already up again and running toward the Ring of Power.

Hurrying after her, Senna scrambled over a fallen branch the size of a small horse. Just past it, a basket of wet laundry was partially crushed. A Witch dress created a ring of damp dirt around it. At first, Senna didn't notice the limp hand still curled around it.

Joshen knelt beside the tree and peered down. He closed his eyes and turned away. "She's gone."

Senna didn't want more memories to seed her nightmares. She kept running.

The Witches were singing. That meant the barrier was up. Nothing and no one could cross until the singing stopped. Drenelle was in the center, singing in her rich alto, which sounded much better than her speaking voice. Other Witches gathered outside the circle, waiting like Senna and Coyel.

Senna searched their faces until she found her mother. Relief coursed through her as her mother's worried gaze met her own. Sacra held her hand over her heart and breathed out in relief. Senna nodded that she was all right.

That relief was shattered when someone cried, "Smoke!"

Senna pivoted and saw a black plume cutting through the bright blue sky.

"One of the trees is burning!" someone out of sight shouted.

"Joshen!" Coyel said. "Round up some Guardians and deal with it."

After sparing a glance at Senna, he sprinted toward the smoke, crying, "Guardians, to me!"

"Steady, girls. The Guardians will control the fire until we can take care of it," Coyel said.

Still, Senna kept an eye on the smoke. The whole island was covered in trees that butted up against each other. She imagined how quickly a fire might spread. How they would all become trapped like a nest of baby birds in a chimney that had sat idle all summer—trapped by the very walls that protected them.

When the song finally ended, the Witches stepped back. Senna gripped the forearms of the nearest Witches, one of whom happened to be Chavis. The barrier rose with a clap of wind that flattened everything beyond it and dragged the smoke outward.

Immediately, Senna felt the connection with all the other Witches. Her sense of the Four Sisters sharpened to a razor edge. She felt the enormous shock wave of water rushing toward the Nafalien coast. Toward them.

Coyel was right. Dangerous as the fire was, it could wait.

Seconds later the singing started again.

> Waters, calm the sea.
> Settle and smooth, not angry be.

The wind twirled Drenelle skyward. The Witches repeated the song until she had all she could hold. Then the woman released it with her own song. Senna felt it rolling toward the waters, felt the song settle the sea like a hand smoothing a rumpled blanket. But their song dissipated long before it reached the end of the wave.

Already drifting downward, Drenelle shook her head in frustration. "Another one!"

> Wind, beat against the wave
> Before the coast her waters raze.

But Drenelle didn't wait until she could hold no more; she released it when the wave was dangerously close to shore—to the nearby city of Corrieth. Senna felt the wind gusting before the city and cutting into the water like scissors through fabric.

The Witches were silent for a moment, Senna knew all of them felt the waters crash against the shore, and the shock of the plants. The wind had deflected the worst of it from the city. But not the docks. An aching hollow opened up inside Senna. People had just died. Many of them. And worst of all, she had friends among the sailors.

The witches sang for the waters to retreat. After more than an hour of continuous singing, they turned their attention to the fire. They sang in a storm. They didn't need a big one, just large enough to cover their island. Still, Senna watched the smoke thicken, watched the first tongues of flames hungrily lick the darkening sky.

A light patter of rain bounced off the barrier. The Witches kept singing as it increased to a downpour. The smoke and flames were lost to the haze of rain.

Finally, Guardians appeared. Sooty streaks ran down their grim faces. Grateful for their assistance fighting the fire, Senna wondered how the island had ever survived without the Guardians. They worked better together, each side shoring up the other's weaknesses.

If Senna were in charge, it could always be like this. She really could change things.

Overcoming her natural reticence would be a small price. Someday, she could become the Head of Sunlight, and then things would finally become better.

But what about the danger looming just beyond her sight? What about the dying land and people of Tarten?

The last of the Witch song cut off, and the barrier dissipated. Almost immediately, the rain let up.

Prenny spoke to Coyel. "How bad do you think Corrieth was hit?"

Coyel pursed her lips. "Our winds and their wall would have deflected the brunt of the wave. But the docks and anyone on them would've only had half that protection."

"By the Creators, Drenelle, why didn't you alert us sooner?" Chavis cried.

Drenelle backed away. "As soon as I sensed the tremor, I warned everyone."

Other Witches grumbled, no doubt wondering how badly their homes were damaged by fire and tremors.

Drenelle lifted her hands in supplication. "I usually sense an earth tremor building for days, weeks even. But this one just happened."

Senna remembered the unholy shriek she'd heard just before Drenelle's warning. There was something unnatural about it. Something forced. She was so horrified she barely registered Joshen's warm presence beside her.

"What is it?"

"It might have just been the sound of the earth tremor. But what if it wasn't? What if it was the foreign Witches' song?"

"What are you talking about?"

Wet and shivering, Senna met his probing gaze. "They sent the earth tremor, Joshen." The more she thought about it, the more sure she became.

"How do you know?"

Using her sleeve, she mopped water off her face. "If they really are the danger coming for Haven, they would want to weaken us first. Weaken us without revealing their presence."

Coyel stepped forward and began issuing commands— something about every Witch checking her Apprentices and Witchlings, and everyone fanning out to look for injured and help with the clean up.

Senna hurried over to Coyel. "Head, what if the tremor wasn't natural? What if those other Witches sent it?"

Coyel pursed her lips. "Perhaps for retribution for you weakening their barrier?"

Senna blanched. She hadn't thought of it that way. Was she somehow responsible for all this devastation?

"Go help the others Senna. There's nothing we can do right now."

9. SECRETS

At a loss, Senna watched as dispirited Witches fanned out to search the island for any injured. And then she remembered Arianis. She wove through the other Witches, searching for the girl's beautiful face. "Have you seen Arianis?" she called back to Joshen.

"No. Isn't she here?"

Trying to generate some warmth, Senna rubbed her arms. "I don't think so. She was upset."

Joshen studied her with a knowing look. "Upset about what?"

Senna winced. "Coyel offered me the position as her Apprentice."

Joshen's eyes widened. "Arianis' position?"

Senna nodded. "I'm pretty sure she overheard Coyel offer it to me."

Anger flashed in his eyes. "Coyel should know better than to treat people so poorly."

Senna glanced around. "Let's check the Ring. If she's not here, we'll search the island."

"I can't. Reden gave me permission to check on you, but then I was to report back to the other Guardians."

Senna steeled herself. "All right. Go."

Joshen didn't move. "This chaos would be a perfect chance for someone to attack you."

Senna shivered. "You can't be with me every moment."

"Did you bring your knife?"

Hesitantly, she shook her head. "I forgot."

Grumbling under his breath, Joshen reached down and pulled a knife from his boot. He slapped the hilt against her hand. He checked the powder in her pistol's pan and cursed. "Damp. I'll have to dig the ball out and clean it before you can use it again." He blew out in frustration. "But you still have the knife. Will you use it?"

She stared at it grimly. "Yes."

"Don't go off by yourself—stay in the Ring of Power and let someone else find her."

After tucking the knife in the loop in her seed belt, Senna started asking other Witches if anyone had seen Arianis. No one had. Joshen had told her to stay with the others, to keep safe. But the look on Arianis' face haunted her.

Knowing Joshen wouldn't be pleased, she lifted her skirts and hurried in the direction she'd seen Arianis go. She passed many Witches and Guardians, all of them helping injured Witches or clearing broken trees and debris from the path.

Senna asked every Witch she passed. Called out to Guardians. No one had seen Arianis.

If the girl was hurt, Senna would never forgive herself.

Just when she'd truly started to panic, she heard someone sniffling. She tipped her ear toward the sound, trying to figure out where it came from. Behind her was the onion-shaped tree house. The noise came from inside. Afraid of what she might find, Senna started up the steps. Arianis was inside, her arms wrapped around her knees.

Senna glanced behind her, looking for another Witch who could help. There were none to be seen. Cautiously, she stepped into the room. "Are you hurt?"

Arianis' head jerked up. Her eyes were swollen from crying. She wiped her nose with the back of her hand and looked away. "No."

Stopping in the center of the room, Senna swallowed. "Arianis...I'm sorry."

Arianis chuckled bitterly. "I have always been the best singer, the fastest learner. Trained from childhood to defeat Espen. And then you came along." She pulled her sleeve over her palm and wiped her cheeks. "And now I'm the one thing I've always been afraid of—average."

Senna was rooted to the spot. She wanted to be anywhere but here. "You'll never be average."

"Average, above average. It's still not the best." Arianis pushed herself up and strode toward the door, but she stopped when she drew level with Senna. "Just remember it's harder to stay at the top than it is to get there."

Senna listened as the other girl's footsteps slowly faded behind her. She closed her eyes. She didn't want the responsibility, the attention. But somehow it wanted her. Shaking her head, she stumbled backwards. Something cracked beneath her weight. She'd stepped on a framed map that had tipped over during the earth tremor.

Absently, she picked it up. It was the desert nation they'd been learning about, Harshen. The frame had broken in the fall. The corner was crushed and part of the canvas ripped. Rain had stolen through the smashed windows and made the parchment swell and the ink run. It was ruined. Discarding the frame, Senna carefully picked up the board the canvas was attached to and set it on the table to keep anyone else from stepping on it.

As she turned to leave, a bit of color caught her eye. Peeking behind the dirty brown of the desert was a splash of faded blue. Carefully, she peeled back the map. There was another canvas beneath this one.

Curiosity suddenly seizing her, Senna tugged back the corner of the top canvas. Sepia had stained the canvas below with age, and the ink had faded. The shores were bound in what must have once been emerald green. Lakes and rivers dotted the land. Senna studied the coastline—one that looked hauntingly familiar.

Horror clutched her throat in an icy fist as Senna laid the newer map over the older one. She folded the desert canvas back to follow the outline of the newer coast. They were the same shoreline. But the rivers, lakes, and green were gone.

Her breathing came fast and hard. With Witch song to control nature, this kind of destruction didn't happen unless Haven *made* it happen.

Suddenly not caring, Senna ripped the newer canvas off and threw it. It spun before settling on the floor. She stared at the map before her. Rolling hills of green, with high mountain peaks capped in white. Rivers and lakes. Cities and rich fields. And in the far right corner, "Harshen" was written in fine calligraphy. Senna reached toward the ornate lettering, but stopped as if touching it might burn her.

Cities dotted the canvas, their buildings enlarged to show strange architecture—roofs with turned up corners and wide porches. She scanned the names of cities written in smaller script. Pennil, Upton, Webick…she froze. In the center of the snow-capped mountains was a city with the most ornate buildings yet, Rinnish—the Sacred City.

"Tarten was not the first." Her gaze darted around the walls of the room, at all the other maps, all the other nations. And she wondered what horrors were hidden beneath fresh canvas—how many dead the Witches had heaped upon the world. "No wonder they hate us."

Filled with a sudden rage, she pulled down another map. Ignoring the pain in her hand, she dug her fingers into the gap between wood backing and frame. It pulled apart with a screech of protesting nails. She peeled back the top canvas. There was nothing behind it.

Senna pulled down another and separated the frame. Nothing. She took down a third map—another desert. The frame gave with a crack, leaving a jagged edge of wood that left splinters in her fingers. Blood dripped onto the maps, leaving garish rivers of red.

She barely felt the pain. There was another map beneath, a verdant land bustling with cities that had been transformed into a desert. Her bloody fingerprints left tracks across it.

Skipping the lands with rich green fields and plenteous water, she pulled down every map featuring a desert. Each had a map of green beneath. Her fingers were raw and her healing hand burned by the time she was done.

There were six of them. Six times the Witches had annihilated an entire region.

Senna leaned against one of the scattered desks, her mind numb with horror. This destruction was not common knowledge.

Of that, Senna was sure. The Heads would know the truth, but she had a gut feeling they'd never admit it.

But there was one woman who might. With a deep breath, Senna gathered herself and ran from the tree house. Outside, it was already past midday. The path she'd chosen was completely blocked by a felled tree. Flying past Witches and Guardians alike, she cut straight through the foliage to another path. Some called after her, wondering if she was all right, if she needed help.

She ignored them until she reached her tree house. She glanced inside. There were a dozen Witches lying on blankets in the parlor. It was well known that Sacra was a former Head of Plants—not because she excelled at potions or plants, but because of her propensity for healing.

Taking a steadying breath, Senna stepped inside. The Witches waiting for treatment didn't look serious. Most were just banged up. A few were bleeding.

She knelt next to her mother. "Mother, I need to speak with you."

Sacra glanced up, her eyes bleary. "Hand me the garku, will you?"

Feeling guilty, Senna studied the injured. She didn't think the foreign Witches would risk attacking Haven again so soon. Whatever was going on with the desert countries could wait, at least a little while. She set about helping her mother with the Healing.

Before they'd finished, the Guardians had brought in another dozen Witches, and the day was tentatively approaching twilight.

Senna washed up and changed her dress before going back downstairs to speak with her mother. Another Witch had come in—this one with a twisted ankle.

Senna handed over the ointment without thought. "I need to speak with you in private."

Sacra's hands slowed. "Now's not the time, Brusenna." Her mother applied a salve for swelling.

Senna fished out the strips of cotton from her mother's satchel. "I know they turned Harshen into a desert, just like Tarten."

The strips of cotton stilled in her mother's hands. "How do you know that?"

The Witch with the twisted ankle watched them with wide eyes.

Senna folded her arms across her chest. "I know of six for sure. Are there any more?"

"I'll be right back," her mother said to the Witch. She grabbed Senna's arm and hauled her outside, beyond earshot. "Tarten is the first in a long time."

"How many?" Senna whispered.

Sacra gestured back to her tree house. "She's hurt, Senna. I think that's a bit more important than your silly questions!"

Senna clenched her jaw. "This is important, too."

Her mother turned to go back. Senna watched her walk away and knew she'd never give up the answers. Some impulse made her blurt, "What of Lilette and Calden?"

Sacra froze mid-stride. She whirled back and grabbed Senna's arm, her chest heaving. "Where did you hear those names?" she said in a harsh whisper.

Her fingernails dug into Senna's skin. She jerked free. "I want the truth, Mother."

Sacra slowly opened her clenched hands. They were shaking. "Where did you hear those names?"

"You wouldn't believe me if I told you."

Her mother squeezed her eyes shut. "Before I ever became the Head of Plants, I was sworn to never reveal the secrets of the Discipline Heads. I *can't* tell you."

Senna folded her hands across her chest. "Can't or won't?"

Her mother met her glare with one of her own. "Knowledge is a powerful thing. For once learned, certain things cannot be unlearned, no matter how much you might wish it."

Senna stiffened. "You kept me in the dark before and it nearly cost me my life."

Her mother sucked air through her teeth. "Lilette...Lilette and Calden were centuries ago, when all of Haven bustled with Witches. Before we were reduced to this" —she gestured toward the abandoned quarter— "pitiful existence."

Senna waited for her mother to go on, but she didn't. "So you would have me remain ignorant?"

Sacra shook her head. "Not ignorant—innocent."

Senna threw her arms out. "Innocence won't save me from

what's coming for me—what's coming for all of Haven."

"But it might save you from yourself," her mother whispered. "You would have knowledge, Daughter, but what if the knowledge destroys you?"

A cold knot of fear wormed its way into Senna's stomach. Was this what the Heads were talking about the first time she'd eavesdropped? Something beginning and Senna dying. "You'll have to trust me to make that choice."

Sacra's eyes were over-bright. "Being Creator-touched isn't a blessing—it's a curse. You are a catalyst, Brusenna. And the change you wreak will use you up." Her mother tipped her face up to study the sky as if it might hold the answers. "I might be able to keep you safe, if only you'll come with me."

Senna was in danger because she was Creator-touched? Her heart pounded with fear. She tried to imagine spending the rest of her life hiding what she was, and running every time the truth was found out. "I can't, Mother."

Sacra let out a shaky breath. "And I can't force you."

Senna shook her head. "I don't understand the connection between me and something that happened centuries ago."

Her mother opened her mouth then closed it again. "Tell me how you heard of Lilette, and I'll tell you what happened between Haven and Calden."

Senna wanted to tell her mother, wanted to share the burden all secrets become. That death and dying lands haunted her dreams. That something dark hunted Haven, something deadly. But her mother would only try harder to force her to leave. She shook her head as she backed away. "I can't."

"The great irony is you berate me for my secrets, Daughter, and yet you keep your own."

Senna glanced up at the sky visible between the leaves. It would be fully dark in a couple hours. She'd wasted enough time. She marched away, feeling her mother's gaze boring into her back. There were so many secrets swirling between them. But Senna had a good idea where to find their answers. And how to get to them.

One thing she knew for certain—secrets were sometimes necessary, but they were always dangerous.

10. Witch Wars

Stumbling over broken branches, Senna checked the barracks, the sparring field, the shooting range. But Joshen was nowhere to be found. Although it seemed everyone she asked had seen him somewhere, by the time she arrived, he'd already left.

When she did finally find him, she was shocked. She heard the unmistakable sound of Joshen's voice, followed by tinkling laughter. Heat built on her skin. She stepped slowly into Arianis' kitchen. The smells of frying fish and lemons filled the air. He sat at the table, laughing about something. They both looked up when Senna came in.

Joshen smiled at her. "Senna, you've got to try this cod. Best I've ever had."

Senna didn't take her eyes from Arianis. Her rich brown hair fell in fetching waves around her shoulders. Her large eyes were the color of cinnamon. Her skin was impossibly smooth, with natural rose hues. She was a soft beauty. The more you looked at her, the more striking she became.

"Senna?"

"I'm sure it is," Senna replied. She knew what Arianis saw in Joshen. He was handsome—tall, with broad shoulders that tapered to a narrow waist. In the lantern's wavering light, his normally dark brown hair appeared black.

But Senna knew things Arianis didn't. He always talked with his mouth full, stole from her plate, and often ate the best bits first. Normally, he was easygoing, but when her safety was concerned, he grew stubborn and bossy. His ears stuck out a bit, and his chin was a little soft, though his neatly trimmed beard and longer hair hid both rather nicely.

Despite knowing all his faults, she still thought he was beautiful.

He smiled and took another bite. "You want some? I'm sure there's enough."

Senna grunted. With Joshen, one could never be sure of enough food. "No. I'm really not hungry."

With a disbelieving shrug, he turned back to eating.

Senna looked Arianis up and down. "Joshen, I need to speak with you."

"I need to report back to Leader Reden anyway." He deftly shoved the rest of his meal in his mouth, tipped back the mug, and nodded to Arianis. "Thanks again."

Senna followed Joshen into the open. He held out her pistol. "I unloaded and cleaned it before loading it again. Try to keep it out of the rain."

She took it silently. "Joshen, why were you at Arianis' house?"

He looked down at her as if she were daft. "You said she was upset, so I came to check on her. She offered me dinner. I've hardly eaten anything all day."

That meant he hadn't finished off a school of fish by himself. Senna tried to cool her anger. After all, Joshen's intentions were good, and he was oblivious to any form of subtlety. Things were what they appeared to be. Nothing more. She took a deep breath. "Joshen, Arianis is using you to hurt me."

He was silent for a moment. "She should be angry with Coyel, not you."

Senna shrugged. "Coyel is well beyond Arianis' reach. I'm not. So you see why she might come after you?"

Joshen chuckled. "Never figured you for the jealous type, Senna."

She blushed. "Joshen—"

He laid a hand on her shoulder and squeezed. "You're reading more into it than there is. But if it makes you feel any better, I'll stay away from her."

Senna wanted to make him understand this wasn't just jealousy, but she didn't think it would do any good. Besides they were almost to her tree house, and she still had so much to tell him. "I didn't come looking for you to talk about Arianis, I came to tell you what I found." She explained about the maps.

Joshen slowed to a stop. "By the Creators."

She held her aching hand—she'd overused it today. She'd have to be more careful. "But there were no maps of Lilette and Calden. I'm going to check their personal library."

He met her gaze and his face hardened. "Why take all these risks for something that happened centuries ago?" He suddenly stiffened. "You're still trying to find a way to lift the curse on your own, aren't you? You're planning to go back to Tarten?"

Her gaze snapped to his. He knew her so well, perhaps too well. "Maybe."

"Senna, we've talked about this!" Joshen pinched the bridge of his nose. "Tarten has a standing order to shoot any witch on sight. It's too dangerous. I want you to swear you'll give this insanity up."

She slowly shook her head. "I can't."

"At least promise you'll tell me before you do anything foolish."

So he could try to stop her? Not really meaning it, she nodded.

He took a step closer. "Say it, Senna."

She stood her ground. "What about your promises? The ones you made as my Guardian—to always protect me and support me? What about those promises?"

"That's what I'm trying to do! You're my Witch, and—"

Anger flushed through Senna. "I'm not anyone's Witch but my own!"

He took a deep breath. "Sometimes you need to trust me, trust I'm only looking after you."

She stood completely still. "And I'm looking after the world."

His face was hard. "I won't let you walk into that kind of danger again. You wouldn't make it out alive."

Guilt warred with the anger charring her insides. "Something's coming, Joshen, and we all have a part to play. It's taken me a long time to accept that, but I have. Now you have to accept your part—accept it or reject it. Because supporting me and protecting me are not always the same thing."

"Accept it? I don't accept it! I won't." He started pacing back and forth, his hands buried in his hair.

Senna backed away. Joshen had been through so much for her, but that didn't give him the right to demand she obey him. She turned and pulled open the door to her house, then stepped in and shut it firmly behind her.

Breathing hard, Senna stood with her back to the wall and peeked out at him. He stood considering her closed door, frustration creasing his brow.

Maybe if Joshen hadn't been so tired, he would have come inside and insisted on personally keeping her out of trouble. But he didn't.

Senna waited until he was long gone before making sure her pistol was loaded. She slipped back out again.

She crossed the island and marched up to the Guardian standing at the elaborately arched cave entrance. It was the man Joshen had been sparring with the day before—Collum. On closer inspection, she saw he wasn't much older than her. His skin was the color of rich earth, his hair divided into little, beaded braids. She found she couldn't look at him. He reminded her too much of Leary—of the fact that she'd gotten Joshen's best friend killed.

Collum raised an eyebrow at the sight of her. "Apprentice Senna, you know you can't come inside unless you've permission."

His soft, rolling accent was like Leary's, too. She tried to swallow around the stone lodged in her throat. "I'm looking for Pogg. Has he finished fishing yet?"

The man's beads clinked as he nodded. "He went to sun himself on the rocks. You might try there."

Senna glanced up at the sky. They still had a few hours before dark. "Thank you."

"Apprentice Senna?"

She stopped but couldn't bring herself to face him.

"My name is Collum. Has Joshen told you that you sailed with my cousin, Leary?"

The world seemed to expand, pressing in on her and robbing her of her air. Collum reached out to steady her. She closed her eyes and concentrated on breathing. "Leary saved my life," she said, shaking her head. She would not cry. "I'm sorry."

She pulled away from Collum and stumbled in the direction the Guardian had indicated. Here, part of the cliff had collapsed, taking a good portion of the staircase with it. She scrambled up the rock-fall until she found Pogg. The mottled green creature reminded her of a frog. He had a wide face with even wider cheeks. Instead of a nose, there were only dark slits that closed when he was swimming.

She collapsed beside him. "I need your help."

Pogg turned slowly toward her. There was no white around his irises, only the cloudy blue-brown that reminded her of the ambiguous color of an infant's eyes. "Seennnaaa?"

He was always slow when he grew overcold. "Do you still have keys to the island's tree houses?" Pogg was a bit like a raccoon in collecting discarded and lost things. His fascination with keys was why Senna had been able to move so freely from one tree house to another during her time alone on the island.

Pogg's clear inner lids slid over his eyes. It took him a long time to answer. "Pogg gets Senna fresh fishes?"

Senna pressed her lips together to keep from shouting. "No. Pogg, do you still have the keys?"

Pogg pushed up so he was sitting like her—he often tried to imitate the actions of humans. He was the last-known Mettlemot, and Senna had seen how much he wanted somewhere to belong. "Fresh fishes betters."

He made a strange sound halfway between a choke and a gargle. He lifted his face skyward and jerked it up and down, almost as if he were…swallowing. He turned to her, his inner lids sliding back. "Sometimes fishes comes back up."

Senna swallowed the bile rising in her throat. "Pogg, do you still have the keys?"

He turned stiffly toward his small tree house. "Yes. Pogg has keys."

She followed him to his tree house and waited at the door. Oily dirt grimed every surface. Useless bits and discarded items were lumped together in groups on the floor or arranged inside broken baskets and wooden boxes. Blankets curled over a nest of leaves were the only indicator someone actually lived in the mess.

Once, Pogg had stayed with her in a tree house, slept in a bed. He'd been untidy, but he'd always smelled like the ocean, not fish grease. But since the Witches had returned, he'd taken to living like this. It was almost like he'd given up now that everyone was safe.

Pogg held up two cups filled with dark- and light-colored stones. "Want to play?"

Senna felt a stab of guilt. She hadn't come to visit Pogg since her attack nearly two weeks ago. He probably didn't even know it had happened. "Not today. I don't have time."

He set the cups down with a sad clank. Then he pulled back some of the leaves that made up his bed to reveal a mess of keys on a ring. Holding them in his mouth, he crept on all fours toward her. He gave her a strange look—well, even stranger than normal. Senna crouched before him. "Which one goes to the Council Tree?"

He sat on his haunches and clutched the keys to his chest. "Why Senna wants them?"

"Because I think someone wants to hurt the Witches."

Pogg made a gurgle that was half warning, half disapproval. He pushed the keys around on his hand, the webbed skin between his fingers crumpled like wet parchment. "This key fors Prenny houses. This keys fors library. This keys fors Witchling house." He went over a dozen keys, while Senna sat in rapt attention. "Ah..." He held up a large, ornate key. "This key fors Council rooms."

Senna took the entire ring from him.

"Why needs all?" He leapt for them. "Gives back keys."

Senna stood and held them out of his reach. "I will as soon as I'm done."

He jumped, nearly bowling her over.

She stiff-armed him. His skin was cold and rubbery. Despite the hours she'd spent with him, the touch repulsed her. Ashamed of her reaction, she forced herself to hold him more firmly. "The Dark Witch, Pogg, she's up to something. I have to stop her."

"Dark Witch," he hissed through pointy teeth.

Guilt twinged her insides for using the creature's hate of the Dark Witch against him—for lying to him. But she didn't think he'd understand that the danger was the same, just from a different source.

Pogg let out a low keening sound. It made her ears hurt.

He was silent a time before he started rocking back and forth. "Pogg finds starfishes in ocean. But Pogg not brings them back."

A wave of loneliness washed over Senna. Pogg had often brought her dog starfish. "Bruke would have liked them."

His movements slow and stiff, Pogg went past her, back to the sun-drenched rocks. She couldn't help but notice how...ragged he looked. "Pogg, why don't you ask for a fire? A bed? There's plenty of room."

Pogg looked over his shoulder at her. Even though Senna had spent a great deal of time with him, his expressions were so alien he was hard to read. "Witches comes back. Not needs Pogg anymore."

Anger touched her. "Go find Leader Reden or one of the Heads. Tell one of them that you want one of the old tree houses by the entrance. They'll see to it."

Pogg continued climbing. He looked so alone.

Senna gripped the ring of keys tight before slipping them into her dress pocket. "Tell Reden you need someone—a Wastrel or a Witchling—to come start your fire every night." Pogg's fingers only had two joints. He was hopeless with a flint and steel.

He didn't respond. Senna promised herself when she returned to the island, she'd play stones with him more often.

She crossed the island in the deepening twilight. Witches and Guardians were still about, repairing fallen trees and patching windows. Senna slipped through them with her head bent and her cowl pulled low over her face. The Council Tree was by the library and the Heads' trees. All of them seemed empty. At the tree's base, she waited to make sure she was alone before using the key Pogg had indicated to open the door.

After shutting it softly, Senna rounded the desk standing between her and the twisted stairs and climbed up.

At the top, she tried the Council Room door. It was locked. Sweat started on her brow. She couldn't remember what the rest of the keys went to, let alone if any of them opened this door. She tried one after another. On the second-to-last key, the lock gave with a snick.

Her heart in her throat, Senna eased inside. Before her was a large window overlooking the Ring of Power. All the other walls were lined with books.

Senna locked the door behind her so she'd have a little warning if anyone came inside. She drew the heavy curtains, then lit a lantern and turned the wick down to a faint glow. She held it before her and started scanning the titles. Her mother had said the first Witch War was hundreds of years ago.

She picked the oldest-looking books and pulled some down. They were all accounts copied from older manuscripts written by a Head of Sunlight. None were quite old enough. Putting them back, she tried some even more faded ones. Finally, she found the one she was looking for—a musty-smelling book by a Head named Merlay, who appeared to be in her mid-thirties.

Senna eagerly started reading. She learned Haven had been exclusively for students once. Adult Witches lived wherever they chose, but most preferred to dwell in Tarten—apparently Haven had been beside Tarten then—so they could participate in the songs that shifted the seasons. There had been two big celebrations in spring and fall to usher in winter and summer, during which time songs were said to fly in the air. Thousands had flocked to see the Witches' singing. Senna couldn't imagine living in a world where people traveled to see a Witch sing.

She skimmed through accounts with dates of the first frost for each country. There were ledgers specifying the perfect amount of snow and rainfall for each region. Witches were dispatched to deal with blights and even a plague of locusts.

Merlay wrote about their difficulty finding enough room for all the new Witchlings and detailed the money coming in from countries to show their gratitude. She mentioned letters asking for Witches to be stationed in regions struggling with poor soil or with a tendency for unpredictable winds, earth tremors, drought, or flooding. And a whole hundred Witches to deal with a newly formed volcano threatening Harshen in the north. That hundred had never come back. The entire ship had sunk when they'd hit uncharted rocks off the coast of Vorlay.

Senna sat up straight and read more carefully.

Before Merlay could investigate, war had broken out between Harshen and Vorlay. Though the fighting was hundreds of leagues away, smoke from the battles had tinged the twilight and morning skies blood red.

And then stories began trickling in of an entire country decimated. By Witches.

It took Merlay months to piece together the truth. How Harshen had exaggerated a dormant volcano's threat to acquire a large group of Witches. Most were either young or old—Witches who'd finished raising or had yet to start their families.

Harshen's king, Nis, had imprisoned and tortured the Witches until they helped him destroy Vorlay. But Nis hadn't stopped there. He'd moved on to another country. Merlay's spies gleaned rumors that he plotted to take over the whole world.

The Witches didn't have an army. Their only weapons were their voices and their Guardians. So they'd made the only choice they could. They'd sealed the heavens, cutting Harshen off from the rains, and threatened to do more if Nis didn't release their Witches.

In response, he'd slit the Witches' throats. The Heads had all voted to let Harshen die. But not all the Witches had agreed with the Head's decision. Some had fought. Led by a girl, barely into her Apprenticeship. Lilette.

Senna gasped. "Lilette." The name rolled off her tongue like a song in the silence of the room. Lilette wasn't a country, but a woman.

Horrified by what the Witches had done, Lilette took those few who would follow her and left for her home country. Calden.

Senna closed her eyes. She wasn't sure she could bear to read anymore.

Hadn't her mother warned her? Once learned, knowledge cannot be unlearned. Senna was beginning to grasp the burden truth could become.

Gathering her courage, she turned the page. Songs now came from two different voices, confusing the elements. The conflicting rhythms grated against each other. Storms whipped up that flattened entire villages, destroyed fleets of ships. Crops froze. Leaves failed to drop before the hard frost killed the trees.

Merlay never actually wrote the words, but Senna felt her fear. Lilette and her Witches' songs were stronger. Strong enough to destroy Haven at any time.

Certain an attack was imminent, Merlay had struck first. She glossed over the details, simply referring to what happened next as "the tragedy," but Senna gleaned enough to understand Haven had struck so hard and fast they had annihilated Calden and every Witch who had fled to it. She believed the entire nation had sunk into the sea.

It might have ended there and been tragedy enough. But it hadn't. The world now feared Witches—feared them or coveted their power. More Witches were kidnapped. More wars broke out. Over a period of fifty years, hundreds of thousands of people must have died.

Now an old woman, Merlay gathered as many Witches into Haven as she could. No more did they travel about healing the lands afflicted by plagues or failing crops. They moved onto the island and went into hiding.

Senna only learned one thing more. Merlay had sent a Witch to discover what had become of Calden. All she'd found were a few helpless pollywog Mettlemots, which were only native to Calden. She'd brought them home to Haven. But the creatures were not meant to live in the colder climate. She worried for their health.

Over the centuries, they must have slowly died out. Until only one remained. Pogg.

Senna knew what came next. Decades of slow decline, until people began to doubt the Witches' power altogether.

And then Espen had come. Espen, who didn't believe Witches should quietly control nature. Espen, who wanted to force the world's respect. Espen, who'd held the seasons for ransom, only letting the rains fall for those with the coin to pay.

Again, the Witches had fought—the second Witch War. Espen lost, but that hadn't stopped her from waging her own personal war against every remaining Witch. The fallout had lasted ten years.

And then Espen had created Lathel—a seed with the ability to turn human flesh into trees that bore the captive Witch's song in the form of a single fruit, the consumption of which had granted Espen the ability to steal another Witch's power.

At first, Haven had sent their most powerful Witches to fight Espen. None returned. So the Witches dug in, went deeper into hiding.

Senna's mother had been the Head of Plants. Sacra had lost her husband and firstborn daughter to the Witch Hunters. When she found herself pregnant, she'd fled deep into Nefalie—to the region known for its hatred of Witches. And there she had remained until the Witch Hunters found them.

Senna closed her eyes, remembering her horror at learning she was the last-remaining free Witch. That if she didn't liberate the others, the Four Sisters would fall into chaos, taking the world with them.

She sat back and stared at the table laden with books detailing the Witches fall from the most powerful and revered entity on earth to the most hunted and feared.

So many must have died. Whole species—including the Mettlemots—must have been lost.

And Senna understood every doomed step the Witches before her had taken, understood why they had fallen into the pit they had. And it was clear they weren't done falling.

"We can't fight the world, and we can't hide from it. They must love us again," she whispered to herself.

The oil in the lantern was running low and the wick needed trimming. Senna rubbed her aching eyes. She was so tired she couldn't think straight anymore. Everything she'd learned was swirling around and colliding in her head like a glass house full of flies.

Ever so slowly, she began to see recognizable patterns in the chaos. If a few pollywog Mettlemots had survived, why not some of the Witches? What if they had escaped and hidden themselves from the world behind some sort of barrier? Surely over the centuries their numbers could pose a threat to Haven. And what if Espen knew where they were?

Senna had to leave Haven, not just to lift the curse, but to discover the extent of the danger facing her Witches. She sat for long moments, staring into the lantern flame and making plans until her eyes burned with the need to blink.

Standing stiffly, she shut the metal clasps and slid the books back onto their places on the shelves. Then she extinguished the lantern and peered out the window. It was fully dark.

Joshen would be asleep by now. Even if he wasn't, she couldn't tell him what she'd learned.

The fallout from the two Witch Wars had not yet ended.

It still might destroy the world.

11. Song Pendant

Senna's mother was waiting for her when she arrived home in the early hours of the morning. Without a word, Sacra followed her up to her room and lay down beside her. Too tired to object, Senna went to sleep.

The next morning, despite her protests, her mother escorted Senna to and from her classes and the island's repair work. Though it had been over a week since she was attacked, her hand still burned whenever she used it much, so the Keepers relegated her to lighter cleanup work.

The day after was much the same. The worst part was, Senna didn't see Joshen either day. She was still angry with him, but his absence hinted something was wrong. Something bigger than their spat. What if he'd been hurt? What if he needed her? On the evening of the third day, she slipped a few drops of sleeping potion in her mother's tea.

Soon, Senna stole out to the sound of Sacra's soft snores.

But Joshen wasn't in his tree house. Or the shooting range. Or the outdoor pavilion where their food was cooked—Senna checked, twice.

"Brusenna?" She started and turned to see Collum moving silently toward her. "What are you doing here?"

"Have you seen Joshen?" she blurted.

Collum's brows drew together. "No. I've been guarding you all day."

She opened her mouth, then closed it again. "I thought it was just Joshen, Reden, and Timpnee. Does every Guardian take turns following me?" she asked a bit desperately.

Collum shook his head, his beads clinking. "No. Only the five of us."

There were *five* of them now? She had to stop herself from wincing. "I need to find Joshen."

Collum looked down at her. He was so tall. "Come with me. We'll see if Leader Reden knows where he's been assigned."

But they couldn't find Reden, either.

Finally, Senna gave up. "If I'm late for class," she said, "Arianis will have me teaching the rest of her lectures for her." That evening, the chesli harvest would begin. Senna wouldn't have another chance to look for Joshen until tomorrow.

Collum dropped behind her as she left the Guardian quarter and hurried to the onion-shaped tree. Despite all their work, the island still looked like the aftermath of a battle. Though the men were nearly done boarding up the last of the windows, glass and broken bits of trees still littered the pathway.

Chavis looked up from gathering broken frames. "This class is still canceled. The earth tremor damaged too many of the maps."

The old maps were well concealed again. Senna knew why Chavis had been sent to clean them up, instead of a lowly Witchling or Apprentice. "Where's Arianis?"

Chavis shrugged. "How should I know?"

Senna tried to remember the last time she'd seen her fellow Apprentice. But Arianis never made an appearance in any of Senna's many work details.

Neither had Joshen. She hustled back outside.

"The chesli harvest begins after sunset. You'd best get some rest!" Chavis called after her.

Senna barely heard her. She fingered her crescent-moon pendant and faced Arianis' tree house, but her feet refused to budge. There was a way to find out without going there, but it made her uneasy. The last time it had been activated was when Wardof had used it to track her. She barely escaped alive that night.

She'd worn it every day since, until it felt familiar against her chest...using it, however—that was something else altogether. Senna's aching hand finally managed to unlatch the clasp. She tapped it against the metal of her belt. The amber vibrated with a sweet tone. The pendant twisted and twirled before slowly lifting. It pointed toward the inhabited quarter on the other side of the Ring of Power. Senna followed it as best she could around trees the size of ships.

She moved deeper and deeper into the Witches' habitation. With every step she took, her heart sank farther into her chest. When she heard the low murmur of voices—one male, one female—she stopped, her heart aching. Her hand dropped, dragging the necklace down with it.

She tapped it against the metal again. It went limp. She clasped it behind her neck with shaking fingers. Not sure if she could deal with anymore unwanted revelations, she considered turning back and pretending she'd never seen this.

Arianis' laughter wiped the impulse clean, propelling her forward. Without bothering to knock, she shoved the door open and stood on the threshold. Joshen and Arianis sat together at the table. Senna smelled honey cakes and something else that was maddeningly familiar, though she couldn't place it.

Joshen rose from the table, his expression tight. "Senna?"

He'd promised to stay away from Arianis. "Is this where you've been the past two days?" Senna asked.

"Yes," he answered immediately.

A flock of angry words filled Senna's mouth before dying and tumbling back to her stomach, where they grew heavy as a mountain. There had to be a reason for Joshen being here. He wouldn't betray her like this. He couldn't.

She inhaled and her breath suddenly hitched. She knew that smell from her potions class. Storming to the table, she tipped back the cup. The color was hard to judge because of the wooden cup, but the golden flakes were obvious.

Dipping in her finger, she tasted it, just to be sure. "Truth serum." She glared at Arianis, song curling around the edges of her throat—a song full of pounding anger. A song that could rend Arianis' tree in half. Senna's body shook with the effort of leashing it. "There are rules for administering this class of potion. Rules you would have learned as a Witchling."

Joshen peeked at the contents in disgust. "Truth serum."

His face blanched. "So that's why I couldn't stop myself from answering your questions, why I couldn't leave."

Senna shot him a glare just as baleful as the one she was using on Arianis. She'd warned him the other Apprentice would use him. Why hadn't he listened? "How long ago did you start drinking it?"

He set the cup down on the table as if it might grow teeth and bite him. "Long enough."

"You had better have a good reason for giving Joshen a potion without his consent." Senna's words came out with a chant-like, dangerous edge—nearly a song. With her sensitivity to the Four Sisters, she felt them perk up, listening.

Arianis tossed her wavy hair over her shoulder and thrust a folded piece of paper towards Senna. "So tell me, Creator-touched, when can the Truth Serum be administered?"

Senna stared unseeing at the paper before her gaze slowly shifted to Arianis. Without having to read it, she suddenly knew. "When did they advance you to a full Keeper?"

Arianis' smile transformed her from beautiful to radiant, but Senna knew she was truly monstrous. "Three days ago. I think Coyel was feeling a bit guilty about discarding me for you. Besides, we need a glassmaker to replace our windows. But our inability to stop the earth tremor and wave will probably anger the Nefaliens. They needed a face no one in Corrieth would recognize as a Witch."

Senna's mouth went dry. She turned to Joshen. "A Keeper may use the Truth Serum when she's considering Guardians."

Anger colored his cheeks. "Without informing me first?"

Arianis smiled gently at him, as if he were a child throwing a tantrum instead of a grown man who'd been tricked into drinking a potion. "You would have resisted had you known. For that reason, the Heads gave me the discretion not to tell you."

Her gaze went back to Senna. "So you believe you've Traveled? And there are hundreds of Witches outside Haven that threaten us? And I never would have guessed you'd seek out Espen. I wonder what the Heads would think of that."

Joshen looked drained. "I had to answer her. And I couldn't leave. I'm sorry."

The potion would make him weak-willed. Malleable. If Arianis had told Joshen to stay, he would have. She addressed Arianis. "Have you forgotten what happened to the last Witch who hurt someone I loved?" Senna felt powerful and dangerous.

Apparently oblivious, Arianis set her jaw. "I didn't *hurt* him."

Again, Senna had to tamp down her anger. Joshen knew nearly all Senna's secrets. And now so did Arianis. "Give me one reason why I shouldn't shove Bindweed down your throat and let you molder like the worthless lump you are."

Arianis had the good sense to blanch. "The Heads would imprison you until you freed me and then banish you from the island."

Fury burned so bright and hot in Senna that she had a hard time forming words. Finally, she said, "I've fought Witch Hunters. Crossed an ocean while blinded by fog. I've been shot and born the weight of men dying for me. Faced the Dark Witch alone. I've seen the Creators' faces.

"I'm not afraid of you, Arianis. And you have no idea how dangerous an enemy I can be."

Fear finally touched Arianis. "The Heads recommended Joshen as my Guardian."

Of course. They wanted to keep Senna and Joshen apart. What better way than to send him away? "Joshen, get me out of here before I do something I can't take back."

He obeyed the command without hesitation, laying a hand on her shoulder. His touch spread through her, cooling her anger. Shaking, she let him lead her from the tree house.

"I have chosen Joshen as my Guardian," Arianis cried out. "He will accompany me or be released from his Guardianship. Is that what you want, Senna?"

Joshen's grip tightened on Senna's shoulder. "I'll talk to Reden. He'll straighten this out."

Senna didn't think there was anything Reden could do. The Heads outranked him. Still, she kept walking.

"I'll tell them about Espen," Arianis called after them.

Senna caught sight of Collum, watching from his position half hidden beside a tree.

"Collum, shut her up," Joshen ordered. "I've got Senna for tonight."

Collum nodded once and strode toward Arianis.

"Do you know he feels trapped here?" Arianis struggled against Collum. "That he longs for adventure, for horses and the open sea? That he has every intention of stopping you if you try to leave the island?"

Joshen whirled around, his hand automatically straying toward his musket. "You're twisting what I said!"

Collum shut the door to any more of Arianis' poisonous words.

Senna studied Joshen, sadness smothering her anger. "But they were your words." He tugged her along. She barely felt her hand in his. "Is it true?"

Joshen's mouth tightened, but the potion compelled him to answer. "I miss my horses. I miss Parknel and the crew. Sometimes I feel as if these walls are a cage."

"And I your captor?"

He spun her to face him. "No."

She knew he spoke the truth. The potion wouldn't allow a lie, unless that person was lying to himself. The thought made her bite her lip. "Would you try to stop me from leaving?"

He swallowed, and Senna could tell he was trying not to answer. Betrayal wrapped cold, steel hands around her heart, freezing her from the inside out. Hugging herself, she brushed past him and started for the clearing.

In two of his long strides he was beside her, his eyes bulging with the effort of keeping the truth behind his lips.

Despite her anger, she couldn't help feeling a little sorry for him. This wasn't his fault. Not entirely. Perhaps not at all. "You can't fight it, Joshen. The potion is too strong."

"Yes!" he blurted. "It's my job to protect you."

His words were like a blow to her stomach. "If *you* couldn't stop me, would you tell the Heads?"

"Probably." She closed her eyes.

The one person in the world Senna had relied on, and he would betray her to keep her safe and useless. She couldn't trust him with any more of her secrets. Maybe her mother was right. "If you're not strong enough without Joshen, you'll never be strong enough with him," she had said.

He rubbed his forehead. "I'm sorry, but I don't care about the Tartens or some foreign Witches as much as I care about you."

He was so tall she had to crane her neck to look at him. "It doesn't really matter. If Arianis tells the Heads about my meeting with Espen, they'll never trust me again. I can't risk it."

He tensed. "What are you saying?"

"You have to go with her. She made sure of that."

His shoulders tensed. "How do you know she won't tell them anyway?"

"I don't. But Arianis crossed a line when she questioned you about me. She would get in trouble too. I think this is just her way of taking something away from me, just like I took something away from her."

Joshen's departure with Arianis would give Senna the chance she needed to escape. But could she really abandon him? Did she have a choice?

He shook his head. "I don't want to leave you."

"I know." And she did. "It's a risk we'll have to take. Besides, it will only be for a couple days. There will be plenty of boats and something besides fish and greens to eat. And you'll have a chance to ride your horses again."

He hesitated. "Senna..."

She smiled, trying to show him she wasn't afraid. She noticed a Witch coming down the path toward them and dropped her voice. "You will go."

Still under the influence of the Truth Serum, he nodded slowly, painfully. "We're to find a glass blower who will agree to work on the island. I'll be back in a day, two at the most."

Guilt pricked Senna's insides. She hated to use a potion to deceive and trick him as Arianis had, hated that their relationship had come to this.

She moved aside to let the Witch pass. But instead of continuing on, the Witch blocked their path. Senna stopped short, surprised that this wasn't just any Witch. It was Drenelle, her face tight with anger. "You Guardians didn't do a proper job boarding my windows. A bat has found its way inside my tree house." When Joshen hesitated, she made a shooing motion in the direction of her tree. "Well, go on!"

He opened his mouth to protest. Senna overrode him. "Joshen, go. I'll be fine." She'd nearly reached the clearing where the Witches were to meet before beginning the harvest, not to mention the fact that she was armed with a pistol and knife.

Joshen strode toward the tree house without a second thought; immediate obedience of a direct command was another side effect of the Truth Serum.

How long would it be before Senna saw him again? She bit her fist to keep her emotions in check. She didn't want Joshen to see how upset she was and become suspicious.

Drenelle rounded on Senna and jabbed her finger into her chest. "And Apprentices aren't to spend time with the Guardians." Drenelle suddenly froze and stared at the hollow of Senna's throat.

Anger burning up her hurt, Senna backed away.

Drenelle matched her movement. Her hand shot out, catching Senna's crescent pendant. She tipped the stone to catch the light coming from one of the windows. "When and where did you get this?"

Senna snatched her necklace back. "I bought it at the Gonstower market years ago."

The woman's gaze never left the necklace. "If I didn't know better, I'd say that was the real one."

Senna's anger was replaced with confusion. "Real one?"

Drenelle's gaze bored into the pendant. "Amber is the most powerful of stones. Wind and sunlight hardens the living blood of trees—plants—and earth turns it to stone. Thus all Four Sisters are part of amber. Only a handful of Witches—the smallest of handfuls—could manipulate it to function like a potion. The knowledge of how it is done was lost long ago."

Drenelle's fingers trembled as if itching to examine Senna's pendant. "There are only five women who succeeded in making a

Song Pendant. I've searched for decades and would give anything to own one, to unravel the mystery of how they were made." She laughed, but it sounded forced. "It's a very convincing replica. But of course, you couldn't have bought the genuine one at a cheap market. Besides, this particular Song Pendant came as a pair."

Senna had to resist the urge to cover her pendant with her hand. What Drenelle didn't know was Joshen had the other half under his shirt while he chased a bat around her house. Senna smiled tightly. No doubt she wore a Song Pendant, and Drenelle would find a way to take it if she knew. "I hope you find one." *Of your own.*

Senna started toward the others she could hear milling just beyond her sight. She felt Drenelle's eyes boring into her back. "Don't you want to know what it was called?"

Senna pasted an innocent look on her face and turned around. "What what was called?"

Drenelle's eyes tightened. She looked pointedly at the pendant around Senna's neck. "It was the Lilette Stone. And it allowed whoever wore it to find the person wearing its mate."

The Lilette Stone. Senna's mouth nearly fell open, but she kept herself in check. If she showed any reaction, Drenelle would grow suspicious. Suspicion would lead to questions. Questions would lead to testing the stone. And then Senna would lose her pendant.

She wasn't going to give it up. Not after the Witch Hunter, Wardof, had used it to track her down and nearly kill her. If anyone had paid for this pendant, it was her. "I just thought it was pretty."

That seemed to convince Drenelle. The Head grunted. "Yes, well, it's nearly full dark. Get to the Ring of Power. It's the eve of the chesli harvest."

Senna backed away. "Yes, Head Drenelle." She pivoted, then jogged toward the clearing, her heart thumping painfully in her chest.

12. CHESLI HARVEST

The vines of the chesli plants twined partway up the trees. Only visible on a moonless night, the flower's fuzzy, pollen-scattered centers glowed golden. Moths and insects of a hundred varieties flitted anxiously from one flower to the next, lugging glowing pollen that dusted the air like a thousand falling stars. Witches surrounded Senna and Mistin, their skin smudged and streaked with glimmering bits.

"Why are we doing this?" Mistin asked.

Sometimes Senna forgot Mistin was even newer to Haven than she was. "Because the chesli only blooms for a few nights a year, during mid-summer's dark phase of the moon. Their pollen increases a potion's shelf life exponentially without altering the potion's properties—it's a catalyst."

With a wince, Mistin rolled her shoulders. "Why can't we gather it during the day?"

Senna sighed. "Because the flowers close during the day."

"We could pry them open," Mistin grumbled.

"They're too delicate. It would kill them and there'd be no seed, and therefore no flowers next year." Senna gathered pollen by brushing a fuzzy cloth inside the flower. After the cloth was full, she shook it off inside a glass jar and went back for more. "Did I ever thank you for warning me?"

Mistin smiled a little. "You're welcome."

Soft trails of light following them, moths competed with Senna for the flowers as they bumped dumbly from one to the next. Her hands were brushed by wings that added their soft powder to her skin. To Senna's surprise, she heard the flower's music. They were calling for the moths, songs that seemed to paint the night with colors of light. The melody was so gentle and full of longing, she forgot about her own heartache and hummed along.

By unspoken agreement, she and Mistin worked steadily away from the others. Soon Senna's skin glowed bright enough that the moths bumped into her as frequently as they did the flowers. As a general rule, she hated bugs. But these moths were so beautiful they didn't really count. They were more like tiny, delicate birds than insects.

A soft touch startled her. She looked down to see a moth skimming along her palm. Another landed on her wrist. She brought the insect close, studying the intricate patterns on its wings. A third moth clung to Senna's smallest finger, its tiny legs tickling so she had to fight to keep from wiggling and scaring the moths away.

She froze and let the moths come. They coated her hands, their wings working as they fought each other to get ever closer. Soon, her hands were covered in moths like living mittens. She must have some in her hair too, because they flitted next to her face, climbing the tendrils of her hair like vines.

She was so caught up with the moths that Mistin's voice startled her. "Do they normally do that?"

"They're lost without the moon," Senna whispered so as not to frighten them.

Mistin was breathing hard. "Shake them off."

But Senna didn't want to startle them. So instead, she sang.

> Off with thee, off with thee, off in the night.
> Fly for the moon and stars so bright.

The music around her fell in harmony with her song, and the moths sprang away from her hands in an explosion of wings. In moments, they were again flitting from flower to flower in mass confusion. None came back to Senna. Her hands still tickling with the memory of their clinging legs, she watched the moths.

Her smile faded when she saw Mistin gaping at her. "Senna, you're *shining.*"

Senna looked down at herself and she was shocked to discover it was true. It wasn't just the pollen and the dust from moth wings. Away from the lantern light, her skin shimmered softly. "That must be why the moths came. They were attracted to the light."

"But why are you *shining?*" Mistin's voice was tinged with fear.

Senna shook her head in disbelief. "It must be the pollen."

Mistin blinked a few times. "Maybe."

Senna flicked her hands, trying to shake off whatever must be on her skin.

Mistin wet her lips. "I'm going to work my way back."

A hollow sadness filled Senna as she watched the closest thing she had to a friend disappear. She slumped down amid the flowers and tried to force the tears back down her throat. She didn't cry anymore. She was past that. She was so absorbed in *not* crying that at first she didn't notice the whirring sound around her.

Something crashed. She jumped to her feet and looked around. "Hello?"

Relieved she had a Guardian assigned to her, she called, "Um, whoever's watching over me, will you come out? Please?" Heavy silence answered her.

Fear spreading through her veins, Senna backed up. "Hello?" This time there was an answer: a steady whirring noise.

"Senna! Drop!"

Reaching for the pistol Joshen had given her, Senna spun around. Reden sprinted towards her, his musket at his side, blood running down his face. Her mind registered the whirring noise. She'd heard it before. A sling. By then it was too late.

The stone connected with the side of her head. There was no pain, only an explosion of pure white light. She was on the ground, her ears ringing and her senses dull.

Senna was only vaguely aware of someone kneeling over her, then hands gripping her under her arms and dragging her away. Blackness curled in from the outsides of her vision. She fought to stay conscious.

Reden shouting again. The unmistakable sound of musket fire. A blur of movement from her attacker. An answering hiss of pain from Reden.

Then Reden was there. He crouched protectively over her, his eyes raking the trees as he poured powder into his musket. "Senna?"

She didn't answer. Mostly because she couldn't drudge up the energy.

"Senna!"

"What?" she tried to say, but it came out as more of an incomprehensible mumble. Her head felt like a watermelon dropped from a cliff. It didn't hurt so much as just felt…scrambled.

Reden gripped her arm and helped her up. "Can you stand?"

Her legs refused to bear weight. He caught her as she fell and draped her over his shoulder. Then he started running. The jarring motion caused her to lose her battle with the blackness. She passed in and out of consciousness. At one point Reden went off the path, running through the foliage. Plants slapped Senna as they went past. The next time she woke, they were on the path again. She didn't understand.

Finally, Reden eased her down to the ground and braced her against him. He pulled her hood over her face like he was hiding her. His breath came in short bursts and sweat rolled down the sides of his face. He didn't bother brushing it away. "I need you to walk, Senna. I can't hide us here."

Why? She tried to respond, but her mouth still wouldn't work.

She forced herself to push one foot in front of the other, swaying as if she were drunk. Her focus was slowly coming back. She climbed up a set of steps almost by herself. Why hadn't Reden wanted anyone to see them? Why was he running away from help instead of towards it? She glanced around. They were in the Guardian quarter of the island, but she didn't recognize the tree.

"Where are we?" Just forming words felt like a triumph.

He checked the door to the tree house, sighing in obvious relief when it slid open. "This is Timmus' place—he's gone with Joshen. We ought to be all right here."

She looked at Reden. His expression was harsh—almost a grimace. He eased her into a chair and then hurried to bolt the door. Senna noticed a steady dripping. She followed the sound to see drops of blood falling from Reden's fingers and scattering across the floor like jewels.

She came to her feet, determined to help him.

In two steps he was in front of her. "Sit down."

She was suddenly nauseous. Her mouth started watering uncontrollably. "I'm going to throw up."

Reden practically carried her to the dry sink.

She retched. He gripped her as if he expected her to fall at any moment. She was too miserable to be embarrassed.

When she finished, he guided her to a chair. She was hot and cold at the same time. He crouched before her and pulled her eyelids open. He stared cursing in Tarten. "Slings can kill a man. If I ever find the dung licker that hit you, I'll show him firsthand."

She almost snorted at the sound of Joshen's favorite curse word on Reden's tongue.

"Your eyes are fine," the Guardian said.

He moved to a shelf. Questions collided with the doubts and fears swirling in Senna's mind, but she couldn't make herself care. She tipped her head back against the wall. She must have passed out again. When she opened her eyes, all she saw was a man standing before her with a knife.

Panic reared up inside her like a striking snake, its venom spilling out her pores. She let out a bloodcurdling scream. Startled, the man jumped back.

"Shh, Senna. Shh. I'm not going to hurt you." He came at her with the knife.

She half sprang, half fell away from him. She screamed again.

Frustration plain on his face, he tossed the knife away. His hand closed over her mouth, cutting off her cries for help. She tried to bite, but he clamped her jaw closed.

She kicked and fought. All the times she'd been attacked before, all the times she'd been beaten and bound—all of it flashed in her memory as hot and harsh as lightning. She nearly choked on her sudden terror.

And then through her fear, she realized the man was whispering her name. "Senna. Shh, shh, Senna. Senna, shh. The knife was to stop the bleeding in my arm. I'd never hurt you. Shh."

Then she remembered. Reden. Not her attacker. Her rescuer. How could she think he'd harm her? She went limp in his arms.

He slowly removed his hand. "Don't scream again. All right? I don't want anyone to know you're here."

Her head throbbed with each pulse of her heart. She cradled her head in her hands. "Why?"

Reden pushed himself to his feet. "Because I'm sure we lost your attacker. Right now, that's your best defense." She saw he wanted to help her up, but he was afraid to touch her. He cautiously held out his hand. "Senna, you have to know I'd never hurt you."

She closed her eyes and tried to force her pounding heart to slow, to shove the panic back into whatever corner of her body it struck from. She started to nod, but stopped at the pain shooting across her skull. "I know. It's just…"

Grimacing, Reden helped her back into the chair. "You don't forget. You never forget. And with the bump on your head, you were confused."

Reden would understand a person might live through a battle but carry the fear and terror with her for the rest of her life. Senna nodded.

"Drink your tea. And hold the compress to your bruise. Prenny supplied all the Guardians with them. They ought to be good."

Senna dragged herself back into the chair. "Tea? When did you make tea? Or start a fire, for that matter."

He poured himself a cup. "When you were out."

She grunted. "If this is Timmus' place, how do you know where everything is?"

Reden raised an eyebrow at her. "Inspections once a week. Discipline is the key of any army, and the Guardians are simply a very specialized army."

Senna held the compress against her head and breathed deeply the strong smell of the herbs. "You were hit too?" She motioned to the blood crusting his head. He nodded and winced as if he regretted the movement.

Mindful of her unsettled stomach, she slowly sipped her tea. "Why didn't you pass out?"

He grinned. "I have a harder head." He unfastened his cloak and threw it in a corner.

She saw the blood staining his sleeve. "What happened?"

Reden grimaced as he tried to peer at the back of his arm. "He targeted me first. I pretended it knocked me out and waited. When he came at you, I fired my musket. Unfortunately, I missed. As I was drawing my pistol, he threw a knife. He's got a wicked aim. I've no idea why I'm not dead."

"I thought the Leader of the Guardians was a little busy to be watching me."

He twisted the wick up on the lantern. The room brightened. He eased his shirt over his head and examined the nasty slash on his arm. He muttered curses in Tarten. "Collum's sick. Joshen and Timpnee are gone with Arianis. Hesten and Deere already had their shift."

Senna dropped her head. "I'm sorry for being so much trouble."

Reden didn't bother responding. His cut wasn't long, but it was deep. She winced. Part of her training as an Apprentice had been the basic care of wounds. But the pig carcass she'd practiced on hadn't been alive. "It will scar worse if you don't have it stitched," she said. "Nor will it heal as well."

He gave her an odd look and gestured to his bare chest. "What's one more?"

Her gaze traced the scars riddling his skin like the lines on a map. Beneath those scars, his body was hard and smooth, the body of a career soldier.

He took a bottle from a shelf and bit off the cork. Immediately the strong scent of alcohol flooded Senna's nostrils. After taking three deep pulls, Reden tamped back the cork. "That ought to tame it."

He gave her a pointed look before twisting the glass of the lantern up to expose the flame. He slid the blade inside.

She suddenly realized what he was planning. Her vision blurred again. "Oh, no. You're not doing that."

"If I cauterize it, I won't need stitches."

Senna felt like she was going to throw up again. "I'll stitch it."

He assessed her. "I don't think you're up to it."

Feeling lightheaded, she rested her forehead on the heel of her hand. "Why not ask for help?"

"Because I don't know who to trust."

She stared at him. "What about the Heads?"

Reden sighed. "We have a traitor on the island—someone in a position of power."

"How do you know?"

"I've been busy."

By the Creators, she was nauseous. "And you think it's one of the Heads?

He nodded. "It's the only option that makes sense. No one else has the influence to force you to stay here, to let someone on the island, and to hide them for this long. Not to mention sending away two of your Guardians, including Joshen, and making the other sick. And at least one of my informants has been intercepted."

Intercepted? Senna decided she didn't want to know what that meant. She considered all of them. Coyel, Prenny, Chavis and Drenelle. Her eyes widened. "Not long before I was attacked, Drenelle took Joshen away and sent me off alone to gather pollen."

Reden rubbed his chin. "Might mean something. Might not. Either way, you're not safe here, and if Drenelle really is the traitor, she'll never let you leave with me. I'm getting you out. Tonight."

She gaped at him. She'd been bracing herself to escape alone. Now Reden was offering to help her. A tight knot of fear loosened in her stomach. "Tonight?"

He gestured to his knife, slowly turning black from the smoke. "Cauterizing is faster."

The idea of sizzling flesh sent her head spinning again. "How are you getting me out?"

He spoke with cold detachment. "I'm going to order the Guard at the entrance to stand down. Then you're going to sing us out."

She was not going to throw up again. She wasn't. "And if he doesn't stand down?"

"Then I will incapacitate him."

She took a calming breath. "And then?"

Reden wiped his sweaty forehead with the back of his hand. "You've already been preparing to go to Tarten."

How many spies did he have on the island? Through fits and starts, she told him her plan. To go to Tarten and lift part of the curse. Find Espen and unearth the secret of these foreign Witches who threatened Haven.

Reden listened, occasionally asking questions. When he was satisfied, he sat back. "We'll need supplies."

She shook her head. "Joshen—"

Reden used the blade to gesture towards Nefalie. "Is in Corrieth. We'll find him there."

Senna closed her eyes. "No. I meant we can't take him with us. He'll try to stop me."

Reden studied her. "You're sure?"

She took a steadying breath. "Very sure."

He gave a curt nod. "Then we won't bring him."

Just as simple as that, she'd abandon the only family she had left, and her betrothed. Haven wasn't perfect, but it was the only home she'd ever been willing to fight for. If they banished her, she'd never be able to come back. "I'm not sure I can leave everything behind."

"If you're right, there might not be anything to return to."

She bit her lip and pushed the thought aside. "They'll banish us both. You know they will."

His silence was answer enough. He wiped the scorch marks off his knife with a clean cloth and held the hot blade to his skin, his face set.

"Just stop!"

He looked at her with forced patience. "When we have everything settled, we can send for your mother and Joshen if you like."

She shuddered. "I can't go yet. There are potions and seeds I need."

Reden worked his jaw, but he would know how important those items were. "Can you get them tonight?" he asked.

"The only person who has all of them is Prenny. The Witches are all over her house harvesting chesli tonight." Senna tried not to wince. She'd stolen from Prenny before. She hated the thought of doing it again.

Reden finally lowered the knife. "How soon can you be ready?"

Senna sagged in relief. "Tomorrow is the second evening of the harvest. Everyone will have moved on to another part of the island. It should be safe to sneak in then. I can steal the potions and we can slip away."

Reden slumped in his chair, clearly unhappy but resigned. "Very well. But only one more day. Whoever's after you isn't going to give up. We need to get out."

Going to the shelf he indicated, she pulled down plants and potions she recognized. She poured salt water on Reden's wound and wiped off the blood. The cut was clean, so it wouldn't be hard to stitch, but touching him like this…it felt too intimate. "What will everyone think?"

"I imagine the Heads will think you've run off to save Tarten, which is partly true. Some might think we ran away together." He showed no emotions at that.

Senna blushed and busied herself heating a needle over the flame.

Reden bit off the cork and took another pull.

"I can give you something stronger than whiskey," she said.

"I need my wits about me."

Her hands shaking, Senna closed the wound with five stitches. Sweat beaded on Reden's face, and his muscles stood out, but he didn't move or make a sound. Feeling sick, she wrapped the wound. Then she drooped in her chair and downed her tea in one swallow.

She eyed Reden's whiskey, but figured her stomach wouldn't be able to handle it. Not yet anyway. Standing on shaky legs, she said, "I'm tired. Take me home."

Reden tossed his bloody shirt in a bucket of water. "No. You're safer in the midst of Guardians. With me right outside your door."

Not safe on Haven. She still couldn't fathom it. "What about my mother?"

His expression remained neutral. "This isn't the first time you've been out all night."

Another blush burned up her cheeks. She really shouldn't be surprised at Reden's statement. He had just admitted to having his own spies on the island. Perhaps one had even spied on her. She considered telling him that nothing had happened, but that was not a conversation she wanted to have. Ever. Especially not with Reden. "She probably knows Joshen left."

Reden drummed his fingers on the table then rose abruptly. "Is that pistol loaded?" She nodded. "Bolt the door after me."

She rose on shaky feet and followed him. "What are you going to do?"

"I'll send one of my Guardians to inform Sacra you are well but won't be coming home."

Senna folded her arms around her middle. "She won't like that."

He opened the door. "Bolt it."

After securing it, she waited for some of the longest moments of her life. Reden's whisper at the door nearly made her jump out of her boots. She let him in.

"There's a bed upstairs," he said. "Take it. I'll sleep just outside your door."

Senna opened her mouth to protest, but she couldn't find the energy. She lifted her skirts and started up the stairs. She chose the room that was obviously unused. The last thing she did before going to bed was shove the back of a chair under the doorknob.

13. A WITCH'S BURDEN

Senna woke to the sound of someone pounding on the front door; its echoes vibrated painfully inside her skull. Squinting, she peered out the window. It was bright daylight outside. How long had she slept?

After moving the chair that was propped under the bedroom door, she eased into the hallway and padded to the top of the stairs.

"What do you mean she's here?" Joshen's voice was angry.

"She was attacked. If I hadn't stopped them, they'd have taken her by now."

"What!"

"Keep your voice down," Reden hissed. "She's all right."

Senna lay at the top of the stairs and peered below.

"You have to let me see her!" Joshen pulled his hand through his dark hair. "Please, Reden. We had a misunderstanding. Let me talk to her."

Reden physically blocked him. "No. She's fine. I just checked on her a moment ago. She needs her rest."

"Fine, I won't wake her. I'll just see for myself." Joshen tried to slip past him.

Reden matched him. "What kind of misunderstanding?"

Joshen blew out. "Things have become...complicated lately. If we could just talk like we used to."

Reden shook his head. "She's sleeping off a concussion. That's more important than you saying hello."

Joshen worked his jaw before nodding slowly. "I have to give

my report to the Heads. You'll tell her I stopped by? Send someone
to tell me she's awake?"

Reden nodded. "If she wants to see you."

Joshen's face fell.

Senna considered calling out to him, but she was still so tired.
Silently, she backed into her room. She fell on her bed, grateful
classes were cancelled the week of the chesli harvest, and went
back to sleep. She awoke the second time to a hollow ache in her
middle and her head pounding in rhythm to her heart. She could
feel the sticky heat of midafternoon.

Not sure if she'd have time to visit the bathing pools, she did
the best she could with a water basin and a wet rag. Finished, she
tugged her tangled hair into a messy braid to hide the lump on the
back of her head.

When she came downstairs, Reden was in the kitchen. He
handed her an orange and a cup of tea. She breathed in the
aroma, easily recognizing the herbs that would help with pain and
swelling. After adding enough milk to make the tea lukewarm,
she gulped it down.

"Joshen was looking for you earlier."

Senna poured herself another cup of tea and rolled the orange
around in her hands. "I heard."

Reden nodded once, clearly uncomfortable. "He knows you
were attacked last night—it'll bring him around to getting you
out."

She hesitated. "Well, I suppose if we don't tell him the rest—
about Tarten—until after we leave." She felt suddenly lighter.
Joshen would be coming with them. She wouldn't have to leave
everyone behind. "Maybe the Heads will think Joshen and I just
eloped. Then they won't be watching for me to subvert their
curse."

"If you were going to elope, why would I come along?"

She sighed. "If they guess the truth—which they probably
will—they'll try to stop me, even from a distance."

"Will they succeed?"

She shrugged. "Maybe, maybe not. It depends on how much
of the curse I can heal." She waited for Reden to demand that

she explain exactly what she could do. When he didn't, her voice dropped to a whisper. "Aren't you going to ask?"

"You'll do the best you can. Nothing I do or say will change that."

Senna peeled away the rind and lifted a section of the orange to her mouth. She almost felt like smiling. This time tomorrow, she would be fighting back instead of bumbling about waiting for someone to take another shot at abducting her. "I'll gather the supplies I need and wrap up my unfinished business. Then we can go."

A Guardian she vaguely recognized was waiting for her outside. He nodded by way of greeting. "Brusenna."

Reden touched her arm. "This is Hesten. He's one of the few in your personal detail. I trust him with this. Our muskets are primed. I'll go on ahead. Hesten will bring up the rear. I already checked your pistol, and your knife is within reach."

Feeling her stomach twisting around her breakfast, Senna nodded. "I have my seeds as well."

"Whichever weapon you need." Reden searched the trees with his eyes. "You're as safe as I can make you while you're here. But be careful."

She left with the smell of oranges on her fingers and a slice of rich, nutty bread that she no longer had the stomach for.

Her mother opened the door with a blanket wrapped around her shoulders. Judging by the dark circles under her eyes, she'd been up most of the night. She eyed the Guardians behind Senna suspiciously. "Where have you been?"

Instead of answering, Senna stepped inside and closed the door to her Guardians. "I want the truth. What happened to my father and sister?"

Her mother blanched. She wandered to her chair and sat on the edge. "A Guardian found me last night and told me you were safe but not coming home. Does this have something to do with Joshen?"

No. Joshen is gone. All we seem to do is fight, and I don't know how to fix it. "They died when you were pregnant with me. I've seen the drawings of them in your money box. That's all I know of them."

Like the sun and moon, their conversations circled around each other without ever touching. "You won't leave this cursed island with me, and yet you'd risk everything you gain by staying—your Apprenticeship, your place in Haven, your *shining* future—all for a boy. What are you doing, Senna?"

I may have already lost him. Refusing to be distracted, Senna sat in the other chair. "Is that what you think happened when you married my father? That because you married him, you lost everything?"

Sacra finally looked in Senna's eyes.

"I won't stop asking," Senna said.

After a long silence, her mother said, "A man in town brought me those sketches after they died." She looked away. "He drew your father's nose wrong. And Arelle's eyes. I remember thinking that when he gave them to me. But now, when I picture my daughter and husband, I see them how he drew them."

Senna waited for her to continue, but she just remained silent and staring. "Mother, they were my family. I deserve to know what happened to them. Please."

Twin tears leaked out of Sacra's eyes. "It was my fault. Espen was hunting us down, one at a time. Men weren't allowed on the island, so your father and your sister were in Nefalie. I slipped away from Haven to tell him I was expecting another baby. He was terrified for me. He begged me to go into hiding with him. But I was a Discipline Head, and the Sisters needed me desperately. "So I left him with your sister and returned."

Senna considered her own future. Duty and family. How did one balance a life where both needed her, but only one's needs could be met?

A sob clawed its way out of Sacra's body. Senna leaned forward and covered her mother's clenched hands with her own.

"The Witch Hunters found them instead of me," Sacra went on. "I was here when I heard. On this cursed island, safe, while my family was in danger. Doing my duty while my daughter and husband were murdered in my place."

Senna closed her eyes, imagining how her mother must have been once—ambitious, beautiful, confident. Senna slid off the chair to kneel before her. "It wasn't your fault."

"No?" Her mother's voice was low. "I chose being a Witch over being a mother. It was a choice I'd made a hundred times. But this time, I was needed. And I wasn't there."

She sniffed and wiped her eyes. "I see you making the same mistakes I did. Sacrificing everything for the Witches, for a boy who loves you. And if it's all taken away, what will you do then?"

Senna almost decided she couldn't risk going to Tarten. Maybe she should just go into hiding until this was all over. It's what her mother had done, though too late to save her father and sister. But Senna's very soul balked at existing in ignorance and fear ever again. She'd been living with doing nothing for weeks, and it was destroying her. "I'll be glad I ever had them at all."

"If you die, what will I do?" Sacra's voice cracked.

Could Senna ask her mother to live with that? It would break her. She searched her face. "Promise you'll release this burden you've carried for so long. Promise me that you'll find a way to be happy."

Sacra lifted her shoulders in a helpless gesture. "I've carried it so long it's become a part of me."

"Then unmake that part of you!"

Sacra grunted. "I'll—I'll try. If you promise to live through all this."

Senna wrapped her arms around her mother's rounded shoulders and pressed her dry cheek against her mother's wet one. "I promise to try." How could she say goodbye? How could she make her mother understand she had to go? That she wasn't repeating the same mistakes, because they'd never been mistakes. They were choices, the best choices she could make with the knowledge she'd had. "Perhaps I'm more like you than I know. I'm glad for it."

Her mother groaned as if the words pained her. "I hope you're better."

Senna kissed her mother's cheek. It tasted salty. "I love you."

Sacra tried to smile. "And I you."

Senna could tell her mother's thoughts were far away. That was probably a good thing. If she were paying attention, she might realize Senna was trying to say goodbye.

Senna went to her room and gathered her things in her battered satchel. Then she refilled her seed belt and wrapped it around her waist. Back downstairs, she paused at the door. "The chesli harvest will start soon."

Her mother waved her on. "You go on without me. I'll be along eventually."

For the first time, Senna understood why her mother had hidden her away in the hell that was Gonstower. Had kept her ignorant and alone. And Senna forgave her for it, as she hoped her mother would forgive her for putting her heart at risk of being shattered, this time so badly she could never put it back together.

14. THIEVERY

Reden, Hesten, and Senna cut through air thick with shimmering bits of pollen. Heavier pieces fell around them like mist, touching the edges of their clothes with luminosity.

Senna threw occasional glances at her arms, checking to make sure she wasn't glowing again. To her relief, her skin remained dull, except for the shining specks sticking to the tiny hairs on her arms.

Prenny's tree house was in sight. Not much farther and Senna would slip inside while the Guardians kept watch. Then they would take one of the boats and escape into the night.

Of course, it was never that simple.

"Brusenna?"

Startled, she looked up to see Prenny pulling her door shut behind her, a freshly refilled lantern in hand. "You don't have a lick of pollen on your hands. Do you think you're above working in the fields now?" Prenny turned on Reden before Senna could respond. "And you two? If you've nothing else to do, I need some help reaching the higher plants." She latched onto Reden's injured arm.

His face tightened with pain, but he didn't pull away. "We've work to do, Head."

"At this hour of the night? Not likely. Besides, no work is more important than the chesli harvest. You two will come with me." She looked over her shoulder. "Keep up, Senna." Within moments, they were in the midst of the Witches again.

"Get to work," Prenny said to Senna as she caught an older Apprentice's attention. "Dorri, don't let her out of your sight."

Reden glanced at Senna, and she saw the indecision in his face. He didn't want to leave her alone or delay their escape, but he didn't want to raise Prenny's suspicions, either. "Don't go off by yourself," he said to Senna.

Who knew how long it would be before Reden escaped from Prenny. In comparison, eluding Dorri would be as easy as pushing a needle through wool.

Hunched over the plants, the Apprentice glowered at Senna. "Well, get to work."

It wasn't long before Senna had her chance. While the others gathered around for a water break, she put a tree between them and stole away. The windows of Penny's enormous four-story tree house remained dark. Senna removed the key from the ring so their clanking didn't draw attention. Moving like a shadow, she crept through the foliage. At the bottom of the steps, she hesitated before lifting her skirt and running up the last few steps.

Her heart hammering in her temples, she slid the key into the lock. It turned with a loud click. She pulled on the hammered metal latch, and the door opened with a groan. After slipping inside, she shut the door softly behind her and hurried to the parlor. At the oval-shaped window, she pulled the heavy drapes closed. Moving by memory, she felt her way toward the stove.

Her foot collided with the corner of a dark lump of furniture in an explosion of pain. Biting back her curse, she hobbled the last few steps and set down a candle nub—plain tallow instead of anything scented that Prenny might notice. Senna lit the candle in the glowing coals of the fire. It flared, orange swallowed by yellow that stained her aftervision with an ethereal glow.

She limped to the cabinet. In the candle's soft light, she saw her reflection in the glass, a ghost who wore guilt on her face. Her dark gold hair seemed to ripple with red and orange, making her an eerie likeness to the candle. Her golden eyes glinted a darker topaz.

Ignoring her specter, she took out a smaller key, inserted it into the cabinet's tiny lock, and opened the cabinet. Her clammy hands left a damp imprint that immediately began to fade.

Senna set down ten glass vials from inside her satchel. Each cork pulled free with an accusatory pop. After wiping her hands on her dress, she reached for the first potion—Ioa. She filled her smaller vials from Prenny's beakers, then placed each vial in her satchel. The beaker she carefully replaced on its dust-free circle on the shelf.

She worked quickly, taking only the smallest amounts. Just as she'd begun pouring the last bottle, she heard the floor behind her shift beneath someone's weight.

"Who's there?" a voice asked.

Senna jumped, spilling precious potion all over the floor.

The woman in the doorway hissed at the waste. Prenny stepped into the small circle of light cast by the candle.

Senna's mind whirled with a thousand lies that could free her, but Prenny would believe none of them. So she kept silent, her insides quivering. She should have waited for Reden or Hesten. With one of them keeping watch outside, Prenny would never have caught her.

The Head's thin lips were pressed together. "Collectively, those potions took years to make."

Senna tipped her head in acknowledgement. "I know."

Prenny snorted. She took Senna's candle, then moved to a small table and lit a heavy lantern. She turned up the wick. Light flooded the room, making Senna blink. Prenny reached inside the satchel and pulled each potion out. She twisted down her magnification lens and read the labels. "By the Creators, these are fighting potions." She pulled her glasses off and pinched the bridge of her nose. "What could you possibly want with fighting potions?"

Senna's tongue felt like a useless piece of cured meat in her mouth.

Prenny locked the cabinet and shook the stolen key at Senna. "Where did you get this? And how did you get in my home?"

Knowing any lie she told might trap her, Senna kept her mouth shut.

Prenny harrumphed and shoved the key in her dress pocket. "In addition to stealing my potions, you've stolen my time.

Chesli flowers only open for a few nights a year. Now, instead of pollinating them, I'm wasting my time with you." She whipped her black cloak around her shoulders and picked up the lantern. "You will come with me. Now."

Senna considered running, but she couldn't leave Reden. And she needed those potions. They were one of the few things she was counting on to keep her alive.

Tugging her hood down to hide her face, Senna moved beside Prenny, who grasped her arm firmly above her elbow. Just before they reached the Council Tree, Senna pretended to trip. She tossed the keys into the shadows of the foliage, grunting to mask the sound of their clanking. Pogg would find them. He always did.

Prenny hauled her up. Without hesitation, the Head marched her back into the midst of the Witches and up to Coyel, who was bent over the chesli plants, her fingers caked with glowing pollen.

"We have a problem," Prenny said. "Where are the others?"

Coyel straightened her back with a groan. She glanced at Senna before sending off two Witchlings to find Drenelle and Chavis. Coyel moved Prenny and Senna out of earshot of the other Witches while they waited for the other Heads to arrive.

Chavis was the last to come in. All of them were smudged with glowing pollen. The chesli plants were so integral to potions that even the Heads participated in the harvest. The four gathered around the lantern to shield its light from the insects swarming the glowing flowers. Senna was trapped inside.

Coyel rolled her neck. "All right, Prenny, what has Brusenna done now?"

Prenny handed her the seed belt. "I caught her in my home, stealing potions."

"Stealing?" Coyel took the belt. She held one of the glinting vials to the light.

Though Senna's heart dropped to her toes, she forced her head high as she met Coyel's baffled gaze.

"How did you get a key to my home? My potion cabinet?" Prenny demanded.

Senna stared at the field of Witches bent over the glowing pollen. Arianis was in the center of a group of girls who were stealing covert glances and sharing hushed whispers. Amid all the furtiveness, Mistin stood unmoving, staring at Senna.

Senna found her voice. "You all seem to have forgotten I lived on this island alone for months. I took the key to Prenny's cabinet and used it to get what I needed to fight Espen."

Prenny's mouth opened and closed again. For once, she seemed at a loss for words.

"And you never gave the key back?" Chavis asked.

Thinking it best to say as little as possible, Senna shook her head.

"What other keys do you have?" Chavis asked.

Glad she'd ditched the keys, Senna answered truthfully, "None."

Drenelle, who'd been quiet until now, touched each of her jewels as if to reassure herself none were missing. "We'll have to search her belongings. All of them. Who knows what other things she has that don't belong to her."

That was certainly something a traitor would say, though they wouldn't find anything. There was nothing to find. Imagining them combing through her underthings and rag chest, she shifted her weight uncomfortably.

"The girl clearly needs a firmer hand," Prenny said. "I tried to tell you she wasn't ready for an Apprenticeship yet."

"Why, Senna?" Coyel asked, a hurt look on her face. "Why were you stealing potions?"

Handling Prenny's anger was so much easier than Coyel's disappointment. "Because I had to."

Chavis took the belt from Coyel and carefully pulled out each vial. Her eyebrow slowly rose. "These are all the potions I'd take if I planned on going to war."

The other Heads all looked startled—all except Prenny, who had begun to look uneasy.

"What do you mean?" Coyel demanded.

"She's pestered each of us in turn to lift the curse. I think it's clear where she was going." Chavis' dark eyes pinned Senna to the ground. "Do you deny it?"

Senna wished she could disappear like ice on a midsummer day. "No." Going to Tarten was only part of it, but she wasn't about to tell the Heads that.

"Where was she going?" Drenelle asked.

Prenny snorted. "She was going to attempt lifting the curse on her own."

Chavis gestured towards Tarten. "What could you possibly think to accomplish except to get yourself killed?"

Drenelle eyed Senna. "You're lucky you didn't succeed. If you had, we would have been forced to banish you."

Which would provide a perfect opportunity to take me captive, Senna thought.

The lantern's dim light cast deep shadows that hid Coyel's eyes. "There's something more, isn't there, Senna?"

Senna stared at Coyel, wanting so badly to trust someone.

"Senna, please," Coyel asked again. "I can't help you if I don't know what's going on."

Maybe Senna was wrong not to trust the Heads. Especially Coyel. Maybe they really would help her. But she couldn't shake Reden's warning. "There's nothing, Head."

Coyel took a deep breath. "Senna, this was wrong, but I can understand why you did it. You will give Prenny back her potions. We'll decide your punishment tomorrow. As for the Tartens, that is not something you need concern yourself with. We are dealing with it in our own way."

Senna ground her teeth. She needed those potions if she was going to Tarten, but now she was going to have to do without them. She started to back away, determined to find Reden and leave as soon as possible.

A voice stopped her. "She's not telling you everything."

When had Arianis wandered over? Senna gave a minute shake of her head, silently begging the girl to hold her tongue.

Arianis looked away. "She's been secretly meeting with the Dark Witch."

And with those words, Senna knew her world would never be the same.

15. Plant Song

Coyel's expression crumpled. "Senna, this can't be true."

Senna wanted to run, hide. But she was tired of deceit. Tired of lies. "I went to Espen for answers."

"She's lying. Trees tell no tales," Chavis said darkly, her thumb absently stroking the butt of her pistol.

Senna met the older woman's gaze. "She scratched her answers in the dirt."

"And what did the Dark Witch say?" Coyel asked softly.

"She said I could Travel because I'm Creator-touched. And she gave me two names, promising me more information if I come to her."

"What names?" Prenny asked.

"Lilette and Calden."

"You're a fool and worse," Chavis said.

Drenelle rolled one of her rings around her finger. "Or the traitor we've been searching for."

"Why would I have myself attacked?" Senna cried.

Drenelle glared at her. "To throw us off, maybe."

Their words cut Senna like an avalanche of glass. She met Chavis' intense gaze. "Before I turned her into a tree, Espen tried to warn me about some other threat. She hasn't lived in isolation on Haven, so I hoped she would know something. She told me of Lilette and Calden. I think some of the Witches escaped the destruction, and they're threatening us now. If I want more, I have to go to Tarten and ask Espen."

Prenny shot the other Heads a look of disgust. "Don't mistake misguidance for maliciousness. Remember, Espen tricked us all once."

"Why didn't you come to us?" Coyel asked.

Senna trembled with humiliation and impotent anger. "Because I overheard you saying you wouldn't tell me anything. And I believe there's another traitor—someone who let my attacker on the island and kept them here. Someone with the power and knowledge to orchestrate all of this. My best guess is it's one of you."

Chavis gave a short bark of laughter. "The girl is mad. Completely and utterly—"

Drenelle stood up straighter. "You're an *Apprentice,* Brusenna. It's about time you remembered that!"

It was Senna's turn to shout. "What I am is a Keeper!"

Prenny's voice went low and dangerous. "You don't deserve the title of Keeper yet."

Senna gritted her teeth. "Keepers *keep*—they don't destroy. So you tell me who doesn't deserve the title."

"You go too far, Senna." Coyel's impervious mask slipped for the second time, revealing just how upset she was. "The course of action you have set for yourself leaves us no choice. We must confine you until we can prove whether or not what you've told us is true. If you've actually conversed with Espen, we must determine how much she has distorted you."

"It's happening again," Drenelle murmured. "Just like it happened last time."

Prenny actually winced.

"What are you talking about?" Senna asked. She never should have trusted the Heads with this. She wrapped her hands protectively over her navel tattoo. No matter what they took from her, they could not take the fact that she was a Witch.

"Does Joshen know of your actions?" Chavis asked, a dangerous edge to her voice.

Senna forced her trembling to still. If she revealed how Arianis had tricked Joshen into revealing her secrets, he would be implicated. Senna would not fail him, not like she failed herself. "No."

Thankfully, Arianis remained silent.

Coyel nodded. "Good. Instead of banishing him, we'll have him permanently reassigned."

"He's my Guardian," Senna said in a broken voice.

Chavis grunted. "Not anymore."

"That's a little harsh, isn't it? The boy is in love with her." Prenny gestured towards Senna.

Chavis' mouth was set in a hard line. "You brought her to us for reprimanding, remember?"

Coyel rubbed her forehead as if she were exhausted. "I think I'm being rather lenient. I should probably banish her. As for Joshen, Arianis has already found him acceptable. He will be reassigned to her—at least until we get all this sorted out." She glared at Arianis. "*You* are excused."

Arianis left without a backward glance.

Senna felt like little bits of herself were crumbling to dust. "I thought you of all people might help me."

Coyel's gaze remained hard and unyielding. "You tell me you're communicating with Espen—the Witch who very nearly destroyed us all—and then expect me to do what? Assign you a Guardian and send you off on your little adventure?"

"We aren't doing this to hurt you, Senna." Prenny's voice was soft, gentle even. "There must be consequences for your actions. And you've proven you're not mature enough to handle all the stress that's been placed upon you. We'll take the information you've provided and conduct our own inquiry. In the meantime, just be patient."

Chavis leaned toward Drenelle. "Go find a Guardian."

Drenelle left without another word.

Senna wondered where Reden and Hesten were. Probably at Prenny's tree house, waiting for Senna to show up. "Tomorrow could be too late," she said desperately.

Chavis motioned for Prenny to move beside them. "You might be the strongest Witch on this island, but you're not stronger than three of us."

A sudden calm washed over Senna, because she *was* stronger. But she didn't want to fight them. Not unless she had no other choice.

"You're tossing handfuls of dirt onto your own graves!" Backpedaling, she wondered if she could really battle these women, and stepped right into a man. Her heart hammering, she whirled around. She recognized the Guardian, but she didn't know him. She started running.

Coyel hustled forward. "Stop her!"

His hands wrapped around her. Senna fought against him, but he was so strong. Her injured hand and head protested the abuse.

Before the Heads could respond, Mistin rushed forward and started beating against the Guardian's arms. "Let her go! Stop it!"

Chavis came forward to peel her off. Mistin kicked and scratched. The other Heads jumped into the fray. Knowing this might be her only chance at escaping, Senna started to sing.

Plants–

Leaving Mistin to the others, Coyel mashed her hand against Senna's mouth.

Breathing hard, Chavis trapped Mistin in a submission hold. There was a matching set of livid scratches on her cheek from Mistin's fingernails.

The fight had barely started and it was over.

Coyel still had her hand against Senna's mouth. "Get me something to gag her!"

Prenny scattered some seeds that grew into long thin vines. The Heads used those vines to bind Senna's and Mistin's hands.

After struggling to her feet, Drenelle tore a piece of frothy lace from her dress. "Here, she can't chew through this."

Senna bit Drenelle's fingers. With a yelp, she pulled them back. Senna started to sing.

Shouldering Drenelle out of the way, Prenny snatched a potion from a special compartment in her seed belt and held it under Senna's nose. The sweet scent of flowers flooded her nostrils. Cutting off her inhalation, she twisted her face away. But it was too late.

"Barbus," she murmured as her body went limp. She struggled to keep her eyes open as the Guardian swung her into his arms.

Something was shoved in her mouth. The colors were wrong, darker and smeared. Sounds came from far away. She tried to understand where she was and what was going on, but she couldn't make sense of it. Was she dreaming? And why did the back of her head hurt so much?

Hastily righting the overturned lamp, Coyel spoke to the Guardian, "Tie them up in separate cellars for tonight. Prenny, you go with him to keep Senna calm."

A cellar? Was she making dinner tonight?

The Guardian shifted Senna in his arms. "Yes, Head."

Prenny bent down and picked up the lamp and Senna's seed belt.

Senna nearly cried out in outrage. What was her seed belt doing on the ground? The vials and seeds could have spilled!

"How long will this stuff take to wear off?" the Guardian asked nervously.

Prenny eyed Senna sidelong. "Not long. We'll know when she starts to struggle again."

Prenny held the lantern aloft to light their way as the Guardian carried Senna down the path. She wanted to ask them where they were going, but her mouth was full of something. Embarrassed, she tried to swallow it, but it was stuck.

Senna was dimly aware of other Witches watching them with shocked expressions. She must look like an idiot with something stuck in her mouth.

Suddenly some of her fear broke free. Death was coming for them. She had to escape. Tonight.

But her hands were tied and her mouth gagged. Knowing she couldn't let the Guardian or Prenny realize she was waking up, she thought hard. All the times she'd heard the Four Sisters were when the songs were the loudest—during an earth tremor, a storm, or the death throes of an entire nation.

So maybe the songs were always there, just so soft she only heard them during a tumultuous event. And if they were there, she could control them. Knowing she'd have to move fast, she listened hard to the Four Sisters. Dimly, she heard drums, winds, flutes, so soft and natural she had mistaken them for the normal sounds of nature.

She began humming the melody, so quietly even the Guardian couldn't hear her. Then she changed the tune. The elements responded as before, shifting to match her. She changed their song, melding them into position.

Prenny paused. "Something feels wrong."

A moth brushed Senna's face. More wings swept across her skin. She felt their clinging legs as they landed on her.

The Guardian gasped.

"What are they doing?" Prenny asked.

The more Senna hummed, the more the moths came, swirling channels of them, dancing about her. Their wings brushed against her skin like the softest kisses.

The muscles in the Guardian's arms tensed. "Head, blow out the lantern."

Prenny hesitated before turning down the wick. She froze. Senna was glowing, a soft light spilling from her in flares of gold. She was so full of the Four Sister's songs, she was drunk with them. She changed one note. In an instant, the vines around her wrists fell away. The wind worked the gag loose. It fell from her mouth into a pile on her chest.

With a warning shout, Prenny grabbed for her vial. Senna switched from humming to singing. Plants knocked Prenny back and pinned her to the ground. Then they wrapped around the Guardian's shoulders, forcing him to his knees. As his arms were wrenched away, Senna stepped free. Prenny's eyes grew wide and frightened. The Guardian gaped wordlessly at her.

Mistin stood rooted to the spot. "Senna?"

Ignoring them, she veered down another path and started towards the sheer cliffs surrounding the island. She was certain she could call up the wind, strong enough to carry her across the ocean to Tarten, but first she had to get clear of these trees.

Suddenly Reden and Hesten were there, with Joshen running at the front of them. Arianis and the other Heads trailed behind him. They must have heard the commotion.

But Senna didn't need her Guardians anymore. With a word, she changed the wind. It twisted a protective cocoon around her, forcing everyone back. In the eye of the storm, some moths clung to her; their furry legs tickling her skin. Others swirled like crisp leaves before a fall breeze.

She picked up her skirts and hurried towards one of the staircases that cut across the surface of the cliffs. One step at a time, she started climbing, moths curling behind her like a wind-blown cloak.

Reden started after her. "Senna! Wait!"

Joshen stared up at her. "What's wrong with her?"

Senna tipped her face up to the moonless night and laughed. There was nothing wrong with her. For once, everything was right. Stepping to the edge of the carved stairs, she called the wind to her. It thickened around her, pulling her hair and clothes up.

"What is she doing?" Joshen shouted.

Prenny tore at the vines, her fingers bleached white. "She's drunk."

"Drunk?" Reden helped cut Prenny free.

"An occasional side effect of the barbus." Prenny yanked a vial out of Senna's seed belt. She threw it at Senna but missed. It shattered against the cliffs. Cool drops splashed her cloak and soaked through to her skin. The scent of flowers engulfed her in a wave.

"What was that?" Joshen asked.

"More barbus extract," Prenny said.

"You gave her more!" Joshen said in outrage.

"I didn't have a choice!"

Warmth and drowsiness enfolded Senna. The wind waited for her command, but she no longer remembered what that command was. It listened a moment more before growing distracted. She felt herself slipping. Into darkness. Into dreams.

"She's going to fall!" Joshen shoved Prenny out of the way and started running.

Prenny sounded close to panic. "She isn't supposed to be able to circle the wind outside of the Ring of Power, let alone one that strong!"

Senna tipped forward. Her muscles turned to liquid and she splashed over the side of the staircase like spilled wine.

16. JOSHEN

Joshen sprinted forward, his heart tearing in two as Senna swayed on the edge of the cliff. He watched from below as she crumpled and tipped over the side, her body as limp as a rag doll.

He tried to catch her, but she slammed into him with such force it knocked him to the ground. For a moment, he couldn't breathe. Holding her to him, he lay there, trying to decide if anything was broken.

"Hold your breath!" Prenny, her face red, ripped Senna's cloak off, crumpled it in a ball, and threw it. She gasped in a lungful of air. "I don't smell barbus."

Reden knelt over them. "Is she all right?"

Joshen groaned and sat up.

"She's unconscious." Prenny's fingers searched Senna's dress. "It appears most of it was on her cloak."

Senna wasn't glowing anymore. For that Joshen was relieved, but her neck was bent back at an awkward angle, her body wilted in his arms. He gently tipped her head into his chest, cradling her to him. He felt the reassuring puff of her breath against his skin. He glared at Prenny. "What did you do to her? Why did she run? By the Creators, why was she glowing?"

Prenny pulled another vial from her pocket and ran it under Senna's nose. She shifted away from the foul-smelling stuff, snuggling deeper into Joshen's chest.

He brushed some of her hair away from her face. "Senna?"

Prenny sang.

Awake my child, it's time to rise.
Find the life within and open thine eyes.

On the song's fourth repetition, Senna's eyes fluttered open. She stared at Joshen in obvious confusion, her eyes glassy.

"It'll take her awhile to shake off the effects. She's basically still asleep." Prenny lifted the spectacles hanging from a beaded chain around her neck. She pulled down the rose-colored lens and stared at Senna. "I've never seen anything like it."

Coyel stepped forward, her face unsure. "I think we should stay with you."

Prenny grunted. "She'll be out for the rest of the night with that much barbus, and we've only a few hours till sunrise. We need that pollen, Coyel."

Coyel seemed to waver. "All right. Let's go back to the harvest. Quickly now."

Reden helped Senna to her feet. "How is this possible?"

Prenny waited until the other Heads had slowly filed away before studying both Guardians, her expression pensive. "She's sleepwalking."

One of the Apprentices hadn't left, though. She was watching Joshen, her face set. Her hands were tied behind her back with what looked like some kind of plant. Sometimes Witches baffled him. Why couldn't they have just used rope?

"What about me?" the girl said.

Prenny made a noise low in her throat. "You were on shaky ground before, Mistin. You're not an adept student, and you're song is barely above a Wastrel. Now you've attacked the Heads. They'll banish you."

Mistin's face crumpled. "Please," she whispered. "I'll try harder. I'll make the Truth Serum this time. I will."

Prenny ground her teeth. "I'm sorry. There's nothing I can do."

Mistin blanched. "I don't have anywhere else to go. My mother and sisters died for being Witches, even though they were just Wastrels. Don't condemn me to the same fate."

Prenny's shoulder's sagged. She motioned to Reden. "Cut her free." With his knife, Reden sawed through the vines binding her.

"What am I to do?" Mistin whispered.

The Head stared at her. "Go to your tree for tonight. We'll come for you in the morning. There's nothing more I can do for you. I wish there was."

Mistin rubbed her wrists. Her gaze went to Senna. "What about her? She's my friend."

Prenny motioned for Mistin to go. "You don't need to worry about Senna. I'll take care of her."

Mistin's gaze narrowed, but she didn't say anything, just hurried back down the path.

"I would save them—save them both—if I could. But it seems that is not meant to be." Prenny made a noise low in her throat. "You'll come with me." She led the Guardians further into the darkness.

Joshen pulled Senna behind him. She followed docilely where he led, her expression dreamy. "Where are you taking us?" Joshen asked.

Prenny glanced back at him. "I could ask you the same thing. I assume you are going with her to Tarten?"

Not Prenny too! Joshen was half convinced every Witch on this island was three-quarters mad. "She is *not* going to Tarten."

Prenny snorted in derision. "Has Senna ever let anything stop her once she's set her mind to it? She'll go, one way or another. The question is, are you going with her?"

Joshen knew if he left, he'd never be a Guardian again. He pushed the thought aside. "I go where she goes." And she was not going to Tarten.

Prenny nodded. "Good. She'll need you. Now come on."

Reden trotted to catch up with Prenny. "Are you sure you want to risk helping us, Head?"

Prenny worried her bottom lip. "Something's happening to that girl. Something that's only happened once before in the long and scattered history of the Witches. And if the Creators trust her, I guess that means we should, too. And if the others won't...well, the Creator's decision overrules the Heads." She met Reden's gaze. "You know it too, don't you?"

He nodded, his face tight. "Yes. It's why I'm going with her."

Prenny's face went slack. "But you're our Leader. The Guardians need you here! We need you here."

Reden grunted. "I believed her when she said she was trying to save Haven. Do you?"

Prenny slowly nodded. "I do now."

"Then my place is with her, saving my charges."

Prenny stepped closer to him. "In Tarten, they call you a traitor. If you leave with Senna tonight, so will Haven."

Reden took a deep breath. "My loyalty was never to Haven." He gestured towards Senna. "It has always been to her."

Prenny's mouth fell open. "From the beginning?"

He nodded.

Prenny sighed. "You've just known it longer than the rest of us, I suppose."

Joshen's grip tightened on Senna's slight hand. He pushed all thoughts of Tarten aside. Right now, his only concern was getting her off the island.

When they reached another cellar, Prenny hauled open the door.

Dank air rushed against Joshen's face. "What are you doing?"

Prenny moved down the first few steps. "You freed Senna and locked me in here. Understand?"

Joshen gaped at the older woman.

Prenny handed him Senna's seed belt and satchel. "She can't steal my potions if I give them to her. See she's safe. And don't come back to Haven. Ever."

Joshen carefully tied the belt around Senna's waist while she stared off into the trees, swaying to music he couldn't hear. He tugged her hood over her face and gently tucked her golden hair out of sight. She was too beautiful and innocent to bear such burdens. "I'm sorry," he said to her.

Reden hefted the thick doors, but hesitated before closing them. "If Senna's right, you'll need more Guardians on the island. I've recruited men in Corrieth. Use the Truth Serum to make sure they're loyal and see they're brought here. More if you can get them."

Prenny covered her mouth with her hand. "I'll do what I can."

Reden shut the door, blocking their view of Prenny's upturned face, and slid the bar home. "Come on."

Joshen tugged Senna after him. "How are we to escape?" he asked.

Reden shook his head. "Leave that to me."

When they arrived at Velveten, Collum was on duty. He looked a bit wan and was hunched over. Reden had said he'd been sick. Still, he seemed alert.

Collum eyed them, his brow furrowed. "Leader Reden, Joshen. What was all that commotion?"

Reden motioned for Collum to step aside. "Let us pass, Guardian."

Collum shifted uneasily on his feet. "Sir? You need a signed pass from the Heads."

"No. I don't."

The Heads' orders overruled Reden's, and they all knew it. Joshen tugged Senna forward so the lantern light spilled across her face. "We have to get her out, Collum. Before it's too late."

Collum opened his mouth, then closed it again.

Joshen took another step towards his friend. "They almost took her again yesterday. And there's a danger coming for Haven. We have to stop it." When Collum didn't respond, Joshen said softly, "Sometimes we have to protect our Witches from their own mistakes—even the Heads. Leary knew that."

Collum glanced around, the beads in his hair clicking. "They'll throw me out, take away my Guardianship. It's all I've ever wanted."

Joshen gritted his teeth, knowing he'd already forfeited the role he'd worked towards his entire life. Now instead of being a Guardian, he would be hunted by them. But it didn't matter, not when Senna was involved.

Reden pulled a length of rope from his pocket. "I'll tie you loose enough to slip free if you're needed."

Collum stared at the rope before slowly raising his hands. Joshen let out a breath he hadn't known he'd been holding.

Reden quickly tied the knots. "If anyone asks why you didn't call for help, tell them the last thing you remembered was the smell of flowers."

Joshen rested a hand on his friend's shoulder. Collum nodded in understanding.

Collum sat down so they could tie his feet. Reden made fast work of the ropes while Joshen tugged Senna into the cave.

Reden retrieved two packed satchels stowed beneath one of the piers. Joshen stepped into the boat and was turning back to help Senna when someone cried, "Wait!"

Expecting Chavis to put a ball in his head, Joshen turned. But it was only that diminutive Witch who'd been tied up with Senna. What was her name? Mistin?

"Take me with you," she said.

Joshen and Reden exchanged disbelieving looks.

"No." Reden handed Senna over to Joshen, who helped her down and settled her on one of the benches.

Mistin took a step closer, but not close enough Reden could grab her. "Take me with you or I'll tell the Heads what you're doing. You'll never escape."

Reden glared at her. "Threatening us is the wrong tactic, little Witch."

Mistin dropped her face in her hands and started crying. Joshen looked away. By the Creators, he couldn't stand it when girls cried.

Reden seemed as unfazed by her tears as he was by her threats. "You're going to be banished tomorrow anyway."

Mistin sniffed loudly. "They'll come for me in the morning and take me to the Ring of Power. All the Witches will gather around me. The Dawn Song will be stripped away, so I'll never be able to come inside the island again. Then they'll take me to Corrieth, give me a handful of upice coins, and abandon me. Please don't make me live through that."

Joshen wanted to shout in frustration. They needed to get Senna off this island, not stand here and argue with some sniveling Sprout!

Reden grunted in agreement. "All right. We'll take you as far as Corrieth. We could use another rower anyway."

Mistin's face brightened immediately. "Thank you! Oh, thank you!" She darted into the boat as if afraid they might change their minds.

Joshen turned his attention to Senna. She stared at the rock wall, swaying. He wondered what she heard. Judging by the look on her face, it was beautiful. A pang of jealousy shot through him. He pushed it away. Her job was to sing. His job was to keep her alive.

"Is your song strong enough to sing us out?" Reden asked Mistin.

"No."

Lot of good she was. Joshen rubbed the back of Senna's hand with his thumbs. "You have to sing for us, my love." It was like she couldn't hear him. "Senna?" When she still didn't answer, he cupped his hands over her ears, blocking out whatever she was hearing.

She blinked wearily at him. "Joshen?"

That was the first time she'd fully focused on his face. The first time she'd spoken. He leaned forward until he was the only thing she could see. "Sing for us."

She half shook her head. "Sing?"

He leaned towards her and kissed her softly. When he pulled back, her eyes tracked him. "Sing us off the island."

She glanced around again in confusion before focusing on the water. Her face cleared. Her song was little more than a whisper.

I ask of thee, plants of the sea,
Take me from the place none but Witches see.

Her voice was so lovely it made his chest hurt. The world seemed to pause, listening. All he wanted was to protect her. In doing so, was he stifling her?

Senna paused, her brow furrowed.

Joshen nodded reassuringly. "Keep singing, Senna."

She stared blankly at him. He smiled at her. She sang again. This time, the world seemed to move in harmony with her.

Before she'd even finished her second song, kelp shot up from the water. Holding Senna tight to his chest, Joshen lay back and tried not to panic. No matter how many times he came in or out of the island, it terrified him anew. Kelp circled the boat, blotting out the lantern light. He felt the boat tip upward.

Joshen braced himself as they pitched forward under the water. Senna gripped fistfuls of his shirt in her hands, a small sound of panic slipping from her mouth.

17. Sea Witch

Senna woke to the feel of something rocking beneath her and the sound of lapping waves. She jerked upright, panic coursing through her. She was in a small boat with Joshen, Reden...and Mistin. They were all breathing hard and red-faced from rowing. Senna gripped the lacquered sides of the craft and pulled herself up. Morning light kissed the tops of the sea, leaving sparks of passion wherever it touched.

Senna's gaze locked with Joshen's. "I...How did I get here? The Heads—they were going to lock me up."

"They still might," Reden answered.

Joshen handed her a skin of water. Why was he here? He'd threatened to stop her before. She drank to wash away the stale taste in her mouth.

"They drugged you with barbus extract. Actually, some of it got on your skin, which is why it put you out for so long. If breathing it can put you instantly to sleep, think how much stronger it is soaked into your skin," Mistin rambled nervously. "It'll take a few hours for the confusion to completely fade."

Shivering in the chill morning air, Senna pulled her cloak tighter around her shoulders. "Where are we?"

Joshen nodded towards a dark smudge in the distance. "Nearly to Corrieth."

She rubbed her numb hip. "How did you get me out?"

Joshen studied her. "Do you remember any of it?"

She closed her eyes. Images flashed in her mind. "Lights,

moths—their wings on my skin—falling." She caught her friends watching her with guarded expressions. "Was it a dream?"

Reden shook his head. "It was no dream." He told her how she'd glowed and about singing the wind into a shield around herself.

Remembering the power that had surged through her last night, Senna closed her eyes and searched for an echo of it. But it was spent. She'd never felt so empty.

"What's happening to me?"

Joshen and Reden dug their oars in harder.

The Heads probably knew she was gone by now. Time was not on their side. Her body still sluggish with sleep, Senna took the seat next to Mistin and grabbed an oar.

"What about your hand?" Joshen asked.

Senna mentally counted how many days since her injury. Nearly two weeks. "It'll be all right if I'm careful." Reden gave her strips of a ripped blanket and she wrapped them around her hands to protect her from blisters. She waited until she had their rhythm, then she started rowing. The strain bothered her, but it was bearable if she used her fingers to grip the oar instead of her palm.

Sweating beside her, Mistin glanced over her shoulder as the city began to take shape.

"Why are you with us?" Senna asked.

Joshen told Senna how Mistin had fought for her. His account evoked Senna's memories, and she felt a stab of guilt. For helping her, Mistin would be banished from the only place she'd ever been safe.

Mistin sighed. "What will I tell my brother?"

"Brother? I thought you were from Dresdan."

Mistin nodded towards Corrieth. "Cord wants to become a Guardian, remember? It's all he's ever wanted." She pinched her eyes shut. "Now he'll have me to worry about."

Reden spoke up. "Then why hasn't he applied?"

Mistin gave a halfhearted shrug. "Because he's not of age yet." All Guardians had to be at least seventeen.

Senna wiped sweat off her forehead with her shoulder. "What will you do now?"

Mistin shuddered. "I don't know. There's nowhere for me to go. Cord won't join the Guardians now. He won't leave me unprotected and alone, but he'll blame me for his lost opportunity the rest of his life." She sniffed loudly and turned to Senna, confusion clouding her dark eyes. "Why would you want to travel to Tarten?"

Senna blew her hair out of her eyes. "I'm going to lift the curse."

"Senna," Joshen growled in warning.

She ignored him. Mistin deserved to know. "You could come with us."

"What?" Joshen cried at the same time that Reden said, "Senna."

Mistin glanced apprehensively at the Guardians.

Ignoring the two sets of eyes boring holes into her back, Senna went on. "We could use your help."

Mistin bit her bottom lip. "But what about Cord? He'll never let me go with you—he's so protective."

They rowed in silence and Senna could practically feel the tension draining out of the men. "What if he came too?"

The tension increased again.

Mistin slowly nodded. "I think he'd like that."

"Absolutely not," Joshen said from behind.

Reden grunted. "This isn't an adventure. It's dangerous."

Mistin's voice dropped to a whisper. "Senna is my friend. I want to help."

Senna turned to see Reden studying Mistin as a commander would assess a new recruit. "Prenny said your song was barely strong enough to bother with."

Mistin's expression hardened. "There are other things I can do. And you need all the help you can get."

Reden heaved at his oar. "What kinds of things?"

Joshen stared at Reden incredulously. "You're not actually considering this, are you? We already have Senna to look after."

Mistin lifted her chin. "I don't need you to look after me. I can fight."

Joshen snorted. "And you think a little thing like you is any good against an army of—"

"I can shoot a musket!" Mistin shouted over him. "After my family died, my brother and I grew up on the streets. We can handle ourselves."

Senna stiffened. As if she needed to be looked after. Joshen didn't seem to notice he'd offended her.

Reden let out his breath in obvious exasperation. "You have a lot to learn about women, Joshen." He nodded towards Mistin. "You slow us down, we leave you behind. Understand?"

Mistin set her jaw. "I won't slow you down."

Joshen muttered something about how it was hard enough having one woman around who was also a Witch. He didn't think he could deal with two.

Senna ignored him.

"We'll need a ship," Reden said.

Joshen grunted. "A ship? It'll be safer if we escape over land— it's a lot less volatile than the sea."

Senna frowned at him. "The only way to Tarten is by ship, and you know it."

He sighed. "We don't have to go to Tarten, Senna. We could—"

She had to stop and rest her hand. She shook out the cramps. "One more word and you'll be swimming to shore."

After a moment, he said through clenched teeth, "Let's hope Captain Parknel has the *Sea Witch* in port."

Senna sang for the wind to carry her song to Captain Parknel, advising him that they needed passage.

Reden waited for her song to end before speaking. "And if he doesn't make it back or his ship was damaged after the earth tremor?"

No one bothered to answer.

Blisters had formed on Senna's hands long before they reached Corrieth. Her scar ached fiercely, but she did her best to ignore it. She surveyed the damage from the storm and the enormous wave of a few days ago. The city itself seemed fairly intact; the high wall surrounding it and the wind must have turned the brunt of the wave. But the port was a disaster. Piers were ripped from their moorings. The ring of hammers sounded everywhere. The hot metal and ash smell of the forges was strong in the air. Worst of all, stranded, broken ships littered the landscape.

What if the *Sea Witch* was one of those stranded ships?

On one of the few remaining piers, Senna followed Joshen out of the boat, her muscles watery.

Mistin sprinted down the wooden planks. "I'll go find Cord," she called over her shoulder. "Don't leave without us!"

Reden watched her go. "Senna and I will see if we can find the *Sea Witch*. Joshen, go to the Two Foals stable and round up some horses and fodder. Meet at the *Sea Witch* in an hour. If it's not at port, we'll meet at McBedee's shop."

"Reden," Joshen called before they'd gone a dozen steps. "Don't leave her side."

Reden didn't bother answering. He let out a long breath, then scanned the docks and started asking around. It wasn't long before they learned the *Sea Witch* hadn't been at port for weeks, but was due back soon.

"You'll have to sing them back," Reden said.

Senna moved to the end of a quiet pier and sang softly for the wind to bring the ship in quickly. In less than an hour, she saw the black ship with the gold letters *"Sea Witch"* carved into the side.

Captain Parknel's ruddy beard gave him away first. He brought the ship in perfectly. Sailors scrambled about, tying off the lines. Within moments, the gangplank was lowered. Merchants from Corrieth came to retrieve their cargo.

Parknel grinned as Senna climbed aboard. He snatched her in a breath-stealing hug. "You brought us back thrice as fast as we left—and that's usually against a contrary wind. You ever want a place aboard my vessel, you have it."

Despite everything that had happened over the past few days, Senna broke out in a smile. Asking for nothing in return, Parknel had transported her to Tarten. He had trusted her, fought for her, and believed in her. Besides Joshen and Reden, he was one of the few people she'd call a true friend.

As soon as he set Senna down, she said, "Captain, we need passage."

He shifted his pipe to the other side of his mouth. "Well, I figured you wouldn't summon us back for a social call." He sobered as he studied Corrieth. "I heard it wasn't as bad as it could have been. Wind rose up and turned the water away from the city. That the Witches doing?"

Senna nodded.

Though Haven wasn't visible from Corrieth, she couldn't help but glance nervously in its direction. "I'll pay for any cargo lost."

He grinned. "You promise to sing a wind to carry us to Tressalay and back for a season, I'll count us even. Where to?"

She swallowed the bile rising in her throat. "Tarten."

Parknel's face fell. "Again?"

But she was no longer listening to him. She could hear music again, just like the night before. Drawn irresistibly to the sound, she found herself leaning over the railing. Behind her, she was vaguely aware of Reden and Parknel working out the logistics of the trip.

The wind's song was growing steadily louder, turning from light and soft to hard and dark. The pace pounded against her skin. She could almost taste the salt spray and feel the coming waves that would batter the ship. "They know I'm gone."

The conversation behind her went on oblivious to the mounting danger. Senna whirled around. "They're calling in a storm, trying to stop us. We must go. Now!"

Parknel started barking out orders. Reden ran to the other side of the ship and shot a glance down the pier. "Where's Joshen?"

"Send someone for him," she shouted.

Men started rushing around the ship, preparing to leave. At the bow, Senna closed her eyes and measured the song's strength against her own. An hour, maybe less, and the storm would swallow up the coast in a fit of rage.

She searched herself for the unimaginable power she'd held mere hours before. But it was gone. Her own songs could buy them a little time, but as strong as she was, she was still no match for a full Witch choir.

She ran to the stern and faced Haven, countering songs to bring in the storms with songs of calm. Her songs were soft and gentle—songs of warm spring days, sunshine, calm seas. The songs coming against her were anything but. They were dark, full of mystery and danger. The two songs mixed into a cacophony of noise—a sound she knew only she heard. Boiling clouds darkened the sky.

Controlling the winds was like trying to tame a half-wild colt. It wanted to streak across the sky, buck playfully with the clouds. Senna sang even more gently, almost a lullaby. The storm stilled, listening. For a moment, the clouds broke apart and a shaft of sunlight broke through.

But then the Witches' Channeler let free another song. Control of the winds turned from Senna. Clouds devoured the sunlight. Thunder boomed. A gust of wind whipped her hair. The storm was too far gone to be called back now.

She stripped her hair from her face and searched the ship. Had Joshen made it back? Had Mistin? There wasn't time to wait for them. "Captain Parknel, we leave *now!*"

He shook his head. "We can't risk the open seas."

"I can keep us safe!" Senna cried. If they didn't beat the storm, she would be trapped in Corrieth. The Heads would come for them.

Parknel studied her, obviously debating. Someone shouted that Joshen had been sighted. The captain growled low in his throat. "All right. But we go now."

Joshen and a stable boy struggled towards them, but the horses they led were fighting their leads, no doubt sensing the ferocity of the building storm and startled by the sound of their hooves on the planking.

"Leave them!" she shouted to be heard over the wind.

"We need them!" Joshen shouted back.

Sailors were still bringing hay on deck, where others waited to haul it below.

Senna stared at the sky as lightning stabbed across the sooty clouds. "We aren't going to make it."

Just then Joshen started up the plank. One of the horses, gold in color with a white mane and tail, reared, terror showing in his eyes. Joshen expertly dodged his hooves. When the horse came back down, Joshen put him in a headlock. "Get me a blindfold!"

A sailor stripped off his shirt. Three men struggled to cover the horse's eyes. Blind, he froze, his muscles quivering.

And then Mistin was there with another man. Locking arms behind the horse's rump, they forced him onboard. The other horses came with only half as much effort.

Thunder shook the world. Horses whinnied. Sailors shouted. The ship rolled with a wave.

"Parknel!" Senna cried. "Please."

The captain pursed his lips, clearly unhappy. "Sailors on board. Shove off!"

18. Wind Song

Sailors hustled to untie the ropes and pushed from the pier with long poles. The sails unrolled from the masts, and the ship took to the open water.

"Watch out!" a man cried from the crow's nest.

A wave crashed into them. Senna gasped as freezing cold water battered her. The ship rolled, swinging back towards the piers. They were going to smash into another ship. Parknel spun the wheel.

Senna's song burst forth, calling the wind to propel them forward.

Slowly, ever so slowly, the sails caught the wind and they began to turn. Another wave hit the ship, tipping sailors from the rigging. They fell, screaming, to the deck. The bales of hay slid, pinning men against the rails. They pushed at the bales, shouting for help until more sailors appeared and freed them.

"No time to haul it below decks," Captain Parknel shouted. "Tie it down before someone else is crushed!"

A solid wall of rain moved towards them.

Mistin struggled to the upper deck. "Can I help?"

Senna pointed to the bow. "You sing there. It'll increase our range."

Dodging sailors, Mistin crossed the deck.

"Tie yourselves in!" Parknel shouted again and again as he and another man strained to hold the wheel.

They cut into the curtain of rain, and Senna was immediately drenched. Joshen snatched a rope and tied it around her waist before doing the same for himself and the men at the wheel.

Senna belted out another song. The ship shot through the hole she created in the storm, rolling down another mountainous wave of what looked like broken glass. Sailors clung to whatever they could hold onto and muttered oaths or prayers or both. Lightning split the sky.

A sailor called out, "Just over eight knots, sir!"

"She'll not take more speed," Parknel called from the wheel.

Halting her song, Senna wiped salt spray and rain from her eyes.

Parknel groaned against the strain of holding the wheel. In two steps, Joshen had the spokes in his big hands. "Senna!"

"How many knots?" Parknel grunted, his face cherry red.

The sailor watched the rope disappearing over the side. "They're moving too fast for me to count, sir."

The wind blew harder, until Parknel's orders were snatched from his mouth so fast Senna couldn't understand him from a few spans away. The waves grew higher, colliding with the ship and slamming Senna onto the deck. The breath was knocked from her.

Water streaming down her face, she watched men rolling across the deck. Some were thrown over the side, and the ropes that held them to the ship strained with their weight. No one moved to help them. No one could.

Rain slashed down from the sky, and Senna realized what Parknel and the other sailors must have known for a while now. They weren't just trying to escape before the storm locked them into port—they were running for their lives. The Heads hadn't just called in any storm. This was a hurricane.

Warm hands gripped her icy ones. Joshen shouted at her, water running down his face in sheets.

She shook her head, unable to hear him over the raging music of the storm.

He brought his mouth to her ear. "Call on that power you had before! When we were on Haven!"

She shook her head again. "I already tried. It's gone."

But she'd promised Parknel she'd get them through safely. She meant to keep that promise. Holding onto Joshen for stability, she sang a soft, gentle lullaby.

> Seas, thy troubles to cease,
> Calm thyself and return to peace.
> Winds rest, for weary ye be.
> Gently, gently blow for me.

She listened for the music to calm, for something to change. After a half dozen repetitions, something did. She could hear herself over the gale. Blinking, she looked up at the sky. It was still raining, but the winds had slowed. The seas were troubled, but not raging.

"Keep singing, Senna," Joshen said. "That's it."

Trembling, she staggered to her feet. As she sang, the seas settled like the scruff on a dog's neck. Soon, sharp sunlight warmed her face. A rainbow glowed before them like an archway to safety. Senna looked back towards Nefalie, where the storm still raged.

Joshen inspected her. "Are you all right?"

Slowly, she lifted her hands. They almost looked translucent, but she thought it was just the cold. "I think so. You?"

Joshen brushed water from his face. His eyes were red from the salt. "Well, I'm not dead, which is better than I expected."

"Master Carver, see to the ship." Leaving the wheel in the care of his second, Parknel approached them, his pipe still clenched between his teeth. He tipped it over, and watery ashes spilled out. He shook it at Senna. "You and I, we have business to discuss."

He turned his back on her and strode down the steps. She cast a nervous glance at Joshen before following. She pulled her heavy hair over her shoulder and wrung water from it, then shook droplets from her hands. Parknel opened his door and squared himself on the other side of his desk, his hands behind his back.

Everything that could be bolted down was, but there were still books, maps, and linens scattered across the floor. Shivering, Senna stepped carefully over them. Joshen came in behind her and stood to her right. Reden closed the door and stepped up to her left, his face pale.

The steady patter of dripping was everywhere. Senna was

getting Parknel's floor wet, but there wasn't anything she could do about it.

"Do you know what that was, Senna?" Parknel asked softly.

Joshen angled himself a step in front of her. "A storm."

Parknel's gaze never left Senna's face. "Do you know?"

Senna didn't need Joshen's protection. Not right now. She stepped up beside him. "It was a hurricane."

Parknel leaned forward, his hands splayed across his desk. "I was a boy during the Second Witch Wars. Two groups of Witches were trying to destroy each other, and we were caught in the middle. The ship sank. Most of the crew was lost, including my father. Only myself and a handful of others survived." He paused. "So tell me, Senna, why did the Heads send a hurricane after you? Why do they want you dead?"

Dead? Senna waited for the devastation to hit, but she only felt a strange sort of numbness, like the time she sang until she lost her voice.

Reden answered, "I don't think they counted on her being able to set sail that quickly. They only meant to trap her in Corrieth."

Parknel's gaze swung to Reden. "Don't take me for a fool, Leader. That storm was meant to kill someone. I almost lost the ship. My entire crew. Everything. You had better have a good reason for risking my men like that."

Joshen's hand tightened on Senna's shoulder. "You didn't hesitate when you helped us before."

Parknel sank into the chair behind his desk. "Before, the world was at stake and Senna was our only hope." He steepled his hands and looked at Reden. "You want my help, then I need to know what I'm getting myself into."

Reden looked at the captain for several long seconds before responding. "There's a traitor on the island. I believe it's one of the Heads. My guess is they somehow manipulated the Circle into sending the hurricane instead of just a storm. Even if they were that desperate to stop Senna, they wouldn't risk damaging Corrieth. They rely too much on trade with the city, and they need the people's goodwill. Even more so after the earth tremor."

Parknel seemed to collapse in on himself. He gestured to the chairs bolted to the floor. "You'd better tell me what this is really about."

Senna remained upright—she didn't want to sit in her own puddle. "The Witches believe they are untouchable on Haven. They're wrong." She took a deep breath and told Parknel the truth. All of it, even about seeking out Espen.

He scratched at his beard. "Why do you think Espen would reveal any secrets to you?"

"I promised to cut her down."

Parknel's gaze held steady. "And will you?"

"I don't know," Senna said quietly. Killing someone who threatened your life was one thing. Killing someone in the name of justice or mercy was another.

"And you're sure these other Witches are a danger to Haven? That they created the earth tremor and sent these men to kidnap you?"

Senna let out a breath in exasperation. How could she explain something so foreign to these men? They'd never heard the music of the Four Sisters, felt her song meld with theirs until she wasn't sure if she was a Witch at all, or simply a force of nature contained in a body of flesh and blood.

She pried her water-slicked hair away from her face. "Have you ever looked into a clear sky and knew a storm was coming? You weren't sure how you knew, but you somehow felt it."

Parknel picked up a cup that rolled towards him with the motion of the ship. "You're saying we're going to have to trust you. Trust you when the Discipline Heads wouldn't. "

She winced. "Yes."

"Very well, Senna," he said with a grunt. "I believed in you when few others did. Wouldn't make much sense to stop now that you've finally begun to believe in yourself."

She smiled to herself.

Parknel tossed the broken cup back onto the floor. "What's my Heading?"

"Kaen's farm."

Parknel rubbed his jaw. "Not far from where we made landfall last time?"

She nodded.

He pulled a chart down. He cleared the debris off his desk with one swipe, then weighted down the corners and started muttering to himself. "No idea where we are." He opened his compass. "Have to head west until the stars come out." He tapped a symbol of rough water and a cloud. "The storm couldn't have forced us to the Darkwell Squalls."

"The what?" Senna asked in alarm.

The captain glanced up. "Hmm. Bah, nothing to worry about. We couldn't have been pushed that far south."

A knock sounded at the door. "Captain, we've a crack in the foremast."

"You've always been rather hard on my ship," Parknel grumbled.

"I'll pay for the damages," Senna said. *Somehow.*

"Yes. You will. I plan to be the fastest ship on the sea for the foreseeable future." Hurrying out, Parknel called over his shoulder, "You'll take my cabin again. Get some rest."

Rest? Everyone was running around in a near panic, and he wanted her to rest. "How long until we reach Tarten?" she shouted after him.

"If we are where I think and we keep up this speed, perhaps four days. If the *Sea Witch* can handle the strain." The last bit was nearly lost in the clamor.

The realization hit her that their journey had finally started. Now Senna could start planning in earnest. She and Reden leaned over the map on the table, studying Tarten. This was the second time she'd had to cross the Darkwell Sea to confront Espen.

Joshen pulled off his cloak and hung it over the back of a chair. "Senna, the Discipline Heads weren't exaggerating. There's a price on every Witch's head. Especially yours. If we really have to find these foreign Witches, fine. But two landings in Tarten are an unnecessary risk."

Anger prickled up Senna's spine. She wondered if her mother and father had these same arguments. The safety of the world balanced against personal safety. She wondered if things had been different in Lilette's day, when the world had reverenced Witches.

Reden frowned at Joshen. "We're going to Espen because Senna knows where these foreign Witches are. We're going to Kaen's because she needs to be inland for the song to be the most effective, and Espen's realm is too risky. Plus we can check on her friends."

Senna was impressed with Reden's knowledge of how Witch song worked.

Joshen pressed his palms into the back of the chair, clearly unhappy. "And then?"

Senna took a deep breath to calm herself. "We discover what we can and warn the Heads."

Reden looked between the two and then headed for the door. "Well, now that's settled, I'm going to see if I can round up some dry clothes. Then I have to test this brother Mistin brought along, see if he'll be of any use to us."

Senna shivered as the wind snaked through the closing door and cut through her damp clothes. She curled her arms around herself. Even her bones felt cold.

Joshen started rummaging around in her satchel. "You're shivering. We need to get you out of those wet clothes."

He found her spare shift and dress and turned around. She pulled her clothes off. They landed with a wet plop on the floor. Hauling on the dry ones, she marveled at how warm they felt over her chilled skin. She sighed and twisted her wet hair up, wrapping a cord around it to hold it off her neck.

Already, the salt was irritating her skin, but a bath would have to wait.

She heard him going through his own bag, pulling out clothes. She looked up in time to see him pull his shirt off. Despite everything that had happened between them, her insides went warm and soft at the sight of his broad shoulders, the cut of his muscles.

To distract herself, she went to the window and watched the purple-black storm receding in the distance—the wind and waves lashing out at each other as if in a pitched battle. She felt Joshen's gaze on her.

"You should rest. I know how much singing like that drains you, and we're going to need you at full strength when we land in Tarten."

Why did everyone want her to rest? Senna sought out her reflection in the window. Her eyes were bloodshot and lined with dark circles. She looked too thin. Her hair was a disaster. She tried to smooth it with her fingers. "I'm fine. I should sing to the wind now so we can cross faster."

"I don't think the ship is ready to handle more speed." He settled his shirt over his broad chest. "Well, if you refuse to rest, will you come below decks with me? I've got to check on the horses, and there's something I want to show you."

She followed Joshen out of Parknel's cabin and into mayhem. Sailors were scurrying back and forth, tying ropes, hauling down ripped sails, and doing other things she didn't really understand.

Senna and Joshen wound their way into the bowels of the ship. It wasn't hard to find the horses—they just had to follow the barn smell and the furious hammering sound.

Joshen trotted forward. Inside the middle stall, the palomino furiously kicked the boards. "Easy, boy. Easy," Joshen opened the stall and stepped up beside the animal's shoulder.

Senna held her breath, her throat constricting with worry. The horse eyed Joshen, his ears flat in warning.

"Joshen," Senna warned.

The animal bared his teeth and lunged. Joshen shoved the horse's face away. Deftly, he threaded two lead ropes through the halter. He tied them to two rings on opposite sides of the stall, trapping the horse in the middle. All the while, he spoke softly. "I'm going to have to take you above deck and work you every day to take the edge off."

"I have a potion that could help," Senna offered, glad she wasn't the one in there with that horse.

"Maybe if exercise isn't enough and the potion is the kind that wears off within a day or two." Joshen brushed his hands on his pants. "Senna, this is Sunny."

She held her hand out for the horse to sniff. He snorted disdainfully. Senna's nose wrinkled in disgust, as she wiped horse mucus off her palm with a handful of straw. "I don't think he likes me."

Joshen took a cloth from the stall and rubbed the horse's already polished coat. "He's from racing stock—one of the fastest horses my father's ever bred, and he has the stamina to match it."

"He's beautiful." Any woman in love with Joshen had to love horses by default.

"Sunny can outrun anything on four legs," Joshen said, pride obvious in his voice.

Senna didn't doubt it. A fire seemed to burn inside the horse, making it impossible for him to hold still. Joshen was studying her, as if waiting for her to make a connection. A sense of foreboding welled inside her. Surely he knew this was way too much horse for her. "I'm sure he's perfect for *you*."

Joshen's gray eyes locked on hers. "He's not for me. I bought him for you."

With an enormous effort, she kept her face blank. "Joshen..."

He sighed and gave Sunny's coat another swipe. "Just give me this, all right? We're going into danger I'm not sure I can protect you from—" He cleared his throat. "Please."

She reached out and took his hand. "If he throws me, I'll be dead either way."

Joshen didn't laugh at her attempt at humor. "He's not mean—just lively."

"Lively, right." Senna tried to smile but it came out as more of a wince. "You bought him? For how much? And when did you have time to get a horse from your father?" His father lived three days journey from Corrieth, and Joshen didn't make much coin as a Guardian.

"I had him brought up weeks ago. And it's none of your business how much I paid for him." Joshen sighed. "He was always meant for a gift, Senna. But now, he's part of an apology, too. I'm sorry for leaving you on the island when you needed me most."

Joshen had given her the most beautiful and most dangerous horse in the world by way of an apology. "I told you to go with Arianis."

He shook his head ruefully. "That was definitely one of those times when I should have ignored you."

She swatted his arm. He grinned and leaned towards her. She took a step back and his grin slipped.

Someone shouted for her from above. A sailor peeked down the stairs. "Brusenna, Leader Reden is looking for you."

Joshen motioned for her to go. "I've got to tend the horses anyway."

She sighed. "We'll finish this later."

19. A Guardian's Sacrifice

Senna emerged from the ship's hold and blinked into the sunshine. Stepping onto the deck, she promptly strode on the hem of her dress and pitched forward. Right into a pair of strong arms. "Oh, I'm sorry!"

The unfamiliar man steadied her but made no move to let her go. She looked up and lost herself in nearly black eyes of a tall, golden-skinned man with long dark hair tied back with a string. His beauty stunned her. Her heart hammered, but not just because of his looks. This was…something else.

"Senna?" Reden said.

She sprang away from the stranger's arms and wiped her suddenly sweaty hands on her dress.

Mistin jogged up to them. She had changed from an Apprentice's plain green dress to a loose-fitting tunic and trousers. "Senna, have you met my brother?"

Her face burning under Reden's scrutiny, Senna shook her head.

"Cord, this is Brusenna, but she goes by Senna because she wants to be new and better."

His eyes were still locked on her. She saw the resemblance. He had Mistin's almond-shaped eyes, though his face had sharper planes. He was shorter than Joshen but taller than Reden, with a wiry build. His dark eyes seemed to weigh everything around him. And they were weighing Senna.

She cleared her throat. "Do I know you? You seem familiar?"

He grinned and his face went from brooding to handsome in a moment, but it was a dangerous kind of handsome. Senna could tell he used his beauty like a tool—an adept tool. "I think I'd remember meeting you."

Mistin glared at him. He turned his dazzling smile on her. She rolled her eyes. "Ignore him. He's a bit of a flirt."

Reden cleared his throat. "If you two will excuse Senna and me."

Mistin grabbed Cord's arm and hauled him towards the bow.

Reden watched them walk away. "He doesn't just want to help us. He wants to be your Guardian."

Senna lifted an eyebrow. "Another one?"

Reden shrugged. "We could use the help."

She studied Cord. "Is he any good?"

"He's somewhat competent." Reden said something in Tarten.

Senna glanced askance at him. "What does that mean?"

He hesitated. "A poor soldier's worse than no soldier."

Senna absorbed this before saying the words that had been bearing down on her since they'd left the island. "Why did you come with us?" she asked softly. "Because of me, you lost your place as commander of the Tarten armies. And now you've lost the Leadership of the Guardians as well."

He spoke carefully. "We teach our Guardians to protect their witches—sometimes from their own folly. That includes the Heads. Three times, you were attacked by strangers on the island. I'm convinced someone with a lot of power is helping them. That means there's a traitor. And if there's a traitor, there's some kind of treachery afoot."

He studied her, his gaze steady. "It all comes back to you, Senna. You're the key to this. So I'm going to follow your lead." He rested his hand on her shoulder. "I'll be Leader of the Guardians again, because we're going to save the Witches from their own foolishness."

She tried not to wince. "Are we doing the right thing?" After all, she'd betrayed those who trusted her. Had risked her mother's happiness and Joshen's love.

"One can't sacrifice a higher law for a lower one."

She stared at him.

Reden nodded to himself. "When you're in that moment of decision, where right and wrong are so mixed up you can't tell which is which, always remember to follow the higher law."

It's what he'd done when he'd sacrificed his home country for the world. "But how do you know which law is higher?"

"It's usually the decision that's harder at first, but better in the long run."

She digested that quietly.

He rested a hand on her back. "Now, how about we lend these sailors a hand mending the sails?"

Senna glanced at him, startled. "You can sew?"

He chuckled. "If I didn't mend my clothes, who would?"

"But you were the Commander."

Reden's warm eyes studied her. "I wasn't always, Senna. Once, I was a lot like you."

***

It was the middle of the night when the cabin door creaked open. Senna's breath caught in her throat, but she couldn't see anything through the darkness clinging to her like pitch. Above the rhythmic sounds of the ship, she heard nothing. She considered reaching over and waking Mistin, but that might alert the intruder that she was aware of his presence.

She reached for the dagger she kept in her seed belt beside the bed.

"Senna, it's just me."

She recognized Joshen's whisper and sighed in relief. He crossed the room and crouched beside her bed.

"What are you doing?" She glanced at Mistin, who hadn't stirred.

"We need you to sing."

Taking one of the spare blankets, she wrapped it around her shoulders and led him from her cabin.

She started towards the bow, but he pulled her back. "Are things all right between us?" he asked.

Her head dropped. "I don't know." Which really meant no.

He shifted awkwardly. "Well then, how do I make it right?"

"Joshen..." She sighed. How could she explain this so he would understand? "I have never believed in myself. Maybe it was because I was taunted as a child, and I came to believe those taunts. Eventually, I didn't need the town bullies anymore—I did well enough belittling myself."

In the moonlight, Joshen's sad eyes nearly undid her, but she continued. "After that, I never had to believe in myself. I had you to do that for me." She went on, her voice barely a whisper. "It's not all your fault, Joshen. This isn't really even about you. I want to be strong. I want to believe in myself. Give me some time to learn who I am."

His mouth pressed in a thin line, and she hesitated. She hated confrontation. Her instinct was to pretend things were fine. But that wouldn't help anything. "I'm not sure I can trust you. You would have stopped me from leaving Haven."

Joshen dragged his hand through his hair. "I was just trying to keep you from getting hurt. And it's not like you're perfect." They were both silent for a while. "So I'm just supposed to accept that I might lose you?" His voice was thick with anger.

She rubbed her face. "I am Witch born. It's what I am."

He took a step towards her. "What you are is my love."

Her shoulders drooped. "Oh, Joshen. You fell in love with a Witch, and there's a cost for that." Her father had paid with his life. "It's even worse for you, because I'm becoming something more than a Witch. I don't know how or what, but I'm not sure any of us will come through this without paying a price."

Joshen turned away, his muscles bunching beneath his shirt. "I know. I've known for weeks. But I can't pay that price, Senna. I can't."

She fought to keep her emotions below the surface. "You're going to pay it whether you accept it or not."

A shudder ran through him. Without looking at her, he strode towards the hatch. "My watch is up. I'll see you in the morning."

Senna watched him go. She wanted to call out to him, beg him to banish her dread with the comfort of his arms, but he wasn't ready. And maybe she wasn't, either. Somewhere, she'd lost herself…or maybe she'd never really found herself to begin with. At any rate, she had to learn to love herself wholly before she could love anyone else. "Good night."

She went to the front of the ship and sang to the wind until it gusted behind her, whipping her loose hair into her face. With a sudden burst, the wind caught her blanket and tore it away from her. She lunged for it, but it was already out of reach. Gasping, she cursed and whirled towards the wind. As if sorry, it snatched her hair from her face.

The damp sea air cooled her hot skin. But it also pressed her thin shift against her body. She wouldn't be alone on deck. Captain Parknel always kept a lookout in the crow's nest in addition to the man at the wheel. She felt eyes on her. Straightening, she saw Cord watching her, his musket leaning on the railing beside him.

He must have relieved Joshen. Cord hefted his musket and came towards her. Hugging herself, she ducked and started towards the cabin.

"Wait."

She picked up her pace.

"Wait." He took her arm.

She kept her face averted.

Gently, he turned her face towards him. He was silent for a time. "What's it like?"

Shifting uncomfortably, Senna stared at the deck and wished he would let her go. She couldn't explain the strange feeling she had whenever he came near. "What's what like?"

"Singing like…that, to the Four Sisters."

The question caught her off guard. No one had ever asked that before. She closed her eyes. Wind was like a half-wild colt—full of wild energy. Earth reminded her of an old man with arthritic bones—slow and sleepy. Water was like a temperamental woman—full of secret moods and hidden places. Sunlight was a playful child—subject to sulks and fits of laughter. And plants… She shrugged, not sure she could share something so intimate with a stranger.

"Well, plants for instance," she finally replied, "They're reliable. Like your favorite musket, I suspect."

Cord folded his arms, pleased with himself. And Senna realized he was trying to distract her from her frustration. It had worked— she wasn't upset anymore. The realization surprised her. She didn't think Cord the type to care about another's feelings.

He rubbed his palms together uncomfortably. "I— did he hurt you?"

She was glad the darkness hid her blush. "Joshen? Of course not."

Cord raised an eyebrow. "Really? Then why were you upset after he left?"

She refused to look at him. "He hurt me a while ago. I guess you could say we're still trying to get past it."

Cord cast a glare at the stairs that led below decks. "Your Guardian should be more careful of appearances. Someone might think there was something more between you."

She shrugged. "There is."

Cord looked at her more closely. "There— what? That's allowed?"

"Does it really matter what's allowed anymore?" Senna started towards the cabin. His hand shot out, gripping her firmly around her arm.

Startled, she turned towards him. He pulled her closer, close enough that her billowing shift brushed his clothes. "Next time you come out to sing, do it a little better clothed." His eyes dropped down to look at her in nothing but her shift. The wind chose that moment to press it against her body. It took everything she had not to cross her arms over her chest.

When he looked back into her eyes, something passed across his face, something that shouldn't have been there. Her body flushed with an uncomfortable heat. "You want to be my Guardian, you better learn to hold your tongue. And your gaze."

Cord's expression hardened, and he dropped his hand. "Good night, Senna." He walked to the upper deck and didn't look back.

Confused and angry, she watched him go. It felt like arrogance to assume he would want her. She was not beautiful—whatever Joshen might say. She was small, with startling golden eyes and matching hair. Strange more than beautiful.

He was at the railing now. And she was still standing in nothing but her shift, glaring at him. Remembering herself with a start, she moved back to the cabin.

She lay in bed beside Mistin, wanting nothing more than to sleep. But there was one last thing she had to do.

She listened to the Four Sister's music. She didn't try to fight it as her soul slipped from her body. Traveling its patterns, she stood before Espen. The woman's branches sagged. She'd lost most of her leaves. "I'm coming," Senna said.

Espen was more awake now. A blighted branch stretched forward and clawed in the dirt. "Tartens kill Witch on sight." She scraped the empty space clear and wrote again. "Another enemy."

Next, she wrote, "More dangerous than Tartens."

"Who?" Senna asked.

"Songs," Espen wrote. "Songs from a hidden land."

Senna curled her arms around her body. "I'll be careful."

20. Senna's Promise

Senna woke with a start to something that sounded remarkably like a dying frog. Mistin was attempting to sing to the wind. Where Senna's song was strong enough to advance the ship for hours, Mistin's was so weak she would have to keep up an almost constant barrage.

Senna buried her head under her pillow. The watch had woken her twice so she could sing to keep up their speed, and it had taken her hours to fall back asleep each time. She was still exhausted.

But there was no blocking out Mistin. With a groan of frustration, Senna pushed herself out of bed and found someone to bring her enough water for a bath. The tub was cramped and the water cold, but at least she wasn't itching from salt water anymore.

She left her cabin and found the deck strangely empty. Parknel stood at the wheel with an expression she'd seen him wear when sailing into battle—like he was determined to go on through tempest, war, or Mistin's singing. Senna chuckled to herself.

Reden and Cord stared at her with pleading expressions. Cord had stuffed wool in his ears. "For love of the Creators, can you make her stop?" he said.

Senna strode across the deck and stood beside Mistin, joining in and singing with her. Within two songs, the wind became steady enough to keep them moving at a swift clip for a few hours.

Mistin turned to Senna with a smile so broad her cheeks almost swallowed up her eyes. "I'm starting to love the sea!"

Senna studied her. There had been a question burning in her mind for a while. "Why did you stand up for me against the Heads? Why did you risk your place on Haven?"

"Ha! They were going to kick me out any day, and you know it. The only reason I was still there at all was because I was their servant, and I hated that." Mistin squinted against the sun. "The only thing they see is the strength of a Witch's song. They never look at the rest of her." She turned her beautiful smile onto Senna. "Besides, you're my friend and you needed me."

Despite her sour mood, Senna found herself smiling back. A friend—she'd always wanted one of those. "Well, I'm glad you're here."

Mistin sighed with pleasure. "I'll take this round of singing, since I know your voice is probably still tired after that storm. You can cover midday and night."

Senna wanted to protest. Mistin would have to sing nonstop to keep the wind going. Senna need only sing a few times a day to achieve the same result. But Mistin would only see her help as an insult.

And her voice did need rest. "All right." Everyone would just have to deal with it.

Senna jumped as a shot fired. She turned to see Cord lower his musket and nod at something Reden said. He reloaded, sighted down the barrel, and fired again. Despite herself, Senna jumped again. She really hated guns.

Reden gestured for the two women to join them. "You need to learn this." He held out a pistol to Senna.

She reached inside her seed belt and pulled out the pistol Joshen had given her. "I've practiced with Joshen a few times, but I've never had the chance to use it. I guess it's not much good in an ambush."

Reden's face was hard. "Not unless it's ready. Takes a minute to load."

She shrugged. "I can sing faster than that."

He handed Senna and Mistin some balled-up wool to stuff in their ears. "Primed, it's faster than Witch song. Different weapons fit different situations, Senna. You should be deft in all of them.

You'll practice every day, twice a day. I'm going to teach you and Mistin some grappling, too."

Mistin didn't accept the wool. "Maybe later. I saw them bringing Senna a bath. I want one too."

Reden's gaze never left Mistin's small figure as she walked to their cabin.

Senna smirked as she started loading the pistol. "Did you have a girl back in Tarten?"

Reden started slightly. "A girl? No. Being married to a soldier is a hard thing to ask of anyone—sending him off, not knowing whether he'll return at all. It's worse when you're a Commander."

It had been a while since Senna had practiced with Joshen. After she'd finally loaded the pistol, she shook her hair out of her eyes and sighted down the barrel. "Why?"

Reden squinted against the sun. "Because Grendi has very little tolerance for a Commander who displeases her. And she's very easy to displease. I lingered longer than most. Still, my time was limited. If I hadn't left with you, I doubt I would have made it much longer."

She fired. "Did I hit it?"

He cocked an eyebrow. "What were you aiming for?"

"The water." She grinned.

He chuckled. "I'm pretty sure you killed it."

She poured more powder into the barrel and promptly fumbled the ball. It fell on her foot and rolled across the deck. Using one of Joshen's favorite curse words, she limped after it.

When she finally caught the ball, she looked up to find Reden watching her, one side of his mouth crooked up.

"Go ahead and laugh," she said with a frown.

He held his hand over his mouth. "I'm not laughing."

She considered throwing the musket ball at his head. Instead, she finished loading the pistol and fired. Despite the wool, her ears rang.

"Not bad. I want you to practice midmorning and midday to increase your speed, until the movements become habit." He studied her. "Why did Joshen take you below decks?"

She rubbed her face. "He bought me a horse. A gorgeous, fast, dangerous horse."

Reden's brow rose. "The palomino?"

She nodded.

Reden took a deep breath and let it out slowly. "Well, the man knows his horses."

If any woman in love with Joshen had to love horses by default, maybe that extended to his friends, too.

"Reden?" she said softly. "Joshen doesn't want me to be here."

Reden studied her sidelong. "How so?"

She fired again. "He doesn't want me going to Tarten. I'm not sure he can deal with all this."

"Give him some time. He's still trying to find his footing—to figure out how to balance protecting you with letting you go into dangerous situations."

Someone cleared his throat behind them. "When you're moving forward, you have to aim a little behind the target to compensate for the ship's speed." Senna recognized Joshen's voice. She turned to find him watching her, his arms crossed over his chest and his expression tense.

Senna rubbed her forehead in frustration.

Reden nodded towards her pistol. "Keep practicing. I'll be right back."

He took Joshen's arm and steered him away.

Senna looked around for another ball to load in the pistol. Reden must have taken them with him. She tentatively approached the hatch.

She could see the edge of Reden's back and hear his tense voice. "Fine. Don't tell me what happened. But I'll tell you this as your friend, you're losing her."

"I'm trying to protect her!"

"You're her Guardian. You protect her from *danger*. You can question her plans, her choices, but you don't threaten her. You don't force her. You follow where she leads and clean up what you can."

"Even if it kills her?" Joshen's voice had grown threatening.

Reden didn't back down. "Being a Witch means putting herself in danger for the world's sake if needs be. That's why they have Guardians."

Joshen didn't speak for a moment. "I love her, Reden. I can't stand by and watch her nearly die. Not again."

"So it's selfishness, is it?"

"What? No, I—"

"You can't stand watching her get hurt so you betrayed her trust? 'Cause that sounds like selfishness to me."

Joshen was silent. "I can't risk her."

"She's already at risk. Accept it and stop being a fool, before it's too late."

Reden turned to go up the stairs and caught Senna watching. He gave her a reprimanding look.

She retreated back to the side of the ship before Joshen could see her. "You took all the balls," she said sheepishly.

Glancing at the pouch at his hip, Reden grunted. "So I did."

"Thanks for speaking with him."

Reden nodded. "You two need each other." He gestured for Joshen to join them. "You know the pistol well enough. Let's see how you do in combat."

Over the next few hours, Joshen taught her how to escape a hold. Specifically, how to block a gag by holding her wrist to her lips. The goal was to protect her song, which would be her primary weapon.

The hurt between them was like a slow poison. Cleansing it would take time, and time was something neither of them had. So they studiously ignored their pain.

Joshen drilled the same four sequences over and over.

"Can't we learn something new?" Senna finally asked.

He circled her. "No time. Better you learn a few things well."

At lunch time, Senna was relieved for an excuse to stop. She retrieved food for the four of them, making a cup of soothing tea for Mistin's throat.

Joshen helped her carry it to where Mistin was singing even more croakily than normal. Reden stood beside her and didn't seem to mind the sound at all. She finished the verse and he said something. She laughed, a sound that was beautiful even if her voice was not. He noticed them and touched Mistin's elbow. She took the tea with obvious gratitude.

Senna passed out travel bread, apples, and salt pork. "Call it a day, Mistin. The ship might need you if I'm stuck in Tarten."

Mistin took a bite of her apple. "That will be difficult, as I'm coming with you."

Cord appeared, his own lunch in hand, and sat beside Senna. She had to suppress the urge to squirm.

"Are you sure you can keep up?" Joshen asked as he took the other side.

"I'll be on a horse, idiot." Mistin glared at him.

Cord chuckled.

Mistin transferred her glare to Cord. Both men clamped up and stared at the deck.

Reden grinned. "In a fight between you three, I'd bet on her."

Senna handed Mistin the pistol she'd been practicing with, and that settled it.

After they'd eaten, Reden gestured for Senna and Joshen to join him in the captain's cabin. Once they were behind closed doors, Reden said, "Senna, we'll be arriving in Tarten soon. I need to know you'll obey me if I tell you to run. If I say return to the ship, you do it."

"Of course I will."

"Even if it means leaving someone behind." She opened her mouth to protest, but he spoke before she could. "Sometimes men get trapped, and there's no way to rescue them, not without losing more men than you save. It's part of the risk we've all undertaken."

The responsibility shot through her. Joshen and Reden were risking their lives to protect her. All they asked in return was that she obeyed them. They both watched her, and she knew they wouldn't go on unless she said it. "If you and Joshen both tell me to go, I will."

Reden nodded. Joshen didn't react at all.

"Land ahead!" came a shout from outside.

Senna hurried to the bow. Captain Parknel came to stand beside them.

"How much longer?" Joshen asked.

Parknel judged the distance through his spy glass. "We'll have to travel up coast for a bit. Sometime early morning."

Senna watched the brown smudge in the distance. "So it begins."

21. Cursed

Everything was dead. What was once a veritable jungle was now little more than brittle, brown rot that no hint of a breeze stirred. Since the Four Sisters had been commanded to lie dormant, there hadn't been so much as a draft since the Witches fled these shores months ago. The stale air made the stink of the moldering corpses dotting the landscape so much stronger.

Unable to believe she had caused this desolation, Senna stepped forward, the dry vegetation crunching like brittle bones underfoot. She searched desperately for some signs of life between the mountains covering the landscape like overturned urns. Cord and Mistin were already out there, scouting for signs of danger. She was glad for Cord's absence, at least. His every gaze felt like an unwanted caress.

Joshen rested a large hand on her shoulder. His eyes never stopped searching the colorless landscape. "Senna?"

He couldn't understand this devastation the way she could. Since her senses had expanded to include the Four Sisters—Earth, Water, Plants, and Sunlight—she felt their absence like a womb suddenly void of life. "Did I really do this, Joshen?"

He finally spared her a glance. "You weren't the only one. And none of you had a choice."

Senna knew that wasn't true. There was always a choice. She could have let Chancellor Grendi kill her and the remaining Witches, and the world would have continued on. For a little while at least.

From atop his own horse, Reden held out her gelding's reins.

She eyed the palomino as it side-stepped nervously. "Are you sure about him?"

Joshen leaned in and spoke low enough that only she heard. "Senna, I'm going to give you every advantage I can."

That horse didn't feel like much of an advantage. "So Sunny's your backup plan if three Guardians and Mistin fail?"

Joshen didn't answer. Senna sighed. She missed the gentle eyes of her old horse, Knight. "All right, but if he throws me, I'm taking Cord's horse." The animal he'd brought for the journey had an ugly, bald face but a gentle nature. Hiking up her skirt, Senna climbed into the saddle.

Beside them, Reden finally spoke for the first time since seeing his ruined homeland. "We should keep moving. There are probably spies watching us."

Senna looked back at him. "How do you know?"

He stared at the landscape. "It's what I would have done."

At his very core, Reden was a soldier—one of the best—so he didn't show emotions the way a normal man would. But they were still there, if you knew him well enough. She'd spent enough time with him over the past months to see his guilt in the unyielding muscles of his face, and in the stiff way he sat in his saddle. After all, he'd helped her destroy his homeland.

"It's not too late, Senna. We can still turn back," Joshen said.

"I spent too much time on Haven doing the smart thing," she replied. "Now I'm going to do the right thing."

Reden didn't say anything more. He wasn't the type to argue. Once a decision had been made, he simply followed it through to the end—whatever that end may be.

They took the agreed-upon formation, Cord and Mistin scouting ahead, Reden in front of Senna, Joshen behind. As they heeled their horses into a gallop, Senna looked back at the *Sea Witch* anchored just off shore. She wished she were back on it, that she didn't have to face the devastation she'd forced onto Tarten.

Moving at a fast clip, they retraced the path she and Joshen had taken months ago. Senna couldn't help but notice the differences. Before, the road was choked with plants vying for sunlight. Now it was bare. The little hut they'd passed before, the one with the cooking fire in front, was empty, the fire pit filled with gray ash the wind hadn't even bothered to blow away.

And here, where they'd turned to avoid the soldiers, the road was littered with decaying plants, none of which had been crushed by footfalls. Sunny leapt a fallen tree, his passing stirring the withered leaves still clinging to the branches. The barn they'd hidden inside so long ago was plainly visible now that the foliage wasn't there to block it from view. It too was abandoned.

Their mounts were breathing hard and dripping with sweat. The small party stopped to let the horses rest for a while before riding on again.

Senna wondered where all the people had fled.

Cord met them not far from Kaen's home. "Mistin and I have scouted the surrounding area. It's clear."

Senna trotted Sunny the rest of the way to the house. Ghosts of memories rose up from around her. She jumped from the saddle. Joshen and Reden moved ahead of her, their muskets primed.

She trailed after them through the two-room hut. At first, she was blinded by the darkness. Opening her eyes wide, she slowly turned around. Their movements had stirred up the dust. The house had the musty smell of a long-abandoned building. Her eyes watered and she sneezed.

Trying to breathe through the guilt crushing her chest, she hurried towards the side room. She started when a rat ran across her foot. She forced herself to push the door aside. The sleeping mats were missing, as was the food that had been in the woven baskets.

They really were gone. Senna bit her bottom lip and willed herself not to fall apart.

Joshen headed back outside. "I'll go check the tunnel. If Kaen left us word, that's where it would be."

Senna closed her eyes and rested the back of her head against the crumbling wall. Where were Kaen and his family? What about his sister, Ciara?

"They still might be alive," Reden said as if reading her mind.

Senna straightened to find him staring at her. "You knew," she said softly. "You knew when you joined us that our curse would do this to your land."

Reden hesitated before giving a curt nod. "I did."

"Then why? Why did you help us?"

He studied the landscape beyond the door, no doubt comparing the desolation to the bursting life that had existed mere months ago. "Higher law, Senna. If the Witches died, there wouldn't be anyone to control nature. And eventually everything would die."

He'd traded his homeland for the world. He had more courage than she did. "We didn't have to curse the land, forbid the storms, stop the seeds from germinating," she said.

"You had to weaken Tarten and more importantly, Grendi, or she would have destroyed you." He said it with so little feeling.

It was such a vivid contrast to Senna, who felt like she was drowning in emotions. She stepped past Reden, back into the stagnant sunlight. "Well then, I think it's weak enough. It's time I did something about it."

From his position as lookout, Cord twisted in the saddle to shoot her a look of disbelief. "I thought you needed a whole choir for something like that."

"She does," Mistin said softly.

Senna winced. She still didn't understand what was happening to her—why she'd grown stronger since consuming Espen's song. So much stronger. Why the night they'd escaped from the island her song alone had been as strong as a hundred Witches'. Or why that power had since abandoned her. "I'll do what I can."

Mistin nodded. "I'll help you."

Cord shifted the horse's reins from one hand to another and didn't answer.

Reden studied her. "You go airborne and everyone within five leagues will see you."

"I know." Senna twisted around, searching for anything resembling a circle of trees. There was nothing. And even if she could, she didn't know how to sing one into existence. Their song wouldn't be as effective without one, but it would have to do.

She listened to the music, or rather the lack thereof. But the Four Sisters were hurting, which meant they were here, cowering from the death and destruction that had been forced upon them. Senna hummed, trying to coax them out. And like wounded animals, they came.

Tipping back her head, she sang in a commanding voice, with Mistin accompanying her.

Wind lift me high,
That my song reach to'rds the sky.

They repeated the song until the wind tugged Senna upward. She needed it to funnel her words up and out. Her skirt swirled around her legs, and she grew lighter. The wind twisted her hair skyward until she thought it must look like a golden candle flame.

She dug deep, searching for the power that had been there before. There. A little pulse of it. To her surprise, her feet left the ground. When she was high enough to see across the tops of the rounded mountains, she switched songs.

I revoke from this land the Witches' decree,
That all storms and plants shall cease to be.
Come to me, storms, gently dampen the earth.
Seeds swell with water to rekindle rebirth.

She sang the song over and over, hoping the Witches in Haven wouldn't notice the decree had been partially lifted. If they did, even from across the ocean, their songs would countermand her own.

When the wind had set her down and left her, she closed her eyes and probed the Four Sisters—Earth, Water, Plants, and Sunlight—with her mind. To her relief, the land no longer felt hollow. She felt a breeze on her skin and the presence of water and plants again. Not as strong as it should be—more like a sluggish resurrection than a full revival. But where there had been only a void, there was now something.

The decree had been partially removed. "It's not right that so much depends on something as fickle as mankind," Senna commented.

"You were able to tap into that power again," Reden said.

All of them stared at her in wonder—staring at her as if she were something more. She sighed. "Not as strong as when I was on the island though. If it had been, I could have restored the land instead of just lifting the curse."

"It was a hundred times more powerful than it should have been," Mistin said.

"Senna," Joshen called as he jogged towards her.

Glad for the change of subject, she looked at him. "Was there a note?"

Nodding, he stopped to catch his breath. "They've gone. We can only hope they're still alive."

Senna let him steer her towards her butter-colored gelding. "What did it say?"

Joshen handed her the brittle parchment. She carefully unfolded it and read Kaen's scratchy handwriting.

My network spies say the Witches have cursed Tarten. That the rains will not come nor the seeds take root. From the way everything is dying, I believe them. We are taking what we can— including the two horses you left—and heading seaward. If nothing else, the ocean should provide fish. From there, we travel north. I'll try to convince the Witch Friends and any I meet to come with us.

Be warned. My spies say the Tarten government is angrier than ever. They are planning retribution. I wish I knew more.

There's nothing for us here. Nothing for anyone.

May the Creators protect us.

The note wasn't signed.

Senna opened her fingers, letting it drift down to decay with everything else. The Creators wouldn't be protecting anyone. They'd given mankind the Witches. If mankind rejected that gift, the Creators wouldn't believe them worth saving.

"Our old horses are alive." Joshen met her gaze, and she knew they were sharing the same memory. All those months ago, when Senna had arrived at Joshen's horse ranch with the Witch Hunters on her heels. He'd sold her the first horse she'd ever owned— Knight. And then he'd followed her across two continents and an ocean to confront the Witch who had defeated all others.

He was still following her.

Senna gave him a small smile. Holding onto those bright memories in this wasted land, she swung onto Sunny's back.

Mistin and Cord galloped out. She wanted to shout for them to stay—she wasn't ready to go yet. But they couldn't linger.

"Come on, Senna," Joshen said. "Any Tarten within a league and a half heard that song. Let's go."

Sunny pranced beneath her. He was an obstinate horse, always looking for ways to outsmart his rider. It made her miss the careful mount Knight had been. She released the tension on the reins. Sunny's muscles bunched beneath her as he galloped after the others.

Reden turned back to make sure they were coming. She didn't meet his gaze again. She didn't think she could.

When they reached the road running parallel to the ocean, Senna saw a dark smudge of clouds in the distance. The rains were finally coming.

"This road will be a mud trap if we don't beat that storm," Reden warned them.

Senna was so focused on the storm coming over the ocean that she nearly fell off when Sunny slid to a stop. Fortunately, horsemanship was another skill she'd improved on.

Reden had pulled up short. Cord and Mistin were pounding back to them. "Soldiers!"

Eating up the distance behind them were at least a dozen red-coated Tartens.

Joshen's horse bumped into Senna's. He cursed.

"They're between us and our ship." Reden seemed to take the fact as a personal insult.

Senna reached inside her seed belt.

Reden backed his sorrel into Sunny. "No, Senna. We have to run."

She looked at him incredulously. "There aren't that many of them. I can keep them at bay."

Reden pulled his musket from its holster. "The only reason they haven't opened fire yet is because they want to keep us from the ship—"

"Until their reinforcements come," Joshen finished for him.

"Back inland," Mistin cried as she reached them. "They'll follow us around the mountain and be forced behind us." She turned her horse and didn't look back to see if they followed.

"It's a good plan," Cord said as he chased after Mistin.

Joshen set his jaw. "Their horses are fresh. Ours are nearly done in!"

"You have something better in mind?" Reden asked. When Joshen didn't answer, Reden took off after Cord.

After a moment's hesitation, Senna followed them. And of course, Joshen followed her.

22. SHATTERED

Two months ago, this stretch of jungle would have been impassable. But now most everything crumbled to dust or shattered like glass when their horses' hooves touched it. Senna wanted to fall behind, work some seeds into the ground, but she had to concentrate on not being swept from the saddle by dead tree limbs.

She heard the soldiers crashing behind them, coming closer with each of her wearied horse's faltering strides.

She had to do something! She snatched one of the potion vials she'd stolen from Prenny's secret cupboard and tossed the contents into the air.

Senna knew the moment the Tarten soldiers passed through the powder. Hacking coughs of men and horses erupted behind them. It might buy a little time.

"Senna!" Joshen shouted.

She whipped around to see a low branch right in front of her. She flattened herself across Sunny's mane. The branch raked across her back. She gasped in pain.

Finally, they rounded the mountain and started back towards the sea. Sunny plunged into the slimy remnants of a stream that stank of dead fish. They followed the riverbed all the way to the sea and climbed the banks. Sunny floundered in the sand, sinking up to his forelegs. The ocean must be close.

As soon as they reached the beach, Senna took Kine seeds from her belt. Standing in the stirrups, she tossed them skyward and sang the wind to fan them out behind her. Then her song changed into something dark and dangerous.

> Kine with biting leaves,
> Flesh and blood and bone to seize.

Trusting Sunny to follow the others, she looked over her shoulder as leaves like razors sprouted along the seashore—the plants were a cross between coral and cactus. She sang until she was out of range, then pulled her horse to a stop. Sunny fought her—he didn't like being left by the others. Keeping a firm hold on the reins, Senna jumped from the saddle.

Unable to slow his horse fast enough, Joshen shot past her. "Senna, you can't stop!"

She frantically dug in the sand and shoved the barrier seed into the ground. The soldiers were pounding up the shore behind them. Joshen didn't know they'd hit her Kine shortly, and she didn't have time to inform him. She started singing again.

> Oh barrier tree, I sing to thee.
> Stop the men who come for me.

Rounding back to her, Joshen leapt from the saddle. He grabbed her arms from behind and steered her towards Sunny. She didn't stop singing. The seed was a full-blown sapling now. Joshen had just managed to shove her foot into the stirrup when the screams started.

But it wasn't the Tarten soldiers screaming. It was their horses. The momentum of the chase had carried the six or so remaining soldiers into the midst of the Kine before the horses had stumbled to a stop. The soldiers were trying to force the horses out. Some were obeying, frantically scrambling, blood running down their forelegs, their hooves shredded. Others were frozen in place, their whole bodies quivering with pain and fear.

Their screams were almost worse than men's screams. The animals were innocent. And Senna was ruining them.

Joshen let out a cry of protest. It took every ounce of determination Senna had to keep singing. As the shade of the barrier tree slowly grew over them, they witnessed the chaos she'd created.

One of the Tartens shouted orders. Abandoning the horses, the soldiers moved carefully around the Kine. To escape, they'd have to skirt into the jungle. And when they came out, the barrier tree would await them.

Senna had bought herself and her friends enough time to load into the boats without being under fire from the Tartens.

The tree was full grown. Senna stopped fighting Joshen and let herself be hauled into the saddle. They took off down the shore. A little bit farther and they found the *Sea Witch* anchored in a cove.

Captain Parknel's waiting sailors took the horses, blindfolded them, and started fighting them into one of the five boats—one for each of the horses—and a smaller, faster vessel for Senna and two of her Guardians. A handful of Barbus seeds in her hand, Senna started off to create a perimeter of plants around them.

She heard running footsteps from behind. Joshen snatched her hand and dragged her towards the boats. "Joshen, I can plant the Barbus! It'll keep the sailors safe."

"No time! They'll be around the first barrier tree before you can even get the seeds in the ground." He picked her up and swung her into the boat.

"Reden!" she cried.

He took up a position beside the boat. The other sailors spread out around him. "We're almost off anyway."

He was right. Mistin's group was already rowing for the *Sea Witch*. Two others weren't far behind. That only left two boats on shore—Senna's and the craft meant to carry Sunny. The sailors were struggling to get him inside. All four of his feet were stubbornly planted, as he refused to get in the boat. Two men linked arms behind his rump, while two more lifted a front leg over the sides.

Joshen grunted. "If the two of you hadn't been so stubborn, we'd be off already."

She ignored him. They were going to make it. That's what mattered.

Sailors shoved Senna's craft towards the ocean. The gritty sand scratched the bottom before they dropped in the water. They drifted while the sailors jumped in and pulled out their oars.

Senna startled at the sound of musket fire. Like blood pulsing from an open wound, dozens of soldiers on horseback broke from the dead jungle. Senna didn't have time to wonder where they'd come from. Balls whistled through the air and hit their boat with a thunk. She ducked as splinters exploded around her. Water poured through the holes.

Soldiers splashed into the water. The sailors and her Guardians aimed their muskets and fired.

Senna had potions and songs, but they would hurt her friends as much as her enemy. She moved before fear could change her mind, grabbing one of the heavy muskets. She swung it up and aimed for a soldier looming over them. But a cry made her look past him.

Soldiers had swarmed Cord's vessel. A soldier lifted his knife to draw it across Cord's neck. Holding her breath, Senna adjusted her aim and squeezed the trigger gently. The musket bucked in her hands, throwing her back.

The soldier fighting Cord staggered backward before falling into the water and sinking. Cord gaped at Senna for a split second before leaping into the boat.

There wasn't time to process what she'd done. Soldiers were all around them. The sailors fought them off with bayonets. Senna reached for her ball and powder.

From behind, hands snatched her, hauling her away from the boat. Joshen shouted and thrust his bayonet up, but the soldier was already out of reach.

Reden grabbed her legs and braced his feet against the boat.

Stretching forward, Senna grabbed one of the pistols from Reden's holster, aimed it blindly at the man behind her, and fired. Suddenly she was free, and Reden dragged her back into the boat.

Muskets fired and one of the Tartens fell from his horse. Still in Reden's arms, Senna saw Mistin standing steady, a musket in her hands, blue smoke dissipating in the rising wind

The other boats started firing on the Tartens. A moment later, the sailors with her opened fire. A handful of sailors abandoned the fight to start rowing. Though their boat was rapidly filling with water, they finally made it out of range.

Shaking, Senna grabbed another pistol. While loading it, she checked Cord's boat. They were rowing for the *Sea Witch*. The Tarten soldiers were firing their muskets, but they were too far away to do much good.

They were safe.

The gun slipped from her fingers and fell with a splash into the water rapidly filling the bottom of the boat.

"Senna—" Joshen began.

"Just row!" She shook so badly she could barely stay upright. Three men in the boat were wounded. Her mind numb, she started tending to them.

It started to rain. The water seeped through her hair before dripping down her face.

One of the men was bleeding out. She pressed a cloth to the wound in his side, but the blood soaked through it. His eyes locked with hers before slowly going unfocused.

Their boat bumped into something. Senna looked up to find herself in the *Sea Witch's* shadow. Dark clouds had finally reached shore. Sailors attached ropes to the boat and began pulling it up.

She felt a hand on her arm, easing her to her feet. "I'm sorry, Senna." Joshen helped her onto the deck of the *Sea Witch*. He wet a cloth and gently wiped her face. "There was nothing you could have done."

She shook her head. She'd been in battles before, but never this brutal, where she'd had to kill a man point blank, where another man had died in her arms.

By this time, most of the other boats had reached the ship. The sailors had managed to load Sunny, his legs splayed skyward. The remaining crew had already loaded the stern cannon and aimed it for the Tarten soldiers, who were staring up at the sky as the rain ran down their faces.

Four sailors were dead. A dozen more were injured. In one of the officer's cabins, Senna treated them with her plants. They thanked her almost reverently. She had to turn away so they wouldn't see the frustration on her face. They had risked dying just to save that stupid horse. Joshen caught her gaze and chided her with a look. She turned back to the men and thanked them profusely for saving Sunny.

She turned to disappear into her cabin, but Cord blocked her way. "Can you help me with this?"

She cringed at the sight of blood spilling from his collarbone down his open shirt. She gestured for him to follow her inside. "Lie down."

He was lucky. If the knife had gone much higher, his throat would have been slit. After giving him some whiskey, Senna washed the wound with salt water and numbed it with some herbs before sewing it as neatly as she could. More herbs for swelling, heat, and infection. Then she covered the wound with clean bandages.

She was proud of herself for not even hesitating on the first stitch; she was getting better at treating injured men. She mixed some tea to speed their healing. While it heated she took a blanket and dried her hair with it.

Cord watched her in silence. "You saved my life."

She shrugged, then set down the blanket and checked the tea. "Your cut wasn't *that* deep."

He chuckled then winced, his hand straying to his wound. "Not for patching me up. When you killed that soldier."

The porcelain lid Senna was holding slipped from her fingers and shattered on the floor. She stared at the pieces, knowing she could never put them back together. A sob burst from deep inside her. She clapped her hand over her mouth to stifle it. She would not cry. She was done with tears.

"He would have killed me. Still managed to cut me good as he fell." Cord stared at the wall. "Killing a man, it changes you inside."

She saw everything in perfect detail. The man slowly falling into the surf. The smell of gun smoke. The soldier that tried to take her...she could feel the bruises forming where he'd gripped her.

Cord shook his head, his dark hair brushing his shoulders. "Some of them stand out more than others."

Senna was glad he wasn't trying to pretend like it was all right.

Cord turned to her, and as he watched her the burning intensity in his eyes surprised her. "Don't look into their eyes," he said. "Don't watch them die. Don't think about them at all. You understand?"

She met his gaze. "It hurts," she said pleadingly.

"It's supposed to. But the less you have to remember, the less those memories will torment you later."

She tucked her hair behind her ears and nodded.

"You'll be all right. Witches might be more subtle than a soldier with a musket, but they're just as deadly."

She watched the storm, water crashing against water. Chaos, and yet order at the same time.

Reden came through the open door. He cringed as he sat in one of the chairs, a haunted expression on his face. "Stop blaming yourself, Senna. In a war, people die."

"Am I really that transparent?" she wondered aloud.

He took the same blanket she'd used on her hair and dried his face. "Not to everybody."

Cord laughed. "Just to her Guardians."

Joshen chose that moment to come in. "You're not her Guardian." His gaze met Senna's. "I need your help with one of the horses. Bring your herbs." He turned and hurried back the way he'd come.

She hustled after him. When they reached the horses, Joshen took one of Sunny's hooves between his knees and looked up at her.

"He bruised his frog."

Senna frowned. "His what?"

Joshen let the horse's leg down. "The inside of his hoof, the soft part."

"Can he still be ridden?"

"We don't have much of a choice, do we?" Joshen pursed his lips, clearly unhappy about it.

Senna watched him, knowing how much it hurt him to push his horses so hard, and that this wasn't the first time he'd been forced to risk them for her.

"Can you make a poultice for him?" Joshen asked. "Something to draw out the pain and swelling?"

"Of course."

"Bring it to me when you're done?"

She nodded.

Joshen grunted and moved away from the horses—away from her. "I need to refill my musket powder and balls. I'll be back."

She watched him walk away. "You're angry."

Partway up the stairs, he paused. "Yes. But not with you. That was too close." He ran his hands through his hair. "You don't know what it's like, knowing danger is coming for you. And I have to stand between you and that danger, not knowing if I'm strong enough to keep you safe."

It was hard to watch him leave, but she couldn't think of anything to say that would make it better. Back in her cabin, she created a poultice for Sunny before turning to the one thing that would ease the ache inside her. Drawing her cloak against the rain, she went to the bow and sang a wind to life.

They rounded a shoulder of land and passed numerous islands. She caught her first sight of people. Even at this distance, she saw their want as they slogged through the wet sand.

A few more hours, and she recognized the bay around Tarten's capitol, Carpel. There was nothing left of the city but the bones of a few buildings sticking out of the earth like an exposed graveyard. It made her heartsick.

23. DARK WITCH

In the gray light of predawn, Senna studied the city of Zaen as the ship sailed into the bay. Memories rose within her, memories that made her pull her cloak close though it was already turning warm.

Joshen squinted at the abandoned city. "We should wait until we can scout it out."

Time grew short, Senna felt it like an itch under her skin. Even though the Witches in Haven had turned their backs on her, she wouldn't do the same to them. "We should go. Now."

His arms crossed over his chest, Reden studied the landscape. "They'll send ships after us. We might be better off getting in and out before they catch up."

Captain Parknel puffed on his pipe. "And if they find us in this bay, they'll block us in."

Cord glanced at the sky. "I vote we scout it out."

"You can't hear what I hear, feel what I feel." Senna closed her eyes and attuned herself to the Four Sisters. "It's like my body is a harp, and the Four Sisters are plucking my strings. The song they're playing is one of fear and desperation. Already, it might be too late to save Haven."

"We can't help them if we're dead." Joshen reached for her hand. She took it wordlessly.

Reden was silent a moment more before he said, "Captain, if you'll send some sailors out to secure the landing. Mistin and Cord, you'll start scouting immediately."

Parknel's teeth ground against his pipe. "All right, let's bring her into port." He started up to the wheel. "All hands man the riggin'! Muskets and cannons at the ready! Keep a sharp eye out, boys!"

Sailors scrambled to tie off the ropes as they docked. The horses were brought up and led down the gangplank. Senna heard the rush of hoofbeats on the wooden planking as Mistin and Cord led their horses into the city. The Witch and the Guardian were armed with as many weapons and shot as they could carry. Led by Reden, sailors spread out to check the area.

Her every muscle tense, Senna waited with Joshen. He cleared his throat. "I want you to know that I'm done fighting this."

She studied his profile, the bulging muscles in his jaw. "This has been hard for me," he went on. "So much harder and asking so much more than I was willing to give. But I understand now. In fighting *for* you, I was fighting *against* you. I'm pushing..." He broke off and cleared his throat. "I'm pushing you away. The very thing I'm afraid of is the thing I'm forcing you towards. I won't do that anymore."

Her voice thick, Senna whispered, "Thank you."

He nodded once. His fingers brushed her collarbone as he picked up the ring she wore next to her pendant. "We're not in Haven anymore. You could wear it."

The warmth of his touch spread through her. "Yes, I can."

A question in his eyes, he reached to undo the cord. Pulling her hair over her shoulder, she turned around. He slid the ring free and held it out to her. She slipped it on her finger.

He smiled that smile that sent her insides soaring—the smile where the skin around his eyes and above his brow wrinkled. The one she'd waited so long to see. Leaning forward, she rested in his embrace.

She realized home wasn't a place. It was here, safe in his arms. As long as she had this, everything would be all right.

Far too soon, a sailor stood at the end of the pier and gave the signal for the all-clear.

Captain Parknel walked beside Senna down the gangplank. "You sure you don't want the rest of us to come?"

She shook her head. "You don't have horses. We'll move faster without you." She squinted up at him. "You'll be all right waiting here?"

He tapped the side of his nose. "I have a few tricks up my sleeve. I haven't made it this long as a captain for nothing."

Feeling eyes on her, Senna turned to find the crew watching her. Parknel nodded a solemn goodbye as he turned back to his ship. A knot of anxiety hardened in her stomach. "We'll be back before they know we're here," she called to him.

He nodded, but she got the feeling he didn't quite believe her.

She and Joshen trotted down the pier, towards Reden and the horses.

By the time their group finally reached the stone streets, Cord was waiting for them. "Mistin has scouted out a half league ahead, just like last time," he said. "She'll relay to me, and I to her. That way we can cover twice the distance. If you hear gunshots, you'll know there's trouble."

Regretting her breakfast of travel bread and salt pork, Senna swallowed several times. "And if there's trouble? What are we going to do?"

"We get out," Reden said.

Circumventing the city wall, they bypassed homes built on the rounded mountain. Even though it had only been a few months since the curse, hovels were already falling in on themselves. Sunny limped slightly, especially when they traversed rocky ground.

The small group crossed into forest bleached white by the unrelenting sun. Suddenly, Sunny shied. Senna held tight to the reins as he reared, his eyes rolling in fright. She gripped his mane so hard her fingers ached. Reden leveled his musket at something behind her. Smoke and burning powder shot from the barrel.

An inhuman scream split the night. Joshen swore.

Sunny bolted, his body bunching and then lengthening beneath her. It took all Senna's skill to pull him to a halt. Still he fought, shaking his head like a fish fighting to be free of a line. She looked back at the others. A great black jaguar staggered from the trees, a yowl passing its lips. Hip bones pushed sharply against its dull coat. Its chest was bloody, but still it came on.

Joshen lowered his musket and fired. The cat fell soundlessly. It seemed smaller just lying there—pitiful, even. How desperate must it have been for food to come after them?

"Anyone within a league heard those shots," Reden growled, as the men reloaded swiftly.

Senna watched the dark shape of the cat until it was out of sight.

Not long after, Cord came galloping back. When he learned the shots were for a jaguar, he grunted. "I'll let Mistin know not to worry. Not much farther now."

They passed through two great mountains as morning gave way to midday. They caught up with Cord and Mistin at the Tangles Trees—a nearly impenetrable barrier of bush-like trees that surrounded Espen's domain. They were mostly dead now, so Senna's song couldn't help them past it. Instead, they had to hack their way through. Senna was covered in welts and scrapes by the time they emerged into the sunlight.

Not long after that, they entered a clearing now devoid of trees. Reden, Cord, and Mistin spread out to check the area. The air was thick and heavy to breathe—another storm was coming; Senna could taste it. When she caught sight of Espen's tree, dread filled her all the way to her fingertips.

Joshen reached over and took her hand. Their eyes met and wordless understanding passed between them. They'd both faced death here.

After dismounting, Senna led her horse forward. Side by side, she and Joshen walked through the clearing and came to stand before the great tree.

It was worse than her last dream. Flakes of bark had fallen off, leaving bald spots. Most of the leaves were gone now. Those that did remain had rusty edges and crusty boils across their surface.

Senna found the bare patch of ground—the same one Espen had written in before—and waited. But the branches trailed listlessly in the wind, and silence filled the air. Were they too late?

"Espen?"

The tree shifted sluggishly before straightening. Leaves fell like scales shed from a lizard as Espen reached forward to scratch in the dirt, "Too late."

Senna clenched her fists to her side. "Too late for what? Stop your foolish games and tell me!"

Espen brushed it smooth again. "Too late save Haven. Calden comes."

All blood drained from Senna's face and pooled in her feet. She steadied herself against Joshen. "Calden? But they were destroyed when the Haven Witches fought them. Surely only a few survived."

The branch Espen wrote with snapped. She continued with the broken tip as if she hadn't noticed or didn't care. "Calden not destroyed."

How could this be? All anyone had found were a few pollywogs where Calden had been. "What do you mean?"

"Haven not only island that moves."

Calden was an *island?* "How do I know you're telling the truth?"

"You know."

Senna did know. The Four Sisters were singing their song, and it was one of foreboding. "When?" she asked.

"Soon."

If the entire island of Calden had survived, how many thousands of Witches must there be centuries later? Senna shook down to her bones. "Where are they?"

"Place of storms," Espen wrote in the dirt.

What did that mean? Senna's hand found Joshen's. "And what's happening to me? Why is it I'm nearly as strong as a full choir?"

Espen's branches quivered, and Senna realized the Dark Witch was laughing. "Don't realize" Espen wrote.

Senna clenched her teeth. "What? What don't I realize?"

"Lilette—" The branch clawed a slash into the ground before going limp.

The last of the leaves fell gently to the ground. "Espen?" There was no answer. Senna took a step forward, grasped the branch and listened for music, but there was only silence.

The Dark Witch was dead, and Senna hadn't even had to kill her. She wiped the blight off her hand.

"Senna?"

She whirled around to see a hunched-over old woman coming past Reden. Joshen started to raise his musket.

"Still afraid of old Desni, I see."

Senna stumbled forward with a cry. "You're alive."

She reached out and took hold of Senna. "You should not have come."

"The others—Kaen, Ciara—are they all right?"

Desni nodded. "They're traveling along the coast until they leave the cursed lands."

All the breath went out of Senna. "But then why are you still here?"

The woman pulled her back the way she'd come. Joshen marched beside her, his eyes alert.

"I'm old and I'm tired," Desni said. "I don't want to fight anymore. I came back to my forest—to the hill my home still sits upon. When I saw the ships full of soldiers coming from the north and heard gunshots coming from this evil place, I knew it had to be you."

Ships full of soldiers? That had to be Tartens, and Parknel was in the bay. By the Creators, were they already too late?

Reden barked out orders. "Mistin, ride ahead. See if the ship is under attack. If not, find some way to warn them. If it is, ride back to us."

As Mistin rode away, Senna gripped the old woman's hands, so fragile they felt like bird bones. Her heart was thumping in her chest, but she couldn't go without telling Desni the truth. "Your daughter, Tiena—she died."

Something in Desni crumbled before Senna's eyes, a stark contrast to the old woman's joy of being reunited with her daughter after Espen's dark songs had forced them apart for decades. "How?"

Senna tried to block out the pain. "She was shot during our escape from Tarten. We buried her at sea."

Desni closed her eyes. "So even the comfort of visiting her grave is denied me."

Joshen leaned low and spoke in Senna's ear. "We have to go."

Desni pushed her towards where Reden held their horses. "Get her out of here. They're hunting her."

Senna swung into the saddle. "Come with us."

The old woman's smile was full of sadness. "No. I will stay to welcome the end."

Reden pushed his horse into Senna's, forcing her back the way they'd come. "How many, how soon?"

"Run," Desni said quietly. "Swift as water runs from the sky."

They turned the horses eastward, Reden in the lead, Joshen bringing up the rear. Their horses were already exhausted, but they pushed them harder. Sweaty foam had built up around Sunny's saddle blanket. His limp was worse. They only had to maneuver around one more mountain before they descended into Zaen.

So close, but the beat of the Four Sister's music pounded out a savage beat. "We're not going to make it."

Though Senna whispered, Joshen heard her. He slapped his horse's rump with the ends of his reins and rode up beside her. "What? What can you feel?"

She turned her fearful eyes on him. "Something bad."

Sunny turned his head back. His nostrils were flared so wide Senna saw the red deep inside. Every vein on his face stood out.

"We have to stop. The horses are no good to us dead," Joshen shouted to Reden.

Reluctantly, Reden eased his horse to a stop and dismounted. "We run beside them."

They jogged on until the heat wrung sweat from Senna's skin.

Cord came galloping back. "We're too late! The way back to the ship is blocked."

"Where's Mistin?" She should have seen them first and come back to warn them. She should be with Cord.

He shook his head. "I don't know."

By the Creators, Senna had insisted they continue. She steadied herself against Sunny's sweaty shoulder. Pushing her worry aside, she focused on the task at hand.

The mountain obstructed most of Senna's view of the ocean. She started to cross the distance. Over the sound of her heart pounding in her ears, she heard the distant boom of cannon fire.

"Senna—" Joshen reached for her. She glanced back at him, and something in her eyes made him drop his hand. "We can't help them."

She grunted. "You forget. You have a Creator-touched with you. *I* can help them."

Joshen and Reden exchanged glances.

"Are you sure?" Reden asked.

She nodded.

"No! Tartens have no mercy for Witches—especially this Witch!" Cord said as he pointed at her. "We have to get her as far away from here as possible. Now!"

Joshen snorted. "Have you ever tried making her do something she doesn't want to? I wouldn't recommend it." He smiled sadly at Senna. "We can try. If you promise to follow Reden's orders."

She nodded eagerly. "I promise."

Cord cursed them under his breath.

Senna climbed back into the saddle and urged Sunny around the mountain. Their view of the sea opened up. Two ships hemmed the *Sea Witch* in. Senna jumped as cannons fired from both ships.

Before her disbelieving eyes, the *Sea Witch* turned into the wind. But that was impossible. Sailing ships couldn't move against the wind. "What—"

Reden pointed to the shore. "They've mounted pulleys to the sides of the ship and anchored them to the shore. They use the ropes to pull them at the angles they need to fire at the other ship."

Senna watched as the *Sea Witch* fired at one of the other ships before pulling hard to the side and firing at the other.

"Parknel does have some tricks up his sleeve." She felt a strange sort of pride in the red-haired captain. It was amazing to watch, but she was distracted from the spectacle by red-orange bursts of musket fire on shore. Sailors had dug in around the pulleys and were defending them from Tarten soldiers.

"Come on." Senna kicked Sunny. He lunged before twisting around. Why wasn't he moving? Then she saw Joshen's hand clamped on the bit. "No closer."

She kicked her horse. The animal spun in a circle, clearly confused and frightened.

Reden snatched the other side of the bridle. They hemmed her in like the ships below hemmed in the *Sea Witch*. "We're outnumbered a dozen to one. You go down there and they'll capture you."

She opened her mouth to argue. Didn't they understand she needed to be closer than this for the sea to hear her song? But then she remembered her promise to listen to her Guardians.

She would just have to do the best she could and hope her song was strong enough to save them. After kicking her foot out of the stirrup, she dropped from the saddle. "No sign of Mistin? She could help with this."

Cord ground his teeth. "I already told you, I don't know."

Part of Senna realized how Desni must have felt. If this was the end, then she would see it through to the last. Senna hiked up the mountain and climbed onto a rocky outcropping. "This will take an incredible amount of control. You can't break my concentration."

Cord, Joshen, and Reden were already stocking the ground with muskets and powder horns. Following their lead, Senna loaded the pistol Joshen had given her and stowed it carefully so as not to spill the powder.

Reden settled in, his eyes scanning the dead jungle for signs of their enemy. "If I give the word, you get back on your horse and run for it. You have to agree to this."

Senna nodded.

Joshen bit off the cork on his horn and filled his frizzen with powder. "I have a bad feeling about this."

Senna spread her arms, listening to the Four Sisters' sluggish songs. She hummed, changing the threads of music. The Four Sisters grew stronger as her song did. She didn't call for the wind to lift her—she didn't want to be that obvious of a target.

Instead, she sang for two enormous waves to rise up on both sides of the *Sea Witch*. The Tarten ships slid away from her friends. She changed her song to the winds. Their sails filled, pulling them away. Men scrambled up the rigging, tying up the sails, but not before Senna had managed to move them out of the line of fire of the *Sea Witch*.

With a pang, she realized it wasn't enough. The ships were already moving back to reengage the *Sea Witch*. And in the distance, more ships rounded the shoulders of the bay.

The *Sea Witch* was safe, at least for the moment. Senna turned her attention to the men fighting on the shore. She had the wind channel a song towards them, warning them to be prepared to flee for the ship.

Focusing on a cluster of men wearing red uniforms, she listened to earth song. Using every ounce of her concentration, she manipulated the song, building up a pocket of energy directly below them. The energy naturally wanted to dissipate, ripple outward. She held it tight, keeping it packed. When she couldn't hold it another moment, she stopped singing. Men and earth flew everywhere.

The sailors abandoned the ropes, scrambling into boats on the shore. They fought their way free and rowed for their lives. Senna kept the soldiers and the ships out of range until they were climbing the rungs.

She started singing again, bending the music until it matched her. She channeled a strong gust of wind at the *Sea Witch*. It shot between the other two ships, gaining speed by the second.

She was so far away, she couldn't be sure, but she thought she saw a man at the stern. And somehow, she knew it was Parknel. They both knew that by moving him to safety, she was cutting off her line of retreat. But if he was any kind of fighter at all, he'd realize their escape had already been cut off by the soldiers on shore and the other Tarten ships.

Reden had said sometimes soldiers had to be left behind to save the majority. Unfortunately, Senna, Mistin, and her two Guardians were the ones who had to be left behind.

Senna locked the song into place so strongly she knew it wouldn't stop until they were nearly to Nefalie. There was no way a Tarten ship could stop them.

Breathless, she shook away the dizziness threatening to pull her under. She stepped to the edge of the boulder. "All right, let's go." She gathered herself to drop down just as everything exploded around her.

She came around on the ground, her ears ringing. Cord was shouting at someone as he dragged her back toward the terrified horses.

"What happened?" she asked.

Cord cast a worried look her way. "Cannon shot the boulder out from under you."

Joshen and Reden fired at Tarten soldiers who were impossibly close.

"Where did they come from?" she cried.

Cord relentlessly dragged her forward. "Rushed us just after the cannon fired. Must have broken away from the main group and crept closer to us as soon as they heard you singing."

Joshen and Reden shot and retreated, then shot and retreated again. Both were loading their muskets when another soldier leveled his gun at Reden. Senna screamed.

Out of nowhere, Mistin leapt from the trees, lifted her musket and fired. The soldier toppled backward.

"Mistin, you're alive!" Senna cried out.

After dropping the empty musket, Mistin emptied both her pistols and shoved them back in her holsters. All three of her guns were empty now. Senna expected her to come back to the horses, but instead, she reached in her shirt. Her motions blurred as she threw a knife. With uncanny accuracy, she cut down the soldiers advancing on Reden and Joshen.

Senna blinked at her friend in shock.

"Get on!" Cord hefted Senna onto the saddle.

She fumbled for the stirrups. Suddenly dizzy, she swayed and grabbed the saddle horn to steady herself.

Under Mistin's furious assault, the Tartens fell back enough for Joshen and Reden to turn and sprint toward Senna, Mistin, and Cord.

"Go!" Reden shouted at Mistin, who had been steadily pressing forward.

She threw another knife before dashing back. She swept up her discarded musket and launched herself into the saddle.

Senna let out a breath she hadn't known she'd been holding. They were going to make it.

And then her hopes shattered around her feet. Soldiers burst from the trees between Senna and her Guardians, cutting off their escape.

Reden and Joshen fought with their bayonets, but they were forced back, towards the first group of soldiers. They were outnumbered two dozen to one.

For half a heartbeat, Joshen's gaze met hers. She could see the realization in his eyes, and she knew. He and Reden were trapped. She dug deep, searching for the power she'd held only moments before, but it had abandoned her. She couldn't sing anything to stop the soldiers—not without hurting Joshen and Reden, too.

Mistin threw a knife, saving Reden's life. "I only have one left." She started loading a pistol.

Cord fired his musket. Half of the second group of soldiers turned and sprinted for them.

"Run, Senna, run!" Reden shouted as he blocked a bayonet stabbing at him.

Senna couldn't move, couldn't take her eyes off Joshen.

"Senna! You promised!" Joshen shouted, grief already tingeing his voice.

Yes. She'd promised that if they both asked her, she would obey. Horror shot through her, burning away all feeling until she was dead inside. "I can't."

Cord reached over and slapped Sunny's rump. "Move!"

Sunny lunged forward with lightning speed. Senna looked back. The last thing she saw was Joshen grunting in pain, his eyes rolling up, before he fell to the ground amid coats of red.

Senna screamed. The Four Sisters were so in tune with her they reacted. The world trembled.

24. Earth Song

Collapsing on the hard dirt, Senna buried her face in her palms. Was Joshen's life the price she would pay for her recklessness?

With a grimace, Cord pulled his shirt over his head. Mistin murmured softly while she examined the splinters sticking out of his back like quills. She pulled them out one by one. Cord winced and grunted each time. Gently, Mistin poured water over the wounds and washed away the blood.

Senna stared. She'd never seen Mistin hold a knife, but the girl's hands had launched several with unerring accuracy. Knives she'd had hidden all over her body. That kind of ease only came from hundreds of hours of practice.

Without warning, a memory washed over Senna like a wave of icy water. An attacker, standing over her and throwing a knife at Reden, a knife that had cut his arm.

Senna's breath came in short gasps. Her gaze swung to Cord. Scars riddled his body. It was so much like Reden's body—more like the body of a career soldier than of an untrained but hopeful Guardian. One scar seemed fresher than the others. It was puckered and purple, newly healed.

She remembered a man chasing her on a moonless night. The gag, so tight it had made her lips crack. Her hand shoving the shard of glass into his guts. Hot blood washing over her skin.

Mistin's voice was a deep alto, easy to mistake for a tenor. Cord's voice was a bass.

With shaking hands, Senna primed her pistol. When she looked up, Cord was watching her, his expression wary.

Numb, she rose to her feet. "It was you."

Mistin glanced up. Some of her long black hair had come loose and partially covered her face. She looked so young, so innocent. How could she have done this?

"It was you two I overheard that night at the tree house. You who attacked me." She pointed a shaking finger at the wound on Cord's side. "And you I stabbed."

Silent, he and Mistin rose to their feet.

It shocked her that they didn't deny it. "Why?" It came out as more of an accusation than a question.

Cord held up his hands. "We never meant to hurt you."

He had an accent now. She'd heard it before—furtive whispers in the night. She reached towards the nearly healed bruise on her head. "So the stone wasn't supposed to knock me unconscious?"

His hand fell. "Well, yes, but we couldn't very well let you sing, now could we?"

"Why?" Her voice betrayed so much hurt Senna wished she could pull the word back into her mouth.

Mistin held very still, as if afraid any sudden movement might scare Senna off. "We were trying to save your life." Her accent had surfaced just as Cord's had.

Senna laughed, but there was no humor in it. She aimed her pistol at Cord's heart.

He studied the gun before his gaze met hers. "You going to shoot me?"

Her hand held steady. "I haven't decided yet."

He stood still, waiting.

Grief and anger made her finger tighten on the trigger. But then she remembered the soldier she'd shot before. The smell of gunpowder. The sudden emptiness. Her muscles went soft. She was not a killer. She backed towards the horses and then took their reins in her free hand.

"Mistin?" Cord said, his voice tight.

She closed her eyes as if listening and whispered, "Just let her go."

Careful to keep her gun trained on Cord, Senna climbed into the saddle, her foot fishing for the opposite stirrup. Suddenly, she noticed the music around her shifting. But that was impossible. Unless...

There are other Witches here, she realized with a start.

She didn't have time to react. The earth beneath her exploded. Sunny hit the ground hard, pinning her leg beneath his barrel chest. She couldn't draw a breath—her lungs felt paralyzed. Sunny rolled until his feet were under him and lurched to stand. Senna's leg was free at last.

She gasped a breath full of dust and coughed. Wind pressed down on her, pinning her to the ground, drowning out all other sounds. A golden flash of horseflesh streaked into the trees.

Joshen had given her that horse. And she'd lost him. Again.

Shaking, Senna listened to the song, took a breath, and began her own. Her song battled with theirs for control of the melody. Slowly, the wind eased away from her. Shaking and bleeding, she pushed herself up.

Mistin stood beside more than a dozen women, their faces twisted with concentration as they battled her songs. They were dressed in long tunics and loose pants—just like Mistin's. Around their waists were seed belts.

Witches. Witches not of Haven. These were the women Senna had felt before, the women who represented a threat to Haven. Calden's missing Witches. Senna had sought them out, but instead they'd found her.

She spun the wind around her, battering the other Witches further away and stealing their songs from their lips before they were strong enough to do any good. Using earth song, she directed pressure to build under them, until the ground trembled beneath their feet. The women collapsed, their faces terrified.

One more song, and it would swallow them whole. Just as they'd tried to do to Senna days before.

Dark, damp, deep, and cold

A knife trembled in Mistin's hand. Her gaze locked with Senna's. Mistin set her mouth. Slowly, her hand fell to her side.

A brief spasm of conscience wouldn't save Mistin from Senna's fury. Not after all her lies and treachery.

Gaping chasm, open fold

"Senna!" she heard Cord shout above her song. He gestured to the east. There were Tarten soldiers in the distance, closing in on them fast.

Did he think she would spare him because of a common threat? No. She would deal with these Witches. The soldiers would be next.

Grit and rock and mineral tang

The ground softened beneath the Witches. They were sinking.

Down to the depths —

Something hurtled into her from the side, slamming her so hard into the ground that the song on her lips shattered into a cry of pain. A gag shuttered the cry. She felt the weight of a man on top of her. More hands tying her wrists. She strained to lift her head.

Cord stretched a hand towards her as if he wanted to intervene, to help her. His expression was full of regret. But he and Mistin had kept Senna distracted while this man had crept up from behind. She glared at Cord with all her pent-up rage as her bonds were tightened.

Cord's chest heaved, his hand falling to his side as the wind slowly dissipated.

Senna was surrounded by men dressed in dark tunics. She hadn't seen them before, but she knew instinctively they were Guardians to these Calden Witches. She was pulled to her feet. Only then did she realize the familiar weight of her seed belt was gone.

Soon it wouldn't matter. The Tarten soldiers were so close Senna could almost make out the details of their uniforms.

Four Witches strode towards Senna without fear. A small army of Guardians fell in behind them. They held their muskets tightly, their faces hard.

"This is Brusenna?" the center Witch asked Mistin.

"Yes," Mistin said, refusing to meet Senna's gaze.

Senna squared her shoulders and glared this new threat down.

The Witch who'd spoken smiled. "Yes. This is her." She stepped forward. She resembled Mistin, but then all the women did. Even Cord had the same look—dark hair and eyes with creamy gold skin. "My name is Krissin," the Witch said. "We've been searching for you for a long time."

25. STRYKER

With a sick feeling of dread, Senna recognized the authority this woman wore like a second skin, so much like Coyel the two could be sisters. Krissin was a Discipline Head—the Head of Sunlight. And Senna realized she'd heard the name before, when she'd overheard Cord's and Mistin's furtive whispers that first night.

"I will offer you a boon, Brusenna. We will remove your gag, on the condition you swear not to sing. Break that promise and you will be violently silenced. Then you will be gagged and bound for the remainder of our journey. Do you agree to the terms?"

Senna nodded once.

Cord freed her wrists before snipping the gag. "Sorry." He held a knot of her golden hair in his hand. He watched her like she was an agitated cobra that might strike at any moment.

She knew better. She would need time to bend the Four Sisters—time she wouldn't have surrounded by Guardians and Witches.

One of the other Heads touched Krissin's shoulder. "They're coming."

Krissin glanced at the coming Tartens, her face going carefully blank. "Take her to the ship, quickly and silently, but before they see her."

Before they see me? But they already saw me, Senna thought.

Five other Guardians flanked her, including Cord. Krissin turned expectantly towards the approaching Tartens.

Realization exploded in Senna's head. These Witches weren't

running, because they were allied with the Tartens. "No," she gasped softly.

Crouched ahead of them, knives in both her hands, Mistin watched her.

"When you went missing before, you were retrieving your Witches." It was not a question.

Mistin nodded, an apology and a promise in the simple gesture. Then she melted into the trees before them. Senna guessed she was acting as some kind of fore guard.

Cord reached out to take Senna's arm. She jerked away. "How could you ally yourselves with them?" He gripped her tighter, relentlessly pulling her out of sight. She fought him every step. "And if you are allies, why haven't you lifted the curse?"

"Because then Haven would know we exist." Despite the fact that she could hear the Tartens conversing with the Witches, she continued to fight him. He hauled her around to face him. "Grendi has more than a horse's weight in gold on your head. We can't protect you if she finds you with us."

Nothing made sense. Grendi wanted to exterminate every living Witch. So why was she allied with them? Senna was an enemy of the Tartens. So why were their allies protecting her?

Senna tried to wrap her mind around the impossible realities. Calden and Tarten had been hunting for her...and now she was helpless against both of them. Maybe it was better if she was captured by the Tartens instead. If she cried out and they found her, at least she'd know if Joshen was...

A sob shook her so hard, her legs buckled and she dropped to her knees.

"Cord, keep her moving," one of the other Guardians growled.

Cord crouched before her. "Listen to me, Senna. Grendi can use Joshen to manipulate you. She won't want him dead."

Tears glazing her eyes, she looked up at Cord. He was close enough she could smell his breath—sweet and dark, like licorice. And she remembered her visceral reaction when she'd stumbled into him the first time they'd met on the ship. She hadn't realized, hadn't understood what that reaction had meant. But somehow her body remembered what her mind didn't—that Cord had held her before, when he'd attacked her on that moonless night and she'd shoved a shard of glass into his guts.

He moved as if to wipe away her tears. She turned away. "I'm sorry I didn't kill you the first time."

His hand dropped. "If the Tartens capture you, they won't have any reason to keep Joshen alive," Cord said, his voice hard. "Do you understand?"

Hope bloomed within her, and she could breathe again. "What about Reden?"

Cord pursed his lips. "Senna—"

She fisted his shirt in her hands. "Tell me!"

He clenched his jaw. "Grendi hates him even more than she hates you."

That meant there was little hope for him. A soft cry of pain escaped Senna's lips. She'd thought she'd accepted that this might not end well. She'd been willing to risk her life, determined to save Haven. And Joshen and Reden had seemed so indestructible that she'd never fully internalized the peril they faced.

The soldiers were dangerously close. One cry, and they would find her.

Senna made her decision. She would go with them until she had a chance at freedom. Then she would find Joshen and free him, no matter the cost. She allowed Cord to pull her up.

Guardians fanned out of sight into the bare trees, moving as silently as ghosts. All Senna heard over the ragged sound of her breathing was the distant waves.

Cord stopped often, giving her water to wet her parched throat. Finally, they reached the city Senna had bypassed on her first trip to Tarten. The geography lessons drilled into her head supplied the name: Epal.

The Guardians emerged from the trees and took up flanking positions. The streets were eerily quiet, but Senna occasionally caught sight of a dirty face watching them. Windblown debris gathered around the buildings, while heavier items remained abandoned in the street. A child's sandal caught her attention. One of the leather straps was broken. Senna couldn't help but wonder what had happened to its owner.

All this destruction—it was partly her fault. She'd only wanted to undo it, find answers to the danger looming over Haven. And now Joshen...Senna stared at her feet and didn't look up again.

They reached the dock and boarded the Calden Witches' boat. The craft was smaller than Parknel's ship and sat higher on the water. Its sails were different, too. The ship looked fast. On its side, *Mirage* was painted in blue.

Cord took her to a small cabin on the main deck. Except for a bed, basin, and chamber pot, it was empty. Senna glared at the man.

Much to her annoyance, he didn't show any reaction. "You should sit. I know you're exhausted," he said.

Though her muscles quivered with fatigue, she stood straight.

Mistin interrupted the tense silence a moment later. She had a tray of food that immediately sent Senna's mouth watering.

Ignoring Senna, Mistin sat on the bed, her legs folded beneath her, then looked up. "You have two choices—eat and keep up your strength, or refuse and grow weaker."

Senna didn't know this confident, powerful woman. Had everything about Mistin been a lie? She must have been the one who attacked Senna with the slingshot.

The girl watched Senna carefully. "If you start to sing, Cord and I will subdue you. This room will be flooded with Guardians. You won't be given another opportunity."

Senna considered her chances. She could certainly get a few notes in before they knocked her unconscious and stuffed a gag back in her mouth. But it wouldn't be enough time.

"Are you even siblings?" Senna asked in disgust. "Or does everyone from Calden look alike."

Mistin narrowed her eyes. "Just because everyone from Calden has dark features doesn't mean we all look alike. But no, we're not siblings. Just friends."

All those stories about Mistin growing up in the streets, her dead sisters and mother. Living a life of fear for being a Witch—all of it had been to manipulate Senna into empathizing with her. Senna clenched her fists at her sides. "Is there anything you two haven't lied about?"

Mistin frowned. "We really are your friends."

Senna had to suppress the urge to hit her. But if she was going to escape, she'd need all her strength and her captors relaxed. She perched on the edge of the bed and started eating. A creamy cheese was spread over thick, soft bread. Atop that, Mistin piled meat with a tangy, sweet sauce. For a time, they were silent except for the sounds of eating.

She'd thought these two were her friends. She'd been wrong. "What's going to happen to me?" she asked finally.

Mistin exchanged a glance with Cord. "We'll take you somewhere safe."

Senna palmed a handful of the berries. They exploded in her mouth, tart and sweet with little nuts inside. "Safe from what?"

"From the Tartens and Haven," Cord said.

Senna snorted. "Who's going to protect me from you?"

Mistin's eyes filled with sorrow. "We won't hurt you."

Ha! They'd already hurt her, numerous times. She studied them both. There was no way Mistin was working alone. Her song wasn't strong enough to sing a boat through the underwater cave that led to Haven. "Who was the other traitor? Drenelle?"

Mistin opened her mouth to say something, but shut it when Cord nudged her, a chiding look on his face.

"What's that supposed to mean?" Senna looked between them.

Cord shrugged before taking the empty tray and leaving the room.

Senna washed her hands in the water basin. Soon, she felt the ship move out to sea.

She was leaving Joshen behind. Who knew what Grendi would do to him? And Reden. If either of them were still alive. Senna lay on the bed as far away from Mistin as she could get and twisted her pearl ring round and round her finger.

Joshen was all right. She was going to escape. She was going to free him and Reden. She repeated it in her head like a mantra.

When the door opened again, she expected it to be Cord coming back. Instead, Krissin stood there—the sound of Witch song drifting in from behind her. Senna sat up. She wanted to sing, wanted it desperately. But it would only cost her what little freedom she had. She had to bide her time.

"Senna, you will come with me. Mistin, stay close." Krissin said.

Steeling herself, Senna followed Krissin out of the room. She was surprised to see twilight coming on. There was no sign of land; the ship must be well out to sea. Judging by the way they skimmed across the waves, they were making excellent time. Black storm clouds churned on the horizon.

Krissin led Senna and Mistin into the captain's cabin and shut the door behind the three of them. Senna retreated to the far side of the room. Mistin shadowed her and watched her every movement warily.

Krissin lit a dozen candles. "Do you know who we are?"

Senna nodded. "You're the Witches planning to take over Haven."

Krissin's face remained blank. "Yes."

"Did you send an Earth tremor after Haven?" Senna asked.

Krissin smiled. "Very good. Mistin informed me your Heads were growing suspicious. We needed a long-term distraction."

"What about the damage you did to Nefalie's coast? The people you killed?"

The smile faded to a frown. "I regret that."

Senna snorted. "Why did you send Mistin and Cord to kidnap me?"

"Because you were the only thing that stood between us and Haven." Krissin poured herself a cup of tea.

"I'm only one Witch."

Krissin studied her. "Yes, but I know what's happening to you."

"What's happening to me?" Senna echoed breathlessly.

The Head looked out the window. "All Witch song influences the music around them. But you—you can hear the music. The strength of your song fluctuates—there are times when you can match a full choir. Other times your song seems almost normal."

Senna shook her head. How had Krissin known? "I don't understand what that has to do with anything."

Krissin leaned forward. "Your Witches don't understand how songs really work. We strengthen the Four Sister's music, bend it if we can. But we can't hear it. You, however, can. And what's more, you can create music."

Create music? Senna couldn't seem to get enough air. Was that really what she'd been doing? "How do you know this? How do you know anything about me? Calden disappeared long ago."

"We have our spies—people like Cord and Mistin—to keep us appraised as to the goings on of the world." The candle cast dark, flickering shadows across Krissin's face. "Long ago, a young Witch became disillusioned with the way Haven ran the world. She garnered a secret following. One night, she stole into the Head's secret libraries and took many of the books filled with Witch secrets. Then she and her followers fled to her homeland: Calden."

Senna already knew this story. "But Calden was destroyed."

Krissin's gaze held Senna's. "Not destroyed. Moved."

Espen's hastily scrawled word's flashed in her mind. "But that would have taken hundreds and hundreds of Witches..."

"Oh, would it now?" Krissin calmly sipped her tea.

Senna's gaze narrowed. "You know it would."

Krissin pursed her lips. She'd been willing to share some secrets. Apparently, this wasn't one of them.

It was true the Witches could move Haven, if there were enough of them, but Senna hadn't known it was possible for any other place. Clearly, Haven's Witches hadn't either. It must be true, because the evidence sat in front of her. "How could you stay hidden for so many centuries?"

Krissin's thumb traced the handle of the tea cup. "You'll understand it better when you see for yourself."

Senna slumped onto one of the chairs and poured herself a cup of tea, adding a generous dollop of clotted cream. "Really, what's the point of all this mystery?"

Krissin smiled. "I will not reveal all our secrets to you, Senna. Know I will not harm you. In fact, all of us have great respect for you and what you've done. As long as you refrain from interfering, you will be treated as an honored guest."

Senna felt the Four Sisters inside her. She could harness them within seconds, sink this ship and every other ship within a hundred leagues.

Krissin must have seen something of this on her face. "Don't. Mistin would knock you senseless, and we would drug you until this is all over. I can't guarantee the potions wouldn't addle your wits or make you a slave to them, either."

Senna swallowed her rage. Krissin was right. She had to wait for the right opportunity. "When I defeated Espen, I thought I was saving more than just the Witches. But that's not true, is it? Hundreds of Calden Witches could have stepped in after we were gone and righted the world. It was never really in danger after all."

Krissin rolled a handful of berries around on her palm. "Give yourself a little credit, Brusenna. We were hiding from Espen just as much as your Witches. She could have overthrown us just as easily as she did Haven." Krissin stood and gestured for Senna to follow.

She obeyed, but only because there was no real choice.

Krissin led her back to her tiny room. "Mistin will stay with you to make sure you don't attempt to sing. Don't test her. She's our best Stryker. I suggest you rest. Tomorrow will be trying enough." She shut the door and Senna heard the lock click into place.

Senna let her eyes adjust to the dark. "Stryker?"

Mistin flopped onto the bed and stared at the ceiling. "Witches trained as fighters." She hesitated. "I told you there is more to a Witch than just her song."

Absolutely exhausted, but still fighting her fate, Senna grunted. "I never disputed that."

"I know," Mistin said softly, her eyes glinting in the darkness. "That's why I'm your friend."

Senna felt like screaming. "Friends don't lie to each other. They don't betray each other. And they certainly don't kidnap each other."

"This friend does." Senna heard the laughter in Mistin's voice. The Stryker rolled over and said seriously, "Not everyone looks at me the way you do. Haven certainly didn't. I'm small. I'm female. I'm young. And worst of all, I have a weak song. But I've found a way to turn all my weaknesses into strengths. People underestimate me. They pass me over as unimportant. This makes me the perfect spy. You don't have to be big and strong to throw a knife or to worm your way in as the Head's secretary."

"Or as my so-called friend." Senna rubbed her eyes. "You know they're not evil."

"This war has been coming for centuries." Mistin's voice had hardened. "When it's over, you'll have a place among us, if you choose it."

A place with these Witches but not with those on Haven. Senna rested the back of her head against the door and slid to the floor. This was what Espen was trying to warn her about. This was the danger coming for Haven.

The island's walls were no protection. Not against Witches.

26. Forbidden

Senna lay on the lumpy mattress, staring at the ceiling and worrying about Joshen. She relived everything that had happened, finding a hundred places where she'd gone wrong, a hundred decisions she should have made differently. Mistin slept soundly beside her. She had considered singing while her "friend" slept, but anything loud enough to be effective in these cramped quarters would surely wake the girl. And she'd seen how fast Mistin could move.

Still, Senna might have risked it. It had worked before, when she'd hummed to the Four Sisters. But now she was in the middle of the Darkwell Sea. Where would she go?

No matter how many times she looked out the tiny window above their shared bed, she saw only the stormy seas. The last sense left to her was listening. She sometimes heard the sailors above the wind and rain. And always the steady sound of a Witch singing to the ship.

That in itself was curious. The woman's song was strong—she should only have to sing every now and then, but she hadn't stopped but for an occasional break since she'd started hours ago.

Her song suddenly ended. There was silence except for booted footfalls. And suddenly, Witch song rang out. At least four of them were singing. In response, wind whipped against the ship, which surged forward.

That many Witches could sing them up to a speed that would snap the mast. "Are they mad?" Senna wondered aloud.

Mistin sat up, listened, and said groggily, "We're headed to the barrier. That means we'll be home by nightfall. When I left, I never thought I'd see it again."

"Where are we?"

"You might have heard it referred to as the Darkwell Squall." With a sleepy smile, she lay back down.

Darkwell Squall—Senna had heard of it, but she couldn't remember where. Was this what Grendi had meant by the place of storms? After pushing back her blankets, Senna knelt before the window and rested her chin against the casement. The dark had a texture so deep it felt like velvet all around her. And still all she saw was the endless ocean and clouds and rain.

Using the illumination of an unseen lantern, she looked back the way they'd come and noticed the slant of the rain and the direction of the waves. The ship was going against both. That must be why the Witch had to sing all night, but that didn't explain the sudden addition of three more.

Senna shifted her line of sight to look ahead and saw something astonishing through the blur of rain. A shimmer of color. A curving wall of bruised green and purple emerged from the storm, stretching as far as she could see.

An intense foreboding crashed over her. If the ship touched that color, something horrible would happen. They must turn around and never come back. The feeling was so overwhelming that it felt as if her brain were shutting down. There was only one thought: *flee*. A small cry of fear passed her lips.

Mistin patted her back. "It'll be over soon."

The room was filled with color as the ship sliced through the wall. Senna was suddenly inundated with music—the strangest music. Cringing, she listened to a song of forgetting and forbidden places.

A moment later it was gone, and she was left with nothing except utter confusion. Even the storm was gone. All was calm and quiet. She looked out the window.

The wall was no longer foreboding. It was a rainbow of bright, liquid colors. Senna finally understood. This barrier was much like the barrier that surrounded the Ring of Power and protected the Witches during their songs. But instead of an uncrossable boundary, this one created fear and a sense of impending doom to keep strangers out.

"How is it possible?"

Mistin yawned. "The currents and winds keep ships away. The storms blind them. If either of those fail, the barrier won't let anyone in from the outside. Even those of us who left—I didn't think I'd ever be able to come home. But that changed a few weeks ago. Now it just scares the hide off anyone who approaches it, but it can be crossed both ways. I don't know why."

Senna's heart beat faster. The first time she'd Traveled, she'd come upon something she couldn't pass, so she'd altered it to let her through. Altered, but not destroyed. "If no one could traverse the barrier, how did you go through it the first time?"

"Getting out is easy. Getting back in is—was—impossible." Mistin rolled over and tugged the blankets around her shoulders, clearly wanting to go back to sleep.

After crossing the barrier, Senna had been attacked by foreign Witches who lived on an island not far from a land with mountains—Calden was just over a day's sail from Tarten. It all made sense.

Beyond the inky sea, buildings gleamed like pearls in the moonlight, with candles shining in their windows. The ship headed for a wide river.

Their speed lagged against the river's drag. Her hand on the casing, Senna almost felt the ship straining to overcome the pull of the water. The Witches' song nudged them steadily forward. They slowed before breaking past the lips of the river and into its mouth.

Senna studied the hushed city. Beams of wood poked through the roofs. The walls seemed to be made of some kind of plaster. Late as it was, she still caught sight of people, all wearing flowing tunics and sandals.

She peered down at the river and was shocked to see Pogg swimming through the water, a fish in his mouth. A cry started from her mouth, but died when she saw another Pogg. And another. She sat back on her heels.

Pogg wasn't the last Mettlemot. He was just lost from the rest of his kind. Senna closed her eyes as the depth and breadth of the Witches' mistakes overwhelmed her. "I'm sorry, Pogg," she mouthed.

She risked looking back out the window. Beyond the city were groves of dark, small-leaved trees. Across the hills, a flock of sheep had bedded down for the night. They looked like a cloud that had lost the sky. Senna watched the landscape change, grow even more barren and windswept. At some point she fell back asleep.

Mistin's hand on her arm woke her. "They'll be coming for us soon."

Senna looked outside again. It was early morning, so early the sun hadn't even awakened yet. The world was grainy and gray, that fuzzy time that lacked clear details. They'd come to another city; their ship was docked at one of the wharves.

Senna combed her tangled hair the best she could with her fingers. She smoothed the wrinkles from her dress and slipped on her boots. She was ready when a group of four Guardians opened the door, Cord among them. Beyond them, Krissin and the other Heads were waiting for the gangplank to be lowered.

Cord smiled, obviously trying to soften the fact that Senna was under guard. "Time to go."

Mistin leaned over. "None of our sea-going ships can go farther than Ilyss. We'll board smaller vessels."

Cord stepped aside, clearly expecting Senna to come without a fight. By the Creators, she wanted to prove him wrong. But four Guardians and Mistin would silence her the moment the song left her lips "I don't trust you." She cut a glance at Mistin. "Or you."

Cord stepped closer, his proximity making Senna squirm on the inside. "When I was hidden and half dead of pain, I overheard them sometimes—your Haven Witches. They accused you of lying, of seeking attention. Even Joshen tried to stop you from leaving. So you tell me Senna, who's the better friend?"

How dare he say anything against Joshen! She slapped Cord, making her hand sting. The other Guardians stepped closer.

"He deserved that," Mistin said quickly.

Rubbing his cheek, Cord motioned for the other Guardians to relax. "Maybe I did."

Krissin glanced back at them. She pulled a vial of purple liquid from her seed belt and held it up for Senna to see. "I will use it if I must."

Senna suddenly felt cold all over, though the predawn air was warm. Yarves would make her mind as malleable as mush. She stepped away from Cord, her hands fisted at her sides until her scar ached fiercely.

Krissin shoved the vial back into her seed belt and strode down the gangplank, her sandaled feet slapping the wood much differently than the click of Senna's boots. Hating her every step, Senna followed. Dark-clad Calden Guardians flanked her on every side and steered her towards the pier.

They stepped into a smaller boat that was intricately carved from fine wood. Senna ran her hands over the inside, searching for the seams where one board met another. With a start, she realized there were none. The entire boat must be sung into shape from a single tree by Witch song.

Stunned, she withdrew her hand. She'd never heard of a song to shape a boat. Never fathomed it. Could it be possible the Calden Witches were even more knowledgeable than the Haven Witches? That they were somehow stronger?

If so, what did they want with her? Why go to all this trouble for one Witch? Krissin was right that the power of Senna's song surged sometimes, but not strong enough to stop these Witches.

The Guardians untied their boat and settled back. The Witches around Senna sang again, and a wind so perfect and precise it only affected their sails drove them forward until they seemed to bounce across the river like a skipping stone.

The first light of day brought men to the river. They paid no attention to the Witches or their songs as they cast nets over the sides of their small boats again and again. Intricate irrigation systems fed the groves and fields of viny plants. Senna watched them in wonder.

Krissin caught her studying the irrigation system. "Though the Tarten jungle is less than a hundred leagues away, our weather is vastly different. Another gift from your Witches. As you can see, we have adapted."

"So this is Calden." The nation the Witches had burned to a crisp and then denied the rains had found a way to survive. Relief swelled in Senna. Even through all the damage the Keepers had repeatedly caused, people found a way to survive. They always did.

"No longer. We renamed ourselves Caldash when we rose from Calden's ashes."

A dozen questions formed in Senna's mind, questions about the Witches' numbers, the barrier, or the songs they sang. "We've been traveling by river for hours now. How could anyone move an island this big? It would have taken thousands of Witches."

Krissin stared across the fields. "Logic would agree with you."

What kind of answer was that? But Senna didn't ask any more questions because asking felt too close to defeat.

With the sun came heat that sapped the moisture from her body. Feeling her skin start to burn, she pulled her cloak over her head. Though it was made of dark material, the shade it offered more than compensated for the added insulation.

Krissin handed out some food—a nutty bread and some sheep cheese that made Senna thirsty. Exhaustion taking hold, she slept.

When she awoke, the air was decidedly cooler. Her muscles were stiff from sleeping on the hard boat. Rubbing her numb shoulder, she sat up and froze. The arid hills were gone. Instead, great mountains towered over her like wizened old men with crops of snow ringing their bald heads.

Shivering, Senna pulled her cloak tighter around her shoulders and looked beyond the press of Guardians partially blocking her view of what lay ahead. What she saw shocked her far more than the sudden change in landscape. A city bloomed between two peaks. A city made of tree houses.

"Where are we?" Senna asked in a daze.

"The city of Lilette—our sacred city," Krissin said softly. She pointed to enormous sentry trees flanking the river. "The only way in is by river, which is heavily guarded by the younger Guardians. If you don't have one of our boats, you don't get in. If you aren't recognized at the city docks, you are promptly taken captive. Most are never allowed to leave."

Never allowed to leave. Senna wet her lips. "Why have you brought me here? What do you want?"

"That isn't for me to decide."

Senna shook her head. "I don't understand. You're the Head of Sunlight."

Krissin grunted. "We run things a little differently here. As Discipline Heads, we control Caldash's weather and preside over our Disciplines, but the Composer presides over the law."

The Witches stopped singing and the boat coasted forward before bumping gently into the dock. Some of the Guardians leapt out to tie it off, while others helped the Witches from the craft.

A man from the city met with Krissin. As they spoke, he peered down at Senna, curiosity and wonder plain on his face, before he turned on his heel and trotted back the way he'd come.

A flock of women were coming down the dock. They wore a less ornate version of the same tunic and loose trousers as Krissin. Senna slowly realized these women were waiting for her. *Had been* waiting for her. As if they'd known she was coming and had been prepared for it. "What do you want from me?"

Krissin nodded toward the city. "The Composer wishes to speak with you."

Senna was ushered out of the boat, down the pier, and into the city. People bustled in and out of tree houses. Guardians, children, Witches—lots and lots of Witches. "There are so many Keepers."

"This isn't even half our number. We live among our people."

"I thought no one could leave the city of Lilette?"

Krissin chuckled. "Only Witches and Guardians. If anyone else comes, they are obliged to stay."

Senna studied the Witches all around her. None of them wore fear on their faces—in fact, they looked peaceful, happy, and prosperous All things Haven scrambled for and fell short.

This was how Haven had been once. Before its numbers were decimated by war and fear. Before Espen had smashed through glass and doors, shattering the fragile remnants of the Witches' already faltering society. Senna wanted to weep for everything they had lost.

The air smelled of savory herbs, sweet flowers, and dry mountain air. Krissin and the rest of the group wove through a forest of tree houses toward the center of the city, where a massive tree rose high above the others. They passed through a vicious-looking hedge, the entrance of which was watched by sharp-eyed Guardians. "We've just passed into the inner courtyard—some men have castle spires, we have our trees," Krissin explained. "Each tree is like a room in a castle."

More black-clad Guardians stood at quiet readiness beside the doors to the largest tree. Noticing Senna's scrutiny, Krissin nodded toward them. "That is the Composer's listening tree."

For a moment, Senna worried they were going inside, but they turned aside, toward one of the adjoining trees.

"And this," Krissin went on, "is the bathing tree."

It looked less like a tree and more like hundreds of saplings twisting and twining their way upward. Mists rose between spaces in the branches. The Guardians took up positions outside while the women hustled Senna in. She gasped when she stepped within. The tree had been sung around a natural spring. A mosaic of tiles created swirling patterns of monochromatic blue. The pool was filled by a thin, steaming waterfall. Towels, soaps, and oils were laid out on sung tables. The walls were covered in thick green moss. The place smelled of a mix of damp earth and expensive fragrances. Senna found it intoxicating.

Much to her horror, the women gestured her to a stool and promptly began to tug at her clothes.

"No," Senna gasped. "I can do it myself."

When the women didn't listen, she shoved one. They clucked their tongues at her. One brow cocked, Krissin held up the Yarves.

Her face set, Senna endured them scrubbing her with soap and pouring shockingly hot water over her head. This was a hundred times worse than her almost-bath with Ciara. Only when they'd scrubbed her skin pink did they let her soak in the pool, but not for long enough.

Far too soon, they were hauling her out again. They anointed her with an oil that smelled of sweet resin. The tangles were worked out of her hair and it was woven into a cascading braid that led to a knot at the side of her neck. She was dressed in a finely embroidered blue tunic and trousers and given sandals in place of her boots. And last, they put a delicate gold cuff of flowers and vines around her wrist.

She stood in front of a mirror, barely recognizing the woman of blue and gold.

"You look like the sun in the sky," one of her women said with a heavy accent.

The women herded her back outside and handed her over to another group of Guardians.

Senna was surrounded in a foreign place, and Krissin still feared she would try to run for it—and that she would make it. Krissin would have been right. Escape was certain, even if Senna had to destroy half the city of Lilette in the process.

Her insides cringed as they mounted the enormous steps to the Composer's listening tree.

Krissin whispered, "It would be very unwise to disrespect one as powerful as the Composer. And please don't try anything foolish. You are in the center of the city of Lilette—you would not escape."

Senna breathed out in frustration. "I could take out a few trees before you stopped me."

Krissin blanched. "They would kill you for it."

The Guardians posted at the ornate entrance eyed Senna warily as Krissin pulled open the door and stepped aside.

Senna wiped her sweaty palms on her tunic. Since her capture, she'd never gone anywhere by herself. And now they were allowing her to see the Composer alone?

Squaring her shoulders, Senna stepped inside.

27. THE COMPOSER

The door shut behind Senna with a resounding thud, and she stopped short. This room was a hundred times bigger than any she'd ever seen. Windows glinted shattered rainbows all over the interior. Plants and vines grew up the walls, their colors and fragrance filling the air to bursting.

She spun in a slow circle, taking in flowers and even trees she'd never seen—not even in a book. But there was no Composer in sight. Senna wandered randomly, searching for the woman. But the plants around Senna distracted her with their mystery and variety. Their songs were different, too, more colorful and spicy than the songs of Haven. She captured a bloom in her hand and inhaled its sharp fragrance.

"It's beautiful, isn't it?"

Senna turned at the voice that sounded worn as if it had sung a thousand songs, uttered innumerable words. It was not a voice that held any power of song. An old woman sat on a beautifully carved planter box, a trowel in her hand. Gossamer lines weaved across her skin like spider's silk. She rooted around in the soil and came up with a rhizome. She brushed it off, scattering dirt on her already-streaked tunic. She sang softly to the plants, her voice as creaky as a new saddle.

Senna took a breath of relief. This woman was obviously just a gardener. "I'm looking for the Composer."

"She's often late. Have a seat and help an old woman, hmm?"

Senna stepped forward, her sandaled feet slapping the floor. Careful of her new tunic, she perched on the side of the box. The woman handed her a spade. "We have to thin these flowers before they choke themselves to death."

Senna began thinning the tightly packed rhizomes. They came out rather easily. The old woman must have loosened the soil earlier.

"These are my favorites," she went on. "They're tough and beautiful. Useful too, as each part is a key ingredient for one potion or another. But their great strength is also their weakness. The roots are so strong they often begin to choke out other plants—which I suppose makes the other plants hate them."

Was this woman mad? Senna dug her hands deep in the dirt and came out with another root—one that looked like a pot-bellied little man. She tossed it into the rubbish bin. "I really should find the Composer."

The woman went on as if Senna hadn't spoken. "Eventually they even begin to choke themselves. The rot will begin in the middle until there's an ugly hole. The rest of the plants will become sickly—there simply isn't enough soil and water for all of them." She dug out another root and held it up. "I imagine that's not much consolation for this root, hmm? Why it and not one of the others?"

Senna's breath hitched in her throat. "We're not talking about flowers, are we?"

The woman tossed the root into a rubbish bin. "Truthfully, there is no answer. The gardener decides."

Senna let out all of her breath in a rush. "You're the Composer."

The woman wiped a bead of sweat from her brow, leaving a streak of dirt across her forehead. "My name is Ellesh. And you're Brusenna. Come for answers."

Senna looked harder and saw what she'd missed before. Ellesh's eyes were keen and sharp as a knife.

The Composer set down her trowel and brushed the dirt from her hands. "Listen and I will tell you the story of a woman who changed the course of history. Her name was Lilette."

Senna had waited so long to hear the full story of what had happened that this didn't feel real.

Ellesh arched her back with a grimace. "Her mother died far from home—a stranger who proved unknown and untraceable. A barren woman took Lilette and raised her. In her youth, the child discovered what she was. She came to Haven for learning, but what she found were women punishing a turnip for not being an apple."

Senna shook her head. "I don't—"

Ellesh's eyes seemed to cut into her. "Some years the Heads were magnanimous women. Others they were downright tyrants, punishing the world and its people for not behaving as they thought they should. In Lilette's day, they were tyrants."

Senna looked out one of the windows at the darkening sky. She pictured it. Women who doled out their songs based on promises of money or power. "The world had its own rhythms, its own song to sing. I know because I've heard it."

The Composer nodded. "Yes. But our voices alter those songs."

Eager to see if Caldash's story matched up with Haven's, Senna leaned forward. "Why did Lilette leave?"

Ellesh sighed. "For many of the same reasons you did. One of the nations rose up against the Witches. Their rains were cut off as punishment. Lilette begged them to reconsider. They refused. So she took those who would follow her and left. She came to Calden. And Haven killed her for it."

Senna mulled it over. "They say I am like her, and they feared me for it. Why? I've only ever wanted to save them."

The Composer was silent for a time. "Because Lilette too saw the Creators." She met Senna's startled gaze. "And she too began to change."

Heat flushed Senna's skin. She stared at her hands. They were dirty from thinning the flowers and scarred from potion burns. Half-healed scabs from the jungle marred her pale skin. Though it wasn't visible, there was blood on them, too. They weren't the hands of some kind of hero.

Ellesh went on softly. "Lilette began to hear nature's music. She grew more and more powerful by the day. Those in authority began to fear her strength, much as they now fear yours. She could have destroyed Haven, but she didn't have the ruthlessness of a gardener. She couldn't bear to thin them."

Senna stared at the beautiful flowers, the naked roots sitting in a bucket to be ground up and used for some nameless potion.

The Composer went to a water basin and meticulously washed the dirt from her hands. "The Haven Witches were afraid of her, so they hurtled a hurricane across the ocean, regardless of ships and people in their path—people who had no experience dealing with such frightening storms, as the Witches' songs had prevented hurricanes for centuries. Lightning bolts shot from the sky. Hail the size of large birds fell from the clouds, crushing everything in their path. Earth tremors rent deep chasms and raised high mountains."

After drying her hands, the Composer reached inside a satchel and pulled out a book. "This is what remains of an account by Jolin Lyon, Head of Plants and a friend to Lilette. It was transcribed by one of her grandchildren. The account itself has been rewritten numerous times as the books have fallen apart." The spine cracked and the pages rustled like dry leaves as Ellesh opened it to a marked page.

"We died by the thousands," she read. "Buildings collapsed around us. Lightning and hail attacked any who dragged themselves from the wreckage. The Circle failed. Lilette braved the storm, creating a Circle alone—as none had ever done before or since. She rose into the rending sky, lightning slamming all around her.

"She sang. Lights came to life around her until it hurt our eyes to look upon her and we were forced to hide our eyes.

"Suddenly, the storm stopped—was pushed back. The sun broke through the clouds and she said, 'I thought we were ready. I was wrong. But someday a Witch will become the kind of woman the world needs. Wait and watch. For on that day, the Witches will rise from our own ashes and the world will be reborn.'"

The Composer shut the book. "Lilette had moved Calden much further south and wrapped a protective barrier around the island. She was never seen again."

Senna washed her hands in the dirty water. "And you think I'm the answer—that I was born to save you?"

Ellesh chuckled. "No. Heroes are not born. They make themselves. The potential to save the Witches has rested in many—including Espen. Are you the one Lilette spoke of? Perhaps, but I'm not going to wait to find out.

"We have been planning our escape from this island for centuries. In cursing Tarten, your Witches pushed the two of us into an alliance. Then you proved the barrier could be destroyed. We won't find a better time."

Senna dried her hands. "But Grendi hates Witches."

The Composer studied her. "Exactly. But the only thing she hates more than Witches is Haven's Witches. I agreed to restore Tarten and destroy her enemy. She's in no position to barter for more."

Thinking of all the women she'd left behind—her mother foremost among them—Senna closed her eyes. "And what makes you think Tarten will keep that promise?"

"Because if they don't, I'll sink all their ships and their lands won't be healed."

With Tarten's army backing them, the Caldash Witches had more than enough strength to destroy Haven. And the Heads were ignorant to all of it. "What do you know of the Witches on Haven? Have you met them? Have you seen the good they do?"

Ellesh nodded toward Tarten. "You can say that after what they did to Tarten? If we don't destroy them, they will annihilate every nation who crosses them."

Senna folded her arms across her chest. "You would be different, would you?"

"Yes."

"Then be different now! There are innocents on Haven—Witchlings and Apprentices."

Ellesh hesitated. "Has your Head of Water not taught you that there are always casualties in war? Do any of them deserve to die?"

"Ironic that you would punish Haven for the same crime you plan on committing." Senna voice was tight with anger.

Her movements stiff, the Composer replaced the book. "After Haven has surrendered, Grendi will turn the survivors over to me. They will be grafted into Caldash."

"You cannot justify the murder of many by the saving of some."

The Composer looked angry. "You freed us, Senna. When you cursed Tarten, you provided us with the army we so desperately needed. Your part in this is undeniable. You are also Creator-touched. I would not risk harming you. Nor would I risk facing you."

Senna wondered if now was the time to act, to sing and warn Haven. But she was inside a tree. There was no clear path for the Wind to escape intact.

"They are hard decisions, Brusenna. Decisions someone has to make." Ellesh sighed. "Perhaps if I fail to restore the world, you will have your chance."

While Senna hesitated, the old woman backed to the door and spoke to the Guardians on the other side. "Bring Cord." She studied Senna. "Mistin has told me much about you. Your Discipline Heads fear you. Your peers mistreat you. Your Guardians oppose you."

Shaking, Senna faced her. "You're cruel."

"You don't trust me, Brusenna. I can't fault you for that. After all, I don't trust you. Only a fool would leave a threat such as yourself in our midst, especially since we don't know how strong you shall become. Some have urged me to lock you away deep in the earth—bound and gagged until Haven has been defeated. Or simply killed outright."

Senna suddenly couldn't breathe. She felt the Composer's knife gaze on her.

"But I will offer you an alternative."

"What alternative?" Senna asked, realizing her chances of escape were slipping by the second.

The door opened, letting in a breeze that stirred the tendrils of her hair around her shoulders. Cord came through, his dark eyes grave.

Ellesh nodded toward Cord. "Take on Cord as your Guardian."

Senna looked from him to the Composer. "I'll take my chances with the cave."

Cord winced. "Don't be stubborn, Senna."

Ellesh held out a small jar of ointment. By the musky smell, Senna recognized it as the potion that allowed a Witch to create a Guardian. "I will permit you to roam about the city of Lilette unfettered."

Unbound...Senna would have a much better chance of escape. Still, she glared at Cord. "I already have two Guardians."

He didn't respond.

She hesitated. Ellesh was far too keen to risk Senna escaping or warning Haven, which meant having Cord as a Guardian was somehow as secure as confinement. Dared Senna risk falling into their trap for the chance of escape? Did she really have a choice?

Obviously reading the defeat on her face, the Composer put the wooden jar in Senna's hand. "Sing."

Senna stared at the ointment, her head spinning. "Fine."

Ellesh visibly relaxed. "The song for our Guardians is slightly different than yours."

"Composer, perhaps—" Cord began.

Ellesh silenced him with a slicing motion. He clamped his mouth shut, but he didn't look happy.

Senna eyed the sheet music Ellesh held out. She sang it once.

Guardian of Sisters and Witch Companion decree,
Bound in purpose and solidarity.

Hesitantly, Senna stepped toward Cord.

His lips were pursed. "Ellesh, she doesn't—"

"Shh," Ellesh whispered. "It is nearly done."

He opened his mouth to say something more, but Senna had the song in her heart now. She walked toward him and began the verse again. Rubbing the potion onto her lips so it would gather the residue of her song, she sang softly. The music of the Four Sisters coiled around her like hundreds of silky threads.

On the third and final repetition, Senna stood directly in front of Cord. She looked up to find the concern on his face replaced with awe. She should have been used to that reaction to her song by now, but it never failed to surprise her. The look of rapture always made her feel like she could never live up to the beauty of her voice.

Ellesh whispered, "Hold the final note for eight counts on the third rotation."

The final note rang from Senna's mouth as she hesitantly rolled up Cord's sleeve.

One.

The strands of thread spun faster. Like a hurricane.

Two.

Cord couldn't see it, but he must have sensed something. His face was filled with a sort of longing.

Three.

Seeing his bare arm, she hesitated. She'd only ever made one other Guardian—Joshen.

Four.

With a pang in her heart, she looked back to Ellesh. The woman motioned for her to continue.

Five.

Senna gazed into Cord's inscrutable eyes. She didn't want to do this. Something was wrong. But it might be her only chance for freedom.

Six.

She closed her eyes and thought of Joshen.

Seven.

Her lips buzzed with the residue of power from the song.

Eight.

She pressed a kiss against the soft skin on the inside of Cord's arm. She pulled back and studied the perfect green imprint of her lips. Suddenly, the white filaments around them snapped tight, jolting Senna into Cord's arms. Only his firm grip kept her from falling.

Quick as a striking snake, Ellesh pressed Senna's wrist against Cord's and shoved a tiny, doubled-edged blade between their arms.

Senna blinked and shook her head. She glanced at her enemies in confusion. Warm, sticky blood beaded between her skin and Cord's. She felt a tingle—like a wriggling feather—between their arms.

Senna jerked free. Beneath the sheen of fresh blood, a waning gibbous had formed on Cord's arm. That wasn't right. It should be a circle. With a start, she realized the wriggling feather feeling hadn't stopped when she'd pulled her arm away. Her heart heavy with dread, she lifted her wrist. Just beneath the shallow cut, a waxing crescent was forming on her skin.

Her eyes traced the partial moon on Cord's wrist. She knew if she pressed them together, they'd form a perfect circle. Ellesh's satisfied smile woke a terrible intuition in Senna's mind. "What have you done?"

Ellesh gestured to the pendant at Senna's throat. "Long ago, we discovered how to incorporate the process used to make the Lilette Stone to alter the potion used to bond a Guardian to his Witch. Now, Cord will always be aware of you. He'll be able to keep you safe."

Her necklace. The necklace that allowed the two halves to always find each other. Somewhere, Joshen had the other half. Senna swayed on her feet. And now Cord was linked to her even more intimately. "Aware of me how?"

Ellesh shrugged. "He will be able to feel your location."

"How?"

"Through the connection forged between your blood."

She turned her fierce glare to Cord. "You knew!"

He stared at the floor.

Joshen. She was bound to a Guardian, and it wasn't Joshen. She ran to the basin of water Ellesh had used before. Senna snatched the soap and scrubbed her skin. Bloody bubbles formed and the water turned pink. She clawed at her arm, trying to scratch the crescent off. Her skin welted and turned bright red, but the mark didn't budge.

Cord's hand closed around her arm. "Senna, it won't come off."

At his touch, something rushed inside her. A foreign awareness. A bundle of emotions. Dread and hope and a cautious longing.

She sagged against the basin, water soaking into the front of her tunic. She could cut her arm off, but it wouldn't break the connection. It was in her blood. "I can *feel* you."

The pendant felt impossibly heavy around Senna's neck. Joshen's ring on her finger seemed to tighten as if sensing the betrayal. "Why? Why would you do this to me?"

He wouldn't meet her gaze. "It was me or someone else. I couldn't bear for it to be someone else."

Her hands curled into tight fists. "So it was a kindness? To tether me forever to yourself?"

He didn't answer, but he didn't have to. She felt his regret building inside her mind. It was a dim echo of emotion, a shadow of true feeling.

Somehow, she was going to escape. She was going to find a way to warn the other Witches. And she was going to free herself from this link.

"Cord?" Ellesh said.

He stared at the floor. "She's plotting her escape."

Senna gasped soundlessly.

Ellesh nodded. "Make sure she fails."

She was as shackled as if she was gagged and bound. Shifting her weight, she hauled back her arm and punched Cord in the jaw. He saw it coming and he probably felt her intent, but he didn't try to avoid the blow.

Pain erupted in Senna's hand. Resisting the urge to cradle it against her body, she ignored the sharp pain echoing from Cord's jaw and stormed past them. She paused at the door. "You're worse than the Haven Witches have ever been. Both of you."

Cord didn't look up from the floor. Ellesh had the grace to look abashed. "It was necessary," she said. "I cannot risk killing or harming a Creator-touched."

Senna stormed out of the tree.

Their voices followed her out. "Cord?"

"She's doesn't have a plan. She's just running."

"Follow her."

He came after her.

She knew because she felt him. As she felt the direction of the sun by the heat on her body, she knew Cord was three steps behind her and a little to the left. But that wasn't all. Cord's emotions seeped inside her. And right now it was so hard to tell where his emotions ended and hers began.

Her body. Her mind. They weren't her own anymore.

She broke into a run to escape the horror, but how could she evade her own blood?

28. Blood Curse

Senna hugged her knees to her chest. Her cheeks felt tight where the salty tracks of her tears had dried. She looked down at the city of Lilette—part city, part forest. The setting sun cast a golden haze over the scene.

She felt Cord behind her, close enough to stop her should the sudden urge to jump off the cliff come to mind—his thought, not hers. Grunting, she stared at the drop a few paces away. It actually wasn't a bad idea. She could launch herself off, feel the rush of the wind all around her, then nothing.

She felt Cord's concern grow. With the scrape of gravel under his sandals, he sat within arm's reach. Her body went rigid. Her hand still ached from hitting him. She didn't think it was broken, just sprained. Still it had been worth it. It might be worth it to do it again.

"No." His voice sounded rough. "It still feels like you dislocated my jaw. And you need at least one serviceable hand."

She glared at him, wanting so badly to hit him again.

"I won't let you," he said softly.

She winced—he'd read her thoughts again, while she was trying her best to ignore the hints of emotions and hurt seeping through. But if he could manipulate the connection, so could she. She concentrated on the small swirl of emotions mixing with hers like a drop of milk in hot tea. His jaw did hurt, right at the joint. He was overwhelmed and frightened, and so very sorry.

She ignored the last bit and explored further. The link between them was more like a leak—like a bit of his emotions and thoughts spilled into the crescent moon on her arm, into her blood, where they mixed with hers.

By the Creators, what would Joshen think? Senna pressed the heels of her palms into her swollen eyes. For the first time in her life, she felt like she knew who she was, what she was capable of. She and Joshen could rebuild their relationship now. But he was gone—captured or...

No! She refused to believe he was dead. He had to be alive. She remembered the way he gently cupped the back of her head, the way his lips felt on hers—hungry and yet somehow gentle. There would be no beauty in the world if Joshen no longer lived in it.

Cord sucked in a breath.

She blushed scarlet. "You dung-licking son of a weasel, stay out of my head!"

He cleared his throat. "You and Joshen...I didn't know."

She cast him a searing look. "What do you mean you didn't know? How could you not know?"

He clambered to his feet and moved as if to go back to the city. He was hoping distance would hide the horror he was doggedly trying to suppress. After a few dozen steps, he remembered he couldn't leave her and stopped with his fists clenched at his side. "I didn't know it had gone that far."

Senna was on her feet before she realized it. Jealousy and confusion and denial poured into her blood in dizzying waves. She stumbled back.

Cord tensed—he must be feeling her dawning understanding. He took a deep breath and then his shoulders sagged. "All I ever saw was you arguing with him. I didn't even know you liked each other anymore. I had no idea you were to be married. I'm sorry."

Shock and disbelief crowded her mind. She stepped back but her foot only found open air. She'd moved to the rim of the drop-off without realizing it. She started tipping back, her arms windmilling to stop her fall.

Before she could cry out, Cord was there pulling her away from danger and spinning her so he stood between her and the edge.

His touch burned—in a very good way. Like she had reconnected with a part of herself she'd lost without realizing it. The link flooded open and information poured through.

He released her a second before she jerked away. But she'd seen what he had in his pocket. Moving by impulse, she reached into his trousers and grasped something soft. She pulled out a square of soft leather and opened it. Inside were golden strands of her hair. Cord had tied a knot in the center.

He jerked it back from her, his face coloring. When he'd cut her gag and accidentally snipped her hair, he'd taken the strands and saved them in his pocket.

Her breaths came in short gasps. "You don't love me. You love my song."

She felt his emotions as he looked at her. Her hair and eyes reminded him of dark honey. The center line in her bottom lip— he wanted to touch it, rub it with his thumb. Her small frame—he wanted to press his body against her. But it was the sound of her voice that drove him.

All these thoughts were his. She pressed her hands against her temples. "Stop it! You don't love me!"

The thoughts kept coming. While Cord had recovered from being stabbed, Mistin had hid him shockingly close to Senna's tree house so he could spy on her. He'd listened to her sing, had watched her from afar for days.

She hadn't thought it was possible to feel more violated. "You're attracted to my body, my song—not me!"

His brow furrowed as he reached for her. "Isn't that how love begins?"

"No!" She shied away from his touch as if it would burn her. "Love is so much more than that. It is a choice you make every day." Inside, she felt dirty, as if she'd somehow betrayed Joshen. She closed her eyes and thought of him again. His dogged concern, the way he swore when he was angry, the way he inhaled his food. He'd left everything to follow her long before he'd ever heard her voice. Their love had blossomed from their friendship.

Not like this. Not based on looks and her voice as golden as her hair and eyes. Her delicate hands. She tried to block out Cord's thoughts. "That's attraction. Not love." She backed away from him.

It was true things with Joshen had been off kilter in the last few weeks, but her feelings for him hadn't changed. She glanced again at the cliff, wondering if she had time to push Cord off it.

"I've trained in combat since I was old enough to hold a stick." He wanted to reach for her, but he knew better this time.

Steeling herself, she held her clenched fists tight to her sides. "You will control your thoughts. I am your Keeper. You will obey my orders and keep your distance. And you *will not* touch me again."

His hand fell. "Very well. Just remember that the Composer's orders supersede yours."

Senna raised herself to her full height. "And if I tell her of your feelings for me and request another Guardian?"

He shrugged. "It's inevitable, Senna. You feel what I feel. Can you imagine living through me even kissing another girl, let alone marrying her?"

She shuddered as she imagined passion seeping through the link. It would be the worst kind of voyeurism. "What have you done?" But he'd already answered that. If not him, Ellesh would have chosen someone else—a complete stranger.

By the Creators, that woman was going to pay for this.

Senna turned on her heel and stormed back down the mountain. She chose a path that seemed to meander toward the tallest tree— the listening tree. She hadn't gone a dozen steps when another tree blocked her way. The path branched off to the left or right. She took the right and found herself heading away from the center. She took the next left and found herself cutting back to the right. As far as she could tell, there were no straight roads. Everything curved and twisted around trees.

The Keepers grew the trees like this to confuse anyone who tried to attack the city—Cord's thought. He was trying to nudge her to take the middle fork. Furious at the intrusion, she took the left. Within a few dozen steps, she was surrounded by Witchlings.

They gave half bows as she passed, their faces alight with wonder.

The strong smell of herbs permeated the air. In a pavilion, girls were mixing their first potions. As Senna watched, one of them tucked a stray strand of her hair behind her ear. Singing softly to herself, she crushed a leaf between her thumb and fingers, rolling it to a pulp before dropping it in. That had been Senna a few weeks ago.

She passed a tree house where Witches were learning their scales—their voices rang with the innocence of youth. Everywhere she went, her pale coloring stood out from the rich hues of skin, hair, and eyes around her. Witches and Guardians alike paused to study her with a touch of reverence in their faces.

She was completely lost by the time Mistin emerged from the trees and stood beside her. "Are you still angry with me?"

Senna planted her fists on her hips. "You betrayed me. I should be in Tarten now, trying to free Joshen and Reden, but you forced me somewhere I can't help them. I saw the way Reden looked at you—like you were something rare and priceless. And you just left him to die!"

Mistin's face darkened with emotion. "I tried to save him! I revealed my knives to save him! But then the Tartens trapped them." Her voice trailed to a whisper at the end.

If Mistin was hoping to make Senna feel guilty, she had failed. "You should have saved them, Mistin! I went into this knowing I might die. I was prepared for it. But not for this!"

Senna took a step closer, her heart pumping madly in her chest. "You spied on Haven. They sent an earth tremor because of your reports. How many people died because of that?"

Mistin cringed. "I'm sorry."

If Senna had a weapon, she would have hurt Mistin. Badly.

Cord reached toward her. "Senna." His unspoken warning poured into her.

She shied away from his touch. "Did you know the Composer planned on violating me?"

Mistin took a step back. "What? Violate you how?"

Senna pointed at Cord. "Ellesh tricked me into making your 'brother' my Guardian. I bonded him."

Mistin's sharp intake of breath proved her ignorance of the Composer's plan. "They only do that to a Witch who's married her Guardian." Mistin eyed Senna's beautiful tunic, the gold bracelet, her elaborate hair.

With a dawning horror, Senna wondered if this was some kind of wedding dress. She yanked her hair out of its pins, ripped the bracelet off, and threw it at Cord.

He caught it without looking and stuffed it in his pocket with the lock of her hair.

She looked for something else to throw at him.

Mistin followed her. "Senna, I'm so sorry. I didn't know she was planning that."

Senna tried not let Mistin's gentle words penetrate her defenses. "Don't talk to me like I'm your friend. We are *not* friends." She found a rock and launched it at Cord. He caught it easily.

Mistin shuffled her feet. "I'm a Caldash Witch. You're a Haven Witch. If we can't find a way to see past our differences, how can we expect any of them to?"

Senna threw another rock.

Cord let it hit him, a dry expression on his face. "Are you finished throwing your tantrum yet?"

Trying to rein in her fury, Senna took a deep breath and let it out slowly. "Only a fool would trust either of you."

Mistin's shoulders sagged. "Our people are enemies, but they're also sisters. Besides, you need me. And as long as it doesn't contradict my orders, I'll do everything I can to help you."

She was right. Senna did need her. Perhaps it was possible to use their relationship to her advantage.

Mistin was silent for a time and then she chuckled. "By the Creators, Cord's head is one I'd never want to be in."

Senna lifted a hand to brush a strand of hair from her face. "I can't find Ellesh's tree. I can't find anything in this place." She studied Mistin. "So how did you find me?"

Mistin steered her down a different path. "You sort of stand out, Senna. All I had to do was ask."

Through the crescent link, Senna felt the smallest thread of hope. She focused on it. From his half dozen steps behind her, Cord was thinking that if she could work with Mistin, she could work with him. She stiffened and shot him a glare.

He was right. The bond between them was permanent. She would have to find a way to live with it.

But not today. Today she was still angry.

29. THE REPLACEMENT

A single eyebrow raised, Mistin looked between the two of them. "Come on. The Heads are asking for you. They're having a big dinner with the other leaders."

"Then what do they want me there for?" Senna growled.

Mistin shrugged. "No idea."

Senna followed her back to the center of the city, into what Krissin had referred to as their castle. Krissin and the other Heads were waiting for her in one of the trees. The Composer wasn't in sight yet, but there were others. Three men and numerous women—about ten in all. Senna couldn't fathom who they could be.

A partial answer came from her link to Cord. The man on the far right was Jarlin, the Guardian's Leader. Senna only received faint impressions about the others. It was as if Cord didn't know them very well.

Senna squinted at him, trying to figure out how this bond worked. She felt a constant flow of his emotions. Every once in a while, his thoughts seemed to slip through, especially if he wanted to tell her something. But even then it seemed sporadic at best.

"Senna?"

She realized Mistin had been trying to catch her attention for some time. "They've set another place for you. I'll see you later."

Senna clamped her hand on the girl's arm. "You're not leaving me."

Mistin blinked and came close enough to whisper, "Senna, I'm not allowed in these kinds of meetings."

"Then I'm not staying either," Senna said through the fear twisting her belly into a knot. She was still angry. But if Mistin was her enemy, at least she was a known enemy. The Composer had invited Senna to a dinner with the leaders of Caldash, and she couldn't think of any good reason for that.

Mistin glanced uneasily around the room.

"Please." Senna forced the words past her teeth.

Mistin set her shoulders and went to speak with a woman Senna had never seen before. She reminded her of Chavis, with her trousers and short tunic, and weapons strapped to her chest.

The woman's head came up and she looked at Senna, who still stood in the doorway.

"Cord can look after his Witch," the woman said.

At the mention of his name, Senna felt Cord, standing against the wall, his hand on his weapon. There were other Guardians with him.

"Cord isn't welcome," Senna ground out.

The woman's eyes widened. After a moment, she gave Mistin a tiny nod.

Mistin found another chair and sat beside Senna, whose middle clenched with hunger.

Across from her, Krissin took a drink and smiled. "Eat whatever you like."

Senna considered refusing on principle. But being weak wouldn't help her escape.

Mistin pointed out the best of the greens—one mixed with a dried sour-sweet berry, candied nuts, and a sunset pink dressing that tasted of onions and wine vinegar. Mistin piled their plates high with some kind of meat drenched in a sticky sauce with more dried berries and nuts.

Senna glanced at the numerous faces around the room. She caught snatches of conversations, everything from intercity trade to orders for weapons, while they ate food Senna had come to consider Witch staples—greens and herbs, berries and nuts, growing things that were easy for Witch song to create.

But where Haven's fish usually was, there was some kind of meat. She bit into it—sweet and sour, like the salad. Why did every nation besides Nefalie think meat needed to be sweetened? "What is this, anyway?"

"Lamb with dried bitterberries," Mistin whispered.

As the warm savor and sweetness filled her, she had to admit she was starting to get used to it. Like it, even. "Joshen would have loved this meal."

She hadn't realized she'd said it out loud until Mistin answered wryly, "He loved every meal."

A sad smile worked the corners of Senna's mouth. "Yes, but he would have especially liked this one."

Mistin squeezed Senna's arm. "When all this is over and we've defeated Haven and Tarten, we'll find him and set him free. And I'll make sure he gets to try each of these dishes. All right?"

Senna stared at her plate, bile rising in her throat. She'd been enjoying herself, while Joshen endured who knew what. She'd even slipped and forgotten to hate Mistin. *Use her, just like she used you,* she repeated to herself.

Senna gestured toward the woman who'd allowed Mistin to stay. "Who is she?"

Mistin bent closer. "Her name is Fallin. She's the leader of my order."

Senna swallowed. "Order?"

"In Caldash, each Discipline has an Order attached to it. Witches can join an Order if their strengths are better suited for it. Mistin pointed to each of the unknown Witches in turn. "Beneath Water are the Strykers—we're trained in the women's art of war alongside the Guardians. We can even become Guardians if we choose. Under Plants are the herbalists and physicians. Merchants are under Earth. Under Sunlight are the teachers."

Senna took another bite of the too-sweet lamb. "So Fallin answers to your Head of Water?"

"No more than the lakes answer to the sea." Mistin took another bite of her food and went on. "Together, the three groups of leaders form the Triad. The Heads' collective vote counts as one, the Orders' vote as another. The Composer's vote is the third." She paused. "Like I told you, here we know that a Witch is more than just her song."

Senna glanced at Fallin. She didn't doubt there were knives hidden in her clothing. "Is it just the ones with weak songs that join an Order?"

Mistin grimaced.

"I'm sorry," Senna said, though she wasn't. "But I need to know."

A bit of the tension eased from Mistin's face. "Not always. Fallin is a level five."

Senna nodded. That was at least as strong as Prenny. "So every Witch is in a Discipline or a specialized Order within that Discipline?"

Mistin nodded. "Yes."

"And if a Witch doesn't wish to be part of any of it?"

Mistin's face went soft with pity. "They won't let you go, Senna."

"They can't keep me here forever." Though she wanted to shout, she whispered it so softly only Mistin could hear.

Mistin's reply was just as soft. "After Haven is defeated, there won't be anywhere else to go. And you're not the kind of woman to abandon your kind. We need you."

Senna's insides hurt. Before she could answer, the conversation suddenly ceased and everyone at the table came to their feet.

Senna looked up as the Composer strode into the room. The woman's presence made her feel queasy.

Mistin tugged on her arm. "You have to stand," she whispered.

It galled her to show respect to this woman, not just for what she'd done to Senna, but for what she planned to do to Haven. Glaring at the lamb, she stayed firmly in her chair despite the murmurs of "Composer."

Shocked silence descended upon the room. Feeling eyes on her, Senna looked up to see everyone, including Ellesh, watching her. But she didn't stand.

With a sigh, the Composer moved to the brazier and filled mugs from a teapot simmering over the fire. She carefully poured and distributed the cups around the room.

Lastly, she held out a chipped cup to Senna, who didn't move to take it from the old woman's outstretched hand.

Mistin shot her a warning look, and the room grew very still.

Ellesh simply set the cup in front of Senna before taking her seat. Everyone sat down.

The Composer blew the steam off the top of her tea before taking a sip. "I have called this meeting to name my replacement."

The Heads exchanged uneasy glances. The Guardians surrounding the room shifted their weight. Senna pushed the mug away.

Ellesh didn't rise to the bait. "Guardians are charged with protecting Witches, Heads are in charge of nature, the Orders with the running of our people. And I" —she took a deep breath— "I am your judge. Our relationship is built on trust and mutual goals. But I have broken that trust."

She folded her hands across her lap and stared at them. "When Haven cursed Tarten, Millay and I knew our time in hiding was at an end. We sent spies out into the world to learn how they were saved and by whom, as well as how to ensure we won the battle that was coming."

Senna guessed Millay was the Head of Water sitting next to Fallin, as both women were dressed like warriors, though Millay looked rather old for it. Senna leaned toward Mistin. "I thought you couldn't cross the barrier until recently?"

Her eyes never leaving the Composer, Mistin answered, "*We* were never able to return, but our *songs* could, remember?"

Senna felt a stab of sympathy for the women who'd left Caldash. She knew what it was like to leave her home, knowing she could never return.

Ellesh looked up and her dark eyes met Senna's. "That's how we learned another Creator-touched had come into being. The cycle had come full circle—beginning and ending with two Witches of unequalled power." Her voice dropped and she seemed to address Senna alone. "So you can imagine my dismay when I discovered you had aligned with Haven. I sent Mistin and Cord to fetch you if they could."

The Composer's gaze felt too intimate. Senna looked away. "It doesn't have to be this way," she said. "Let me talk to them."

"You know they won't listen." Ellesh's voice was thick.

Senna closed her eyes. Ellesh was right. Caldash's alliance with Tarten had forever destroyed that hope.

Krissin cleared her throat. "I don't see how you've broken our trust, Composer. We all agreed to this."

Ellesh sipped her tea before carefully setting the cup down. "I bound Brusenna to a Guardian."

Krissin winced. Gasps and murmurs of conversation flooded the room.

"But that's only ever done by Witches who've married their Guardians!"

"The poor girl."

"No wonder she refused to stand."

Senna felt more than heard the unease from the Guardians at her back. A sharp spike of shame flowed from Cord.

One of the Heads spoke up louder than the rest. "Your actions served a higher purpose—surely we can understand that."

Ellesh's gaze was distant and unfocused. "I doubt Brusenna would agree."

She felt the weight of their stares, the heft of their silence.

"On the brink of our war, we must think to the future. After we have defeated these Witches, we will ask them to join us, but we must give them something in return. One of them will take my place."

Senna looked up sharply. Ellesh's dark eyes were on her. "Haven will need some proof of our intentions. Brusenna as our Composer will accomplish that."

Krissin said carefully, "Composer Ellesh, she is still a child."

Ellesh grunted. "No. Just young. She will make mistakes, but no more than I did. Than I still do."

Krissin opened her mouth to argue.

Ellesh held up her hand and stared Krissin down. "She is Creator-touched, Head. Have you forgotten what that means?"

Senna straightened under all the scrutiny. It meant she had been chosen by the Creators. She could hear the Four Sister's songs, create her own songs. It meant power.

Krissin made no more arguments.

Ellesh stared at Senna and seemed to speak to her alone. "I offer you everything you've always wanted. A chance to change the Witches for good. A better way of living. Witches who are respected by their people. Witches who are powerful and good and do not abuse their power."

Despite her animosity towards these women, Senna's spirit stirred. Ellesh was right about much of it, but there had to be another way.

Ellesh lifted her tea. "To our Composer in Training."

The women all slowly raised their cups and tipped them to their lips.

Through her stunned haze, Senna felt Cord's worry and heard Mistin's whispered voice. "Drink it."

Senna stared at the brown liquid. She considered refusing, but what had Coyel said weeks ago? A position of power would mean the chance to change things—to protect the Haven Witches who survived. The power to make sure all the Witches were treated as equals. The mug felt as heavy as Senna's heart as she lifted it to her lips. She forced down a couple of hasty swallows, but couldn't finish the rest. It was too bitter. And somehow familiar, but she couldn't place it. She suppressed a grimace as she plunked the cup down on the table.

Ellesh watched her. "You must finish it." Senna tipped the cup to her lips and pretended to drink.

The Composer bowed her head. "After the battle is over, I shall step down, and Brusenna shall take my place." She looked up at the many faces in the room. "If any object, I will hear you now."

To Senna's disbelief, no one did. Ellesh nodded. "Very well. Let it be written in the Chronicles of the Law."

Millay rose to her feet, her hands splayed across the table. "As you know, I sent out orders this morning for our ships to stand ready. Even now, the last of our seeds and potions have been sent downriver. We begin moving out tonight."

Low murmurs rose from those seated, but it was not the chatter of surprise or frustration. All of these women had known what was coming.

All except Senna. She slipped the cup beneath the table and poured the contents onto the floor. A small act of defiance, but it was better than nothing. She rubbed her eyes. It had been a long few weeks, and she was exhausted, but she had to drudge up the last of her reserves to find a way on those ships. If she could just manage to escape from Cord first.

She felt him watching her. No doubt he already knew her thoughts. There had to be a way around that. The impossibility of it made her limbs feel so heavy.

"And now, I must apologize to you again, Brusenna." Ellesh surprised Senna by speaking from beside her. She took Senna's cup and examined the dregs.

Not liking the way the woman towered over her, Senna stood. She was surprised how hard it was to keep from swaying. "For what, Ellesh?" She refused to call the woman by her honorific title.

The Composer motioned for Cord to come closer. "For drugging you."

Senna sucked in a breath. She tested the unnatural heft of her limbs. Her heavy eyes. And she remembered the bitter tea. "But everyone drank the same tea," she protested.

"The sleeping powder was already in the chipped cup."

Senna felt Cord behind her, his hands outstretched in case she fell. But she hadn't swallowed it all. That single act of defiance might save her.

But Cord would know that. She met his gaze and pleaded through the link. In return, she felt his fury, but not with her. Instead, his anger was directed at Ellesh.

His conviction spilled into her. He wouldn't tell the Composer and give the woman another reason to violate Senna. He would watch her carefully and keep her safe. He promised it to himself and her even as Senna pitched into him.

In one smooth movement, he held her limp body protectively in his arms.

Ellesh rubbed her face tiredly. "I have done two great wrongs against you, child. I'm sorry for that. But it's better this way. Better you wake long after we're gone. Too far away for you to catch up to us. Too far away for you to interfere or risk yourself. Still, I am sorry."

Senna was finding it difficult to concentrate. "When I am Composer, I'll make you pay for this."

Ellesh chuckled dryly. "We'll see, Brusenna. We'll see."

30. Forever Sleep

Senna woke to the sound of pacing. She sat up with a start. The drug still pulled at her, but she fought it with every bit of determination she had. It was still dark out. Maybe it wasn't too late. But before she'd even reached the door, Cord was there. Knowing the link was betraying her every idea, she tried to think of a way to escape without actually *thinking* of a way to escape.

Cord took her arm and steered her toward the bed. "Go back to sleep."

She was afraid if she lay down again for even a moment the warm bed would capture her. "What right do you have to even be here?" It wasn't appropriate to have a man in her bedroom.

He blinked as if he was having a hard time keeping his eyes open. "The bond is considered practically a marriage anyway."

Ignoring that, she narrowed her gaze at him. He seemed nearly as tired as she did. Was it possible the potion was affecting him as well, perhaps diluting its potency between the two of them? She hadn't even drunk all of it.

Was that why he'd been pacing earlier? To try to stay awake?

She thought of potions she could use, but she didn't have any potions—or seeds. All she had was herself.

She missed Joshen so much. She remembered another time when sleep had pulled at her, dragging her down to its soft depths. A song had saved her. It had been magic, not of power or potions, but the magic of one soul connecting to another.

Softly, she sang a lullaby her mother had sung to her as a child, when she was free from danger and betrayal.

Magic rings and moonbeams,
Star giggles and shadow schemes,
Gallantly slip the singing streams.
The lion basks in the flower's beams
In the garden of your dreams.

Cord slumped against the doorway. Behind him, there were more Guardians assigned to watch her, but they were staring glassy-eyed at the fire.

With a start, Cord rubbed his face and looked at her blearily. "What are you doing?"

Firmly tamping down any thoughts of escape, she sank into the bed to allay his fears and sang again. It had an immediate effect. Behind him, one of the Guardian's heads tipped back. The other rested his forehead on the table. Cord slumped forward, his eyes closed.

Focusing fiercely on the song, Senna sang again. Cord's legs buckled. He caught himself with a start. Half asleep, he glanced at her, his mind fighting to wake.

Hoping against hope that it worked, Senna rose seductively. She crossed the room one swaying step at a time. She didn't let her voice falter or hitch as she reached out and took his hand.

The connection between them surged again—the joy of finding something you never knew you had lost. He followed the seduction of her song. She had him captured in a spell. She didn't question how. She pulled him down on the bed beside her. Propping herself up on her elbows, she sang over and over. It wasn't enough. But it hadn't been that other time, either.

With the vibration of the song still powering her lips, she kissed him, softly, gently. Her lips held enough residue from her songs to push him over the edge. With a slip of a sigh, he eased into sleep.

A surge of triumph coursed through her. Cord shifted. Reining in her emotions, Senna hummed the lullaby. She crossed the room, then stepped out and eased the door shut behind her, keeping her thoughts firmly on the song.

The two Guardians in the main room were sound asleep—one was even snoring. Keeping her steps light, Senna took Cord's cloak and draped it across her shoulders. It was much too long for her, sweeping the ground, but it would keep her warm and hide her light coloring in shadows.

After tugging the hood low over her face, she gently pushed the door open and left the tree house. Just to be sure, she kept humming the song.

Hoping a little distance would mute her link with Cord, she moved directly away from the tree. She put a few dozen paces between them before starting in the direction where she thought the shore was. The city was eerily empty. She walked for far too long before stopping to look around.

After all she'd been through, she was going to fail to escape because she was lost! Pressing the heels of her palms into her eyes, she tried to force her sluggish mind to think.

How did the Caldashans find their way? Senna remembered walking with Mistin and Cord. They had glanced around quickly, like they were seeing some sort of sign, but what?

Senna studied everything around her, trying to figure out which path would lead in the right direction.

But Mistin and Cord had never looked at the paths. They'd looked at the trees. Senna stopped short. Moss grew on the trees' north side. She glanced up and caught glimpses of stars in the sky. She'd spent enough time on a ship to understand how to read the stars, at least a little. Now she knew which way was north. With this new way of looking at things, she made a left and headed towards the river. She didn't watch the paths—she watched the moss and the stars above her.

Senna didn't know how long she'd traveled when she saw a woman running through the trees, a package clutched to her chest. Moving on instinct, Senna broke into a run after her, careful to keep a safe distance. Soon, more girls had joined the first. Senna hurried to catch up with them. Breathing hard, she was careful to lag a little behind. By the time they reached the docks, there were nearly ten of them.

There was only one riverboat remaining. The rest of the Witches must have already left on their journey downriver, where larger ships waited to take them to sea, and from there to Haven. She had to find a way aboard this boat and then a seagoing ship if she wanted any chance of stopping the Caldash Witches from destroying her home.

"About time," a Guardian huffed. "The other boats left long ago."

The girls answered with a chorus of "I'm sorry"s.

Senna kept quiet; she didn't want her accent to reveal her. It was dark enough that the shadows hid her features. Still, she kept her cloak pulled low over her face and stayed right on the heels of the girl in front of her.

Quelling her hesitation, Senna stepped into the boat.

The Guardian climbed in after her, obviously not pleased that theirs was the last boat to leave. "All of you try to get some sleep. We'll be transferring to the ships early in the morning." He finished untying the boat, and he and the other Guardians took up positions around the perimeter, steering them downstream.

Senna lay on the floor of the boat, which was lined with straw and blankets. Some Witches were sitting up, watching the city of Lilette grow smaller by the moment. Others had already lain down. Senna found a place facing the side of the craft and put her back to the others. She wrapped Cord's cloak so it completely covered her and finally gave into the pull of the potion.

Some time later, she woke with a sudden surge of panic. Her left side was soaked. Apparently, the boat leaked. Unable to help the groan that escaped her lips, she sat up. It was early morning, so early the darkness was still thick and soft like rabbit fur.

The small boat maneuvered into the dock. Large ships towered above them.

As far as Senna could tell, there was nothing to justify the fear splitting her insides apart. But the panic didn't ebb. Then she realized it wasn't hers. Cord must have woken up and discovered she was gone.

To her relief, the connection didn't feel as strong as before. She had a vague feeling of Cord's direction, but she couldn't be sure of the distance. Hopefully, his link was as fuzzy as hers. She tried to keep her mind blank.

Sleep still clinging to her like a sickness, she stumbled to her feet. Shivering, she joined the columns of Witches who had climbed out of the smaller crafts to enter the surging, shouting chaos surrounding the docks.

Sailors were everywhere, directing the Witches from the small river crafts to board dozens of enormous seagoing ships, working the pulleys that loaded pallets of cargo, and scrambling up and down masts. One of them was probably the ship Senna had arrived on not long ago.

Any moment now, someone was going to glance under her hood and get a good look at her face. Ducking her head even lower, she mumbled an apology to the sailor and went back to the boat to pretend to look for something.

The Guardian from the night before caught sight of her in the boat. He worked through the throng toward her. "Here now, hurry up. You have to stay with your choir. They'll leave you behind and then we'll have no end of trouble figuring out where you should be."

He held out his hand to help her out of the boat. Knowing her pale skin would reveal her, she pretended she didn't see it and climbed out herself.

He watched her warily, the first hints of suspicion touching his features. He took her elbow. "Come with me. I'll make sure you catch up."

She had to get away from him. Now.

At that moment, the men loading a crate of cargo with pulleys and horses gave a shout, ordering the Guardian and Senna to stop. The crate wobbled unsteadily. The Guardian's eyes were finally off her.

"I remember where I put it now," she mumbled to hide her accent. He shot her an annoyed look but let go of her. She did the only thing she could. Moving out of sight beside the boat, she sat down and slipped off the pier into the water. The shock of the cold drove back her exhaustion.

Her sandals and clothes weighed her down and made swimming impossible. She unlatched her cloak and let it drift down to the bottom. She dove, managing to stay underwater until she'd put the ship between her and the too-curious Guardian. She came up on the other side and took a silent breath as he called for her in confusion. She doubted he would shrug off her disappearance, but there was nothing she could do about that.

Glad her time as a seal had taught her that ships usually had rungs up the side, she found them and hauled herself out of the water. Her clothes felt heavy and her limbs tired. The metal was slick under her sandals. Halfway up, she slipped and banged her shins on the rungs.

Dangling by her hands, she scrambled for purchase. She finally managed to haul herself up to the top rung. But the deck was swarming with Witches, Guardians, and sailors. There was no way she could climb over the rail without someone noticing. After hooking her arms around the top rung, she waited for things to settle down.

They didn't. Even after the ship left the docks and moved downriver, she was stuck. Dawn finally came. Eventually, her clothes dried and the sun baked the shivers out of her. Soon after, she was hot, and her recently dried dress became damp with sweat instead of river water.

Cord's panic seemed to have settled. She felt him moving toward her. He'd left the city of Lilette, his attention focused singly on her. Still, she didn't think he'd catch up to her before they reached the open seas.

She tangled her arms through the rungs and dozed when she could. She grew painfully thirsty and desperately needed to empty her bladder. No matter how much she shifted, some part of her was always numb.

More than once, someone on the riverbank gaped at her. There was nothing for it but to wave and smile. Bewildered, they waved back. She saw lots of Mettlemots and was dismayed that, other than size, they all looked just like Pogg.

It was midday before they reached the open sea. The traffic on deck began to slow, and Senna started to hope she might sneak on board. But then a wind message came from the city of Lilette. Its meaning was garbled, barely discernible. All the Witches with any power of song or knowledge of war had already left, which led Senna to believe it had been sung by the weakest of Witches— Wastrels. They would've had to spend the entire morning singing for a single message.

She felt a little sorry for them, even if their song had betrayed the fact she was missing and presumed onboard one of their ships.

This announcement was followed by a heartbeat of silence, and then Krissin's voice rang out, "Have the ship searched. Now."

Senna readjusted her grip on the rungs and hoped they wouldn't think to look over the side. After searching for what felt like hours, the ships rang with the confirmation that no one had seen Senna.

They were out in the open water now, fast approaching the shimmering barrier.

Senna's sigh of relief caught in her throat when they passed through. She was lost and afraid and alone. And then they were on the other side. The sudden storm bit into her flesh, but she barely felt the wind's teeth. She was too consumed by horror at the sight of dark ships stretching as far as she could see.

An armada bearing Tarten's red flags. At this distance, Senna would be hard to make out, but that wouldn't last for much longer. She couldn't stay here, not where any Tarten could look out and see her. She'd rather take her chances with the Witches.

Gripping the next rung with shaking hands, she peeked over the side. There were people everywhere and nowhere to hide. "Might as well get this over with," she muttered to herself. She hauled herself up and over the side. Her muscles had cramped into place. She straightened herself stiffly.

Everyone on deck froze.

Krissin moved first, marching over and gripping Senna's arm, a phalanx of Guardians at her back. "Foolish girl! Do you know what you've done?"

Senna was too tired to care. "I'm thirsty, and I need to relieve myself."

"We should take her back," Krissin's Guardian said.

Krissin pursed her lips. "How long do you think it will take for the Haven Witches to feel our songs? We've passed the barrier. We mustn't stop now." She glanced at the Witches standing a little ways back. "Sing to those in the city of Lilette. Tell them we found her, and make certain none of the Tarten ships hear the song."

"If the Tartens find her, they'll kill her," the Guardian warned.

Krissin sighed. "They couldn't possibly know she's here."

One of the sailors called, "Head, a Tarten captain is requesting to board."

Krissin's skin went a chalky gray. "Our ship? But if they meet with anyone it should be Millay. She is the Head of War."

The sailor shook his head. "They've already put a boat in the water, Head."

Krissin pointed to two Guardians. "Get Brusenna out of sight. If she tries anything foolish, knock her unconscious."

The Guardians grasped Senna's arms, hauled her into one of the officer's small cabins, and told her to keep quiet. Then they shut the door.

Senna found and used the chamber pot. Then she waited in the dim, cramped room, sweat starting down her back. Soon, she heard voices on deck. Unable to hear or see anything, she perched on the edge of the bed.

It wasn't long before the door was pushed open. Krissin stood looking at Senna, her face hard. She nodded to the Guardians. "Go on deck with the others. Be ready for trouble." After they left, she shut the door behind them. "Somehow the Tartens know you're onboard."

Waves of dread rushed through Senna with each heartbeat. "What? How?"

She felt Cord reacting to her fear. She pushed the interference aside.

Krissin shook her head. "I don't know. But if I don't bring you out, they'll call off our alliance. And if they don't attack us immediately, Haven will. We've already revealed ourselves to them. Either way, it'll mean war—a war we might not win. I can't save your life at the cost of hundreds more, Creator-touched or not, next Composer or not."

Senna rested her head in her hands and then started when Krissin shoved a waterskin, hard bread, and salted lamb into her hands. "Keep it next to your breasts. That's the safest place for it."

"Unless they rape me."

Krissin faltered. "Try and stay alive until our battle with them is finished. We'll monitor the ship they have you on and try to negotiate for your release."

Senna doubted she would live that long.

Krissin held the door open and gestured her out. Unused to the brightness, Senna squinted at the dark figures on deck. When she recognized them, she went as still as a grave. Grendi narrowed her eyes. With wings of white at her temples, her thick black hair was piled in elaborate twists on top of her head. The silk of her sleeveless dress rippled like water. In her hand, she held Joshen's section of the crescent-moon pendant. It stretched and twisted toward the pendant at Senna's throat.

"No." The denial left her mouth before she could stop it.

Grendi delicately took the pendant and tapped it against her metal ring. It immediately went limp. Her smile was wide and predatory. "Brusenna. How fine to see you again. I'm so glad you crossed this abominable barrier so we could find you. We have much to catch up on."

Cold talons of fear wrapped around Senna's soul. "What have you done with Joshen?"

Grendi tapped her lips thoughtfully. "Joshen, Joshen. Ah, yes. The Guardian who refused to tell me all about you, no matter how much we tortured him. It wasn't until I found the old woman—what was her name? Desni— that I finally learned the secret of your pendant." Grendi carefully tucked the pendant in her dress pocket. She turned to the soldiers next to her. "Bring her in the other boat. Bound *and* gagged."

Rough hands seized her. "What did you do to him?" Senna screamed. "What did you do?"

Grendi slowly turned, her face unreadable. "I offered them forever sleep or more torture. They chose to sleep."

Senna's muscles melted and she collapsed, barely feeling the pain as her knees hit the deck. "No."

Grendi watched her, satisfaction etched in her face. "Torture is a complicated art, Brusenna. The line between pain and death is very thin. And the human body can only take so much."

Hatred burned in Senna's chest. Words poured hot from her mouth, seeming to coat her tongue with ash. A song that could set the very world on fire.

Ember to flame
Scorch and burn
To Cinders and ash

"Stop her!" Grendi screamed as smoke rose around her feet. Waves of heat roared up from the ship, hot enough to blister Senna's knees through the thin fabric of her dress.

A sharp blow to the jaw silenced her song. A gag was shoved in her mouth, her wrists bound with rough cords. As they dragged her away, she cast a glance back at Krissin.

The Head of Sunlight looked away, shame coloring her cheeks.

31. WATER SONG

Senna was too horrified to cry, too horrified to think. She only knew she wanted to die.

Joshen was dead, and it was her fault. After all, she'd dragged him to Tarten knowing full well how dangerous it was. Her eyes refused to focus, sounds became muddled, and her body lost all feeling. She was so full of pain, her senses were shutting down.

Through the link, Cord kept trying to reach her. She ignored him as she would a fly ramming a window.

Grendi stepped so close Senna could smell her sickly sweet perfume. She watched in satisfaction as they hauled Senna's hands above her head and tied her waist to the foremast.

"We'll be in Haven in two days. And then you can watch your people—your home—fall apart around you, as you made me watch mine."

Senna wet her lips. "You promised Ellesh you'd turn over the survivors. You break that promise, and she'll sink your ships."

Grendi leaned in so close her hair tickled Senna's face. "Let her sink them." She observed Senna's sickened expression. "When it is over, we'll hang you and display your body in Tarten until you crumble to dust with everything else." She stepped back and addressed the soldiers around her. "No food. No water." Then she turned and was gone.

Senna closed her eyes, her body racked with sob after sob.

***

For two days and a night Senna was tied to the mizzen mast. During the day, the sun baked her skin. Blisters formed during the night. Her tongue swelled in her mouth. She couldn't work up any saliva or tears, so she kept her eyes and mouth closed.

Her arms felt like dead weight above her head. She tried to wiggle her fingers, but she couldn't tell if she succeeded or not. Perhaps her hands were already dead. She couldn't drudge up enough emotion to care. She couldn't sit, couldn't rest. She was thirsty—so thirsty.

She actually took comfort in Cord's presence, more so the closer he came. She was able to retreat into him just a little. Even though she was sharing her suffering with him, he seemed to take it gladly. She suspected that without the link, she'd be dead already.

She must have dozed, for when she woke again it was night. She was hyperconscious of the waterskin under her tunic. She felt the liquid through the bladder, heard the slightest slosh whenever she shifted.

Under cover of darkness the night before, she'd tried for hours to reach it, until the blisters around her chin had cracked and oozed down her shirt. She had to try again.

She wiggled her chin under her filthy tunic and stretched her tongue under the gag, trying to curl it around the waterskin's neck. She dropped her body weight, using the pressure of the ropes to force the bladder further up. She worked for hours, until her neck cramped and something wet ran down her neck—more fluid from her blisters, or perhaps blood.

Suddenly, she realized someone was standing in front of her. Her Tarten guard. How long had he been watching her? Surely he knew of the waterskin's presence by now. He studied her, his face drawn. He looked furtively around before carefully pulling the waterskin free. He held it to her lips.

She was so shocked she gaped at him.

He nudged her and she drank, water dribbling out the sides of her mouth because of the gag. The water tasted wonderful, and her body absorbed it like parched earth. When she'd drained the waterskin, the guard carefully tucked it back out of sight. His movements slow and gentle, he reached inside her tunic, pulled out some of the hard bread, and slipped it in her mouth. The gag was too tight for her to chew, but she managed to soften it enough to swallow.

She tried to catch his eye to give him a nod of thanks, but he refused to look at her. When he'd fed her all the bread, he took up his position again.

Eventually, she slept. And unlike last time, she knew when she woke up, she'd still be alive.

She stirred at the distant sound of thunder. She blinked the sleep from her eyes, then squinted into the distance. Black clouds rolled toward them, lightning leaving jagged images in her aftervision. She felt a change in the air—a heavy kind of expectation. A hurricane.

Through the link, Cord felt so close she knew he must be on one of the Caldash ships. She had the presence of mind to wonder how he'd caught up to her.

Closing her eyes, Senna listened to the Four Sisters' songs— oppressive chanting that twisted the Sisters' natural songs into something dark and sinister. The Haven Witches were trying to force the ships back. The Caldash Witches were countering the storm, creating unnatural pockets of calm for the armada to slice through.

The two opposing songs clashed, creating chaotic noise that grated against Senna's ears until they felt raw. She clenched her teeth, trying to think past the shrieking cacophony.

The wind surged toward them. The ship scaled a wave as big as a mountain, until it seemed they were climbing to the sky. They slowed near the top. Senna was certain they weren't going to make it. She imagined them sliding back, the craft rolling over.

The ship clung to the top of the wave at a standstill. Suddenly, they rushed down again, sending Senna's stomach into her throat. They smashed into the trough. Spray exploded across the deck and slammed into her. It was so cold it stole the breath from her lips. She gasped, water streaming down her face and stinging her eyes.

Tarten sailors flashed in and out of sharp relief with each flash of lightning. A bolt shot through the sky, heading straight for their ships. But before it hit, another bolt cut into its path. The two collided with a percussion that shook the air and made Senna's ears ring.

The war had begun.

For what seemed like hours, they fought their way through the storm. Helpless as the ship she'd been anchored to, Senna tipped her face to the rain, letting her mouth fill with water until she felt nearly normal. If only she could stop shivering.

And then, through the unnatural twilight, she saw waves shattering white against distant cliffs. Haven.

Senna wanted to scream at the Haven Witches to move the island. She could imagine the scene. Witchling messengers running everywhere. Witches singing in the Ring, firm in the belief the Tartens and their Witches could never cross their walls. The Haven Witches would see it as a siege, one they would simply outlast as the sea battered their enemy's ships into pieces.

When the ships were in range, the captain shouted orders for them to turn the broadside cannons on the cliffs. Senna didn't understand. Surely they didn't think they could beat down sheer walls hundreds of feet thick with mere iron balls.

Cannon fire boomed beneath her feet, but instead of cannon balls, modified anchors arched through the sky, ropes trailing behind them.

A few anchors exploded in a deadly rain of shrapnel against the cliffs, and some bounced harmlessly to the sea. But a few caught hold. A wave hit their ship, pushing it away from the cliffs, dragging its anchors back into the water. The anchors were hauled back and fired again. This time they held.

Senna's apprehension suddenly, inexplicably spiked.

Guns strapped to their backs, Tarten soldiers were tied to the ropes. They climbed hand over hand from the ships toward the waiting cliffs. There was no one to stop them. A cry left Senna's lips, a warning the Haven Witches would never hear. If she hadn't been tied to the mast, Senna would have fallen to her knees. The guard who had given her the water turned to look at her, pity in his eyes.

With a mighty crack, one of the anchors gave way. The guard's head whipped back around. On deck, the sailors grabbed the rope and heaved it across the deck, hauling swamped soldiers back toward the safety of the ship. Before long, the half-drowned soldiers sprawled across the deck, gasping for breath. There weren't nearly as many as had left. At least half of them must have drowned.

The cannons were fired again and the sailors started across it for the second time. The rest of the anchors held.

By the time the Haven Witches realized their peril, it would be too late.

Senna pictured Haven as it had once been, shining and filled to the brim with Witches and Guardians who were lauded for their power and skill. If Tarten succeeded, Haven would be a burned-out ruin of ash and rot.

She couldn't bear it. She pulled at her bonds. They cut into her chaffed wrists, but they wouldn't give. She sagged against the ropes, letting them take all of her weight. It was hopeless. She'd done everything she could, and it hadn't been enough.

Suddenly, lightning struck the side of the ship. Electricity jumped across the water-soaked deck, sending a shock through Senna. She could smell burning, hear shouting, and feel the tremble of dozens of running feet, but she couldn't see what was happening.

A soldier shot past her, his fist colliding with the man guarding her. She tried to wrap her mind around the idea of one Tarten soldier attacking another. But the man who turned to her wasn't a Tarten soldier.

It was Cord, the too-small soldier jacket half-buttoned over his chest. With his dark features, he could easily pass for a Tarten in this chaos.

Kneeling over the semiconscious guard, he yanked a knife free of its ankle strap.

"Don't!" Senna cried through the gag. She couldn't bear for Cord to kill him.

With a grunt of exasperation, Cord reversed the knife and hit the guard on the temple. He pulled the unconscious man out of sight, then pressed up against her and peeked past her. The warmth of Cord's body suffused her with beautiful heat.

His breath stirred across her mouth as he spoke, "I don't think anyone noticed." His face twisted as if the sight of her pained him. "I'm so sorry, Brusenna."

He cut the gag from her mouth. Her jaw trembled as she closed it for the first time in two days. His sharp knife cut through the ropes holding her hands. Her arms dropped down in front of her, so heavy she couldn't lift them, but the skin on her wrists wasn't black, just a lurid purple. At least the tissue was still alive.

"How?" Senna had to shout to be heard over the storm.

"Did you think I wouldn't come for you?" Cord cut through the bonds tied around her waist. The knife sliced into her skin and she didn't care. With a sudden burst of ropes, she was free. Unable to support her weight, her legs buckled.

Cord guided her to the deck, where she collapsed in a wet heap. Kneeling before her, he braced her up and pulled the rest of the ropes off her.

The feeling in her arms and hands was coming back, thousands of white-hot needles wheedling into her skin. "How did you catch up?" she asked through the pain.

Cord ruthlessly rubbed the circulation back into her hands. "The Composer went into a fit when I told her you had escaped. She put me in a smaller, faster vessel and made sure I caught up. Krissin and I watched you from our deck. She even sent a bolt of lightning to hit this ship—nice distraction, huh?"

"But how did you get onboard?" Senna's voice sounded broken and disused.

He brought out another waterskin and held it up for her to drink. Lukewarm, rich broth filled her mouth. The taste brought her out of her stupor. She grasped the skin and chugged greedily.

He watched her, guilt at letting her slip away from him seeping through the link. "I swam."

She choked, wasting the wonderful broth. She caught some in her hand and slurped it up without shame. "Through this?"

He nodded.

In these freezing, thrashing waters? Just to save her? That's what must have caused her spike of apprehension earlier. She'd felt his fear when he jumped into the water. She dropped her gaze. "You shouldn't have. It was too dangerous."

He peeked around the mast and watched the Tartens. "We need to get out of here."

Senna felt stronger than she had in days, but she still couldn't seem to get warm. She looked past Cord, at the sea rolling as if a giant, invisible hand stirred the surface. "How? I don't think I can swim in that. I don't know how you did."

He pulled a vial from his trouser pocket. "With this, we can make it back to the Caldashan ships."

She recognized it immediately as Ioa, the potion that allowed a human to take the shape of a seal. She took the topaz-colored potion from him, the glass slick under her fingers, and studied the hundreds of soldiers dangling over the open waters like laundry on a line. They were almost halfway there. "I have to warn Haven."

His arms on her shoulders, he pushed her back against the mast. "You can't stop this. No one can. All you can do is help the survivors."

"There won't be any survivors. Grendi doesn't care if her lands are restored or her ships sunk. My mother's in there, Cord."

He flinched as if Senna's words had burned him. And through the link, she could tell they had.

"If we leave now, we can warn the Guardians. They can reach the cliffs," she said more gently.

Cord lowered his head. He'd known what her answer would be when he freed her, and he'd come anyway. "I have to take you back with me, Senna."

Impulsively, she took his hand. "Come with me to Haven! Help me save them."

"You go back and you'll die with them. And that's if they don't throw you in a cellar to rot first."

"I can only control my actions, not their reactions," Senna replied. "But I have to live with both."

He opened his mouth to argue, but voices spoke, close enough she could make out their words over the tempest. Cord pressed her against the mast.

"You may come with me or not, but I'm going," she said right in his ear.

He felt her despair, as she felt his. He peeked around the mast and said in a harsh whisper, "I could stop you."

Her breath came fast. "I saved your life. And in return, you have done nothing but hurt and violate me. You owe me this."

He winced as if she'd punched him. "I just saved you. We're even."

She stared at him as water ran down both their faces. "We'll never be even. If you truly loved me, you wouldn't have stolen everything I cared about. You wouldn't stop me from saving the people I love."

Cord gazed at her as if seeing into her soul, and she realized he was probing the link. "But you love Joshen?"

She felt herself dying inside. "You and Ellesh took him away long before the Tartens killed him. You know that." It was the truth, much as she loathed to admit it.

He slowly nodded. "All right. But change us quickly."

Senna hauled her sopping-wet dress over her head and knelt shivering in her shift. Cord ripped off the Tarten red and stood before her, his chest glistening with rain and ocean spray.

She sang softly so the sound of her words wouldn't reach the Tartens. Her lips tingling with the power of the potion, she rubbed the oils off them and drew lines of the residue from Cord's forehead to his navel, her finger sliding effortlessly across his hard body.

He looked at her, his eyes hungry, and she realized the water had turned her shift nearly transparent, so much so that she could see the faint outline of her crescent-moon tattoo through the cloth. Cord gripped her face in his big, warm hands. He tipped forward and pressed his lips against hers. The warmth of it was overwhelming, but Senna could only see Joshen, think of Joshen.

"I had to know what that felt like." Cord pulled back and looked into her eyes. Sadness seeped through the link. Her thoughts had betrayed her. "Someday, you'll only think of me when I kiss you."

The idea sent a stab of grief through her. She tipped her head back and watched him. Was he really in love with her? She didn't think so. With the idea of her, maybe, but not really with her. "It wasn't the first time we've kissed."

He grunted. "That doesn't count. You tricked me." He released her as a shudder of pain took him. The Ioa was beginning to work.

Quickly, Senna sang the potion for herself. She dragged a line of potion down the center of her body.

Cord doubled over, a groan slipping from between his lips.

"What was that?" a voice asked.

A man rounded the mast and gaped at them before reaching for his sword. "What are you doing with the prisoner?"

In one smooth movement, Cord threw his knife. With a grunt, the man collapsed. A second man shouted for help. In two steps, Cord had the knife in his hand again, and the second man's warning fell silent.

His skin rippling, Cord clenched his jaws shut, a barely contained scream thick in his throat.

More Tartens rushed them. Cord fought them off, his knives flashing. Senna's skin shivered. She felt the first tremor in her bones. She grabbed Cord's arm. "Quick! Before it's too late."

Keeping her behind him, he backed them toward the banister.

"The Witch is escaping!" Someone yelled.

Wrapping her arms around Cord's middle, Senna threw them both over the side of the ship.

32. VELVETEN

Senna's bones thinned and elongated as she plummeted. Half-transformed, she hit the surface so hard her skin stung as if she'd fallen into a bed of nettles. Her bones reformed as she writhed in the sea's cold embrace. Slowly, so slowly, the pain receded. For the first time in hours, she didn't feel bone-deep cold.

Righting herself, she gathered her bearings. The sea was dark and full of bubbles, making it difficult to see and harder to swim. The current yanked her furiously this way and that.

Cord curled his tail under him and stared at it in disbelief. She swam to him and bumped him with her nose. He gaped at her with liquid seal eyes. Using her sensitive nose and whiskers, Senna swam toward the smell of seaweed.

When she reached the side of the island, she swam until she found the telltale sign of seaweed growing in the shape of a gibbous moon. She discovered the entrance to the cavern—a black mouth almost completely obscured by seaweed—and swam forward.

Something lunged out of Velveten's mouth. Senna only had time to register the flash of steel in a burst of lightning before Cord threw himself in front of her. His back arched and he let out a bark of pain.

Pain reeled dizzily through the link. The metallic taste of blood filled Senna's mouth above the salty, mineral taste of the water. With horror, she saw a harpoon sticking out of Cord's side. Rich blood clouded the water around the wound. Senna pivoted, searching for their attacker.

Flaring his limbs and then pulling them tight like a frog, Pogg shot through the water. He was already loading another harpoon. Haven must have sent him to guard the entrance from any Witches in a seal's disguise. She barked at him, but he couldn't understand.

Gently taking Cord's flipper in her teeth, Senna pulled him through the water, pumping as hard as she could for the entrance. She shivered. The realization that she felt cold shot through her—the first sign the potion was wearing off. There was no way she could swim the distance as a human. She had to get them out of the water or they would drown.

Out of the corner of her eye, she saw Pogg aim the second harpoon. She dove, taking Cord with her. She bit too hard into his fin. Blood seeped into her mouth, but there was nothing she could do. The harpoon sliced through the water above them. Senna shot forward again. Her skin shuddered and a tingle started in the middle of her tail, where her legs ached to split. Using her fins to steer, she pumped her tail, weaving along the bottom of the sea.

Pogg aimed at her. She put on a burst of speed and shot into Velveten's mouth as another harpoon embedded itself in the rocks behind her.

It was pitch black inside. Senna had to rely on her keen sense of smell and her whiskers to guide her through the cavern. Far above her, she saw a circle of wavering firelight. The tingling in her tail became painful before her skin split apart. Fins became feet and hands.

Her speed floundered as her spindly legs kicked at the churning water. She gripped Cord under his arms and pulled for the surface. Already her lungs were burning. She wasn't going to make it, not with Cord's extra bulk.

He wanted her to leave him—wanted it without restraint. But she couldn't bring herself to abandon him, and he was too weak to fight her.

Pogg burst into the cavern behind them, the harpoon clutched in his hands. He aimed it at her before his eyes went wide. He dropped the harpoon, then snatched Senna's and Cord's shoulders with his padded fingers and burst upward. It wasn't a steady progression, but one filled with stops and starts.

Senna's vision was beginning to go black around the edges. She touched Cord, using the link to tell him how sorry she was.

Pogg put on a final burst. Suddenly, Senna broke free of the water and took her first desperate breath. Pogg shoved her toward shore. Her muscles were locking up from the cold. Knowing he would see to Cord, Senna swam for the dock.

"Helps her!" Pogg cried.

"Pogg?" a voice called uncertainly.

"Helps!"

Senna tried to pull herself onto the dock, but her muscles refused to bear her weight. Panting, she dug her numb fingers into the wood. She felt the vibration of footsteps. She looked up to see a dozen muskets pointed at her face. It had happened so much over the past few days that she simply waited for whomever it was to decide whether or not to shoot her.

"Brusenna?"

She forced herself to look past one of the black barrels to the face of the man holding it. "Collum?"

He set the musket down, then gripped her arms and hauled her onto the dock. "Brusenna? What? You've been banished. How did you get past the Tartens—swim in this freezing water?"

She pointed to Cord. "Help my Guardian. He's hurt."

Two of the Haven Guardians bent to take hold of Cord.

Climbing up beside them, Pogg trilled a high-pitched keening that made her ears hurt. He hugged his knees and rocked back and forth. "Poggs not knows seals was Senna! Poggs not knows!" He repeated it over and over again.

Collum's eyes widened. "Who's this?"

Senna crawled to Cord's side and gaped at the harpoon sticking out of him. "He needs a Healer."

"You're the only Witch who isn't fighting." She recognized the speaker as Beck, Reden's second.

Shutting out Pogg's wails, she searched desperately for some kind of solution, but if she didn't heal him, no one would.

The harpoon had lodged deep into Cord's side, and blood leaked out around it. His face was gray instead of its usual warm brown. His lips were a dusky blue. He gasped for each breath, as if he couldn't fill his lungs.

A mountain of inadequacy crushed her heart. This was so far beyond her skill. "Cord," she breathed.

He couldn't seem to focus on her. Confusion and loss rolled through the link. He reached up and touched her face to reassure himself she was really there. She couldn't help but wince at the sight of the bite marks in his hand. "Senna?"

She studied the harpoon helplessly. "I can try to pull it out. If I can get the bleeding stopped, I might be able—"

Cord winced and took a shallow breath. "No. Leave it."

She opened her mouth to argue.

"You came to warn them," he reminded her.

"I have to—"

"Senna, I'm dying." Each word seemed to cost him.

His words wounded her deep inside. He had to be wrong, and yet she knew he wasn't. She felt it. His body was slowly shutting down and taking the link with it. There was nothing she could do for him.

He smiled and brushed her cheek with the crook of his finger. "You care. I can feel it."

She bit her lip to keep from crying. Holding herself together with the last gossamer threads of her determination, she faced Beck. "There are Tartens heading for the cliffs. You have to stop them!"

Her eyes widened as she really took in the dozens and dozens of Guardians—so many that Velveten was full. "Where did you all come from? What are you doing here?"

"Guarding Velveten," Collum answered.

She pointed toward the nearest stairwell. "They're not coming through the pool! They're coming from the cliffs."

Beck shook his head. "That's impossible. Any ship that got close enough to use ladders would be smashed to pieces against the cliffs. The only way in or out of the island is that pool!"

Senna gritted her teeth in frustration. "They fitted cannons with some kind of modified anchor and ropes. The Tartens are climbing them towards the cliffs right now!"

Beck gestured to two Guardians. "Tomes and Thayer, go scout those cliffs."

She shook her head. "You don't have time for that. They were more than halfway there when we left."

Beck studied her. "The Heads don't trust you. How do I know that dozens of Tarten boats won't surface the moment we leave the caves unguarded?"

She held out her wrists, raw and bruised. "I risked my life to escape and warn you." She saw by his expression it wasn't enough. She grasped for anything else that might convince him. "Reden trusted me enough to come with me when I left. He did it because he knew only I could save Haven."

After a moment's hesitation, Beck started shouting orders, "Double-time for the cliffs. Keep your musket under your coat until you need it—damp powder means a worthless musket." The Guardians hustled from Velveten. "Pogg, get back in the water and watch for any more seals who might really be Witches!"

Pogg paused in his mournful trilling to turn to Senna. "Poggs not knows."

She took a steadying breath. "I know you didn't. Go. It'll be all right."

Pogg jumped into the water and sank, the water cutting off his high-pitched keening.

Beck paused at the cave mouth. "Collum, keep her here and watch the entrance. If she tries to escape, shoot her. If the Tartens come, collapse Velveten."

"But Leader, that was our last resort."

Beck shook his head. "If she's lying, it's our only resort."

Senna lifted Cord's head onto her lap and stroked his hair. His cold hand squeezed hers. "Go. Help them," he said.

She didn't know tears were running down her cheeks until one dripped onto his face. She brushed it away. "I can't leave you."

He squeezed her hand. "Didn't. Stayed with me. In the water."

She felt as if her insides might shatter. A part of her was dying with him. "Cord—"

"Go." He pressed something into her hand. Senna looked down to find the Ioa potion in her palm.

"You might...need...it."

She shook her head. "No."

"Now...we're even. You saved...my life. I saved...yours, twice. Yes?"

She nodded as a tear ran down her nose. She brushed it off with the back of her hand. "We're more than even."

He grunted and the corner of his mouth quirked. "You'll succeed. Known it...from the beginning." His eyes rolled up and he was still except for his shuddering gasps.

The place he'd gone—she couldn't reach it through the link. Bending down, she pressed a kiss to his forehead, and this time, she thought only of him. When she pulled away, the link between them was gone.

Thunder boomed. A flash blinded her, but she didn't blink.

Collum started beside her. "By the Creators, that was close."

Senna cradled Cord in her arms. He had betrayed her. He had saved her. In his own way, he had loved her. How could she leave him? But the Guardians couldn't keep the Tartens back forever. There had to be less than two hundred of them—no match for Tarten's thousands.

If the Witches' songs were added to the Guardians' guns, they might be able to slow them long enough to move the island. Senna couldn't help Cord, not anymore. But she could still help her Witches.

She looked up at Collum. "You won't leave him alone?"

Collum shook his head. "Not if I can help it."

Gently, she laid Cord's head down. "Goodbye, my friend. I hope to see you again someday."

His eyes averted, Collum held out his cloak.

She remembered her sopping wet, nearly transparent shift. Embarrassment seemed such a small thing compared to men dying. "No. Cover Cord with it."

Collum didn't move. "I'll find a blanket."

When she didn't take it, he took a deep breath. "He doesn't need it, Senna. Not anymore. You're freezing."

Grudgingly, she took the cloak, shivering at the lingering warmth. "You're not going to shoot me?" She was banned from Haven after all, and he had his orders.

He pursed his lips. "I trust you."

She almost wished he didn't. Men who trusted her ended up dead. "You'll keep him safe?" It was a futile question. Nothing could ever hurt Cord again. But she had to ask.

Collum nodded. "I will."

Forcing herself not to look back, Senna left the smoky light of Velveten for the murky light of the storm. Lifting the bottom of her cloak, she ducked her head against the onslaught of rain and ran through the island. She heard all the Witches, their song so well matched it sounded like a single voice. The choir stopped and Senna recognized Chavis' forceful voice as she released the combined power of their songs.

Heat and light and power,
Strike the ships beyond our bower.
Lightning bolts to turn aside,
Waters roll back the enemy tide.

Senna reached the Ring of Power as Chavis finished the song. Light and sound exploded around her, throwing her to the ground and knocking the air from her lungs. Unable to draw breath, she watched as arcs of electricity shot across the barrier. They diminished before stopping altogether.

In a handful of heartbeats, dozens more lightning bolts streaked across the sky and shot beyond the cliffs. Some were intercepted and arched harmlessly across the clouds. Others seemed to hit their marks. Thunder shook the world.

As Senna struggled to her feet, Chavis was already singing another song.

A counter song rose from beyond the cliffs.

Chavis paused to draw breath, and Senna shouted into the expectant silence, "The Tartens are on the island!" Over two hundred pairs of eyes riveted on her. A few days ago that much attention would have paralyzed her. But shyness seemed another silly thing in the face of men dying. "We have to move the island now."

Stunned silence followed her pronouncement. Drenelle waved her hand, her rings flashing. "Pah! The Tartens are just men. It's the Witches we have to fear."

Dozens of women erupted into speech at once.

"How did she get on the island?"

"What makes you think you have the right—"

"It's a lie!"

Above the cacophony, Senna's mother cried out, "Brusenna?"

Their gazes locked for a moment, long enough for Senna to see the relief and regret on her mother's face.

"Silence!" Coyel shouted.

Drenelle said, "We've been over this. All we have to do is sit tight while they beat their fists bloody against our walls."

"Tarten soldiers have nearly reached the cliffs—too many for our Guardians to hold off. You have to move the island."

Chavis stroked the butt of the pistol strapped to her chest. "That's impossible."

As if to punctuate Senna's words, musket fire bloomed along the cliffs. All the Witches' minds were linked, so they moved as one to turn and see the battle illuminated by spills of lightning.

Prenny gaped at Senna. "By the Creators, she's right."

Like snake eyes, the gems on Drenelle's fingers flashed with a lightning strike. "It's a moot point. Our song isn't strong enough to move the island. Not anymore."

Coyel studied her. "You're absolutely sure?"

Drenelle nodded.

Chavis closed her eyes as if she were in pain. "You shouldn't have come back, Brusenna."

Senna ignored the grief in her voice. "With my song, you're strong enough."

"No!" her mother shouted.

Chavis snorted. "No Witch is that strong. Besides, you expect us to give control of the entire Circle to you? I think not. Even if the Tartens are on the cliffs, we'll collapse the ground beneath their feet, blast them with lightning."

"Your Guardians are up there!" Senna threw her hands out at her sides. "Besides, the Caldash Witches will protect them!"

"Caldash Witches?" someone said.

"Calden Witches who renamed themselves Caldash after Haven tried to destroy them centuries ago. They've been hiding behind a barrier."

There was a heartbeat of stunned silence. Only the Heads seemed to understand.

Prenny spoke up for the first time. "We didn't listen to her before, and look what's happened. I'll not stand by and watch you make the same mistake again." The old woman slowly stood, careful to keep her connection with the other Witches. "You are afraid of her—of what she's becoming. I understand that. I was afraid too. But Brusenna is not Lilette."

Chavis rounded on Prenny. "And if the song isn't strong enough and disintegrates after we release it? The island will collapse in on itself and we'll all die!"

Senna thought of Cord. Joshen. Reden. All dead for helping her deliver this message. She'd faced worse than old women's fears, and she'd come out stronger for it. She wasn't afraid anymore. "Perhaps you deserve the fate coming for you." She pointed at the others. "But the Witchlings? The Apprentices? All the other Keepers? I came back for them too. And if you deny the truth, perhaps they won't." There was a time for insurrection. Perhaps this was it.

"You're asking us to trust your word that you're strong enough?" Chavis asked.

Senna narrowed her gaze. "Yes."

"I don't." Chavis twisted to look at Drenelle. "You?"

Drenelle shook her head. "The kind of power to move that much earth...we've nowhere near what it would take."

Senna squared herself in front of Coyel, who held the sway vote. "It always comes down to this, Head. You and me."

Coyel studied her. "And if you manage to move us, what then? The Tartens will just come again and again."

"You'll have to abandon Haven and go into hiding or join Caldash," Senna said.

"As if we can trust Caldash," Prenny ground out.

Drenelle winced as a bolt struck dangerously close. "Now that we know how the Tartens plan to invade, we can defend against them."

Coyel held herself as still as death. Finally, she slumped as if the weight on her shoulders was too much. She eyed the women around her. "This song requires us to move to the cliff's rim. Spread yourself behind our Guardians and use wind to buffet the Tartens back. When the Guardians are behind us, we'll create a corporeal barrier." She paused. "And Brusenna will move the island."

"No!" her mother shouted as she broke the Circle, running to stand between the Heads and her daughter. The barrier flickered into fragments that dissipated like a rain of dying stars. "I'll not let her die."

Die? Senna didn't understand.

"You promised we wouldn't use Brusenna this way—that we wouldn't let her die! We all did," Prenny barked.

Coyel watched her mother, and Senna saw the friendship that had once been between them. "If she's right, she's the only one strong enough." The Head shifted her gaze to Senna. "I'm sorry."

Sacra fell to her knees before her daughter. "A singer has never lived through moving an island, Brusenna. Not even Lilette."

Senna knelt in the wet grass and encircled her mother in her arms. "You knew from the beginning I would die, didn't you?"

"I tried to warn you." Her mother's body trembled. "I knew Haven would use you up for its own purposes, just as they did me. It's one of the reasons I kept you away from them, why I tried again and again to get you off this island."

Love bloomed in Senna's breast like the promise of a rainbow after the storm has passed. "It has to be this way."

"No!" her mother cried. "I'll do it. I'll sing the song."

Senna noticed the outline of a pistol beneath her mother's coat. Looking up, she saw that all the Witches wore one. They would have one shot before the rain dampened their powder and made the guns useless. "You're not strong enough, Mother."

"No! I won't let you!"

Sadness was like a raw wound inside Senna. It was obvious her mother would never let her go—she couldn't. Senna looked at the others for help and found Prenny singing softly under her breath. The old woman flashed a violent purple potion at her as she sneaked toward Sacra.

Yarves. The potion would take away her mother's free will. The effects were permanent, unless the antidote was given in the first few hours.

Senna closed her eyes. It was the only way. She nodded slightly.

Prenny pressed her mouth to Sacra's before she could fight back. Her eyes went blank. Prenny ordered Sacra to the cliffs with the others. "I'll look after her," she promised.

Senna watched her mother go, her heart like a cold stone in her chest. "Tell her I'm so sorry."

Prenny nodded curtly and hurried after her.

Coyel grasped Senna's hand. "We aren't touching this time, so our minds won't link. Are you sure you remember the song?"

Senna smiled bitterly. "Even if I don't, I can move the island."

"No, you can't!" Drenelle shrieked. "I'm telling you, it's impossible. We're all going to die!"

"Spoken like the traitor you are," Senna cried.

Drenelle jerked as if she'd been slapped. "Traitor? I'm no traitor."

"No? When I was first attacked, you tried to stop us from searching for my attackers. The second time, you sent Joshen away, giving them the perfect opportunity to take me."

Drenelle held up her hands. "That's ridiculous."

Coyel eyed Drenelle suspiciously. "Drenelle?"

"I swear, I'm not working with Caldash."

Coyel stood stiff and unsure before seeming to make a decision. "You'll stay next to me until we can sort this out."

Drenelle went pale. "It won't matter. If she tries to move this island, it will all break apart."

Senna groaned. It was foolish leaving Drenelle free, but there wasn't time to argue the point.

Coyel took Drenelle's arm. "She's Creator-touched. That has to mean something." She turned to Senna. "Goodbye, Brusenna."

Everyone else had already gone. Senna was alone, and she was going to die. The thought frightened her, made her sick, but she didn't try to run.

Instead, she thought again of Joshen, dead for her. Of Reden and Cord. Her father and sister, whom she'd never even met.

And she realized most of the people she loved were already with the Creators. She would be joining them soon. Maybe there was nothing to fear after all.

Senna tipped her face up to the rain as her apprehension melted away.

She was ready.

33. TRAITOR

"Brusenna!"

Chavis strode across the green toward Senna. Arianis trotted behind her. Quick as a striking snake, Chavis pulled the pistol from her holster and pointed it at Senna from underneath the protective covering of her cloak. "I'll not let some silly majority vote get us all killed. Arianis, tie her hands."

Senna blinked in surprise. Arianis' mouth moved wordlessly, like a fish ripped out of the water.

"Arianis!" Chavis shouted.

Arianis jumped and hauled out some rope.

Senna shook her head. "I'm the only one who will die."

Chavis chuckled darkly. "I've trained for war my entire life. Don't pretend to tell me how to manage a battle."

Arianis wound the rope around Senna's already-raw wrists. The rough fabric dug into the scabs, breaking them back open. Senna hissed through her teeth. "How many people have to die, Chavis?"

Arianis tried to gag her, but Senna locked her teeth just after the rope had passed her incisors—something Joshen had taught her. It was obviously the first time the other girl had ever attempted to gag anyone, for she didn't seem to notice her mistake. Neither did the Head.

Chavis was careful to keep her pistol out of the rain. "Don't. Lecture. Me."

Arianis' hands were shaking as she tied off the knots. "They'll miss me if I'm gone any longer." She wiped her palms on her cloak. It was obvious she didn't want to be a part of this.

Chavis gestured for her to leave. "Fine. Go. I'll meet you at the cliffs."

Arianis hesitated, her gaze riveted to Senna. She started to slowly back away.

Refusing to beg, Senna watched as the other girl turned and ran.

Without the Witches' songs to counter the lightning, bolts slammed into the ground all around them. Chavis motioned Senna to move away from the Ring of Power. Where was she taking her? Ducking her chin, she managed to work the gag off.

Senna heard the unmistakable sound of a hammer cocking. "You sing one syllable, and I'll kill you. Do you understand?"

Senna believed her. Rain streaking down her face, she begged, "Please listen. I have to move the island or we'll all die."

Chavis ignored the plea. "How did you escape from the Tartens, anyway?

Senna's breath snagged in her throat. "How could you know that?"

Chavis stiffened. "Know what?"

"That it was the Tartens I escaped and not Caldash?"

Senna didn't realize she'd stopped moving until Chavis shoved her with the barrel of her gun. "You said it yourself."

Senna stumbled forward. They were inside the trees now. The wind lessened. Great drops of rain that had collected on the leaves plopped on Senna's head. Lightning ripped apart light and shadow, leaving jagged edges. "No, I didn't. The only way you could have known is—" She whirled around.

Jabbing the pistol at her chest, Chavis shoved Senna to the ground.

More pieces fit together. "When I defeated Espen, she had every Head's seed in her belt—except yours."

Chavis took a step back, her pistol aimed at Senna's heart, her eyes as dark as midnight. "You don't know what you're talking about."

"I was wrong. Drenelle's not the traitor. You are! You let Cord and Mistin on the island!"

Something shifted in Chavis' expression, and Senna realized the Head wasn't trying to force her to go anywhere. She was just staring. Cold realization shot through Senna. Chavis hadn't brought her into the trees to tie her up in some cellar. She'd brought her here to kill her.

Terror tore through Senna, caging her voice inside her throat. Not that it mattered—Chavis' bullet would stop her heart long before any song took effect.

Chavis must have seen the understanding dawn on Senna's face. "It's not what you think. When I first read the records, I realized what monsters we had become. Espen had the power to control us—to rein us in. So I worked for her, helping her from the inside."

"Why are you telling me this? Why not just shoot me?"

Something in Senna's gaze must have betrayed her disgust, for Chavis' face tightened. "I want you to know that I wouldn't kill you unless I had no other choice. I was out looking for you when you found Espen. She thought she could out-sing you. Pride always was her downfall."

"My mother and the others always claimed the traitor had been killed. Did you murder her, Chavis? Did you kill an innocent woman?"

Chavis' face registered no emotion. "No. I just made her look guilty after she was already dead."

"And what about Caldash?"

She shrugged as if it didn't matter anymore. "They found me, but you had to ruin that, too."

Senna shook her head, desperate now in a way she hadn't been just moments ago. "Traitor." She put all the venom she could in the word.

Chavis grunted. "Caldash will do a better job of controlling the world—you know it as well as I. Besides, they're stronger than us, especially with Tarten behind them. There was no way we could win this war. But if we surrender quickly, with few casualties, and are grafted to Caldash, we can overthrow the Tartens. It is better this way."

Senna hated that Chavis' words made a sick kind of sense. Caldash would do a better job. They were more cohesive, less corrupted. They didn't discriminate against Wastrels, instead making a place for them. The power of ruling was spread between the Heads, the Orders, and the Composer, each group checking the others. And they had learned to live in cohesion with the rest of the world, something Haven hadn't managed in centuries.

"There won't be any prisoners," Senna said. "Grendi doesn't care if every soldier she has dies. She's bent on revenge."

Chavis frowned. "That can't be true."

"You underestimated Tarten."

It was obvious Chavis didn't believe her. "I really hate to do this, but as I've told you many times before, casualties are a part of war."

Senna kept her eyes wide open. She wanted Chavis to see the life draining from them, wanted the image to haunt her for the rest of her life.

Chavis took careful aim. Musket fire cracked. Senna held her breath, waiting for the pain to envelop her, for the world to go dark. Instead, Chavis' face contorted and she pitched forward.

Bewildered, Senna released her pent-up breath. Then she looked past the Head and saw Arianis a little way off, black powder smoke drifting from her pistol as she watched Chavis die. "That ball wasn't meant for her. It was for the Tartens."

Senna struggled to her feet, wanting to shield Arianis from the curse she'd wished for Chavis. Using her shoulder, she propelled Arianis away from the sight of Chavis in her death throes.

Arianis was white-faced and eerily calm. She looked at Senna, pulled a knife from her seed belt, and began cutting the rope from her hands. "I hated you, Senna. You had everything I ever wanted, everything that was always meant to be mine. And you didn't even want it—I think I loathed you the most for that." Arianis stared unseeing at the knife gripped in her wet hand. "I wanted you to know how it felt, so I tried to take Joshen."

Senna turned at the sound of Witches calling the wind down on the cliffs. It had begun, and she had her own part to play. "For what it's worth, thank you for saving my life." She started back toward the Ring of Power.

Arianis reached out and gripped her hand. "Just so you know, it didn't work. No matter how hard I tried, he only wanted you."

Senna stiffened. "It doesn't matter. Joshen is dead."

Arianis covered her mouth with her hand. Unwilling to hear any words of pity, Senna fled, stumbling through the landscape that was seared into her pupils every time lightning shot to the ground.

Her borrowed cloak was so heavy with water it tripped up her feet, so she tore it off. She was drenched anyway. Lightning stabbed at the edge of the cliff, and Witches fell screaming from the rim.

Senna reached the Ring of Power, her heart pounding as if it was trying to escape death by beating out of her chest. Lightning flashed so bright that the world went dark. She screamed in terror, but the sound of the bolt was so loud she couldn't hear her own voice.

When she opened her eyes, a black spot singed the ground not far from her. It smelled of wet and burning. Shaking, she stumbled to the center of the Ring. She tipped back her head and sang.

Wind lift me high,
That my words reach to'rds the sky.

The wind grew stronger than she'd ever felt it before. It snatched her so swiftly it knocked the breath from her. She shot upward, rain dripping from her body, into the turmoil of clouds and lightning. The crackle of electricity lifted the tiny hairs on her arms. She sent a prayer for the Creators to keep the lightning at bay.

Still singing, she looked below. Behind the Guardians, the Witches were using the wind to drive the invaders back. The Guardians in the front line fought with bayonets. No one used muskets—the rain must have rendered the powder useless. But they were losing ground instead of gaining it.

Senna took a deep breath, and her song grabbed a current of wind. She hurtled it like a spear. It struck the Tartens with such force it threw them back, but it also hit Haven's Witches. They stumbled and collapsed to keep from being driven off the cliff's edge.

Senna used all her concentration to try to shrink the wind to a precise stream, but it was like channeling a river through a funnel. The wind lost nearly all of its power. The Tartens struggled to their feet and started forward again.

Haven's Witches rallied, calling forth their own protective barrier of wind. Without the worry of harming her own Witches, Senna redoubled her efforts, and the gale slammed into the Tartens with enough force to drive them from the cliff, plunging them into the churning waters.

The songs around her shifted. The lightning gathered into a tremendous strike against her. She wrestled control from the Caldash Witches and twisted the bolt down onto them, hitting a ship square on. Though soaked, it erupted into flames. Their bodies alight, men dove into the water.

And in that moment, the tide of the battle shifted into Senna's hands. The truth of it was undeniable to Tarten, Caldashan, and Haven alike. It made Senna sick.

Looking away from the battle, she reminded the wind to keep her afloat and redirected her song at the last of the Tartens clinging to the edge of the cliffs.

She listened to the storm and changed the song slightly, enough so hail rained down in white sheets upon the ships and Tartens. Men ran for cover or fell screaming into the sea. Not a single hailstone fell upon the island.

Haven's Witches spread out with the Guardians behind them. Below Senna's dangling feet, the barrier swelled between the Witches' outstretched hands like ice freezing across a pond, until it encompassed the island.

The Witches started their song. Power poured into Senna until her fingertips tingled. Closing her eyes, she drew upon the strength of the Four Sisters. The might of the sea, the richness of the earth, the blinding brightness of the sun, the force of the winds. Before, that much energy would have overwhelmed her after a few songs, but now she soaked it in like cracked earth soaks in rain.

Songs rose up from the Caldash Witches as they tried to wrest the control of the songs away from Senna. But they were like raindrops attacking the sea—she just absorbed their power into her vast reservoirs. She waited as it filled her, listening to the songs around her. When the time came, she needed to know the exact melody and words to shift Haven.

She could hold more song, but she sensed she had enough to move the island and more. There had been enough violence,

enough death, for one day. With a few soothing words, she calmed
the sea and the storm. Hesitantly, those on the ships left shelter
and stepped onto the decks. A few more moments, and sailors
and soldiers poured from the holds. Senna pressed a gentle wind
against the ships, pushing them back to safety.

But the Tartens and Caldashans stubbornly tied up their sails
and threw anchor.

So be it.

Her voice rang across the island and sea like the clearest bells.
Sailors on the ships dropped to their knees. Some threw down
their weapons.

Senna's heart sang with hope. But then the men's commanders
started shooting those who resisted. Senna cried out in horror.
More men dropped to their knees or threw their weapons into the
sea. And more of them died. The cannons started firing modified
anchors again.

Tears streaming down her face at what she was about to do,
she sang.

> Haven, raise thy stakes.
> Winds, a path to make.
> Earth, compact thy soil.
> Plants, thy roots uncoil.
> Waters, thy waves divide.
> Take us to a home we can abide.

The barrier began to twist around the island, slowly at first,
then faster and faster until everything was a blur of color and
motion. Senna pulled the barrier in until it fit snugly against the
cliffs, sheering off some of the rough edges, making them smooth
as glass. Senna finally understood why the island had always been
such an unnaturally perfect circle.

But she was not within it. The song to move the island only
worked from the outside. And when it was gone, she would
remain behind with nothing waiting below her but chaos.

She sang again, and the world grew brighter. She blinked
against the blinding light coming from below. Confused, she held
out her hands to shield her eyes, only to find they were the source.

She gaped as strange filigrees of light, like honey with glittering
bits of sugar, swirled from her skin. As the song within her grew,

so did the lights—almost as if the songs were spilling from her. She looked out. Witches and Tartens alike had paused in their fighting. All of them were turned toward her.

The ships stopped firing at the cliffs. The commanders stopped shouting orders. The world held its breath.

"Brusenna!"

In the stillness, someone called her name from the ships. She searched among them until she saw a knot of Tartens. Grendi stood in the front, her beautiful dress torn and her hair hanging in limp knots. In her stance, Senna saw defeat. Grendi had lost, and she knew it. Knew she was going to die.

"I've won." Senna's words came out as a song.

At a gesture from Grendi, the soldiers behind her thrust two men forward. Senna squinted at them.

Grendi grabbed handfuls of their hair and pulled their heads back. They were bloody and beaten, so bruised and swollen they were nearly unrecognizable as men.

But then one of them locked gazes with Senna. He was too far away to make out details like the gray color of his eyes, or the way his skin wrinkled when he smiled. But she knew the way he moved like she knew the melody of the wind.

Joshen. And beside him must be Reden. They were alive!

Grendi had to scream to be heard. "You move the island and they'll die with us."

Senna shook her head. When she'd faced Espen so long ago, she'd declared that if she had to choose between the world and Joshen, she would choose Joshen.

She looked down at Haven, at the Witches who were still singing to keep the barrier intact. They would all die if she let it go.

Her gaze found Joshen again.

"They'll kill me anyway!" he shouted.

One of the Tartens cuffed him.

Senna cried out. Either way she chose, people she loved would die. Joshen had all of her courage and none of her powers. He'd risked everything, suffered so much. He had more heart, more bravery than she did.

She searched for a familiar face on the ships, but she couldn't find Krissin. Her heart wringing inside her, she cried out, "This is what your Composer has aligned herself with? This is the choice you force upon me?"

A shudder convulsed through her. The wind grew weaker. She sang softly, strengthening it. When she looked up, she knew what she had to do. She had to have as much courage as Joshen.

In the space of a blink, angry gray clouds boiled in the sky. Senna hurled down a barrage of lightning, striking Grendi's ship and the soldiers on it.

Joshen and Reden rolled away from their captors. Reden swept up a sword from a fallen soldier. They limped to the other side of the ship, where Joshen worked at their bonds. The ship exploded beneath them as the fire reached the gunpowder. A wave swept them off the burning ship.

Senna bit her knuckle as she watched them, so small and helpless against the might of the freezing waters. And then she saw a boat moving toward them. Inside was a small girl with dark hair. Mistin.

Perhaps she was Senna's friend after all. But even as Mistin reached out an arm to the Guardians, Senna knew it was futile. When the island disappeared, a wave would rise up. All the ships would be swallowed by the raging sea. She hadn't saved them. She'd only delayed their deaths.

Always serve the higher law. Reden had told her that. Choose what is hardest now, but better in the long run. Closing her eyes tight, Senna turned away. *As brave as Joshen,* she mouthed to herself. *As brave as Reden.* She concentrated on the barrier. The Haven Witches hadn't stopped singing since they'd created it. It was strong enough now. Her song changed.

Haven, raise thy stakes.
Winds, a path to make.
Earth, compact thy soil.
Plants, thy roots uncoil.
Waters, thy waves divide.
Take us to a home we can abide.

The light that had gathered under her skin shot out, striking the barrier, which flashed with such brilliance she had to shield her eyes. When she looked back down, there was only a gaping, concave hole. Her skin no longer glowed. Her voice felt broken.

A great wall of water trembled, hesitating as if feeling for the walls that were no longer there. Then it rushed forward with a roar, dragging the unfortunate ships with it. And she was in the epicenter. She realized the water would reach the heart and explode upward, toward her.

Wind, lift me higher!

The wind tugged her up even as the sea surged beneath her. Senna threw her arms over her face. Water slammed into her, tossing her like a child throwing a doll.

It slowly began to fall back. Gasping, Senna sang for the wind to keep her afloat, but her voice was raw and overused. The power she'd wielded had left her bereft and hollow.

She was slipping, the wind's hold on her lessening. Looking down at the chaos of sinking, burning boats and the debris-filled sea, she tried in vain to locate her Guardians, but it was impossible.

The air grew thinner and weaker by the moment. Senna tried to claw her way up. The speed of her descent picked up until she was freefalling. She would join so many who had died this day. Like Cord. He'd given his life to save her.

But that wasn't all he'd given her—the vial of Ioa! She fished it out of her pocket and dumped it down the front of her face. Gripping the vial so tight her fingers turned white, she sang with what little strength remained in her.

She flailed her hands and legs, trying to slow her descent toward the freezing cold Endall sea.

As the choppy waters rose up to meet her, she threw the bottle and twisted so she was feet first. She screamed as she hit the water. Her bones cracked, whether from the impact or the potion, she wasn't sure. Then her flesh shifted. She didn't know if she would change soon enough, or if the change would be enough to save her.

Then it no longer mattered. Something pierced her hip, and pain ripped through her. The world went dark.

34. Waiting Blackness

Senna awoke to grit against her cheek. Something tugged her back and forth. She hurt everywhere. Dimly, she recalled reaching Nefalie's coast just before passing out. With a groan, she opened her eyes. The water and rocks beneath her were red with blood. Her blood. Debris and worse littered the shore around her. She tried to push herself up. White-hot pain shot out from her hip.

Steeling herself, she tried again to push herself up, but she was so cold her muscles simply locked up.

A huge swell crashed over her, shoving her higher onto the shore. Gasping in pain, she dug her fingers into the rocks to keep from being dragged back out with the retreating wave. When the sun had warmed her a little, she pulled herself a bit farther out of the water. The movement caused the pain to gnaw at her anew, and everything faded away.

Her senses returned after a time. She carefully shifted so she could see her hip. What she saw made her stomach roll. Through what little remained of her shift, she saw the garish white of her hip joint, skin and muscle hanging around it like the tattered ends of a flag, the flesh bleached white from sun and salt.

Hissing through her teeth, she locked her legs together and dragged herself forward, waited for the agony to lessen, then pulled some more. She wasn't sure how many times she repeated this process, but finally she was out of the water.

The movement had caused the wound to bleed again. Senna ripped off a strip of her shift and pressed it into the wound. The world started spinning as blackness edged in from the outside of her vision. She was going to pass out again. Knowing she was on the verge of bleeding to death, she dug her wound into the rocks below her to compress it.

For a time, she was insensible with pain. She came around a bit when she threw up salt water. Her tongue felt as dry as week-old bread. She lay back, wishing for darkness to take her from the pain. When she opened her eyes again, she had to squint against the warm sun that had baked the cold out of her, and somehow made her hip hurt so much she thought she would die from it. She struggled to sit up, but she was so weak she barely shifted. The pain drove her toward the waiting blackness.

"Is she alive?"

"Yes, Head."

Senna struggled to open her eyes. It was dark out, and the air stank of death. Krissin lifted Senna's tattered shift; her face went gray. "You're lucky we're the ones who found you instead of the Tartens." Senna didn't bother to answer. "You've lost a lot of blood. The shore is soaked with it."

Senna worked her tongue over her dry mouth. "Water."

Krissin pursed her lips before nodding to one of the Guardians standing over her. He held a waterskin to her mouth. She drank, the cool wetness sliding down her raw throat. She coughed at the foreign feel of the moisture. The Guardian pulled back. She cried out and reached for the waterskin again. He gave her some more.

"Slowly," he chided.

Krissin shook her head. "Why did you move them? They've done nothing but betray you."

Senna lay back against the rocks, feeling the water spread through her like its own kind of warmth. "The Tartens would have killed them." Her voice came out thready and weak. "There wouldn't have been anyone left for me to be a Composer over."

Krissin stood and brushed off her knees. "You haven't saved them, only delayed their destruction. Because of our earth senses, we know where you sent them. Why to the Tarten coast, right above Caldash?"

Senna closed her eyes. She hadn't known where she was sending them. The song hadn't dictated a location. But it didn't really matter. She'd sacrificed Joshen to save Haven, but in the end, she hadn't saved either.

When Senna didn't respond, Krissin asked, "Is Chavis dead?"

Senna nodded carefully.

Krissin sucked air through her teeth. "She was supposed to convince Haven to join with us. I don't see how that can happen now. You might have just sentenced them all to death."

Senna's heart beat a lonely echo in the hollow of her chest. She willed it to stop, but it went on despite the pain, both inside and out, that threatened to destroy her.

"With that injury, you may never walk again." Krissin nodded to two of her Guardians. "Take her to the Healer. See that she is cared for."

Someone made a sound of disapproval. Senna couldn't see who.

"I won't have a Creator-touched dying because I refused to treat her," Krissin responded. Then she turned and left.

"The Creators don't want this!" Senna cried even as one of the Guardians slipped his hands beneath her. She drew breath to say more, but he lifted her. A hollow ringing sang through her head, and there was only the pain.

35. BURNING

Senna remembered waking when they gave her bitter opiates. Though the drugs made her sleep, the pain didn't recede. In fact, it grew, increasing until she was certain her bones were crumbling to dust. Eventually, even the lure of water couldn't make her drudge up the will to swallow. When they tried to help her drink, the water ran down her cheeks and into her damp hair.

She heard their worried voices. They knew she was dying. She knew it, too, and she didn't care. She welcomed the fever, the hot infection that spread its poison through her blood.

She came to her senses suddenly and saw a woman standing above her. She was as beautiful as a sunset over ripe fields. She looked vaguely familiar, but Senna couldn't place her.

"Do you *hear* the breeze across your skin?"

Senna thought it an odd question. After all, she was dying. But the answer seemed important. She concentrated and heard the distant sound of woodwind instruments. The wind drifted across her, caressing her and soothing away the fever. The sound of sunlight and wind. She managed the barest of nods.

The woman's face lit up, seeming to glow from the inside. "Come, dance with me and the Fourth Sister, Sunlight. Let us take you away from the pain and sorrow." She held out her hand.

Senna recognized her. The Creator who'd gifted her with Espen's song. She controlled Sunlight. Senna took her proffered hand without question.

The pain was gone as if it had never been. Music rose up around her. She clung to the woman as the sound lifted her. They danced, twirling like a pair of autumn leaves on a breeze until she grew dizzy. They skimmed across meadows and low hills like a rock skipping across the water.

The music shifted from light and playful to darker and more insistent. The tempo increased until she was driving across open seas in a stampede of storms. Finally, they reached mountains, and their frenzy cooled as they rose. They crested the top and drifted down until Senna rested on the baked sand. The desert filled her with a warm and delicious heat.

She slept to the sound of the deep, sonorous song of the earth. When she was rested, she opened her eyes to find another woman—this one with ebony skin and wild hair. She smiled at Senna, her eyes like chips of onyx. Another of the Creators. "Come, and I will show you the beauty of the First Sister, Earth."

A part of Senna wondered if she had died.

The Earth Creator cocked her head, listening. "Can you hear it?"

Senna listened to the rumbled lullaby of the earth. It spoke of cover and quiet and hidden places in drums. Secrets of sparkling diamonds and shining gold with the tinkling of chimes. The pacing of the drums picked up, and the woman smiled so broadly her white teeth gleamed. She took Senna's hand and pressed it against the hot sand. "A mountain aches below. Can you feel it?"

Senna closed her eyes and felt the earth's pulsing heartbeat as the drums pounded out their rhythm. "Yes," she breathed. "I feel it."

Without the need to confer, they began to sing. The earth rumbled, shifting and growling. With a great shuddering, it exploded beneath them. The ground shifted under Senna like a crest of water. She rode the wave upward until she stood at the mountain crest.

Still singing, she stared at the space between her feet, feeling something hot and surging beneath her. She lifted her eyes in question.

The Earth Creator nodded. "Yes."

Senna sang and the mountain split. Red magma gleamed deep below. She dove inside it without a splash. It didn't harm her—

Somehow she'd known it wouldn't. She saw nothing in the hot darkness, but she didn't need to. She swam through the earth's veins, into vast wells of water that tasted of minerals and sulfur. There were gemstones the size of her fist that chimed like cymbals when she touched them, but she left them where they lay. They were the earth's hidden treasure, and hidden they would remain.

Always, the Earth Creator was by her side, guiding her. Finally, they entered a pool of water heated by underwater magma. They shot out of a spout, and though Senna still couldn't see anything, the water changed. It tasted of salt and fish. The ocean.

The Earth Creator was gone. The Water Creator had taken her place. The woman gripped Senna's hand. "You've spent time with the Second Sister, Water," she sang. "But there is much you've never witnessed."

They rode underwater rivers and found lakes within the sea. Senna saw fish no bigger than her fingernail that pulsed with a rainbow of colors. She swam in turquoise oceans with dolphins and sang with the whales in water so dark it was green black. She explored reefs with fish that wore color like flowers trying to attract bees. She crossed vast oceanic deserts where nothing lived for leagues in every direction.

And then a wave carried her forward and set her in a land of verdant pine forests. Their music was rich with deep, chaotic brass. It was also more complex than any of the other melodies she'd heard. An undercurrent of life pulsed through the music.

"And last, you meet the Third Sister, Plants." A woman dropped down from a high branch, bits of moss clinging to her red hair. "You feel how full it is?"

Senna nodded. The woman took her hand, and suddenly they were on a sparse, rocky plateau. Gray-leaved olive trees grew in the thin soil. The music here was steadier, but more sparse—like the plants themselves.

The Creator watched Senna silently. When she seemed satisfied, she took her hand again and brought her to a vast continent of death—Tarten. Senna crouched and held a hand over the earth. She pulled back as if stung, a hiss passing through her teeth.

"You feel the difference between this and the desert?"

Senna nodded. The desert song was muted but healthy. This, though…

"Sometimes it's a raw, stinging pain. Others, a deep, throbbing pulse that shoots out like a wind-whipped ember." She crouched next to Senna, her hair now the color of baby grass. "But if you listen, you can hear the Four Sisters' song."

Senna waited and listened a long time. Finally, she reached out and took hold of a flaking tree. She felt it more than heard it—a faint buzz of life deep within the roots. Her voice joined the Creator's.

The two called in a storm, dampening the soil before adding their voices to the dying song of the plants. The music of earth, wind, water, and plants swirled all around her.

And she directed it, adding her voice to the mix until a symphony arose, coaxing the music of the plants back to life. Stalks went from a dead brown to a bright green. Tentative leaves uncurled and broadened. Seeds soaked in the water and forced roots into the rich soil. Flowers bloomed, their thin, sweet fragrance filling the air.

Senna listened beyond the music for any sound of life beyond their voices. There was nothing. No hum of insects or cry of animals. Exhausted, she sagged against a tree.

Then she realized the Plant Creator was gone. In her place, the blonde Creator was back. "Now you understand. Our power—the music of the Four Sisters'—is everywhere. Always. Keepers bend the songs of the world to *keep* it."

Senna cast outward, listening. The music was strong and steady around them, but beyond was the hollow emptiness—the pain of unhealed lands. "We didn't heal all of Tarten."

The Creator shook her head. "No. That would have taxed you too far."

Senna studied the woman. Without the aura of power she wore like a cloak, she looked very normal. And very young. Senna's quick eyes picked out distinguishing features. And suddenly she realized who she must be. "You're Lilette."

The Creator smiled. "Yes."

Senna's mind raced over what Krissin had told her. "You lit up like a newborn star. When the light faded, you were gone."

Lilette nodded. "It is what the Caldash Witches are saying of you back on the Nefalien shore."

Senna shook her head in disbelief. She had lit up before she left to ride the winds? "Am I dead?"

"You are more than dead. You are transformed. You have been judged worthy to become a Creator." Lilette took her hand and suddenly they were in a castle made of stone that seemed to have grown from the earth. Intricate stone branches and leaves climbed the walls.

Senna placed her palm on a stone plant. It was warm, thrumming with song. "It's alive," she breathed.

"More alive," Lilette corrected. "We woke it up. As a Creator, you can do the same. Build your own worlds and populate them with your people. Or stay here with us and keep this world beautiful."

Senna couldn't begin to comprehend the enormity of Lilette's offer.

"Come. I have something to show you."

Trailing after her, Senna ran her fingers along a vine so intricate she felt the tiny veins. Stars grew out of the ceiling, diamonds and sapphires glittering from their centers. Lilette stepped out onto a garden balcony and pulled apart some of the branches to reveal a small pool with water as clear as the finest glass.

"See for yourself."

Senna moved to the edge and leaned over to look at her reflection. What she saw shocked her to stillness. Shining like polished gold, her hair flared like flames around her head. Her dress shifted with the blood orange of coals, and her skin shimmered.

Hesitantly, she touched the fabric of her dress. Her hands sank into fire and ashes. It wasn't fabric at all, but real fire. It felt pleasantly warm and full of power.

"Let your aura go," Lilette whispered.

The sweet seduction in Lilette's voice made it easy to obey. Senna relaxed. Light flared from her skin. It curled at the edges, a delicate filigree of song made visible. "I'm a Sunlight Creator." A God with the power of creation in her body.

Lilette laughed. "That's why I'm here with you and not one of the others. You shall be my Apprentice."

Senna had trouble forming coherent thoughts. "But I never chose my Discipline."

Lilette tipped her face toward the light that drenched everything in gold. "Sunlight chose you. It has been fusing with you ever since my lips touched yours. The process of transforming a mortal into a Creator must be slow and steady so as not to overwhelm your weak flesh—though you've no doubt noted that at times the power flared more strongly than others."

When Senna had heard the Four Sisters' songs for the first time. When she'd sung her own circles. When she'd nearly lit the Caldashan boat on fire. And finally, when she'd moved the island.

Lilette took a deep breath. "And so I will offer you the same choice that was once mine. Spare yourself the pain and hurt of mortality. Come with us and dance on the wind, sleep deep in the earth, swim in the seas, and grow gardens of such beauty as to make mankind weep."

Senna closed her eyes and felt the music strumming inside her. Joy sang through her, but there was also a hard kernel of sadness. Her mother, truly alone in the world. "You left your Witches behind," Senna said. "They needed you."

Lilette inclined her head. "Yes. After I moved them, I created a barrier so Haven could do no more harm. I hoped that with time, they could become something better. When I met you, I thought perhaps you could bring them together. Apparently, that was not to be."

"So I failed."

Lilette smiled gently. "No. They failed. Not you."

Senna stared up at the impossibly blue sky. "Why did you stay?"

"My love was here. It made the decision easy."

Senna closed her eyes. Joshen—she'd tried to save him, but what chance did that little boat have? And there were others. Cord. Her father and sister. "Can I see them?"

Lilette gestured gracefully beyond the balcony. Senna stepped closer. Below was an entire city made of the same living stone. Trees and flowers and plants mixed among them like old friends. And there were people. Hundreds of them.

"It would not, I think, be right for you to meet your father and sister. A brief moment would be cruel—unless of course you chose to stay. But there is another."

Senna turned at the sound of footsteps. Cord smiled at her, more beautiful than she'd ever seen him. With a cry of joy she ran to him and hugged him hard. In wonder, she felt the wholeness where his wound had been.

He reached out and lightly touched her healed hip. "Such things don't come with us."

Senna turned to Lilette. "What about Joshen? And Reden? Where are they?"

Lilette's brows dropped down. "They aren't here."

Confusion and uncertainty welled inside Senna's breast. "But surely they didn't survive. That wave was taller than any mountain I've ever seen. "

"They have not passed from the mortal world."

Senna didn't know whether she felt relieved or horrified. "Why did Grendi let me think she had killed them?"

Lilette's face hardened. "What better way to wound your Guardians than to force them to watch you suffer? What better way to hurt you than to let you think them dead?" Senna tried to imagine Joshen watching her at the mizzen mast for nearly three days, while she thought he was dead. And him unable to tell her differently.

She took a measure of comfort from Cord's solid presence beside her.

"Grendi does not have a place waiting for her here." Lilette fingered a bright blue flower. Yellow pollen stuck to her finger. "I knew love during mortality, and I watched him die. So my decision was not hard to make." She sighed. "You could wait for Joshen. We do not feel time the way mankind does. It will seem a matter of days, not decades. If he is worthy, he will join the Guardians after his death, safeguarding the souls of those who have earned a life in our everlasting gardens."

Cord took her hand. "Stay with me?"

Tears filled her eyes. Cord brushed them off her cheeks and stared at the gold on his fingertips. "Even your tears are filled with songs."

She saw her future unfold with Cord. No pain or sorrow. Joshen would eventually move on. He would be happy again—he wasn't the kind of person to stay sad for long. "Isn't there still a chance I could save them?"

"If you return, it will be to your battered body. The power of a Creator will fade quickly, leaving you with little more than your own song." Lilette pursed her lips. "We whispered warnings to the Keepers through you. And for it, they banished you. They are not worthy of more chances."

Senna remembered all the hurt and pain the Keepers had caused her. But there were kindnesses, too. Gentle nudges and laughter.

Lilette walked to a climbing vine and picked a white flower growing along its base. "You would give up all this beauty and peace to go back to them who hate you?"

Senna hesitated.

Cord tucked her hair behind her ear. "Is it Joshen?" He didn't seem angry, just sad.

Senna looked up at him, her eyes imploring. "Not just him. There's my mother, too, and the others.

"You needn't fear for the world's coming death, Brusenna. It is merely a change for the better. The Witches will not end. Those who have earned their place will come here. Those who do not will go somewhere else."

Senna's sorrow was like a slow burning coal in her chest. "But it would mean decades of slow decay. What kind of life will they live until then?"

Lilette didn't answer.

Senna took a deep breath. "I have to go back."

Lilette sighed as she tucked the flowers she'd gathered behind Senna's ear. "You have made your decision. Very well."

Cord studied her, his brow furrowed. Bending down, he pressed a kiss to her forehead—just as she'd done for him as he lay dying. "I will tell your father and sister stories of you." He cradled her cheek and smiled as if he understood and it didn't pain him. Then he turned and left, walking with a light step until he disappeared through the garden.

Lilette reached out and placed something solid in Senna's palm. "I believe this is yours."

Senna stared at her complete moon pendant. The cord was gone, but other than that, it was perfect. The last time she'd seen it, Grendi has used it to find her. A wave of relief tumbled over her. "You made this a long time ago, didn't you?"

Lilette nodded. "So that my Guardian and I would always be able to find each other. Until he went where the pendant could not follow, but I could." She sang softly.

Senna watched in awe as a chain of gold grew through the loop.

Smiling, Lilette reached forward and snapped out the waning gibbous. "Joshen can still use the other half." Pushing the gibbous back in place, she gently clasped the chain around Senna's throat. It felt warm and familiar.

"It's so beautiful. Thank you." Senna fingered the waning gibbous that had been Joshen's. In addition to her ring, it was the closest connection she had to him. "But Joshen doesn't have his piece anymore. How will he find me?"

Lilette looked sad. "He'll have to use his wits, just like everyone else who is lost."

Senna was silent for a time. "How will I find the Witches?"

"I will take you. But remember, time moves differently here. Four days have passed. The Tartens and Caldashans have already crossed the ocean and resumed their attack on Haven. They've nearly breached the last of the island's defenses."

Lilette wrapped her arms around Senna's neck. The Creator's aura flared a blinding white. When the light faded, Senna found herself aloft in the sky. Lilette was withdrawing and fading. But she wasn't alone. A tall, masculine shape moved beside her, and they were holding hands.

Her Guardian. Lilette had followed him in death, while Senna had returned from it to find Joshen.

Below her was Tarten. Men were locked in a pitched battle; smoke was thick and acrid in her throat. Ships rose and fell on an angry sea. But they were looking up at her now, their faces slack with wonder.

Senna shone like the sun, her dress the orange red of glowing embers, her hair flaring around her like flame.

She caught the sight of green dresses. Witches. She saw into their hearts. They had abused the power given to them. Instead of harmony, they had sought discord and chaos. They'd proven themselves unable to bear the burden placed upon them.

She listened to the music all around her. The muted hum of brass, the high cry of the strings, the thrumming of the drums, and the confused chaos of the woodwinds.

Senna sensed the pain waiting for her at the end of her songs, but there was no time to dwell on it. Power rapidly leaked out of her. She would need every last drop of the energy still strumming through her to accomplish her task.

She let her aura flare. She sang and the Four Sisters went silent. She pulled a cord of music here, changed a note there.

Slowly, the Four Sisters' melody melded to hers until every sound, every pitch blended together into a symphony of might. Senna set the boundaries of the climate, creating self-contained orchestras of sound.

When she was finished, the sound of the rich music all around her had wilted like a frostbitten bloom.

She had taken the Keepers' ability to control the climate and returned it to the Four Sisters. She knew the price of her song— hurricanes, floods, earth tremors, hard winters, and inadequate summers. From now on, Witches would be able to curb the weather, but not rule it. They would be able to stir the earth, but not rend it. Shift the waters, but not lift them. She left them the ability to control the plants.

That done, her song shifted to Tarten. She restored every plant, every flower beyond the lands she had already healed with Lilette. As she sang, her aura faded, and her immortality and immeasurable power diminished, slipping from her body like water from cupped hands.

Pain came in her power's wake—a deep ache in her hip that spread down her leg and up her side.

She sagged, her strength nearly spent. She was almost mortal again. The music that had become such a part of her had gone silent. She felt empty, spent like a guttered candle. She spoke to those watching her. "Why? Why were you not as you were meant to be? Songs meant to protect were used for destruction and gain. And so I have bridled much of your power, and all the world will suffer for it. But no more than the suffering you've already caused. And perhaps you will one day be worthy for that power to be restored."

She flicked her wrist and waves rose up, carrying the Tarten ships away. Then she called upon the wind to carry a single figure toward her. Grendi. Though weak, Senna was still a Creator. She looked into the woman's heart and saw hatred and malice like a hard chunk of tar. Grendi's veins ran with it. And there was more.

Senna's eyes widened. "You are a Witch."

Grendi flinched as if she'd been slapped.

Senna read the woman's soul like a diviner reads tea leaves. "A witch with no power—a Wastrel who watched her sisters and mother bend the world to their will while you stood in the shadows, powerless and alone."

"They were an abomination! A scourge I vowed to exterminate!"

Senna winced in disgust. Grendi had aided Espen in her hunt to imprison the Witches. When their plot failed, she'd tried to slaughter them. She would have succeeded if the Witches hadn't razed the city and cursed Tarten.

Then, instead of using Tarten's dwindling resources to evacuate her people from their dying lands, Grendi had plotted Haven's destruction.

"You will never stop, no matter the cost." Senna loathed the words she knew must come. "The world cannot survive your hatred."

She sent Grendi back to the ground, where she sang Bindweed around her. Swathed inside a cocoon prison, the woman would be unable to escape or be freed by anyone but Senna.

The power Senna had left was so little—a drop in the vast ocean she'd once held. All that remained was the agony. Blood dripped down her leg. She felt the fever robbing her of health and strength, the infection poisoning her blood.

Perhaps she would be returning to the Creators sooner than she thought.

Steeling herself, she dedicated the land to the Witches.

City of Witches–Ashfall
To all who need healing, we call
Potions or plants to end a drought,
Purchase wind to secure a trade route.

Then she directed her power at Haven.

Wastrel or power abounding
All have a place, all bear power resounding.

The last of a Creator's power slipped from Senna. She was a Witch now, as before, one exhausted beyond any mortal's endurance. The pain in her body was a dark pit of fire and burning.

Burning.

Blackness invaded her vision. The symphony she'd sung slowly faded to echoing silence. The wind lost its direction. She was falling.

Falling.

Falling.

Hundreds of Witches joined together in song.

The wind roared to life under Senna, catching the edges of the dress that had gone out like a spent coal, and cradling her as she drifted down.

Down.

Down.

Down

Only partially conscious, she was aware of the dozens of hands that reached out to bear her gently to the ground. Then she remembered no more.

36. Ashfall

Golden sunlight drenched the city. A playful breeze lifted Senna's hair and sent gooseflesh down her back as she looked out over Ashfall. Her memory of her time spent with the Creators was dreamlike and distant. It was hard to imagine that she'd created self-contained orchestras of sound in so little time, that it had been four months since she'd fallen from the sky.

She sat in the garden balcony at the center of the tree palace that rested at the top of one of the domed mountains. The Witches had connected the trees with branch bridges. Vines and flowers ran along every border. At each corner of the magnificent grove were four enormous single trees—one for each Discipline—built to honor either Plants, Water, Sunlight, or Earth.

Perhaps it was a poor copy of Lilette's palace of living stone, but it was still the most beautiful this world had ever seen.

From there, the yet-to-be-built city was divided into quarters dedicated to one of the Disciplines. Each would someday be paved with mosaics—some of sunbursts, some of trees, some of gusting winds, and some of great mountains. Even now, Guardians were laying patterns of stones to form the streets.

Everywhere was the sound of Witch song as the Keepers grew tree houses for shops and homes. All their songs also happened to nourish the rest of the plant life.

Trees and flowers burst to life everywhere, filling the air with their sweet fragrances.

Senna rested at the pinnacle, in a tree that was the highest part of the city. The balcony opened to all four directions, letting the wind through as she strained to hear the slightest hint of music from the four corners of the world. But the world echoed with a resounding silence.

"They're here to see you. Do you wish me to show them in?"

Senna shifted to see her mother watching her. "Yes, thank you."

Instead of summoning them, her mother came forward to take Senna's hand. "Don't look so sad."

Senna stared at their intertwined fingers. So much to forgive, by both of them. But they were trying, and they had something neither had felt in a long time: hope that they could begin again.

"It's just hard to adjust," Senna replied. To being mortal again, to losing most of her precious connection to the music, to living in a world that was a mere shadow of the one beyond. One where, even surrounded by people, she was alone. And then there was the constant pain. It was bearable now, but the damage was permanent. She would never walk without a cane.

Her mother's eyes softened with understanding. "You made a great sacrifice coming back for the Witches, coming back for me." When Senna didn't answer, her mother whispered, "Don't give up on him yet."

For four months, Senna had been left to wonder what had happened to Joshen. The price was so high that she still questioned whether it had been worth it, whether she should have stayed with the Creators. "I haven't. Not yet."

Her mother opened her mouth as if to say more, then seemed to change her mind. "I'll see you for supper tonight." With a reassuring squeeze and a soft goodbye, she left.

Moments later, Coyel, Prenny, Krissin, Millay, and Reden crossed one of the bridges surrounding the balcony on four sides. The four women were the new Discipline Heads. It had taken two months of haggling, but Krissin had finally agreed to take over the position as Head of Earth. She was actually better at it than Drenelle had been.

"Composer," they murmured.

Krissin and Millay stood a little apart from Coyel and Prenny. But they'd arrived together, which was an improvement over last week. Senna hoped that someday, the two factions of Witches would become one.

Reden's hard gaze met hers. He and Mistin had turned up in Tarten not long after Senna. Since their boat had flipped in the ensuing chaos of Haven's disappearance, they hadn't seen Joshen. No one had.

Senna tore her gaze from Reden and looked at the others. She had seen into their hearts, and sometimes she felt like she knew them better than they knew themselves. "Your reports?"

They shifted. All but Reden still seemed in awe of her. That awe led them to obey her unquestioningly, which frightened her. Senna had seen people with the best of intentions make mistakes. Even simple misjudgments could be rectified if they were made by a group, which is why she'd kept Caldash's structure intact. The Orders, Guardian Leader, and Heads held equal power with her.

Though Reden wasn't awed by her, he still treated her like glass—as if he were afraid anything but the gentlest handling would shatter her. "Some animal life has been seen," he said. "Judging by their condition, a few have survived the curse. Others are coming in from beyond Tarten's borders. We have put the call out for soldiers to outfit our army, and many of the Tarten soldiers have answered. I'm still looking for a general to lead them."

Senna nodded. Reden hadn't wanted the army to be a separate entity from the Guardians. But when given the choice of running the army or the Guardians, he'd chosen to remain the Guardians' Leader if she let him pick the general. "Did you ask Mistin?" Senna asked Reden.

"I did, Composer. She does not want the position. Instead, she prefers to remain with her Order." Reden actually blushed.

Senna had to suppress a smile. It seemed he had finally found a woman willing to accept his soldiering ways.

He cleared his throat. "You still need to choose a personal Guardian, Composer Brusenna."

Senna held her hand out to forestall any arguments. "I will choose a Guardian when I'm ready for one."

He pursed his lips and nodded, clearly unhappy with her refusal to replace Joshen, but knowing better than to press the issue further. That was wise. Senna wouldn't allow more speculation on the subject. "Coyel?"

The Head came to stand beside her and stared out over the city. "Composer, it's been done as you directed. The adult Witches have been relocated to Ashfall. All the students, both Witchling and Apprentice, have been moved to Haven and the school has been expanded. The call has been made that every Witch, regardless of level, is welcome. Already many of the empty tree houses have been filled."

Krissin spoke up. "And the administration of our government has been successfully moved to Ashfall."

Millay spoke for the first time. "Are you sure we should put a price on our songs?"

Senna smiled to herself. Finally, one was willing to voice the question all of them must have. After all, the Second Witch War was fought over the subject, and Espen was the biggest proponent for monetary gain for songs. "We must put a value onto our songs for people to respect them. I wish it were not so, but people value that which they must struggle for, and put little value upon that which they receive for free.

"We will make ourselves the world's most valuable commodity." She saw the Heads uncertainty and braced herself for bad news. "Speaking of, have any more come for our cures, songs, or services?"

Prenny and Coyel exchanged a glance before Coyel answered, "A few for Witch healing plants and potions. They leave as quickly as they come. But just this morning, Nefalie asked that we destroy a pestilence in the Urway City State."

Senna rubbed her palms together, considering. "While they may not like us, Nefalie has had centuries to get used to us, I think. The rest of the world still fears and mistrusts us. As they should. It will take decades to earn their trust."

Krissin licked her lips. "Our coin goes fast—building an empire does not come cheap. I don't see how we can keep offering our services as Witches to the entire world when no one is paying."

Senna smiled to herself. "It's impossible for a Witch to starve. We'll be fine."

The sound of shouts made Senna peer down to the courtyard. There was a bit of a struggle, but she was too far away to see what was going on. Still, she trusted the Guardians to deal with it.

"When the world begins to trust us, they'll pay for our services. Until then, no one is to be turned away. They pay with coin if they can. If they cannot, they pay with their labor. City streets need cleaned. Refuse needs to be hauled out and buried. Gardens need to be kept."

The commotion moved beyond her sight. She furrowed her brow, wondering what was going on. She turned to see Prenny staring hard at her. "Yes?"

Prenny glanced quickly at Coyel before meeting Senna's gaze. "Well, Composer Brusenna, things have been going smoothly, but…"

Senna sighed. "But?" When Prenny didn't answer, Senna leaned back into her chair and rubbed her aching hip. "Prenny, I think I liked you better when you thought I was some upstart Sprout."

Prenny snorted. "All right then. Some Witches aren't happy about us taking on Wastrels. They think it's beneath us."

Senna dropped her head so they wouldn't see the rage burning up her face. "I'll not have them called Wastrels. They can still connect to the Four Sisters, even if they cannot control them. That makes them Witches. Desni couldn't recognize a note, yet her innate sense of plants and potions and her skill as a healer rivaled anything a Witch with a strong song could claim. If Drenelle cannot see the worth in that, she doesn't deserve her position as an instructor at the school."

Senna still felt guilty for falsely accusing the Head of treachery, and later for practically ordering her to stand down as Head of Earth. Just as she felt guilty for sentencing Grendi to be hanged and Ellesh to remain imprisoned on Caldash for the remainder of her days.

Senna's thoughts turned to Desni. Under torture, the old woman had revealed the secret behind Senna's pendant, allowing Grendi to locate her. But Senna couldn't find anger for the old woman in her heart. She'd made too many of her own blunders to blame Desni for the secrets she revealed in her darkest hours. Instead, Senna felt sorry for her. The task of teaching Witchlings might be just what the old woman needed to pull her out of her grief.

Coyel spoke softly. "You know some of the lower-level girls will be ridiculed."

Senna traced the grain of her chair's wooden arms. "It will not be tolerated. Every woman deserves the right to prove herself, to live up to the fullness of her potential. No one has the right to deny them." She turned to face the Heads. "Bring Desni in. And find others like her. The students need examples of teachers who are strong in other ways, especially those from the Caldash Orders."

Prenny crossed her arms over her chest, a calculating look in her eyes. "I'll make sure it's done."

"See that you do," Senna said with a smile to soften the command. Prenny might be ornerier than a gut-shot bear, but Senna was starting to like her.

The oppressive silence was suddenly interrupted by a faraway echo of music. More than anything, Senna ached for the lost songs. She tipped her ear toward the sound, listening. With a sigh, she motioned for one of them to pull the bell.

Her mother came up a moment later.

"A hurricane is building off the coast of Menette," Senna said. "Assemble the Witches on duty."

Sacra nodded. Within moments, Witch song drifted from the inner courtyard. Senna listened absently. "If that is all?"

The Heads made their goodbyes, but not Reden.

"What of Pogg?" she asked.

Reden made a sound low in his throat. "He's not adjusting well to Caldash."

She took a deep breath. Pogg had spent so much time trying to be a human, he didn't know how to be a Mettlemot. "Does he still want to come here?"

"Yes."

"I suppose we'd better let him, then." Senna traced the scars on her palm. "Have you found Kaen and Ciara?"

"I received a missive this morning. They're being brought here, and they still have your horses. Kaen said having the animals saved their lives when they fled."

"Joshen will be glad."

Reden stood beside her for a long time, his hand on the pistols strapped to his waist. He had many more scars than before. And he seemed infinitely older and quieter, but his heart was still strong and loyal as ever.

Knowing what he wanted, she sighed. "I can't, Reden." She forced herself to face him. "I can't give up hope that Joshen will find me. Not yet."

She saw the phantoms of remembered agony play across Reden's face. He and Joshen had been tortured nearly to death. "When our boat sank, I came up right on top of a barrel. I saw Mistin and Joshen. They were both in trouble. I had to make a choice." His voice caught. "I chose Mistin." He'd never told her this before. "When I turned back, Joshen was gone. Senna, he drowned."

She clenched her hands into fists. "No. Lilette said he was alive."

Reden was silent a long time. "It's been four months."

Senna shook her head. "I know."

"I'm sorry, Senna, but someone has to say it. What if he died after you left Lilette?"

She clutched the Creator's promise that Joshen was alive. She just had to wait for him to come to her. She rubbed the pendant at the base of her throat. *Please, Joshen, be alive. Find your way to me.*

"I wish it would have been me," Reden said softly. "Joshen was the better man."

Senna spoke in a whisper. "He wasn't perfect, Reden. None of us were. We all made mistakes."

Reden stood there for a moment, as if hoping she might change her mind, admit Joshen was dead and take on a new Guardian.

Senna closed her eyes and listened. The music floating around her was so beautiful, it made her heart ache, but it was a lonely, sad kind of beautiful. Or perhaps it simply reflected her mood. But as the Witches' singing continued, the hurricane settled and the music faded to nothing.

Finally, Reden sighed. "Have you walked today?"

She shook her head. "Not yet." She held out her hands for him to help her up. She gritted her teeth and slowly let her bad leg take some of her weight. He helped her a few steps, until her hip had warmed up.

"Do you want me to make a round with you?"

She shook her head. "No. I'll be all right."

He made no move to leave. After taking her cane from him, she started out on her own. "Go." She hated that he still didn't leave, but stood watching her.

With the limp, drag, and tap of her cane, Senna started down the bridge that led to her favorite room in the tree houses. Her hip ached and sweat broke out across her face.

Finally, she reached the room. Bright murals were being painted on the walls. All of them reflected pivotal moments in Witch history, and Senna was in a good deal of them. She tried not to mind. After all, the Witches needed to remember the brink of destruction they'd played with.

As if of their own accord, her feet took her to her favorite wall. Smelling strongly of paint, the newly finished section depicted her standing at the pool with Lilette. Though Senna had done her best to describe the scene and the painter was brilliant, it was only a shadow of reality. She'd come back to save the Witches. Well, now they were saved, but she still didn't have Joshen.

Moving a little farther down, she peered past the painters as they worked on the next wall, which depicted Joshen carrying her through Haven the night they'd escaped. His expression was fierce and protective. Her body ached with the need to be held by him.

She startled at a yip. A flustered Guardian she half recognized crossed a bridge toward her—she thought his name was Chan. In his arms was a squirming puppy. A wolfhound puppy. She froze, remembering Bruke.

The Guardian stopped before her and bowed. "Composer Brusenna, there's a man at the gates who claims to know you. He insisted we let him up. Of course we couldn't. He begged that this gift be brought to you. He said you would understand."

Senna felt herself soften. She reached out and took the squirming puppy from the Guardian's arms, her mind barely recognizing what her body was doing. It looked so much like Bruke that she caught his wiry fur in her hands and inhaled the warm smell of him. The puppy whined and struggled in her arms. She bent to set him down, wincing as her hip caught. He immediately squatted and piddled on the floor.

An inexplicable smile spread across her face.

The Guardian went cherry red. "Composer Brusenna, I'm so sorry." He picked up the dog.

She took the puppy from him. The dog's hot little body immediately settled in her arms. Handing her cane to the Guardian, she took his arm and let him help her back the way they'd come. "This man, what did he look like?"

The Guardian opened his mouth to answer, but Reden's voice overrode him. "Senna?" He stepped onto the bridge, obviously looking for her.

"Yes?"

"Senna?"

That was another man's voice, one she recognized. Her head feeling light, she leaned heavily against the Guardian. As if sensing her distress, the puppy licked her, his tongue leaving a cool spot on her skin.

Joshen stepped around Reden and started across the bridge toward her.

Her mouth came open, a small cry drifting from her like the last leaves of autumn. She was so overwhelmed she couldn't move.

Obviously misinterpreting her cry, Chan moved between them and leveled his musket.

Joshen stopped, desperation on his beautiful face.

Reden rolled his eyes. "Stand down, Chan. This is Senna's lost Guardian. He's come back to her."

Chan shot her an uneasy glance before lowering his musket and backing away.

Joshen took a hesitant step toward her, his face unsure. He was thinner. A livid scar cut across his cheek, and he walked with a limp. "I figured I'd already given you a ring and a horse. The next best thing was another protector in case you sent me away again."

Leaning against the railing for support, Senna released the puppy before her unresponsive arms dropped him. "Joshen." It was the only word she could manage. It was the only word that mattered. She shook her head. "I was starting to think you were dead."

"I came as fast as I could." He ran his hand through his hair. "After our boat flipped, I lost Reden and Mistin. The waves were so high and I was hurt. It was impossible to swim. I was drowning. Something slammed into me and I grabbed on. It was a chunk of shattered mast.

"Still, the water was so cold I should have died of exposure in moments, but I managed to sit on the mast with only my legs dangling in the water. I found a flat of wood and used it to paddle and push away most of the dangerous flotsam.

"I found an island with this hidden bay and nothing but seals. I had to abandon the mast and swim for it. I barely made it before my muscles cramped up. I built my own boat out of the wreckage that washed ashore."

She shook her head in disbelief. "That's the same island Wardof was trapped on."

Joshen grunted.

She closed her eyes. "I saved the Witches and left you to die. Can you ever forgive me?" And that wasn't even all of it. She'd practically forced him into harm's way, and for his service, he'd been tortured and nearly killed.

He brushed away her tears with his thumb. They weren't gold anymore, just salty. "It was the right thing to do."

She leaned forward until her head rested against his chest. His arms came around her. She inhaled deeply the smell of him— horses and the sea—and reveled in his closeness.

And once again she had the sense that this was where she fit, where she would always fit. She was finally home.

"I've heard so many things. Are they true?" he whispered into her hair.

She tipped her head back to look at him. "Most likely. But I'm just me again."

He grunted as he cupped her cheek in his hand. "Senna, you've never been 'just' anything."

She stretched up and kissed him softly. "I love you."

He took her hand in his. "I know."

Suddenly aware of the numerous eyes watching them, she glanced back to see the painters staring at them as if memorizing the scene. One of them was furiously drawing with a piece of charcoal.

Somehow she knew there would be a new mural soon, and she and Joshen would feature in it.

THE End

GLO·SSARY

Apprentice: A Witch with a fair amount of training/schooling who has also chosen one of the Disciplines to study and belong to. Traditionally sponsored by a full-fledged Witch.

Creators: A God who, like the Discipline Heads, rules over one of the Four Sisters, but on a much larger scale.

Discipline Heads: Leaders of the Witches and representative of their order or Discipline. By name: Head of Plants, Head of Sunlight, Head of Water, and Head of Earth.

Disciplines: An order, of which there are four, specializing in one of the Four Sisters.

Four Sisters: The elements the Witches use to manipulate nature. Namely: Wind, Water, Earth, and Sunlight.

Keeper: An adult Witch trained in all the Witch arts and belonging to one of the Disciplines. Called a Keeper because of their special duty as "keepers of the earth."

Wastrel: A wasted Witch, or a witch who has little or no power to manipulate the Four Sisters.

Witchling: A very young and/or untrained Witch. Sometimes called a Sprout, which is derogatory.

Acknowledgements

Novels are a journey of two parts: the author who writes them, and the reader who reads them. Without both, the process fails. And so I must thank all the many readers who have begun this journey with me. I'm grateful for the kind messages, reviews, hugs, and support (and yes, for buying the books).

Big thanks to my alpha and beta readers for their invaluable insights and even the occasional disparaging sarcasm: Julie Slezak, Carrie Knudson, Michelle Argyle, JoLynne Lyon, Cami Checketts, Steve Diamond, Cathy Nielson, Rachel Newswander, and Andrea Winkler. Witch Born is better because of you.

For all the bloggers and reviewers who have taken a little time to write a review, share the love, or spread the word: thank you.

Thanks to Eve Ventrue, Linda Prince, Robert Defendi, and Kathy Beutler for making Witch Born shiny.

Thanks to Derek for being superdad during deadline crunch time, and to Corbin, Connor, and Lily for not caring one bit.

To my biggest fans: Gayle and Gordon Stuart and Donna Cornia, everyone who's ever met you knows you have a granddaughter and niece who writes the best books ever written. It makes me smile every time I meet one of them.

ABOUT THE AUTHOR

A mber Argyle grew up with three brothers on a cattle ranch in the Rocky Mountains. She spent hours riding horses, roaming the mountains, and playing in her family's creepy barn. This environment fueled her imagination for writing high fantasy.

She has worked as a short order cook, janitor, and staff member in a mental institution. All of which have given her great insight into the human condition and have made for some unique characters.

She received her bachelor's degree in English and Physical Education from Utah State University.

She currently resides in Utah with her husband and three small children.

CPSIA information can be obtained at www.ICGtesting.com
Printed in the USA
LVOW12s1020240314

378678LV00003B/120/P